Steve Emecz started writing in the middle of the Australian desert in 1994 and the character Max Jones was born. Cut To The Chase proved a hit in 1998 and Cuban Cut followed in 2000 after many letters to Steve's publishers at the time (Hamilton) asking for Max to return. However, as critics were divided about the first book Steve took a slightly different path with the sequel. Steve heavily researched the second book travelling several times to Eastern Europe and even as far as Cuba. The result was a more polished thriller that found more favour with the reviewers. Cut To The Chase however remains the favourite with many readers – perhaps as it has a lot more humour than it's darker sequel.

Several reviewers had commented that Cut To The Chase "reads like a screenplay" and in fact a copy found its way to a Scottish production company who arranged for Steve to convert the book into a film script a few years ago – the film reached casting stage at one point but still awaits the several $m required to bring the story to the silver screen. Maybe one day someone will bring Max to life.

These days Steve does more editing than writing being heavily involved in the publishing company MX Publishing which specialises in NLP (Neuro linguistics Programming) and has one of the leading titles for learning difficulties in the UK. Seeing Spells Achieving has helped thousands of children tackle Dyslexia. Recently Steve co-wrote "Enabled" with a disabled lady called Ruth Merry with royalties going to the charity he and Ruth have fundraised for since 2001 – Leonard Cheshire Disability.

www.mxpublishing.co.uk

Max Jones

in

Cut To The Chase

&

Cuban Cut

Steve Emecz

First published in 1998 and 2001

By Hamilton & Co and MX Publishing, Ltd.

© Copyright 2008 Steve Emecz

ISBN 9781904312338

Published in the UK by MX Publishing

335 Princess Park Manor, Royal Drive,

London, N11 3GX

For Andy

Acknowledgements

There are many people that deserve thanks for their help writing these books, though some will appreciate me not mentioning them in person – they know who they are. As I method write, liking to visit the places and experience the things my characters do, the writing process has left me with wonderful memories, a few scars and a dislocated shoulder.

In terms of family I owe a debt to my mother Sophie whose prolific letter writing got me hooked on story writing, and my wife Sharon who forced me to persist in getting my first publisher. Finally, a big thank you to my brother Charlie, who has greeted every bit of writing with enthusiasm.

1

'............and that made twenty three. 'Some 'informal' 'nothing-to-do-with-work-or any-form of business whatsoever' dinner this is. If he mentions the fact that he can do us a nice deal on our life insurance once more - however subtly, nonchalantly or unintentionally, I'm going to put that exquisitely prepared stroganoff over both his inflated head, and that supposedly quiet, yet overpoweringly loud, Italian suit - better still I'll just smack him one'.*

It had been a tough day. Max had invited this colleague of Jan's over for dinner simply because it may further the career she desperately wanted furthered. He wanted so much for her to be content, but what do you do when a bloke like this comes over and invades the perfectly ordered chaos that their Thursday evenings are, and have always been. Although they had been divorced for four years now, Max still had dinner at his wife's house every Thursday, well most of them anyway. He knew that this is what was what being a good ex-husband was all about. Though he didn't remember standing at the altar saying 'in sickness and in health and in total and unequivocal boredom while a prat in blue rimmed "designer spectacles" prattles on about the benefits of getting the new BMW 'J' series.'

A pathetic and completely unbelievable excuse later, and Max Jones retired gleefully to his study; spare room upstairs that has a desk in it, to nurse a purely medicinal bottle of scotch. Most Thursday's he ended up in the spare room as he would inevitably miss the last tube back to his flat. Several of his friends were concerned by how he kept touch with Jan in this way, as if it was somehow holding him back from finding someone new. Maybe there was some truth in it, but he couldn't help the fact that they were still friends. If he was honest with himself, that's all they had ever been and it had been far too easy for her career to get in the way of their marriage.

St. Paul's Cathedral. He could see its dome from here. The sun had already disappeared over the jagged London skyline on this evening late in June and Max really had had a bad day. It wasn't totally due to the thoroughly unwelcome visitor downstairs. To be completely frank with himself he had messed up. Yes, not for the first time he had pissed off someone that was on the 'Do not, under any circumstances piss anyone on this list off' list. What had begun as a quite ordinary day had turned somewhat sour....

2

Late as usual, but by a miracle of modern technology (actually less traffic on the north circular road) by a mere twenty minutes. The empty coffee cups piled precariously high in a bin that even the most agreeable of office cleaners refused to venture near to, greeted Max as he stumbled through the door and planted himself behind the large oak desk. Any self-respecting criminal worth his salt would immediately recognise this figure as an undercover policeman. Basically this was because no other vocation allows such an extent of disorganisation from its workforce. Well, they'd be wrong. He was simply one of the most unusual deputy accountants of a hospital this side of the Thames. He had not started out in this line of business, oh no, and it was due to the culmination of events too numerous, onerous and lacking in credibility to mention. If any of them gain relevant status they shall be revealed.

He glared at his 'In' tray. It was full as usual with letters from the 'Compuluv Dating Agency' offering him the perfect partner for the price of a phone call, 'Draino' the miracle all-in-one, house, garden, garage, and cat cleaner, and of course several credit card companies offering a special gift if he introduces a friend to the wonderful world of plastic debt. These he placed carefully (as carefully as you can from nine feet) into the pile in the corner where they nestled quietly on top of an answering machine he had never used, with the rest of the post that had amassed over the last few months.

Around Max the walls were covered with charts, rows of books and the odd picture of the type you find at a car boot sale and find yourself haggling over the price tag of £1.50. Many of them were not Max's but had been left there by the person before, or indeed before that.

A finely tuned mind would have guessed on this evidence that neatness and order didn't play too prominent a part in this burly man's life, and they would be right this time. Having decided that lifting his pen before the morning's fourth cup of coffee was a sin his dishevelled taste buds were in no state to commit, he called to his secretary for his usual brew. It was then that the phone rang. Not an unusual thing for a phone to do, but pretty rare in the case of Max's because he normally left it off the hook to give the impression he was busy. Regretting the first mistake of the day he lifted the receiver.

He could almost smell the caller's aftershave down the line. It was his boss's personal assistant. Despite the fact that the subject in question carried most of the administration of the hospital on his shoulders, Malcolm Pitts was still an A1, numero uno prat. This extensive character assessment Max had put together over the last three years that the 'devils advocate' had been there. Incredibly creeping, energetically irritating, he just wanted to get to the top of the heap. He would get there too, just as soon as the old duffer snuffed it or retired to the seaside with his bucket and spade. All he had to do was keep brown-nosing and succumbing to the boss's every whim.

"Nice to see you in at this early hour Jones" - he never called Max 'Max', it was always 'Jones' - *'egotistical little git'* thought Max, not for the first time.

"You'll actually be doing some work then? I know it's against your religion". (Subtle pause for emphasis) '*..git'* "but we have some extremely important visitors coming into the research lab today. I've sent you a memo with all the details," he added as he put the phone down.

'The NHS has more administrators than patients,'
Max thought. He was usually content with the daily task of getting sick people well again. Simple concept, but we are still dealing with one of the largest bureaucratic dinosaurs left in the country. The research centre they had was made up of a few dedicated professors who specialised in rare areas of brain cancer. They were good too. They had found cures and preventative treatment

for a number of strains. Still, rather than continue funding this life-saving work, the men behind closed doors at Whitehall were considering turning the place into a research centre for plastic surgery. Not the kind that rebuilt the shattered lives of burns victims but the 'cosmetic' kind. Curiously the transition seemed to have gone on hold the past couple of months. Research that pays for itself they said. Max didn't follow the same train of thought. The only people who would benefit from the new centre would be those with enough money to pay for treatment themselves. Although not a fervently politically active man, he tended to follow his own personal theory for life - "If you're a little person avoid the foot - if you can make a difference, kick the bureaucratic establishment's ass at every possible opportunity." Not the sort of epitaph you would want on your headstone, but being headstrong and stubborn were among his best qualities.

Sally came in with the coffee. She was OK though. Young, and still harbouring some innocence. No, not in that sense. Naivety takes many forms. Max chuckled to himself as Sally set the coffee neatly on the corner of the desk, smiled and winked at him.

"No messages sweetie," she called as she slipped out of the office. What she was doing here Max couldn't fathom. Her appearance was more akin to the reception of a hairdresser, but she was an excellent secretary and a pretty good sort too.

Max glanced out of his window that overlooked the entrance to the East wing. An extremely important looking car pulled up to the doors. Out of it stepped three men. The first looked up at the grey sky above and shook his head. This and the sunglasses led Max to believe he was an American. The other two dwarfed the first as they formed a miniature 'v' shape and headed toward the large wooden doors. They went straight in as if they owned the place. More evidence that they were from across the water. He noticed too that a second car that had been following the first pulled up some way down

11

the street. Its occupants stayed put. Max didn't much like Americans on the whole, especially those in dark suits and sunglasses. Deciding that the day wouldn't be complete until he had executed his personal special blend of red tape, Max got up, carefully retrieving the steaming coffee as he made for the door.

3

Monday. Max awoke displaying an unexpectedly large amount of timidity for a man of his size. The curtain was wide open and rare London sunshine was gushing in. He vaguely remembered the alarm having gone off and hoped that was a nasty dream. Sadly, in a repeat of most Mondays, he had greeted the shrill tones of the alarm with a murmur and a thump of his fist onto the perpetrator of the disturbing noise. Had he been a primed Olympic athlete, getting ready and to work on time from his present state would have been an amicable challenge. As he could not, even in the dimmest of lights, be mistaken for an athletic specimen, he met the prospect of lateness with a shrug and headed to the bathroom. The tiled room that greeted him resembled most of the rest of the house with the predominance of antique objects. He looked in the mirror and paused for a moment to assess the face that stared back at him. There seemed to be a little more grey in the brown hair that was swept back from his brow. He could see the telltale signs of a second chin and sighed. He leaned a little closer to examine the bags under his eyes. That'll be the scotch. He'd always got away with that in his younger years as his light blue eyes snatched the attention from pretty much any other feature on his face. His ex-wife had begun to nag him to use a moisturiser – Max smiled as he looked at the nearly full tub that sat on top of the cabinet. Max liked the security that came from familiar things. He reached for a razor that could have graced the parlour of Sweeney Todd it was so well imprinted with the passage of time. Although Max's chin could have been polished off by an electric razor, or even a modern wet blade, in a quarter of the time, the solid brass handle and silver detailing did transform the simple act of shaving into somewhat of a performance. Liberal amounts of balm were required after a quick shower to treat the battle scars inflicted by the monolithic weapon.

Within half an hour Max stood at his front door, key in hand with a dreary sky slowly choking what had seemed a buoyant sun. His ground floor flat was located on a quiet road just off the high street in the North London suburb of Finchley. He'd chosen the location because it was just far enough from the house he had lived in for a decade with his wife to require a conscious decision for a visit but still within a short hop on a tube. His journey was only really interrupted by a police roadblock conducting random breath testing. *'Good job they don't try mine,* Max thought. The hastily micro-waved onion bhaji he'd had for breakfast gave his breath a potency that would make even the least nasally sensitive policeman keel over. To describe the busy London roads to anyone who has sampled them is unnecessary, but for those that haven't the phrase 'Kamikaze pilots in cars' should suffice. Each inch is fought for and Max's car bore many small scars where he and a territorial adversary had pushed stubbornness that little bit too far. Max collected his thoughts and tried to focus on the meeting he was going to be late for. "Oi," he screamed at a bike courier who managed to tweak his mirror with his backside as he careered past.

'No wonder it's the job in London with the worst life expectancy' he thought. He'd been in emergency on a number of occasions when a young lad's mountain bike had been no match for a truck or a bus. The impending meeting didn't ruffle Max as the same rituals seemed to be played out each week. Max would give them the information they'd asked for and by the end of the meeting the various decisions concerning the running of the hospital would have been made and minuted and the tea and biscuits wheeled in. It was uncanny that the decision-makers, stuffy middle managers in the most part, appeared to have their decisions and opinions in the briefcases they brought

with them to the meetings. The figures that were displayed by Max did not seem to affect said opinions and thus a heated discussion never ensued. The proceedings went along the lines of 'having one's say in turn' to reassuring choruses of mumbles. He'd often thought how amusing it would be, to him at least, to come to the meeting with two sets of figures. The correct ones would be preceded by laughably false figures which Max would present with solemn sincerity - he could see their faces now. 'A stunned silence befalls the room - the heads turn and looks are thrown at other committee members until, prompted by a tactful elbow, the youngest manager splutters into voice like an old motorbike on a frosty morning. Two or three of the others try, pathetically, to adapt their rigid ideas to no avail. Then I deliver the second set of figures'.

The horn of the car behind him woke Max abruptly from his daydream, the reprimand coming as he hadn't shot off the moment the green light had turned. Although this was one of the things that annoyed Max most - people's inability once behind the wheel of a car to exhibit rational thought and behaviour - his energy was at a low ebb and he put the impatient git out of his mind. Max grabbed another extra strong mint and finding it was the last in the packet, reached for the glove compartment which revealed a dozen or so further packets which constituted about a week's driving supply. He attempted, as ever, to suck the aforementioned mint but soon resigned himself to crunching. By the time he reached the East gates of the hospital, the second packet was almost gone. The sun was peering cautiously through the clouds and the time was twenty past nine. *'Not too bad for a 9am meeting,'* he thought. The porter acknowledged Max's lumbering through the doors with a large grin. The wards looked busy as he walked quickly past the melee of sick, injured and supposedly sick and injured people clogging the corridors. Max's brief journey up to the third floor was marked with many smiles and a few comic taps on watches. Finally reaching the meeting room door he was met by a tea trolley rattling frantically. The trolley was propelled by a small round aged lady whose name was Alice and whose diminutive stature made it look as though the trolley was moving under its own steam.

"Ah gentlemen, it appears that we are blessed with the presence of our learned colleague who we have to thank for a second breakfast while we were waiting".

The face behind the voice was small, round and looked like a weasel sucking on a lemon. Max grinned an apologetic grin and set his case on the table next to the cold cup of tea that had also awaited his arrival. The room he was in was fairly long and narrow. The centre was occupied by a large sturdy looking table with a dozen chairs seated around it. At the head of the table was the weasel - Alec Farmers - who was tapping his pen impatiently on the table and accompanying himself with intermittent sighs and tuts. His pen was gold, his suit hand made and his ideas somewhere further right than Thatcher. He had been running the hospital a good few years before he was actually given the top job. This was largely due to the influence he exerted through his many business contacts. His P.A. Malcolm sat grinning at his right side. Malcolm wore the same suit Max had seen him in every day for the last three years and he was sporting the same tie. He remembered briefly the surprise at the Christmas party when he'd turn up in a different tie. Same suit mind, just a tie that was a slightly different shade of blue. Living the dream. Max found himself grinning and stopped abruptly. It was Max's privilege to present the costs first as these were then made to seem insignificant in comparison to Farmers' stirring words on profits, expansion and private enterprise. So without much ado Max got his papers in order and silenced the tapping and rumbling by clearing his throat.

".......and that gentlemen is the future of medicine".

Farmers' last words had been heard so many times before they fell largely on deaf ears, though the creepier among those present (led by Malcolm) gave a smattering of applause. The routine over, Max headed for his office.

On opening the door he found the same serenity that greeted him most mornings. In the bustle of the hospital his office remained steadfast in its ability to be quiet and peaceful. Briefcase on desk and mug in hand he re-emerged onto a scene of animated gestures as Sally was in the middle of a telephone conversation. It was quite evident that the person on the other end was taking little or no part in the discussion, as there didn't seem to be any pauses in her speech. She didn't appear to either notice or mind Max's presence until a further minute had seen her voice grow steadily louder, and the phone slammed down rather hard. By then Max was holding two steaming cups of coffee. He handed one of the mugs to the sobbing Sally.

'I bet he's dumped her.'

"Have you finally dumped him?" Max asked

"Yes, he's a complete sod."

'Yep, he's dumped her - here comes the background story.'

"He was just soooo jealous," she sobbed

'In other words, he wasn't liberal minded enough for her to wear less material than a handkerchief to a night-club,' Max thought

"Well a lot of these young men are far too self-conscious," he offered.

"Tell me about it. I don't see a problem with a lycra top and a miniskirt."

'Neither does most of the male population,' Max thought. It seemed amusing to him that while these young guys chased Sally in her various non-imagination provoking outfits, once dating her they decided she needed to cover up. As Saturday night was clubbing night Max had lost count of the weeks that had begun like this.

4

The young officer moved from the silver lift and passed through a corridor whose bright lights emphasised the dullness of its colour. The sparse design met him at each turn of the winding route until he came to what appeared to be just another panel in the wall. Lifting his foot off the floor he placed the sole against the wall. A small click was followed by the appearance of a small screen. He placed his hand on the screen which lit up. Once it had satisfied itself that the person in front of its wall was appropriate the remainder of the panel disappeared revealing yet another passage. *'Flash bullshit,'* the young man thought. He kept the thought to himself as these walls not only had ears but eyes as well and his lips could always be read. The third door he came to had a simpler opening device - namely a handle, and after a brief series of knocks the young man entered. Although the man on the other side of the room lost twenty years to him it was not difficult to see that his physique and frame matched his. He had his back to the door and was looking at a map screen of some sort located on the back wall.

"Sit down Easton," he said without turning around. His voice was deep and a little melancholy. The younger man sat with his arms crossed and the folder he had brought with him on his lap. His cap hid most of his dark hair which was cropped very short. Still without turning around, as if to add emphasis, his superior continued.

"As you have no doubt digested everything in that file, I'll cut to the chase. Although this may seem a cushy assignment on the surface - baby-sitting a few scientists and surgeons - you will have noted it is marked with a code 3.

Why this is the case, is of little concern to me and will be of none to you. But it is there for a reason. You should feel honoured to get something like this after only a few years with us."

'Oh great, a month in dreary London watching over a bunch of eggheads,' thought the young man as he let his eyes drift to the map on the screen.

"If this goes without a hitch I'll recommend they push you up a couple of levels," the older man said as he turned around. His face was suitably worn and hardened with a few noticeable scars. Easton could almost imagine the man in front of him with M16 in hand, tramping though the jungles of North Korea or Vietnam. Although he never mentioned the above conflicts it was widely known that he had been decorated for his conduct in both.

"Your name is now Sherman Jeffries and you are with the Institute of Medicine of New England. Considering you studied medicine next to law you should be able to carry that one off. You have a wife and a two-year-old son called James. All your papers and personal effects are in the package on the desk. As your file states you will be in London for a month, though this could be extended."

"Extended?" asked Easton surprised.

"Yes, extended. Due to the medical nature of the operation, no pun intended, it could take longer."

"May I ask how much longer?"

"You may, but as my medical expertise doesn't stretch past basic first aid you are unlikely to get a straight answer."

'Great, so I could be stuck there for months,' he mused.

"I know what you're thinking, that this is a real piece of crap to be thrown, but our work isn't restricted to terrorists and revolutionaries. At least you'll not be dodging bullets and sleeping in ditches," he grinned.

"One question Sir. The file mentions a partner. Am I at liberty to know who I will be going with?"

"Oh you'll find out on the plane – it's in the package. Don't panic, you know him quite well."

At this, he handed the package to the young officer, who took this as the sign that the brief meeting was over. He saluted his superior and with the file and package lodged under his arm he ventured into the corridor once more.

5

The kickback from the Baretta pistol felt good in his right hand as he pummelled half a dozen bullets into the approaching soldier before ducking behind the low stone wall off to his left. The cold air drifted over his face as he paused, making him aware of the beads of sweat slipping down his brow. Counting to three he threw himself to the ground six feet away and released the remaining bullets into the second figure. A mortar exploded somewhere behind him and showered him in earth. It took a split second for his eyes to adjust in the smoke. Scanning the horizon for a moment he located the awaiting transport and broke into a sprint. He discovered another enemy in the boggy earth but somehow he managed to vault the ramshackle fence in his way. Only a few yards to go and suddenly he felt a thud in his right shoulder. Looking down he saw the yellow patch and swore out loud. The run slowed to a walk and he approached Major Hava with a stern expression.

"Sniper you fool!"

screamed the major as he got within six feet.

"Apart from missing him in sector two the rest was pretty good….for a lard-ass agency nancy-boy,"

The Major sneered as his old friend saluted and handed over the weapon for inspection. Anders smiled and climbed into the jeep. It felt damn good to keep his skills up. Although the training facility was mandatory for all operatives once a year, he found himself back in Hawksville every few months. He was annoyed at having missed the presence of the sniper cut-out, but had hit every other target on the range. The adrenaline rush had been severely lacking in the last few assignments and he wondered if the next one would contain any excitement.

6

Tuesday. Max took a long gulp of his steaming coffee. Between his mint addiction and preference for boiling drinks he had assumed his taste buds would disappear completely before he reached thirty. That hadn't happened and Max often pictured them as armour-plated. He's spent much of his younger life in South London where his parents had both been teachers. His gruffness was attributed by his wife to his somewhat tough childhood. Although it was one of the golden rules of being a teacher's son, the closeness of the school where his father taught and the fact that it was the only Roman Catholic one for miles had led to him attending there anyway. He could recall the exact number of tiles in the Deputy Head's office (423, four cracked) he had been there so many times to receive a short sharp whack with the cane or training shoe that he'd had plenty of time to count them. From the first year there he developed a survival instinct and often resorted to his fast sense of humour – the de-facto defence of the ostracised. Despite being a large lad there was not much that could protect him from the fifth form lads that had received lines from his father. Max looked down at a scar on the back of his hand and rubbed his fingers over it absent-mindedly. The branch upon which his hand had been impaled was located on a tree half way down a hundred foot ridge behind the school that a gang of kids had decided Max should travel down at great speed. His mother had wondered just how such an injury could have come from playing football – in fact by the age of fourteen there were few bones left in his arms and legs that had not been broken in one way or another – to Mrs. Jones football was indeed one of the most dangerous pursuits imaginable. By fifteen Max had grown so big that it was only the biggest of lads that would dare take him on and joining the boxing team had helped cement his reputation as well. His father had a strong hand in sending him off to military college where he'd continued with the boxing alongside a light dabble into martial arts. He was far too bulky to be effective though and he'd concentrated more on his studies than his extra curricular activities. To many of his friends he was an enigma. He had a passion for numbers but a dislike of paperwork, process and authority.

The whistle of the kettle made him look up. Sally had not touched her coffee yet and was already making him a second cup. As he stepped into the main office he exchanged a pile of typing for the aforementioned coffee and returned to his desk. Any visitor to his office would find Max's door open at all times. If the door was shut it meant he was out. From the doorway you could see a huge desk dominating the centre of the room and around the edges various office machinery, each with a pile of paper covering it. Max's theory here was that no dust could collect on said equipment if they were shrouded with paper. He of course knew exactly where everything was, but to the casual observer the scene was one of cosy disorder. On his desk was a PC which hid within its dull grey casing how organised this man really was. Despite being apathetic toward the dreaded machines for many years Max became computer literate with a vengeance with the advent of the 'stand-alone' PC. Although it was linked, for certain applications, with the hospital's mainframe and a local network inside his department, what lived on his PC was largely his business and that's the way Max liked it. Rumours abounded within the hospital of his computer skills but one visit to his messy office was usually enough to dispel these. In case of further prying eyes Max had installed an intricate protection system that in an establishment like St. Mary's was vastly over the top. It was more for his peace of mind than serving any functional value. However, hidden behind the mass of codes and passwords were files containing Max's figure

24

work on the running costs of the place since he had been there. They showed the current boss in a very unfavourable light. Farmers had massaged the figures for a number of years. Max kept these as security for the time when he might need them. Farmers didn't like Max and on the occasions Max had stood against his wayward ideas on the grounds of common sense he had warned him that his days were numbered. Max knew, for instance, that the investment from the Italians three years before had been an unmitigated disaster. The true costs had been hidden and Farmers had come out of the fiasco without a mark. Max had been the first to push for, and get CD ROMs in to the department. His PC also had a removable hard-drive of which he had two backups. On the hospital records only one of those was shown. The other lived in a post office box in his uncle's hometown of Melksham. Now this may seem a little paranoid, or at the very least over cautious, but Max was familiar with Farmers' methods. Many a member of staff in his way had been given the bullet prematurely. Max liked this job and no little jumped up git in an Italian suit was going to take it away from him. In true tradition though, Max left the PC un-dusted and the desk un-cleared. This further fuelled the impression that the machine was there for occasional use and nothing else. He was sitting beside the PC working on his notes from yesterday's meeting. Though the sun was still fighting a losing battle with the clouds the office was fairly bright.

7

Matheson air force base....10:30pm. Two figures are walking across the tarmac towards a transport plane. Their silhouettes against the myriad of lights inside the control tower reveal one is slightly shorter than the other and they are both carrying large bags. The back of the plane is open and the two figures, both silent, disappear into the belly of the plane. The plane makes one stop-off at JFK to pick up fuel and it is there that the two figures re-emerge, minus the caps and bags. The younger man has short dark hair, deep blue eyes and is wearing a very plain grey suit which looks out of place on his shoulders. The taller man is perhaps fifteen years older with a face that nature had not been altogether generous to. The passage of the last twenty years is imbedded in the stern wrinkles and furrowed brow. He doesn't smile and his eyes are hidden by mirrored sunglasses despite the fact that it is the middle of the night. He, too, is wearing a conservative suit and they look like two businessmen about to board a commuter train into the city.

'I'm determined not to mention the sunglasses,' Easton thought. *'He's bound to give me a lecture, but he couldn't be less conspicuous if his hair was green.'*

"The sunglasses are fine - it means that people think my eyesight is impaired and that gives me another edge."

'Gees was this guy telepathic or what. Nope, it was me looking over out of the corner of my eye.' He tried to change the subject.

"You looking forward to London?" he asked as enthusiastically as he could muster.

"Oh sure, I get two lots of baby-sitting this time," came the terse reply.

'I ought to know better. If he's quite happy to act like a monk I guess I shouldn't bother to try and make conversation,' Easton thought and turned his thoughts toward breakfast. This was the fourth time he'd been paired with Anders and he had yet to shake off the 'rookie' tag. You had to respect the man. More senior, more skilled, and still alive at the age of forty-five in a profession where the odds were heavily stacked against growing to a ripe old age. Nevertheless, Easton was frustrated at being treated like a kid. He was damn good. Why else was he where he was by the age of thirty. But that didn't count for anything with Anders, oh no. You had to have survived at the hands of the PLO, had a number of near fatal wounds and lost a finger, toe, testicle or earlobe during either warfare or torture of some description. He had to admit that the previous three missions they had been paired together had been fairly routine and had gone almost to plan. The exception had been the last one, where Easton had almost been caught. A fact Anders would never let him forget. He had been standing by the swimming pool and had watched Easton's premature exit from the hotel room's second floor window. The hotel had been in Jakarta, and the impromptu exit due to a double-cross by their contact there. They entered the domestic terminal via an inconspicuous door near to baggage claim and went to the bar. Four hours later a bus took them to the international terminal and flight BA127 to London Heathrow.

8

Thursday. It had been an uneventful afternoon and the sun had almost decided to call it a day. Max stared at the computer sheet on his desk. The yellow highlighted figures stared back at him. Part of him wanted to just add a few notes and slip it into Dr Reimer's tray. He would get it back in a couple of days later with a plausible reason the cost committee would be happy with. Another part, the stronger part, was angered by the channelling of funds into the research centre. Decision made, Max got up and walked to the photocopier by the window. All cost rises of 40% or more were highlighted and this week's list had twenty of them. As the copier kicked into life he glanced out over the car park. How the face of the hospital had changed over the last twelve months. The plush new wing with its fancy security system, wards that look more like hotel rooms. "...This is the future of British medicine - private research will fund an increased level of patient care." Farmers' words as he had cut the tape at its opening still clear in Max's memory. The lights were all out but the dim glow of all manner of computer wizardry at rest lit the parking places outside. There always seemed to be plenty of cars at night too. Probably all the commissioned professors working through the night researching the next breakthrough in plastic surgery. Max chuckled to himself as he pictured a life-size Barbie doll sitting behind the reception. He slipped the copy back into the folder and the original into the bottom drawer.

There is an uneasy quiet that people associate with hospitals after dark. As Max walked the stairs and corridors toward the new wing, the small hives of activity that surrounded the sisters going about their duties were like oases in a dreary desert. Peaceful though. Max liked this time of the day. There wasn't that same air of illness or presence of suffering. The bleach smell was the same but Max was almost immune to that by now. He reached the security doors and was greeted by a pleasant grin.

"Hiya Max. They sure got you tied to you're desk these days."

"Merv. When's the next shipment of rum coming from your brother?" Merv had the best Jamaican connections in North London and could get the best rum this side of Kingston Town.

"Next week man. Don't tell me you drunk those two bottles already," he chuckled.

"Almost," said Max as he ran his pass through the decoder.

"I need to do a bunch of sections this week. We're really up against it with the end of the budget this month." Although he knew exactly where he wanted to go, Max went through the motions of pulling the sheet from the folder. Merv was a long-standing part of St. Mary's and he and Max had always got on well. They shared the same taste in rum. Max shuffled the sheets and read out as he came to each new section.

"Hey, you know I can't get you into G section - you can leave that one with me and I'll get Dr.Reimer to sort it out for you tomorrow," Merv said.

"Oh OK," Max replied shutting the folder and walking towards the inner door.

"Shit, I almost forgot. Dr Reimer wants these figures typed by Monday. Any chance you can swing the section for me. It'll only take a minute," Max pleaded.

"Well I'm not sure..." Merv said contemplating the idea.

"You can come with me if you like?" Max offered.

"OK, I'll get Barry to take over here," Merv smiled.

Merv was small for what Max assumed, judging by other acquaintances, the average size of Jamaicans is. His beard was short and liberally specked

29

with grey. The grey had yet to reach his hair, which was still as dark as coal. Max suspected that this wasn't entirely due to strong follicles. He looked fairly distinguished in his 'mock policeman's' uniform that all security staff had to wear. *'Under duress,'* Max thought. Merv was quickly relieved by Barry who in contrast was a plain, expressionless, thin, tall man with whom a long discussion was limited to a couple of sentences. An avid collector of dead insects apparently. *'Wouldn't surprise me,'* Max thought as his smile was returned by a forced blank grin that seemed to defy all the other muscles in the young man's face. Max followed Merv through the buzz of the security door and down a long brightly lit corridor.

"I remember when this was a children's ward," mumbled Max.

"Yep, sure is quieter," laughed Merv, "but it hasn't got no life any more - unless you call them machines a'clickin and a whirrin all night lively," he frowned.

"I bet even Barry gets bored with this," said Max.

"Hmm, difficult to tell, man," replied Merv as he slid his security card through another door lock. The card was met with a small beep and a green light. *'Star bloody Trek,'* Max thought as the door panned slowly back to reveal a smaller corridor with three doors either side in perfect symmetry. The floors and walls were a dark grey and the door frames only a marginally lighter shade. A far cry from the plush, plant-dominated reception area and the private rooms that the punters actually got to see. Max remembered back to his visits to RAF Morton and expected his friend Carl to greet them as Merv threw the latch on one of the doors. The innards of this fortress were little different to other labs Max had seen on his travels. More attention to detail perhaps. The main lights were on, possibly triggered by the lock. Everything was bathed in a sharp white light. *'It probably looks the same in the daytime,'* Max thought as he walked to the first storage unit and checked its contents. There was something macabre in the organs encased in their various containers. Of course they weren't visible but Max could see their images in the wording on the labels. He supposed that once you've seen more livers than a Pavarotti fry up of a morning, then it was natural for the mind to override the weaker sense and allow such a deeper sight. In much the same way his neighbour Daniel was able to evoke Max's taste buds with the most graphic descriptions of a gourmet meal he had recently prepared. Max slowly redressed the whiteness of the page with strokes from his red highlighter as the resting places and uses of the various stocks revealed themselves in the cabinets. With all but one of the items on the list checked Max motioned that yet another door needed opening. Merv handed him the pass without moving from the stool he had found. His distant gaze didn't alter as Max opened the thick metal door that was marked only with the letters B.R.I. The door opened not onto another room but a small storage area. Its walls were sliding doors of glass. Max quickly identified where the substance had been employed and noted the relevant details against the text on the sheet.

'I expect they'll put bar codes on these one day,' Max thought as he compared the shelves to those in his local supermarket. The inner door clicked shut and Max made a low rumble in his throat which stirred Merv from his gazing into space.

"On the beach again?" Max whispered as Merv clicked open the door.

"Yep, with me rum bottle sittin in the ice bucket and the young ladies playing volleyball in the sun," he grinned revealing a row of white teeth a man half his age would be proud of.

"Just another three years," he added.

"As few as that. You make me feel old," Max laughed.

"Not so much of the old you young puppy. 'Experienced' is a far better word," Merv laughed.

"Well, save me a deck-chair," Max shouted over his shoulder as he passed through the final door manned by the ever alert Barry.

As Max turned the key in his office door he thought of his impending drive home, no traffic but plenty of road works. It was a matter of minutes before he'd keyed in the necessary details. It would be flattery to describe him as a touch typist but a number of years in front of the 'infernal machines' had quickened his pace. As he went through Max corrected any obvious mistakes in spelling etc. *'Sally's had a bad week,'* he said to himself. The young lady in question, he remembered, was having another man crisis and her attention was wavering. Three d's in acidic did seem a touch excessive. She had even left out the date when Mr.Verdkyll had passed away, but seeing as the tissue that occupied his jar in the lab was less than 24 hrs old Max keyed in "Thursday 10pm" as a rough guess. *'That way she won't get dragged over the coals on Monday,'* mumbled Max to himself as he put the papers in his top drawer and silenced the computer with the flick of a switch. *'Maybe then I'll have a quiet start to the week instead of tears and woe with my first cup of coffee,'* he thought.

9

"Get that bloody smile off your face missy...!"

The large woman behind the voice was Sister Mary, and everyone knew it. Her request, or rather order, was directed at a young nurse on the opposite side of the bed. The nurse's red hair was straight, long and cascaded over her shoulders when it was loose but on duty was tied into a neat bun. She had a natural gleam in her green eyes, which incidentally went with her hair to a tee.

"You know Mr.Mortimer needs stern treatment," the sister continued.

'Or neutering,' thought Kathy.

"Yes Sister," she said as if the last comment had been an order too. To this the sister gave an indignant 'humph', spun on her heels and headed down the ward looking for the next victim of her sharp tongue. Mr Mortimer was almost a regular. He had a tiny feeble five foot four frame but caused most of the commotion on the ward. He suffered from an endless stream of minor strokes, and while in the hospital dealt out his fair share of strokes too. Student nurses screamed, doctors tutted and the rest of the onlookers were usually quite amused. Kathy could handle him though. She referred to him as being in his 'second adolescence'. His frown was still there as she looked at him.

"My arms are too short and your bum's too small," he complained

"Thank you for the compliment, I think," she smiled. She gave him his pills, he refused. She finally got him to take them by telling him they were hallucinogenic drugs. Had his memory been better he would have remembered her using the same trick a few days earlier. She'd had a ticking off from the sister to whom Mr.Mortimer had complained that his LSD fixes hadn't worked properly. Kathy looked to her left and saw the 'old battle-axe' taking a piece out of Max. She liked Max. He was down to earth and funny. Now if he were ten years younger, half the size and looked different then there'd be no stopping her. It was rumoured that Sister Mary had a soft spot for him. *That narrows it down to almost any part of her anatomy'* Kathy thought. She saw his eyes dart in her direction, as if a cry for help. She smiled and walked over to the animated sister and interrupted.

"Oh Max,I've got some urgent paperwork from Dr. Coulemans for you."

"Ah yes," Max said feigning urgency.

"I've been waiting for that, can I come and get it now?" he said.

'Sharp as ever,' thought Kathy.

'Wonderful,' thought Max.

"Of course, I'll take you through," Kathy said grabbing his arm quickly before Sister Mary could open her mouth again.

They scuttled off down the ward and into a quiet corridor and slowed to a walking pace.

"Thanks," said Max

"Oh, just my good deed for the day," she replied in the soft Welsh accent he liked so much.

"You know she fancies you...?" she continued with a grin.

"Hmm," he frowned "I had hoped that was a vicious rumour spread by an enemy bent on revenge," he said breaking into a smile.

" 'Fraid not. Anyway, how are things, I haven't seen you down here for a few days."

"I'm sorry, I've had so much extra figurework. That new research centre generates more hassle than the rest of the place put together."

"I guess it does," she said. There was that smile again.

'I must change the subject' Max thought as he felt himself staring at her eyes.

34

"Anything much happen this week?"

"Not much. Mr Mortimer is back again so Sister Mary is being a pain. There's a new young doctor, no he's not my type, and we lost Mr.Verdkyll."

" Ah yes, rather sad that," Max said trying to sound sincere even though he hadn't known the man personally.

"Yes, he had been battling cancer for two years, always bubbly and friendly."

"Cancer?" Max stopped in his tracks.

"Yes, lung cancer," Kathy repeated looking puzzled.

"Why do you ask?"

"Oh nothing, just that one of the patients in the neural section had a similar name and also died on Thursday."

"Can't be the same one then, Mr.Verdkyll didn't die until Saturday. Well, they turned his machine off with his wife's permission. The son was there too, very sad."

"Must be a different chap," said Max dismissing the point.

"So, you free for lunch?" he asked hopefully

"My my, you don't come and visit me for a week and then expect lunch. Well I might be in the canteen at one, and if there aren't any other free tables I might just sit next to you," she smiled.

Max looked at Kathy and could picture that hair over her shoulders. He often wondered what would have happened if they had met earlier – like when he was ten years younger and more available. They had found out within a week of Kathy joining the staff that they had been at the same University just a year apart. Their groups of friends had overlapped an they found that they could even recall the same legendary student nights out but by some twist of fate they couldn't ever remember meeting. They had shared one passionate clinch at the previous Christmas party but had not talked about it since. It might be his imagination, which considering it was Kathy was highly likely, but

35

he wondered if that had been the defining moment that had led her to put him in the category of 'mate' rather than colleague she'd like to have an illicit affair with. Shame.

"Why thank you," Max grinned and pushed through the doors into X-Ray.

10

The doors on the conference room clicked to a close and the short man reached for the phone and dialled the number. After a series of clicks a voice came on the other end.

"Yes. I told you never to call me at this number unless it was serious," the voice snapped.

The short man glanced at the closed door.

"Yes well, I think it is. One of the staff has been nosing around our research area," he said quietly.

"What, a doctor you mean?" the voice answered concerned.

"No, an accountant. Jones" replied the short man.

"And that worries you? Very well, I'll deal with it. We can't take any chances with what is at stake. Not a word to our two boys. We don't want them knowing any more than absolutely necessary. Right?"

"Yessir," the short man replied and slowly replaced the handset. He looked out of the window across to Jones' office and felt a pang of guilt. Was he being too cautious or was there really a danger that he would uncover something. He dismissed the idea with the thought that if there was a problem, it was about to be solved.

11

Max kept telling himself that being sent on a conference visit to Belfast was a good sign for his stagnant career. He was nursing a particular flat cappuccino watching the people rushing around. He was early for the flight. Not an unusual feat for most, but for Max this was a remarkable achievement. When he was born he was a week late, and to be honest, that was the beginning of an illustrious record of the same. At university a seat at the back of the main lecture theatre that was closest to the door was designated Max's so as to cause the minimum of disturbance to the other students when he rolled in. He had even been late for his own wedding. An argument with the best man over the quickest route to the church led to them being stuck on the Chiswick flyover behind an accident. The two of them finally arrived on two bikes commandeered from the local post office. This time though it turned out he had little choice but to be early. Farmers had told him to check in at 6:30am for the 7:00am flight. He duly arrived at the Aer Lingus desk at around ten past seven assuming he'd catch the next one at 8:00am. The young lady behind the desk was amused at his apologies for being late.

"But you're two hours early," she had grinned.

"You're booked on the 9:00am flight."

It was then that he checked his ticket for the first time. Sure enough, 9am. It had meant that he could have breakfast which was a result. He walked over to the brightly lit café. He looked through the glass counter and although he resented paying six quid for a couple of overdone eggs, sausage and bacon that had sat under a heat lamp for an eternity he ordered and sat down. He would have plenty of fun people – one of his favourite pastimes on account of being able to do it sitting down and requiring very little energy. Of particular interest was the group of football supporters that looked as though they were about to fly off to Holland or somewhere. Their paraphernalia, hats and scarves etc. suggested their team was Arsenal, but it could have been any team playing out there and this bunch of lads would have been along for the ride. They were proud to be British, hence Union Jacks were sewn to virtually every item of clothing. On reflection, Britain may not at this particular moment in time be equally as proud of them. All were drunk to some level, and the most unfortunate was unconsciously laid over a pile of bags and rucksacks with a dopey grin on his face. Unfortunate, because without consciousness his guard was down and two of his 'friends' (the term is used loosely here) were taking great pleasure in trying to wake him using just their flatulating talents. Max grinned as the larger of the two lost his footing and collapsed taking the other with him.

'Probably find he's a chartered surveyor or a lawyer in the week,' he mused. A security guard looked over briefly at the noise but thought better of any action. The other group of interest was four nuns. *'Always good for a laugh, nuns'* Max thought. They were seated not far from the patriotic louts at the side of the cafe. Apart from the odd disapproving look and tut they didn't seem to react much to their surroundings.

'Couldn't do that,' he thought. *'Tough break being a nun. You can't have a bad day, can't swear, drink, get into fights, go bowling, have a decent vindaloo - tough break'.* He realised his mind was wandering and checked his watch. Seven forty-five. He might as well go and check his bag in. It had been short notice for this conference and he'd had to go down to the dry cleaners at the last minute to pick up a suit.

'At least they'll have some decent whisky when I get there,' he smiled to himself as he handed his ticket and bag over.

"I'm afraid we've had to move your seat sir," said the green suited lady ever so politely.

"It's still inside the plane I trust," Max grinned but quickly realised it was too early in the morning to be flexing his wit.

"Er, yes, they've moved you forward to business class," she said with a smile.

"Well, I'll let it pass just this once," said Max in mock horror and strutted off as if he was in a really bad mood. This got a laugh from its target but a bunch of puzzled looks from the queuing passengers.

It was a small plane. Max disliked them normally as being the size he was, he never seemed to have enough leg room. But not today! Business Class. He glanced around the small section of perhaps twenty people. Four women, very well dressed and the rest men in suits and ties. He looked down at his choice of travelling attire. The jacket didn't really go with the trousers, the shirt was creased, no tie, and *'Oh bollocks,'* one navy sock and one black one.

'Well, if this plane crashes on a desert Isle then the girls won't be fighting over me,' he thought. *'Luckily there aren't many desert islands in the Irish sea,'* he added to the thought and grinned. The steward and the stewardess went through the life-jacket routine, no one paid attention. The moment they got the drinks trolley out though they became the central attraction. Max resisted the temptation to have a straight scotch, but had one with ginger ale instead. *'It's not like it's ten year old malt,'* he thought as the steward placed the open can on his tray table. *'Oh balls,'* he thought, downed the scotch and offered the can of ginger ale to the bearded chap next to him. He declined, but very politely. So politely in fact that Max considered altering his long harboured opinions of red bearded people. *'Nah, still looks dodgy,'* he thought as he reached for the magazine in his seat front. 'Popular Yachting'. He placed it carefully back in its compartment and closed his eyes. It must have been a smooth flight because he only woke up as the wheels were touching the

ground at the other end. He let out a huge yawn as the plane taxied and pulled to a stop. The passengers started to stumble off but the guy next to him was still fast asleep. *'Probably had a rough night,'* Max thought as he picked up his briefcase and walked out of the plane through the tunnel into the terminal. He had all afternoon before the conference opened that evening and he quite fancied a nice lunch and a gentle walk around the sights of Belfast. At the moment he need the loo. He spotted them just across the way and scuttled across. He checked himself in the mirror. He must have had his head lying to the left on the seat because his hair was all squashed on that side. A shower and spruce up at the hotel should do the trick. As he walked through the door he stepped into a scene of commotion. There were a lot of people shouting, and a few running toward the gate he had come from. He passed a couple of ambulancemen as he crossed to the cafe. Deciding to go for an Irish coffee (well when in Rome) he sat down in the corner and placed his order with a wave of the hand and some elaborate miming to the girl behind the counter.

"Excuse me, Sir". The voice came from a young looking security guard standing near to his table looking slightly nervous.

"Yes sonshine, what can I do you for?" Max replied looking up and finishing his coffee with a gulp.

"Would you mind coming with me, Sir," the young chap said slowly and quietly, almost as if he didn't want the other cafe customer to hear. *'Probably want me to point out a drunk guy on the plane that kept touching up the stewardess. There's always one.'* Max grinned. Max took one step out of the door and felt his briefcase snatched out of his hand and was thrown to the floor by a number of pairs of hands. On the way down the group of people in front of him was a blur, then a sharp bang on the ground. The last words he heard before the darkness closed in were

"Er, he's not moving much Sarge."

12

The lights were bright. He closed his eyes again. His head hurt and he was lying down. He felt a hand on his shoulder and heard a female voice he didn't know. He tried to open his eyes again, still too bright. It didn't take a genius to work out that he was on a hospital bed of some sort, but how did he get there. His nose hurt too. He tried the eyes again - he could see a figure seated at the side of his bed.

"Welcome to the land of the living, Max." He knew the voice but couldn't place it. He slowly made out the face. Matthew Banks, his lawyer. He hadn't seen him in years. *'Must be getting some compensation for this accident,'* Max thought. Matthew looked solemn, but then he always did. Matthew had a round pleasant looking face with small brown eyes that resembled a puppy dog that were made slightly larger by the thick gold rimmed glasses that sat high on his nose. Even through the positive greeting Matthews' brow was creased in a frown. Max couldn't remember seeing his face without those frown lines.

"So what do you think I'll get?" Max said cheerfully. Matthew nearly fell of his chair.

"Look Max, I don't know why you did this, well the news reports said way, but this is serious, you're looking at fifteen years."

"Er, what are you talking bout, I'm not getting any compensation for my fall?" Max was very, very puzzled.

"Reasonable force." Matthew said slowly.

"What, breaking my nose and knocking me unconscious?" Max snapped.

"You don't remember, do you?" Matthew said surprised. "Oh shit," he added.

"What's with the 'Oh shit', you never swear Matt," Max said sitting bolt upright in the bed.

"The guy next to you on the plane was a political activist for Sinn Fein," said Matthew.

"The IRA?" Max said stunned.

"Yes. He was poisoned and dead as a dodo by the end of the flight. The police had an anonymous tip off it was you and that you were armed - hence the 'reasonable force.'

"But that's crazy, why would I kill him, or anyone for that matter?" Max was struggling to find words.

"Max. I'm you're lawyer. If you tell me you didn't do it that's fine, but they found traces of the poison in your case".

"A plant," Max said blankly.

"And pictures of the man at your house, work, even diary entries pointing to it". Max swallowed hard, this had to be a very bad dream. "Look Max,if you didn't do it, and judging by the expression on you're face you didn't, then someone extremely clever had some reason to kill this person and they chose you for the fall guy."

(Matt watches too much American TV for his own good).

"But why me?" Max said still in shock.

"Who knows?" came the reply as Matthew took a buff coloured file out of his briefcase.

"They'll be charging you formally soon. The trial is set for the day after tomorrow. You made a lot of headlines and it looks like they want to get it over and done with as quickly as possible."

"What do I do?" Max asked blankly

"Well," Matthew hesitated

"Their evidence is clean cut but it is likely to go to a jury so I suppose there's always a chance. They do have some pretty damning video evidence which won't put the jury on your side."

"What?" Max asked puzzled once more.

"I've seen it. That anti-IRA march you took part in."

"But that was twenty years ago," Max pleaded.

"Yes, but you did thump a policeman."

"Oh yeah, after he belted me with his truncheon. I was never charged, he even bloody apologised!" Max said dismayed.

"I know, but the news footage of the march only shows the bit where you smacked him one," Matthew said slowly.

"Great" Max said burying his head in his hands.

"Look. I've spoken to the prosecution. They will go for a deal. It's not fantastic, but in the circumstances I have to admit I didn't expect anything."

Max sat up straight and took a deep breath.

"OK, what's the score?" he asked not wanting to know the answer.

"If you plead guilty they'll go with severe mental trauma and cut it down to manslaughter. Eight years in a secure institution. You'd probably be out in four or five."

"Oh just four or five years" Max shook his head.

"The alternative is they'll push hard for murder. On the strength of the evidence you will get life, with parole at about year nine."

"Either way I spend the next five years behind bars?"

"Yes. Look Max,if there was another way I'd find it, you know I would. I've been through their case. It's watertight. They've made it look meticulously planned and that the only thing that let you down was the tip off."

Max looked him square in the eyes.

"Not guilty," he said quietly and sternly.

"I was afraid of that," Matthew said forcing a smile, "which is why I drew these up." He reached for the file.

"Character statements from six pillars of society and my opening address," he said, placing them on the table next to Max who forced a smile.

"Oh, and I brought you these," he added pulling half a dozen packets of extra strong mints from his pocket.

"Don't eat them all at once," he said as he stood up and left the room. The click of the locks on the door left Max in silence and he stared at the white walls around him. He reached for the file and opened it. The first name was 'Jason Collinson', Mayor of Croydon. Max read the testimony slowly. It was glowing. He hadn't seen Jason for a couple of years, they'd sort of lost touch. As he read the words over again he smiled. Maybe he had a slim chance after all.

13

"That's him," said James pointing to the television nestling on the bar. The younger man glanced over his shoulder and looked at the photograph displayed on the screen. It wasn't a particularly flattering photo. Max had been hung over when he had that passport picture done for a holiday in Spain. It was all messy hair and stubble. Standing slightly over six feet with very thick set broad shoulders and close shaved blond hair James was a few inches shorter than his colleague but it was easy to see form the body language of the younger man who was in charge.

The volume on the television was turned low and he only made out the words

'....IRA.......peace process.....chilling precision.'

"James," said the other man quietly, "are you thinking we should kill him, maybe?"

James crossed his arms on the table in front of him and leaned forward.

"Maybe. But first I'm going to ask him why he did it."

14

He had butterflies in his stomach and a sick feeling in his throat. His chest was heavy and his collar size shrunk three sizes too small. Max ran his fingers over the highly polished wood of the bench outside court number nine. There was a faint muttering of people coming and going along the corridors. Smiles were uncomfortably absent. Women and men in dark blue and grey suits looking so stern they could have been born that way talked to each other outside each set of doors. *'I'd like to get hold of the bastard that designed these corridor floors,'* he thought. Marble-like stone that meant a constant clicking of at least two or three pairs of high heels and the deeper thuds of the flat black conservative shoes that were the order of the day. His suit suddenly felt out of place. Was it too light? Would the judge think that he was a frivolous man? Max wished he'd worn that dark blue suit that had languished in the back of his wardrobe since his uncle's funeral two years before. The thought triggered a memory and he remembered back to the only other time he had been on the wrong side of the law, and been caught. It was ten years before and he could see the alleyway as clear as the night it happened. He'd been drinking with a couple of his friends after work. This was in the days before the regeneration of the town centre and some of the pubs by the water were great fun but could get a little edgy on a Saturday night, especially if one of the London teams was in town for a game. It wasn't unusual for pubs to close early and barricade their doors when faced with a drunken angry crowd of supposed football fans. It was near closing time and a group of around a dozen visiting fans came crashing into the pub and the landlord ushered the locals out. There was no point in calling the police as at the time they tended to let things play out and turn up after things had calmed down by themselves. It all happened so fast. One minute they were having a quiet pint and the next a chair was being used as a mallet by one of the thugs on whoever was unlucky enough to be in the path towards the bar. Richard, one of Max's friends and the mild one of the bunch didn't even see the chair coming as it crashed down on his head knocking him out cold. Without a thought Max steamed in and despite his lack of fitness, his size and brute strength surprised several of the shaven headed yobs and he managed to lay half a dozen of them out before he himself was beaten unconscious with table leg. He'd woken up in the back of a police van and had eventually faced a charge of grievous bodily harm (GBH) that had been reduced to drunken and disorderly. He'd shattered the jaws of two of the thugs and the judge had told him at the time he'd been lucky as his reaction, which he'd claimed to be self-defense, went well beyond 'reasonable force'. Max unconsciously fingered the scar on the back of his head left by the table leg and looked at his watch again. Five minutes to go now. The time does go slower. Deep breaths, he should at least look calm. *'Now there's an organised man,* Max thought. *'He's got a dark blue suit, black briefcase, silver pens in the top pocket nestling next to the matching handkerchief. A wonderfully conforming paisley'.* He wished he hadn't worn that tie either. If this were the wild west then there would have been a dollar sign stamped on his forehead. This is not how it works in the films. Where was the bustling group of supporters for the condemned man, the snarling of teeth, cute stenographer and eerie classical score? His ex-wife Jan kept popping back into his mind. He wasn't even allowed out of his cell to hold her. They had held hands through the bars. She had worried how suspiciously fast the case had come to court. She told him everything was going to be all right but bar a miracle this would be a short sharp trip to the Isle of Wight and the Maximum security prison. The two guards next to him on the bench suddenly stirred and lifting him up via the cuffs they walked Max to the door. The time they had been sitting there they had been like gargoyles. Going through the two fairly plain wooden doors could not have led to a more stirring scene. The courtroom erupted and the public gallery seemed awash with angry faces and placards. As he lifted his eyes they met those of a young lady who was screaming abuse. He managed to make out the words 'Scum' and 'Peace wrecker' from the taunts. One of the officials quickly ordered the court to be cleared and Max could see people being dragged out by the hordes of policeman present. Within a minute the public gallery was empty apart from a group of news hounds eagerly scribbling away at their pads. As Max was shown to his seat still connected to the two officers he looked over at the prosecutor's table. Dark suit, paisley ensemble - Mr.Organised.

'Oh Shit,' thought Max. Not for the first time that day.

From where he sat Max was probably ten yards from the jury that had been selected to seal his fate. As he cast his eyes over the two rows of six he wished he could change places with any of them. There were four women and eight men (though one of the latter could have passed for one of the former judging by what he was wearing). They all seemed eager to avoid eye contact with him; understandable in the circumstances. Max's two escorts, still handcuffed to him, look bored already.

'Not much scope for job satisfaction,' thought Max looking at the two of them.

"Do you mind if I have a mint?" Max whispered to 'Leftie,' as he had dubbed the officer attached to his left arm. The officer forced a smile and reached into Max's top pocket to retrieve yet another new packet of mints. That was the third that morning. They'd seen him go through a whole packet in his cell when they went to get him and another on the way here.

'*Mmm, taste a bit off,*' Max thought as he crunched away. 'Rightie' had decided to go for a mint as well and also wondered why they tasted peculiar. As the officer fell forward his head just missed the bench in front of him. Max was a little taller and the whole court turned as the thud of skull against wood rang out.

15

It was dark and wet and the little bit of light there was seemed to be fighting a losing battle. By squinting the two men could make out the open hatch above them. One of them walked directly below it and looked up. About ten feet above him the dim light of the laundry room was visible.

"Are you sure they'll bring him here?" he asked as he turned around.

"Put it this way, I wouldn't want to be standing where you are now when they do," came the reply.

Most stretchers are designed for one individual. On this occasion there were two bodies squashed in a haphazard way still connected to a third who was in turn wedged at the back of the ambulance. The doctor and nurse made it a very cosy five as the driver wound round another corner. The nurse was alternating between the two horizontally aligned men checking they were still alive while the doctor frantically examined the remains of the packet of mints. The other conscious passenger was anxiously searching his brain for a plausible explanation as to how a prisoner in his charge and his colleague had been poisoned. His position had been further embarrassed by the sudden disappearance of the man with the keys to the handcuffs (an officer with quite sever bladder problems who was holed up in the loo at the time of the two men's collapse). His radio crackled into life.

"Romeo Victor this is Alpha One. Do you read?"

"Roger Alpha One," he replied quickly.

"The officer with the keys to the cuffs is at the emergency doors of the hospital, please inform the ambulance crew."

"Roger Alpha One," he said and looked at the doctor who nodded that he'd overheard.

The receiving crew at the hospital had been told to expect two cases of poisoning. They were mildly curious as to why a police officer (well he had to be a type of copper as he appeared to be desperately trying not to look like one) with a bunch of keys was waiting with them.

"Bet you don't get this sort of excitement down at St. Judes," Alex grinned to the new boy Simon who'd been transferred over from there the day before.

"Oh sometimes," he smiled, "Don't forgot we're just down the road from the Milwall football ground. Things can get a little racy of a Saturday afternoon."

"I can't find anything yet," said the doctor in a frustrated tone.

I wonder what I'll wear for Jimmy's work do,' thought the nurse as she checked their pulses once more.

"Still alive and sort of kicking," she said as they turned through the gates of the hospital and screeched to a halt outside the doors to emergency.

"Do you think they'll be long?" asked the young lad in the dim tunnel. He was sitting on the trolley and watching the drops falling from the ceiling.

"I shouldn't think so," said James as he looked at his watch. By his calculations their package should fall from above in the next five minutes.

The man with the keys lunged through the ambulance doors and unlocked the handcuffs. He sneered at the officer still pinned to the back wall and leapt back out to give the attendants a hand.

"I've got this one," Simon shouted yanking the slightly larger of the two men onto a stretcher. Alex reached for the other and spun around to find that Simon was already speeding halfway down the corridor.

The scene outside the hospital doors was bedlam. Two dozen police officers trying to keep a mass of journalists at bay. Puzzled patients looked on as a succession of policemen scuttled down the corridors heading for the emergency room. Simon rounded the next corner and stopped the trolley in front of the utility room door. He turned around and braced himself. The door opened, the trolley was pulled in and after a hollow thumping noise Simon slumped to the ground and was dragged inside. A few seconds after the door clicked shut Matthew rounded the corner closely followed by a group of policeman and officials and flew down toward the emergency room.

There was no lock on the inside of the utility room so he had to be quick. The man on the trolley was quite a size so he manoeuvred as close as he could to the opening of the laundry chute and pushed him in feet first. It was quite a squeeze. He swore under his breath as he wedged his shoulder against the motionless lump and pushed.

The doctors in the emergency room watched calmly as the doors flung open and Alex flew in. They transferred the officer to the operating table and attached a host of tubes.

"And the other one?" enquired the taller of the two doctors in a sharp voice that didn't sound at all interested. A number of hovering faces turned and scanned the room which wouldn't have concealed a small sausage dog let alone an eighteen stone man on a trolley.

The body was stuck halfway down the chute. The person who pushed it there was blissfully unaware of this until he followed it and felt a bump as his feet hit its head and dislodged it. The makeshift ramp in the laundry room did its job though as the body rumbled down and slid straight down the hatch into the sewer piping. Arriving moments later, the man leapt off the ramp, dismantled it and followed down the piping shutting the cover as he went. The thump was slightly louder than the splash (but it was a close call) as Max's body landed in the sewer. He was about to take his second trolley ride of the day but sadly he wasn't going to remember this one either.

By the time the three plain clothed officers reached the laundry room, and had put two and two together (more cynical commentators here would suggest

53

that for plain clothed policemen this was an achievement in itself) the body on the trolley had covered a few hundred metres through the sewer, been lifted out through a manhole in a back street and dumped under a blanket in the back of a plain white transit van. Another five minutes and the van was on the south circular. Another ten and it had become a blue Renault.

Max had always been sceptical that you could tell a lot about a person from their eyes, but had never been in a situation in which to put it to the test, until now. The three men that he could see in the back of the van were all wearing masks and looking into their eyes he saw nothing but harsh concentration. It is amazing how in all the big-budget thrillers churned out by Hollywood no one has ever mentioned that being scared witless and having adrenaline running rampant through your veins in fact enhances your senses tenfold. At that particular moment, with the feel of cold steel against his temple, Max's sense of smell was equal to that of a blind man. Unfortunately, the position of the pistol meant the revealed armpit of one of his captors - the sweatiest of the bunch. As his eyes plunged into darkness from a painful thud against the aforementioned temple Max made a mental note. *'Add to the important to remember list; If you encounter a crazed paramilitary with a personal hygiene problem, keep it to yourself...........'*

16

'A chair. A room. Four walls. A table. Body tied to the chair. Man coming through the door with a cloth pad, pushing it over my mouth. Darkness......'

17

Max was beginning to get annoyed with the process of regaining consciousness. This time the effects of the chloroform had given him a splitting headache much like a hangover. He was in the back of a van again. The first thing he noticed was that he was breathing through his nose. This was directly attributable to the thick piece of tape that had been wound across his mouth. His hands were tied behind his back too. There were two men in the back of the van with him and Max could hear the third, the driver, talking loudly in the front. The van was moving. The younger lad he recognised from the previous van ride. The other was different. Conversation was out, so Max tried to examine his surroundings. It was a different van from the last, smaller and more compact. It had no sliding door and a single hatch door at the back. The two men both had stern expressions on their faces and pistols on their laps. The younger one realised that Max had woken up and grinned at him. He then tapped the butt of his pistol against the palm of his left hand. Max looked over at the other man who was larger and stockier. His clothes were rougher and almost exclusively denim.

"What do you think you're looking at scum?" he sneered at Max and gave him a hard punch to the ribs. Max tried to cough which was impossible with his mouth taped up. The result was a lot of heavy breathing through his nose and his eyes began to water. For the first time in his life Max wondered whether he'd be better off dead. People sometimes say it but it takes a lot to make you actually think it. He thought fate had been listening when he felt the impact of the lorry which threw him onto the floor. He heard some shouting before another bang as the van bounced off the central reservation onto its side and was pinned there by the lorry. He was bounced around like a rag doll. A montage of blurred images that he later suspected had been his life flashed before his eyes and then nothing but green. He squinted. They had stopped moving. He heard more shouting and out of the corner of his eye he could see the back door being forced open. The younger lad was being carried out covered in blood. Max realised the green colour in front of him was the shirt of the other man who was slumped in front of him. He managed to get onto his knees and shuffled out of the back door and into the sunshine. The scene was chaos. About a dozen cars had been going too fast to avoid the lorry and were across the carriageway at all angles. Many others had pulled up and were helping people out of their cars. The screams of a man with a broken leg diverted most of the helpers' attention to his red estate car which was wedged underneath the side of the lorry. Max managed to slip into the ditch in between the carriageways unnoticed and slowly made his way along it. After fifty yards he got off his knees and stood up cautiously. The traffic was backing up now and he could hear sirens coming closer. Running with your hands behind your back is somewhat of an art form but Max managed to make it across the other carriageway and into the woods boarding the motorway. His progress through the trees and bushes was more cautious after he fell flat on his face the second time. He need not have panicked as the other three from the van were in a pretty bad state and were being attended to by a couple of ambulance crews. After stumbling for half an hour he came to the edge of the wood which met the back of a small industrial estate. He slowly approached a large brown building. Tired, aching and surprisingly hungry Max staggered in through the warehouse door of a furniture importers. The store man could scarcely believe his eyes as Max slumped into a chair outside his office. A cut over Max's left eyebrow had left a streak of dried blood down his face and he looked very worse for wear. The store man shouted to the secretary for the first aid kit and the two of them slowly removed the tape from Max's mouth. After spluttering for a while he forced a smile.

"What the hell happened to you?" asked the store man as he cleaned the cut carefully with a damp pad of cotton wool.

Within two hours of the police's arrival at the scene of the motorway pile up the phone in Anders' hotel room rang and his contact at New Scotland Yard gave him the location. The firearms in the back of the van had been traced to an IRA cell that was operating on the mainland. After a half dozen calls Anders and Easton vacated their rooms, settled the accounts with cash and made their way to the car parked across the street. At the same time a dozen office workers in the Oxford area took an unexpected afternoon off.

The cup of tea and half a packet of digestive biscuits had put Max in a better frame of mind. He wasn't sure the two that had just cleaned him up had believed his story and he was a little worried that they had reached for the phone to call the police the moment he had stepped out of the door. He wasn't going to take any chances and as soon as he was around the corner he climbed over a fence and headed off through a field of deep grass at a quick pace. He had no cause for alarm as the store man was currently filling the secretary in on a similar incident in his family when his cousin had been caught by his wife with his next door neighbour. He'd got away with a broken nose and a couple of black eyes. This guy had been less lucky. Fancy torching his car and dumping him in the woods. Relatives could be so vindictive.

18

The slow monotonous beep of the machines would have cured even the most committed insomniac. The man in front of her was a shadow of the man that she had stood by for thirty years. The room was cold to the eye despite the obvious attempts to create a sense of comfort. The promises of the doctors rang hollow in her mind. Was he going to get better? Her heart held out hope but her mind had long given up. Countless operations had chipped away at her faith in him regaining consciousness and coming home once more.

19

The smoke was beginning to get to Pete. If he could choose a place to be on a Sunday afternoon this would not be it. The pub was large and this was the busier bar - the 'lounge bar'. Most of the clientele were older country types but there were two or three groups of younger people and these were the focus of his attention. Pete didn't look too out of place in the busy bar. He had chosen jeans and a back sweater with a stripy collared shirt underneath. Smart casual, office manager type out for quiet pint on the weekend look. He glanced over at the mirrored back of the bar at his reflection. He looked perhaps a little young for the character, but about right for his twenty seven years. Dark brown hair that he was trying to have in that kind of messy but smart look. Short at the sides and back with a bit spiky on top. It was the look that his father had duly expected him to be sporting after university. Some job in the city, banking, finance, something with a future. He remember how his father hadn't been able to hide the disappointment in his face when Pete had proudly announced his first job in journalism. At least Pete had kept up with the sport, which is something that they shared. Tennis and Squash, a couple of times a month. He dreaded the monthly conversations in the bar after a game when the subject of work, and 'getting a proper job' seemed to come up every time.

If the rumours were true and he could get more information then maybe he could finally get shot of the tin-pot local paper and get touted by one of the nationals. The 'Wessex Warbler' had never carried a story as strong as this and it was half written already. 'Satanic Sacrifices in the Home Counties'. He had plenty of background. Now if he could get an interview with a worshipper, or get himself invited to a sacrifice... This last thought lifted his spirits considerably and he sipped his pint and moved over to a stool at the bar. Unbeknown to him the group next to him were pig farmers.

"...........and that'll mean we get two to slaughter in one go," said the man in the Argyle sweater and green boots. Pete's ears pricked up and he listened more intently.

"But you'll have to be careful - you know how the blood gets everywhere," the other man warned and motioned with his arms

'*This is great!*' Pete thought and leaned yet closer. '*The tip off was right, and they seem so brazen about it all.*' Unfortunately the stool he was sitting on was not designed for leaning and before he could do anything Pete felt himself falling backwards. Its quite amazing how far three quarters of a pint of lager can travel with the slightest provocation. Before Pete had even hit the floor most of the liquid had passed over the saloon bar doors and slammed into the back of a large man dressed in leather bikers gear. As he hit the floor, the glass hit the large man in the back of the head. Pete's fall had gone unnoticed in the noise of the lounge bar but the commotion in the next bar was considerable. The leather, and now beer clad, biker after a brief dizzy moment had rounded on a well dressed man standing next to the saloon doors. He had been laughing at something his friend had just said and was waiting for his next drink from another mate at the bar. To the wounded man the laughter and empty hands were more than enough evidence and he shook his fists and began pushing the man into the wall. The smaller man rallied and with two swift jabs he caught the heavier man full on the chin putting him swiftly onto his backside. The rest of the bar had begun cheering as the biker got clumsily to his feet, shook his head and charged at the man again.

Meanwhile Pete was on all fours moving quickly through the maze of feet in the bar. He could see a door and was going to get to it as quickly as possible. He was almost there when a lady decided to change position on her chair and move her stilettoed feet. Pete saw them coming and closed his eyes and braced himself. Nothing. He opened his eyes at a squint and saw the heel neatly placed between his finger and thumb. A bead of sweat glistened on his brow as he gently removed his hand. A few more shuffles and he was through the doors. He'd been on his knees for so long it didn't occur to him to stand up and he aimed for the next door he could see. He found himself inside a telephone booth and this prompted him to stand up. He could hear the rumpus going on in the bar but it was fairly faint. He picked up the receiver quickly and pretended to be listening to someone on the other end. There was someone in the booth next to him and instinctively he tried to make out what the man was saying.

"Yes it is important, I've already said that......yes I'll hold." The man sounded agitated. It didn't sound too interesting but Pete didn't fancy going back into the bar just now.

"Yes, I want to speak to Kathy. It is a matter of life and death."

'Hmmm, that sounds better,' Pete thought.

There was a brief silence then the man continued.

"Hello Kathy? Yes, yes its me.... Yes, I'm fine.... No I can't, they'd find me if I said...I just wanted to say I was OK and alive. Is everything ok there?.......I thought they might have......What men took what files?....Which patients?...Mr Verdkyll!... I knew it!.....I'd better go.....I'll call again soon, please tell Jan I'm OK, they've probably tapped my home phone and hers...."

'Sod sacrifices,' Pete thought *'This guy's on the run from someone, don't know who but I'm sure as hell going to find out.'*

He heard the receiver go down in the next booth and waited until he heard the adjoining door open. It was then that he saw him. The same man as on the 10 o'clock news the night before. Max something or other - hit man who had broken free.

'Wow what a story!' he thought as he slipped out of the booth and the side door of the pub following the big man's footsteps.

Two men left the lounge bar half a minute later. They headed down the same lane as they left the pub. Pete had seen him go down this alley but it was long and deserted.

'Surely he couldn't have reached the other end so quickly,' he thought.

His eyes nearly popped out of his head as a large hand shot out of a gap in the fence and grabbed his throat. Within a second a gate opened wide and Pete was pulled inside and the gate closed quickly. He saw the face close up now. It was rounder than it looked on the telly but the dark hair and dark eyes were unmistakable. The man motioned to him to be quiet and Pete strained his eyes toward the fence. He could hear footsteps moving past and within a minute the grip around his neck was released.

"You're not going to kill me?" he stammered.

"Hell no," Max said, "but they might," he added motioning to the alleyway.

"I think they think you're with me," he smiled.

Pete considered this for a moment. "You're Max Jones aren't you?"

"Yes," Max replied, "And you are?" he asked sarcastically.

"Pete, but who are they?" Pete asked, forever the reporter despite the fact he was moments from mortal danger.

"The IRA I assume - well they seemed pretty annoyed I managed to get free."

"The IRA?" Pete said with genuine surprise. "Did they break you out?" he asked.

"Yep, it was just as much a shock for me too," Max whispered.

"Did you kill that guy then - the one on the news?" Pete couldn't believe he was having a whispered conversation with an alleged hit-man, down an alley.

"No, I was set up," Max replied.

"I knew it!" Pete whispered with an air of satisfaction.

63

"I'm the only one in the office that bet on you being innocent," he added smugly.

"I'm touched," said Max and still with sarcasm. "Now look. You'd better get your ass out of here or you'll end up six feet under, which is probably where I'll be before the day is out..."

Before Max could finish they heard a man shouting from the other end of the alley. Max bolted and climbed over the wall a few feet behind them. Without thinking Pete followed. His feet landed with a thump, which he felt mostly in his knees. He saw the large man disappear around the corner of some houses and with the excitement of a kid on Xmas morning he ran after him.

If he were to be chased by the IRA again Max would probably not choose a motorcycle as his getaway vehicle. However, the petrol station beckoned and the gleaming Honda, which had thoughtfully just been filled by its owner, was sitting there with the keys in it. Pete stopped dead as Max leapt on.

"You surely don't intend on taking that," he blurted out but before Max could answer a bullet rattled the row of oil-cans next to the pump. Despite being half his size Pete seemed to get his hands all the way around Max's waist in an instant and the engine roared into life. The bike wobbled left and right for the first 100 yards or so as Max got used to the controls again. It had been a good ten years since he'd ridden a bike as a motorcycle courier. There was that kick again! The rush of wind and weaving around the tight corners of the little village Max was in his element. His face broke into a broad grin, in complete contrast to Pete whose first time on the back of 750cc of Japanese steel gave him the look of person reaching the highest peak of a roller coaster. The two figures had switched their feet for a somewhat faster Rover. A few miles out of the village on a straight piece of road Max motioned to Pete to pass him the spare helmet. He could have assumed this was to protect his face from the wind, but it had more to do with drowning out Pete's cries and moans. An inquisitive herd of cows watched closely as the bike followed now by the car sped past a small farm. Max was having far too much fun to pay too much attention to the danger behind. Thoughtfully though they gave him the odd reminder of the small coned cylindrical type. Max felt Pete's grip tighten considerably and his right leg drop away. He'd gone quiet too. He'd been hit. As abruptly as it had begun the fun-ride stopped. Max focused his attention on the predicament. How was he going to lose the car? Should he get off the main roads where the police would surely be looking for the stolen bike very soon? He also needed to find a doctor for Pete. The next road sign triggered something in his mind and he opened up the bike even further. As soon as the speed increased it was slammed down by the back of a 16 wheeler blocking the road ahead. Go around on a blind corner or get shot - easy choice - he threw the bike out into the middle of the road. *'Isn't that just great,'* Max thought as the oncoming truck rounded the corner. "Breathe in!" he screamed into his helmet - plenty of room - OK, so both of the mirrors had been torn off the bike in the process but at least the car couldn't follow. Hard left, then right, left again. He took random turns for perhaps ten minutes. Max pushed the bike until his heart finally stopped racing. *'Well if they're still with us they deserve to get us,'* Max thought as he pulled in behind a farm building. He was relieved to hear only the cackling of a couple of chickens as he turned off the engine. Removing his helmet he looked back at his passenger. "Pete you OK?" - judging by the expression on his face that was a pretty dumb question. Pete's leg was bleeding as he gingerly got off the bike. He managed a small grin as Max slapped him gently on the back. *'I'm going to die,'* Pete thought as he looked at Max. *'if this bloody bullet doesn't kill me his driving will'.*

"I've been better," he muttered.

"OK I'm sorry, but I know someone who'll sort this out for us," said Max

"What a doctor?" Pete replied surprised.

"Sort of," Max paused "He used to be, he's a vet now."

"Oh great, just wheel me in next to Flossy, Daisy and Lassie," Pete groaned.

"It'll be fine," Max said reassuringly. "I met him at a piss up at a Union conference, he lives about forty miles North of here in Tilverton".

20

After washing the wound under a tap inside the barn and covering it with a clean handkerchief Max helped Pete back onto the bike and slowly edged down the small lanes. It had now begun to get dark and Max decided to keep the bike for it was easier to hide than a car, and besides, he didn't know how to hot-wire a car. The journey to Tilverton was slow but without incident and they soon pulled up by the phone box at the edge of town.

"Hello, 45728." the voice was deep and friendly

"Hello Angus, its Max.....Bournemouth last year, remember?"

"Max you old sod, of course I remember! It's not every day I get arrested for indecent exposure."

"Ah yes, the midnight swim, well we had had a few beers," Max grinned

"It's great to hear from you, but aren't you supposed to be a wanted dangerous criminal on the run?"

"What do you think," Max laughed, "me, a hit-man?"

"Of course not, only kidding. Is there anything I can do to help?"

"Well actually, a cup of tea would go down a treat. We're in the phone box opposite the clock tower. You did say that if I was ever in the area."

"Great! Harbouring escapees happens to be one of my favourite pastimes - follow the road out of town up the hill and take the second left - we're the first place on the right."

"Thanks mate," Max said and put the receiver down gently with a heavy sigh. He looked out at Pete who was propping up his head with his hands. *'He's a good lad,'* thought Max. His jeans were torn in a number of places and where they weren't bloody they were covered in mud.

"Hey Pete," he called over, "fancy a nice cup of tea?" he said smiling.

"If there's a brandy in it," came the weary reply.

Within five minutes they had pulled up in front of a small cottage to be met by a goat that was wandering around the front garden. The flicker of an open fire reached them through a porthole window next to the front door. Max reached for the large brass knocker and gave a series of thumps. Almost immediately the door opened and was filled by a tall bearded man sporting a huge grin

"Max, I heard you come up the lane. What are you riding? Sounds like a tank."

'His handshake is as strong as I remember it,' Max thought as he retrieved his hand from the big man's grip.

"Angus, I've got someone with me. Pete this is Angus. Angus, Pete. He's picked up a bit of a scratch, do you mind taking a look at him?" Max asked as they walked through into the hallway.

"Sure, I'll get Anne to sort out my bag," Angus smiled.

"This is Pete," Max announced as he ushered the limping Pete into the warm lounge. Anne emerged smiling and carrying a large black bag. She was very different to her husband, small and pretty, her dark brown wavy hair touching her shoulders. Strong arms though. Angus towered over even Max although his size was softened by the thick brown beard hanging below his messy mousy hair. The thick grey woolly jumper and cords made him look almost cuddly, which is an achievement for a man of 6'6".

"So 'e fall of the bike then?" enquired the big man as he showed Pete to the small sofa in the corner of the room. Max held back his reply as Angus looked at the outstretched leg. His smile suddenly left his face. "Max, for God's sake he's got a bullet in his thigh!" he frowned as he turned round to Max who was perched on the edge of an armchair.

"I suppose you wouldn't believe that it was from a freak duck hunting accident?" Max offered lamely.

"What do you think, and before you answer that I don't think I really want to know," Angus sighed reaching inside his bag.

"I suppose not, but can you fix him?"

"I can't promise he'll be able to enter the 'Miss Lovely Legs' pageant this year but the bullet is fairly accessible. I think it must have hit something else first as its not too deep. I had a similar wound with the Jones' mare and a pebble last week."

"Oh great," Pete groaned softly.

"Here's your tea young man," Anne smiled as she handed him a large cream coloured mug.

Pete drank the tea and watched as Max and Angus chatted with great animation and frequent bouts of laughter recalling their exploits in Bournemouth. He'd begun to like this big guy Max Jones. He could come across a bit brash, and OK he was really stubborn, and I suppose he could do with a few evening classes at charm school, but deep down he was an OK guy. There was no way he was a killer. The goings on at the hospital did reek of something and he was sure that it was all linked with Max being set up. It was very well done, but the question was, by whom. It was going to be a fantastic story he thought. Mmm, nice cup of tea.

"So, where's the anaesthetic," Pete piped up.

"You've just drunk it," Max laughed and Pete joined in as he felt his eyelids go heavy and the room slowly drift into darkness.

21

Pete awoke to the sound of a cow mooing. It seemed pretty loud and as he squinted and put on his glasses he turned his head toward the window.

"MOOOOO..." It was definitely a cow and a large one at that. It was standing outside the window with its head through the opening and approximately six inches from his face. Its focus appeared to be the vase of fresh flowers on the bedside table.

'Where on earth am I?' Pete thought as he looked around the small room. It was very cosy. A lot of floral designs with everything matching, from the curtains to the tablecloth. He wasn't unduly worried as it looked like a nice enough place. The cow and lack of noise suggested he was somewhere in the countryside. It took a few more moments before the previous day's events came flooding back to him. The dull numbness of his left leg signalled his complete return to consciousness. He took a deep breath - clean air!

'This is a great story,' he thought. He was on the run with one of the most notorious criminals of the past few years, been chased by the IRA and shot into the bargain. No more 'Local fisherman catches Wellington boot' stories - no more standing in the pouring rain on a Sunday afternoon watching Melchester Junior 11 get hammered by another equally obscure team of young louts. The sun was out and the smell of a country morning fuelled Pete's appetite for adventure. The cow was now more than half way through the flowers and paying him little attention. He'd lived near the countryside all his life and had almost become oblivious to its beauty. His visits to farms had, in the majority of cases resulted in getting covered in mud and/or having abuse

thrown at him. Farmers, like most people have an almost in-built dislike for journalists. He was about to attempt to leap out of bed when the door opened and a tray appeared in the gap. At first the steam from a pot of tea obscured the face of the person holding the tray, but nevertheless the cow instinctively knew who it was and hastily withdrew its head.

"Good morning young man," said Anne smiling.

"Hello," replied Pete glad to see the friendly face almost as much as the huge breakfast on the tray. This was, in all possible definitions a 'full' English breakfast.

"You're quite a lucky chap you know," Anne grinned as she laid the tray across his lap.

"It's not common around here to have received a bullet and been around the next morning," her grin turned to a laugh and Pete joined in.

"Thanks for the hospitality," Pete said thinking it sounded naff but not really knowing what to say.

"Oh, that's OK. Angus does have some unusual friends I'll give him that. Max is a great fella though, heart of gold," she said as she left the room. This suggested he should eat, and he wasn't going to argue. He was starving and got stuck in.

The path ran alongside the hedgerow that separated the cornfields from the grazing land. It wasn't wide enough for two people and as Angus walked through the knee deep grass in his boots they glistened with the morning dew.

"What now?" he asked.

Max was walking slowly with his hands in his pockets and a thoughtful expression on his face.

"To be honest, I'm not altogether sure. I know I'm the subject of an elaborate set-up, I have very little proof and virtually no expertise with which to validate the little I have. Both the police and the IRA are looking for me and

71

I have already got one person shot." At this last sentence he paused and Angus quickly added,

"Yes, but Pete came with you voluntarily remember," he said firmly

" I suppose so," Max agreed but that didn't detract much from the fact that it had still been his fault.

"I need to find someone with knowledge in the neural area. Maybe they could piece together what these people were up to," Max said as he started walking again. They were now half way down the narrow path which lead to what could be loosely described as a barn of some sort.

"If you need to stay a while, the offer's open," said Angus putting his arm on Max's shoulder.

"The lad ought to rest a couple of days. It was only a little nick but he could do with taking it easy," he added. Somewhere back toward the cottage a cock crowed loudly prompting both men to turn around just in time to see Anne emerge from the house waving frantically what looked like a newspaper.

They had made second page news. The rundown of the chase down country lanes, the stolen bike and Max's 'kidnap' of an unknown hostage would probably have made it to the front page except another Royal crisis had broken overnight and the papers were all jostling for position with different 'Exclusives'. The Telegraph carried the headline 'One is not amused' next to a picture of the queen they'd managed to dig up where she had a frown on her face. Max read their story intently. Despite containing a surprising amount of accurate facts it has been glamorised considerably. He was flattered at being described as an 'expert' biker and Pete was annoyed at being labelled 'anonymous'. The one good thing was that the paper suggested that he had fled west into Avon, probably to Bristol or Gloucester and that area was being monitored heavily by the police. That put him a good 150 miles away from scrutiny.

72

22

This was embarrassing. Easton knew it. Anders knew it. The latter was on the phone in a small hotel in Berkshire. The call was transatlantic and the person on the other end was not amused. Apart from standing at a phone booth in the pouring rain on a biting Brooklyn morning, he was getting little out of a stubborn Anders as to why things were not going to plan.

"He'll be dead within a week," Anders snarled and put down the receiver. He was embarrassed more than he had ever been in his career. The saga had dragged on for months now. He would have put a bullet in the guy's head long ago but the agency decided on this IRA thing. Very messy. It had run perfectly but with such an unpredictable group as the IRA they should have been more careful. Now they had the man at the centre of it all running loose around the countryside. At least the British had assumed the IRA had been behind the previous day's chase. That was how it must stay. He was sure that Max didn't know what the hell was going on. Heck, even they didn't know the half of it. As far as the rest of the world was concerned this Max character was going to leave this earth at the hands of avenging IRA gunmen. It would have to be soon though, as the longer it went on the more loose ends there would be to tied up, and he was already bored with England.

23

In the four days that Max and Pete stayed at the farmhouse the focus of the media remained strong. Each day every available newspaper was bought from the village store by Angus, much to the bemusement of the shop's grey-haired owner. Speculation was rife as to Pete's identity, and names of missing persons from all corners of the country entered and left the fray with quick succession. Various theories as to why the IRA had not killed Max outright were being bandied about, from the amusing to the ridiculous. One paper had on the Monday run the idea that the IRA wanted to find the people behind Max as they felt he was just a pawn in some large international conspiracy. This was quickly forgotten the following day when Scotland Yard released a statement.

"It has been made known by a source within the IRA that abduction of Max Jones was not sanctioned by the main leaders but carried out by a hard-line faction whose sole purpose was to avenge the murder for which he was being tried."

The media and the British public seemed to take this as almost read. Most sources now reported that Max had left the country and he had even been spotted in Geneva of all places. Max smiled at the thought of being in Switzerland.

'A *bit wide of the mark,*' he thought as he sipped a steaming mug of cocoa. Pete sat opposite him in a fireside chair with his cheeks a healthy glow from sitting so close to the open fire. He was cutting more pieces from the day's papers and scribbling notes on them. He finished with the scissors and struck up a conversation.

"Where are we off to then," his voice sounded light as ever and his strength had definitely returned.

"I am off to try and clear my name," came Max's stern reply.

"I thought you might try that," replied Pete as if rehearsed. He continued in a confident tone.

"Firstly you need help, especially in getting your side of the story across."

"Yeah but...," Max tried to argue but Pete was on a roll.

"And secondly, I know where you've been, what you have done and where you're likely to go."

"You mean you would turn me in?" Max said sounding hurt. This didn't deter his young friend who grinned and added, "The story gets written Max - as soon as we part company."

Max shrugged and sat back in his chair. He admired this lad and although it was a cliché he reminded him of a certain stubborn lad he once was. The major plus point was that he fervently believed in Max's innocence. He was a good partner to have, even if the sole benefit was to keep Max sane.

"Thanks for the choice," Max said quietly as he stood up and went to the kitchen. He looked out of the window at a clear starry sky. Jan would be watching the stars too. He could picture her on the balcony at the back of the house - sitting there in dressing gown and quilt and the dulcet tones of Smokey Robinson filtering through from the lounge. He'd left messages at her work every day of his recent freedom. He knew to talk to her was too risky - who knows who would be listening. He sighed as he poured another steaming cup of cocoa into a mug.

"OK," he said slowly as he returned to the living room.

"This is for your ears only, I'm not going to tell Angus and Anne which way we are going." Pete nodded and perched on the edge of his seat.

"There is a lecturer at Southampton University, a neurology expert . He owes a mate of mine a favour and I think he'll help."

"How?" Pete's pen was poised and Max had his complete attention.

"I need him to find a reason why those behind the research are so anxious to keep the tests they are doing on people's brain tissue quiet, and why they were taking the tissue while they were still living."

"You mean they were taking parts of people's brains while they were still living?" Pete said with a look of horror and disgust on his face.

"Uh huh, well sort of. All of the patients I can remember, except the last two, had life threatening illnesses and were being kept on life support systems," Max replied.

"And the last two?" Pete was fascinated and his pen was working overtime.

"They had come in with neural problems, but not necessarily fatal. They were obviously getting desperate."

Pete opened his mouth to speak but paused and seemed to be thinking.

"Any proof?" he asked

"Some," Max sighed, "but it's of no use until I find out what research they would have been doing. It's secret enough to kill for."

"Could it be cancer or HIV or something like that?" Pete suggested.

"I suppose so, but we're scratching around in the dark. Hopefully this guy can give me a better idea," Max smiled.

"And then?"

"Then we take another look at my proof to see how much it's really worth."

The additional time spent at Angus and Anne's had been put to good use. The bike had been painted and a number plate from an old cycle and sidecar switched onto it. Max had cut his hair short and dyed it jet black and both he and Pete had a complete change of clothes. This latter point was achieved with some difficulty as although Angus and Max were roughly the same size, Pete was much smaller. He was kitted out in a wool sweater that had shrunk in the wash and some of Anne's jogging bottoms. They also had matching raincoats.

As they sat on the bike in the misty morning sun, Angus smiled and shook both of their hands in turn. *'They won't win any fashion prizes,'* he thought.

"I'd never recognise you," he said trying to keep a straight face.

"Its not really you I'm worried about," laughed Max. He turned the key and the bike kicked into life and purred like an oversized kitten. They had exchanged helmets and Pete was now wearing a blue one and Max the red. They both shook violently as Max guided the bike down the lane. It was 5am. They would be well on their way to Southampton before anyone was on the roads. Had they not had their helmets on they may have heard the flock of sheep bleating as they pulled onto the main road. Twenty miles further on, had they been looking for it, they may have seen a green four door Jaguar pull out of a small lane and take the same A40 turning they made. It was going to be "an overcast of day with afternoon showers," well at least according to Radio 4 and that was good enough for Max. Sure enough, after they had completed over half of their journey and they had found the M3 it began to drizzle. Max decided to stop off at a motorway service station for a quick break.

The service station was busy and Max and Pete finally found a table in the corner of the packed café. Max had swapped his helmet for a peaked cap and Pete smiled as they sat watching the hustle and bustle.

"You look more like James Herriot every day you know," Pete smirked.

"That's rich coming from a person with the colour co-ordination of a blind chameleon," Max replied with a large grin on his face. This isn't going to be as bad as I thought Max mused as he gulped down the steaming coffee.

'Only 60 miles to Southampton, we should be there by 11,' he thought.

"I've never actually seen one of these places busy," Pete piped up.

"Well you haven't lived then," Max said sarcastically.

"Its great for people watching though don't you think?" Pete added

"Suppose so," Max agreed. He was too busy thinking to chat, but Pete seemed to be in the mood to talk so he made an effort.

"I see what you mean. Take that guy over there by the counter. Yeah, the tall one. Its raining, dim and dull and he's wearing sunglasses indoors."

"Hey, maybe he's got eyesight problems?" Pete suggested

"Nah, more like social problems. He looks like a raincoat pervert."

"OK, Mr Expert, how about the man at the table in the corner. He looks more normal. Tell me about him," Pete smiled.

"Ah yes. Young, short black hair and a really dull suit. I reckon he's 26 if he's a day and a sales rep."

"What does he sell?" asked Pete who was enjoying the game.

"Shower curtains and sometimes watches."

"What out of a suitcase!" Pete laughed.

"Oh yeah, and his name's Kevin."

"OK, the girl at the next table from him?"

"Blonde, 22. Training to be a scuba diving instructor."

"Definitely," Pete laughed again.

"OK, now a really tough one. The two badly dressed guys sitting at this table."

The voice was deep and threatening and accompanied by the barrel of a gun firmly pressed between Max's shoulder blades.

"That's a toughie," Max coughed.

"Max Jones and Pete Smalt, two smartasses currently training to be corpses," Anders said quietly. Pete looked anxiously over at Max.

"It's the dopey one with the sunglasses," he said through clenched teeth.

"Shit, how'd he get over here so quietly," Max said under his breath.

"Maybe he's wearing trainers," Pete said trying to stay calm.

"When you gentlemen have quite finished. Get up slowly and walk to the exit. No funny stuff, we only want to ask you a few questions," Anders said slowly.

Max got up slowly as instructed but after taking two steps spun round and threw a right jab toward the man wearing sunglasses. Max issn't quite Mike Tyson and Anders saw the punch so early he could have sent a postcard to it, and even got a reply. As he side-stepped it connected with Pete's chin full on and sent him sprawling across a nearby table. The previously noisy café went quiet and Max stood there gasping at what he'd done. He felt a tap on his shoulder. He turned round to see a group of truck drivers who, sitting at a nearby table close by had seen the 'attack' on the young lad.

"Oi, arsehole, why don't you try someone your own size," said the first guy whose tattoos were probably the most attractive thing about him. Roughly Max's size the man's clenched teeth were at the centre of a pockmarked face covered with a few days stubble. This challenge brought a small volley of cheers from the other tables. The man stood up to face Max head on. Max glanced at Anders who had taken a step back with his hand inside his coat pocket.

'Oh well,' Max thought and after feigning a shrug promptly head-butted the large man in front of him square on the bridge of the nose. While he fell to his knees screaming with blood pouring from his face his mates piled in. Within the space of ten seconds the centre of the café looked like a rather violent rugby scrum. Pete slowly got his senses back and the first thing he became aware of was a damp serviette being dabbed on his face. He opened his eyes and squinted.

"My glasses," he said and began fumbling around.

"Here you go," said a soft and sweet voice. He put them on and looked at the young lady whose table he was spread over.

"Thanks," he said awkwardly. He was embarrassed and she was pretty which made it worse. She had short brown hair, gorgeous brown eyes and soft red lips. He realised he was staring and blushed. She smiled and blushed too. The sound of a glass being smashed on someone's head brought him abruptly back to reality.

"What's your name?" he asked quickly

"Elizabeth," she replied shyly.

"Hey, Romeo," shouted Max from near the counter. The brawl had turned into a free for all and Max was currently entwined with a bearded man in a checked shirt. Pete leapt the adjoining table and bounded across to him. He shoved his hand over the counter to try and find a weapon and found a cappuccino tube in his hand.

"Coffee?" he asked the man politely and placed the end of the tube down the collar of his shirt. He flipped the switch and the man let out a yelp as the steaming coffee flowed down his chest and he quickly removed his hands from around Max's throat. Max jumped up and looked towards the door. There was dopey with the sunglasses again. He looked to the other side of the café at the large plate glass window and their bike, which stood on the other side of it.

"Oh bollocks," he said and ran at the window throwing his shoulder at the glass. It's amazing how far back someone bounces off a double glazed window.

"Toughened," Pete smiled as he helped Max to his feet. He grabbed one of the metal pepper pots from the counter and hit the large pane right in the bottom corner. The bang as the unit shattered was huge and Pete grinned.

"Always wanted to do that," he shouted as he jumped through the frame and clambered behind Max onto the bike. The tyres spun in the wet as they sped off. Easton stood nonchalantly against the green Jaguar as Anders ran out of the café doors.

"Very smooth," said the young man as he got into the driver's seat.

"Just stay with him," Anders growled as he slammed the door and the car squealed toward the exit.

In normal road conditions a 750cc motorcycle and a V6 Jaguar would be fairly evenly matched. However, it was raining and if you were a gambling person the word JAGUAR would be carefully etched on your betting slip. The mitigating circumstances in Max and Pete's favour were that they were two minutes ahead, there was a lot of traffic on the motorway and the bike could weave where the car could not. Also, British drivers have an in built fear of motorcycles and an equally strong dislike of people wealthy enough to own a Jaguar.

The two minutes turned into merely one on an open stretch but as they progressed to the coast, Easton could make no further gains on the bike, much to Anders' frustration. As the car squeezed through gaps most people wouldn't try and put an electric bubble car through, Anders knew better than to criticise Easton's driving. With the reverence usually reserved for fighter pilots, Easton had already gained the reputation of one of the best drivers of any four wheeled vehicle in the agency. Anders was glad to be in the passenger seat. His Beretta lay on his lap. It always had a new magazine and he had added a silencer. They were too far from the bike to get a clear shot but he wasn't unduly worried, it would only be a matter of minutes.

"Shit," exclaimed Easton as he caught the blue flashing lights of a police car in his mirror.

"Didn't you see him?" enquired a genuinely surprised Anders.

"Hell no, it's an unmarked car, the blue lights are in his grill of all places," came the reply.

'What a waste of a good bullet,' Anders said to himself as he wound down his window.

A minute later two policemen stood looking at their crumpled Vauxhall sitting in a ditch by the hard shoulder wondering how on earth a car with new tyres had got such a severe puncture. Two days later a single bullet wrapped in a neat sample bag would land on an embarrassed US ambassador's desk courtesy of an extremely pissed off New Scotland Yard.

Max's mind was racing. He didn't know Southampton very well. In fact his memories of the place were very vague. He'd been on a few pub-crawls down near the dock areas whilst visiting his friend Mark at the old university down there. He smiled to himself as he remembered clambering around the shipyard after the pubs had closed. It had been winter time and the moon had given them plenty of light for exploring. They'd climbed aboard a yacht that was moored there and had been nabbed by a security guard. Ah, but the docks will have changed if Dover and Ramsgate were anything to go by. All ferries, hovercrafts, 24hr restaurants, and French speaking stewards everywhere. The commercial docks wouldn't have changed too much he hoped. He remembered lots of concrete buildings and alleys - lots of places to hide. It wasn't much of a plan but it was all he had. He caught a brief glimpse of the Jaguar again in his mirrors but the rain was getting heavier. They were still there. The traffic now slowly came to a standstill. His heart leapt at a sight that would normally get him mint munching. A traffic jam, which he could pass through but they couldn't. He weaved through the cars but unfortunately the jam only lasted a mile or so, it was only a shunt. He began to breathe easier, well slower at least. *'If I can only get to the next exit wherever it goes,'* he thought. It was then he saw the Jaguar careering up the hard shoulder.

'Bastards,' he thought *'I'll have to stay on now and go back to the original idea.'*

Easton's eyes were firmly fixed on the bike. He needed to get Anders a second or so to get a clear shot.

They passed the final exit and the motorway ended at a set of traffic lights. Red. Max was just able to see the green car about ten rows back. He edged through the first few rows until they were right on the line. It seemed like an age before the amber light came up and they shot off.

"Keep your eye on them," Easton said calmly. It was an unnecessary statement as Ander's steely eyes were fixed firmly on the bike.

"Second left," he said.

"What, the docks?" exclaimed Easton "Are they trying to catch a ship or what?"

"There is a reason," Anders said quietly as the car slid around another corner, "but I'm not sure what. Those stiffs in Washington ought to choose their decoys a little more carefully. He's still alive after run-ins with us and the IRA - not many people could lay claim to that," he added with a hint of respect.

"He can damn well ride I'll give him that," said Easton as they bounced over a mini roundabout.

Pete was in complete ignorance of the position of the car. He knew they were still with them. Max wouldn't be riding like this if they weren't. They had just passed a police car which hadn't moved. Had Max seen it? Were there more? He was itching to stick his head out and look but he knew better than that. Max had pre-warned him to stay close in and to hold on extremely tight. He had done and was still alive - which was plenty of persuasion enough. He was scared but the excitement was keeping the fear at bay.

Both Max and Anders had seen the police car. Both had noted it as unimportant to their current task in hand. By the time they reached the entrance to the commercial docks they had passed another three. Anders was still unmoved but Max was beginning to panic. '*I'd rather be locked up again then be found at the bottom of a river somewhere with a bullet in my skull,*' he thought. They squeezed past the barrier to the docks and seconds later the Jaguar shattered the barrier prompting the entrance to be quickly blocked by a number of awaiting police cars. The dock has three levels and Max took the upper one on the premise that he'd rather be forced down than up where he would have nowhere to run. Anders' window was now fully down, and the barrel of the pistol resting on the side mirror. The rain was really pouring and Max was switching from right to left. It was difficult to get a clean shot at them. The local police had the dock surrounded and as the bike and car weren't going to go anywhere they were quite content to sit tight and wait for the armed unit to arrive. Max did a neat little left and fake right and Easton lost him.

"Damn," he shouted as he slammed the gear leaver into reverse. They backtracked to the last point. Max had ridden a circle and was now riding next to the edge of the dock. To the right of them was a thirty foot drop to the bottom level and the quayside. Anders picked up the gleam of the bike off to the right and motioned Easton to stop. As the bike came into view between two buildings he grinned as he got them in his sights. He had them and squeezed the trigger.

Max felt a thud in his side and the bike toppled over the edge. As they disappeared from sight Easton sped forward and within a few seconds they had reached the point where it had gone over but as they went to get out of the car there was a large explosion. They reached the edge to see thick smoke bellowing from below. The bike had landed on a stack of fuel drums and the latter were now scattered over the quay and in the water which was alight in a number of places, as was the quayside itself. There was no sign of the bike or its riders.

"Goodbye Mr Jones," said Anders coldly as he stood in the pouring rain still sporting his sunglasses. Easton cleared his throat as he saw the dozen or so armed policemen with their guns trained on them. Anders calmly placed his gun on the bonnet, sighed, and he and Easton sat on the front of the car with their hands held high. The first heavily clad figure to reach them was handed an official ID which prompted him to curse under his breath and slowly troop back to his colleagues. It would take a few minutes to check out but no doubt it would turn out to be kosher. At least they wouldn't have to clean up the mess.

24

The crane driver loaded the last huge crate of vodka deep into the hull of the large ship. It was near the end of his shift and even the thumping tones of Def Leppard on his headphones couldn't keep him from thinking about his tea. He picked up his copy of The Sun which had been propped open in his cab, probably the reason why he didn't notice the gaping hole in the last crate he had loaded.

25

The two men stood motionless at attention in front of the large oak desk. No light entered the room as there were no windows and this added to the uneasy silence that had been present since they had been ushered in. The person in front of them was in a large chair behind a pile of folders and strewn documents, wearing a forced smile and had crossed arms.

"So, which one of you two marvellous gentlemen would like to explain this one away to me, eh?" The voice was stern yet feminine and its owner was a woman of forty-five with straight brown hair cut into a long bob. Christine Pemberton was the CIA station deputy and until two hours before she had been having a half decent day. A half hour briefing on a conference call with several senior figures and she had been instructed to read the riot act to two errant agents. She had worked her ass off for the last three years to develop good relations with the Brits and today's events had put here progress back months and months. The two men remained silent and the Christine took this as a definite sign to continue.

"At the last count we had 200 policemen at the scene in Southampton, fourteen people arrested at a service station and £15,000 pounds worth of damage there, a quay covered in bits of Honda and no definitive result."

'Oh, oh,' thought Anders, *'the search for the bodies must have been completed and come up blank.'*

"I trust you realise we are being pushed very hard to reveal the identities of the two men on the motorcycle, and before I forget Mr Anders, although the Brits haven't linked this with you I am pretty certain this is yours too," she added placing a single .35mm bullet on the desk in front of him and raising her eyebrows inquiringly. Anders stayed expressionless and spat out a regulation, "Yes Ma'am."

His unwavering response threw her a little and she continued slowly after reaching for a folder in front of her.

"I don't want to hear any talkback to this but you are both desk-bound for two weeks," she said in a determined tone. No reaction.

"If you include the car you shot off the road, we are looking at a lot of money I've got to explain away to the Brits, plus all the media speculation which we do not need. You must assume that the two 'amateurs'," she lingered on the word, "are still alive and kicking."

'Sure,' thought Easton, *'from a long drop and a fire that took three hours to put out.'*

"MI6 have confirmed that the surrounding area was combed by their people but as the body search wasn't completed until this morning they could have slipped through."

"As the sea was too rough to do the search until 36 hours afterwards, the bodies could have been washed many miles from the original spot. Besides, neither of them was exactly renowned as a powerful swimmer," said Easton.

Ms. Pemberton, as she preferred to be known, looked the young man straight in the eyes and replied in a cold voice.

"I'll ignore that little outburst Mr Easton in recognition of your limited experience in the agency, and the fact that you are probably right." Still staring she added. "Nevertheless, I and my superiors have had a bellyful on this one and you boys are going to cover your asses. Besides, off the streets you are far less costly."

She handed the folder to Anders, sat back in her chair and pointed toward the door.

26

'*Hmm, death is cramped.*' Max was semi-conscious, in complete darkness, cold and surrounded by smooth cylinders which felt like they were made of glass.

'*Ow! Yep, definitely glass.*' Exploration of his surroundings would have to be a bit more cautious. Ah, there was a soft bit. The soft bit emitted a low groan as it was prodded, and after a few more prods Max came to the conclusion that it was Pete.

"Pete," he whispered.

"Max?" came the confused reply. There was an uneasy silence as neither of them wanted to be the first to cast aspirations on their current location. Both remembered the bike crash fairly vividly but didn't know how or why they had ended up where they were. Max continued cautiously with his search and after climbing over countless bottles he reached a wall. The wall was made of wood and well able to stand up to Max banging on it. He turned around and did the same in the three other directions with the same result.

"Max," this time Pete's voice was much clearer.

"Yep," Max replied from a few feet away.

"Do you know where we are?" he asked, knowing it was a silly question.

"In a big box full of bottles, some of them broken," Max offered.

"They're vodka bottles Max - the liquid inside is a spirit, you can tell by feeling the cap, and it hasn't got much of a taste, except the burning sensation of course," Pete added.

"Very good Sherlock - you want to tell me how we got here?"

"Now that's a bit beyond me. Perhaps it's a bizarre prison cell, the product of an ill and twisted criminal mind?" Pete laughed.

"And perhaps," Max added sarcastically "God is a vodka drinker and this is his idea of purgatory."

Pete laughed again and Max joined in. As they fell silent again Pete became aware that they were moving. Well, the box that they were in was sort of moving. He didn't have much time to contemplate it as a wide shaft of light appeared above them and both covered their eyes. He could hear voices but still the light was too strong for his eyes. The voices were coming nearer and as he squinted he could see about five feet above them a hole in their box. The light came from above this opening and slowly he made out the silhouette of a couple of figures standing on top of their box peering in. Pete stood up slowly shielding his eyes from what he now guessed was the sun. As he reached his feet, his head protruded from the opening and his arms were grabbed on either side and he was hoisted up. The two men, were now distinguishable as sailors - *'We're in the hold of a ship!. Hence the movement,'* he thought. He could see through the large hold door and next to him was a ladder which led to the deck. The two sailors were in the middle of a heated discussion and kept pointing at Pete and the hole in the crate. Pete leaned over and signalled to Max to come up. Max's head popped up through the hole and he whispered to Pete.

"They're Russian, I think," he said, to which the two sailors paused and pointed at Max. As Pete struggled to help Max out of the crate one of the sailors shot up the ladder. The other produced a large knife and motioned that they should sit down, and presumably, not move. The man holding the knife looked more menacing than his weapon. He stood nearly as tall as Max and his bare arms were as thick as tree trunks. On the left arm there were a number of tattoos including one of a knife not dissimilar to the one he was holding. The surface area of his left biceps may well have left the tattooist with a

90

shortage of ink, as the right arm was bare, apart from the abundance of black hair that is. Max and Pete sat down without a thought and it was Max who spoke first.

"Do you remember falling off the bike?" he asked

"As I recall, you fell off and as I was attached to you I fell, too."

"Did you get the sense of falling a long way?" Max asked.

"Now that you mention it, as we parted company with the bike the ground just seemed to open up."

"Yeah, we were over the edge of the quay. I can only assume that somehow we landed on this crate."

"I won't even begin to try and work that one out," Pete said shaking his head slowly.

"But how did we come to fall off the bike?" he added.

"That's the weird thing," Max replied. "It felt like a push, almost as if I had been shot, but I can't feel any pain."

Pete looked worried. "It could have hit a nerve and you could be bleeding or getting infected, or anything." At this he stood slowly and checked Max over. He could feel the tattoo man's eyes following his every move but he carried on.

"Hey, that's my wallet," Max chuckled as Pete felt his right hip pocket. As he worked his way round to the left one he saw a neat round hole and paused. There was a large damp patch around the hole.

"OK, I've found it," he said in a serious voice. Max stopped smiling as Pete reached behind the jeans. Max clenched his teeth and as he squinted his eyes he actually looked quite constipated. He opened his eyes as he heard Pete start laughing loudly. He was holding Max's now very dented hip flask. He held it up to Max's face and Max saw the bullet firmly embedded in the antique silver. He took the flask and after putting it under great scrutiny shook it and declared,

"Good job, it's still got some left in it," to which Pete frowned.

"Well, it's 18 year old single malt scotch, bloody good stuff," he added.

Their relief was cut short by a short burst of Russian and the threatening waving of the knife. Their friend with the tattoo didn't know what these mad Englishmen were up to but he suspected it had something to do with being locked up in a box for two days. They seemed to calm down after his actions which was just as well as the most savage act committed with the knife to date was the butchery of a batch of innocent cabbages and cauliflowers. He was the cook but these two idiots were thankfully unaware of this. He was as puzzled as his crewmate on how the hell they ended up in the hold. Still, it was the captain's problem and no doubt he would show his face soon enough.

Max and Pete sat quietly with fairly cheerful expressions on their faces. Max fiddled with his penknife trying to free the bullet from the flask. It was a fairly large one as hip flasks go - leather and silver and engraved 'Good Luck Max - Croydon Branch' except now it was C.........n Branch. He'd been given it fifteen years ago when he had left a company south of the river. Pete watched intently and was as engrossed with the retrieval as Max. Neither of them noticed the well-built, well-dressed man come down the ladder and stand before them. He was one of the two crew members on the ship that spoke a bit of English.

"Good afternoon, gentlemen, my name is Captain Yarun," he said in an impeccable southern counties' accent.

Max and Pete were startled at the sound of their own language and immediately embarrassed at not noticing the arrival of their host. They both stood up and Max extended his hand which was shaken firmly. It quickly became apparent that the greeting delivered so expertly constituted most of the captain's vocabulary. His neatly groomed handlebar moustache matched his almost completely grey hair. They managed to glean that he wanted to know what they were doing on his ship. They were as much in the dark on that subject as he was and after lots of explaining, including animated visual displays, the captain reluctantly accepted that he was stuck with these two for the remainder of the voyage. He hauled the other English speaker - a small kitchen hand called Balof whose mastery of the English language strayed into double figures word-wise. It was from him that Pete enquired their port of destination. They eventually received the reply of 'Newcastle' but from his rantings they assumed it was a round-about route. This was fine with them as the captain had sent for a mop and bucket and knife and fork and had demonstrated in a bizarre form of charades that they could earn their keep on the ship. The deal was struck over a bottle of vodka taken from the very crate they had begun the journey in.

Easton sat patiently behind a desk full of papers in a small hotel room in Southampton which they had hastily converted into a temporary office. A laptop computer with a small printer attached sat on the desk in front of him and it was this that held his attention. Anders sat in one of the armchairs reading 'The Times' - he didn't care too much for computers but had to admit that they made things easier. Easton was a whiz on those things and as he read, he could hear Easton tapping away furiously once more. They had been there for two days now compiling all the possible routes out of Southampton. There was still no sign of the bodies but that didn't worry him. They would stay here for another few more days, file a report then head home. Job done. The tapping stopped and Easton stood up and went to the kitchen. He emerged a couple of moments later with two steaming cups of coffee. Anders set the paper down and carefully spooned three spoons of brown sugar into the mug and looked over at Easton who was now setting the printer in motion. The Brits had done themselves proud keeping all this out of the papers. None had linked the bike chase with Max Jones though some had mentioned it briefly. The Times had run a piece on how sources of theirs had suggested the fugitive had fled abroad. Anders was pleased with this as it would remove any further attention in the UK.

"That's the ship report," Easton said as he sat down. He flicked through the sheets of printer paper as he sipped his coffee.

"A grand total of two hundred and twelve vessels, of twenty seven nationalities."

"How many destinations?" Anders enquired casually.

"Seventeen," replied Easton.

"Ouch," came the reaction to that.

"That's quite a few countries to cover. Lots of paperwork," he added shaking his head.

"Yep, I suppose we'd better get onto it. There are seven major nations and ten minor. What do you fancy?"

"I'll take the majors," Anders replied in an apathetic tone. It made sense though. Anders had more contacts in the big countries than Easton and they covered over a hundred and fifty of the ships on the list. It was a boring routine. They would contact the local agencies in those countries, quote the ships to check and sit back and wait. They had missed four ships that had already reached their destinations but the next one didn't arrive until tomorrow. He'd been in England for three months now, and despite the long phone calls to Cassie his fiancee, Easton was getting fed up. She was marvellous, a trainee lawyer with gorgeous blonde locks that cascaded over her shoulders. They planned to get hitched at the end of the year. It seemed so close. She had accepted his career quite easily as she worked long hours and studied endlessly so didn't have too much free time either. He looked over at Anders engrossed in his paper. *'Not the ideal stand-in partner,'* he thought. *'About as much conversation as a trappist monk on valium.'* This last thought made him smile as he tapped a few more keys and brought up the fax module.

Two hours later the contacts had been made and the wheels set slowly in motion.

27

"Fishk!" was the greeting as the cook's mate placed two steaming plates in front of Max and Pete. The latter dived straight in pausing only to salt his potatoes. Max sat and looked at the stew sitting on the long table in the dining area. He hated fish - he always had, and it was all they had eaten in the last four days. He was also concerned that their journey was taking so long. Every time he ventured onto deck (which wasn't very often) either the visibility was atrocious or all he could see was blue sea and sky. Pete was loving every minute. He'd grown up on fish apparently and had found that the main activity on the ship was chess, which naturally the little sod was bloody good at. He had to admit though that their hosts had been very good and he couldn't swear that had he been in captain Yarun's position he wouldn't have just chucked them overboard. He made up his mind to try and find out more about their route. They had docked once but decided that it was better to wait until Newcastle to jump ship. In return for their passage they were basically doing any task that needed doing. He had spent yesterday afternoon peeling potatoes and this morning in the boiler room helping out the engineers. Last night had proved to be a scream. Some crew members had decided on a bit of a party and the living area which normally consisted of rows of bunks dimly lit and dingy had been transformed into racks of bunks less dimly lit, a cassette player and a crate of vodka. The music consisted solely of 'The Beetlies' as they affectionately referred to them. Within an hour they were all singing along with the words. He was sure he would never forget the rendition of 'She loves you yeah yeah yeah'. That vodka was good stuff too as his head kept reminding him. Oh yes, and after the singing came the dancing, well sort of.

Max had insisted, he couldn't remember why, on learning Cossack dancing. The lads readily agreed to teach him and a slightly reluctant Pete also took part. Abbot and Costello, Laurel and Hardy and even the Marx Brothers could all have learnt from them last night. When he wasn't knocking tables over it was people he was toppling. He landed on his bum more times than he would care to mention. He couldn't remember getting back to his bunk but Pete had told him that three of the crew members had carried him there. He ate the last forkful of lunch and had to concede that as fish went that was pretty good. Pete had long finished and was already into a game of chess with one of the officers. They had the afternoon and the evening to themselves and Max decided he would pop up and see the captain. This was a bit of a drawn out routine as he had to communicate his wish to one of the crew who then arranged for him to go above deck. The first few times had been tougher as the word 'captain' meant nothing to most of them and Max had to resort to mime again. Now he asked one of them who disappeared and returned within a couple of minutes nodding his head. The captain's cabin was at the head of the ship almost directly behind the bridge. He was seated at his desk looking at some charts when Max entered. He rose and beamed shaking Max's hand firmly.

"Sit, sit," he said and pointed toward an armchair. As Max went to sit down he saw the laid out charts and stopped. The one on top showed the African continent and the surrounding seas. Curious, Max pointed at the map and shrugged his shoulders. The captain pointed at the cape and said simply.

"Last night, dock."

You could have knocked Max over with a feather. He tried to hide his shock, swallowed hard and asked enquiringly,

"Newcastle?"

Captain Yarun smiled and reached for another chart. This one showed South East Asia and Australia.

"Newcastle," said the captain pointing at a large town north of Sydney on Australia's east coast. He pointed to a dotted red line, which led from there under Tasmania and out into the ocean.

The ship's doctor could find nothing wrong with the Englishman and no reason as to why he should be so white. He had fainted for no apparent reason whilst talking to the captain.

'These bloody English can't hold their vodka,' he thought as he handed the big man a cup of coffee.

28

"Keep tabs on them. I want to know everything they do. Be careful though, they may appear like two monumental screw-ups but they are actually two of the agency's best." *'And lord help the agency if that's true,'* he thought as he turned back to his scrawled notes on the blackboard.

"Anders," he continued, "is a bit of a slippery bastard but basically clean. Easton could do TV commercials for detergent and be the cleanest thing on the screen." He paused looking at the small group in front of him. They were young, by his standards and still eager. He felt annoyed at giving them another 'no result' assignment but they had to be kept busy - his superiors had already begun hinting that 'staff cuts' were on the way. He continued, "If something stinks," the *if* echoed in the minds of each of them, "my instinct tells me it will be further up. As usual this is a closed unit. The room is clear and the brief is unknown outside these four walls." At this last remark he nodded toward his superior who occupied a seat behind the group. At first, his penchant for sitting in on the briefings had irritated Martin, but he'd got used to it.

"Don't dig too hard until you get something, but when you do I'll be waiting. The detail, and there is a stack of it, is in the folders. They also include everything I have told you this morning in case any of you had a rough one last night." He glanced at Perez as he said the last remark which broke a few smiles. Perez was teetotal and she'd had many a comment like that thrown her way. Drinking was an accepted part of the life of an internal affairs agent. At least it had been in the predominantly male dominated agency. Martin was one of the 'Old School' who took the influx of a number of excellent female recruits into the teams with difficulty. The fact that she didn't share their love of beer, whiskey or indeed baseball made her a prime target for smartass remarks. They seldom went further than that though as the ladies had proved that they were more than holding their own. Angie Perez was no exception, and had plenty of respect from her four male colleagues. The team had been together nine months and worked very well. The department now covered all law enforcement and other agencies. The most identifiable success to date had been cracking a powerful corruption ring in the Chicago police force six months ago. The last dozen or so assignments had come up empty. This was positive of course in that those being investigated came up clean, but made the team feel that their efforts were misdirected. They were given a week at the beginning of each case for initial investigation, and at the end of if nothing had surfaced then they moved onto the next one. Not an ideal method but these were the days of 'efficiency' and 'correct use of taxpayers dollars.' The meeting closed, and as with all the cases before it, the team left to individually examine the facts.

Four hours later they met up again. This time the venue was the back of a poolroom downtown. Sam Matthews, the most senior of the team stood up and the others hushed. At six foot four he was also the tallest member with light brown hair and blue eyes. It was his ability and leadership that held the respect of the group not his size. He spoke as he always did, clearly and with authority.

"Well, two of the team will stay here in The States. Unless there are any other suggestions, Andrew and Juan would be my choice." There were nods of agreement. "Angie, Tom and myself will head to England and keep tabs on these two guys from there."

"You think there's anything in it?" The question came from Tom Jilney, a tall athletic man with blond hair whose gold rimmed spectacles looked peculiar set against his large frame.

"Its difficult to say," replied Sam.

"There are a number of things which puzzle me," he added to murmurs of agreement. "But I'd like to hear what you all think first."

The first to speak up was Juan Manilt. He was Puerto-Rican by descent and a virtual wizard with anything electronic. He had classic dark Latin looks and a deep lightly accented voice in which he continued.

"The official word from the agency is that the two are in England to add weight to the search for Max Jones after initially going there as chaperones for some research work."

"Correct," replied Sam.

"Yet, from the accounts of the events at Southampton it appeared that they planned to take Jones back in a wooden box."

"That's a bit presumptuous," argued Tom.

"Anders and Easton would argue that dealing with someone like Jones you had to be ready to strike first," he suggested.

"Except that he had a hostage," added Juan.

"That hasn't always stopped the agency before," said Angie with a solemn face.

Juan nodded and said, "Our sources add that they are putting considerable effort in the possibility that Jones is still alive and kicking."

"So they screwed up and now they've got some desk duty for being bad boys?" Sam said casually standing up and pacing around.

"I think it's one of two things. Either, as you say, the agency has assumed Jones is dead and the continued activity is to make a point," he paused, "or there is another reason they want him and they can't ignore the possibility that he is still alive."

"No chance." It was the first time that Andrew Kettles had spoken. He was a fairly quiet man with mousy hair, small frame and a razor sharp mind.

"They think he's dead. The reason I'm so sure is that that they are searching, but not very hard."

Angie smiled and nodded, "Yeah, they've not put the net completely tight out there," she agreed. Sam nodded and took control of the meeting again.

"OK. So we have two agents who outpace the rest of the forces to find this guy. Then they screw up and lose him once in Berkshire. Then they find him again only this time they are a little too eager to stop him getting away and making themselves look stupid again." He put the facts out as the agency would have done themselves.

"I don't buy it," Angie said. "They've been sent on a mission which should have been classed level two, for some reason given a high level three and they are putting far too much into it. I know the situation with Northern Ireland is a biggie, what with the large Irish contingent over here, but there must be another reason why they want him."

Sam grinned. That was the second time Angie had snapped at him more energetically than normal. *'This'll be a long opening meeting,'* he thought and made a note to try and find out what else was on her mind.

29

The sun was setting and demanding everyone's attention. The clear sky, calm water and still wind assured it would get it. Max stood on the upper deck smiling at the beautiful shimmering bay that stretched before him. Barely a mile away the hustle and bustle of the busy port seemed like the other side of the world. He fidgeted uncomfortably in the unfamiliar outfit that sat snugly on his large frame. Dark blue trousers, black boots and a thick navy sweater, Max the Russian sailor. The outfit was topped off with a navy bobble hat. He hadn't shaved for a week and a half and had a rough look about him. He was happy with the way he looked, it was the language that he was worried about. In order to get past immigration at the docks the captain had arranged for him and Pete to assume the identities of two of the crew. To this end Pete's hair had been shaven to make him look similar to one of the kitchen hands. Large sailors with beards and dark hair seem to be in abundance in Russia so Max had no problem finding someone he resembled. All of the ship's crew had 'day passes' which enabled them to leave the ship whilst it was in dock unloading. The two members whose identities they were using would be concealed and thus the full quota of crew would pass through immigration in one bunch including Max and Pete. Neither of the two selected spoke any English, which was probably an advantage. To get them by they had spent the last two days learning as much as they could. The method was simple. They went for accuracy rather than vocabulary or grammar. They found those words which they could pronounce perfectly and ignored those which they had been hopeless at. The result was a mix-match of words and phrases that sounded foreign but would have any Russian speaker questioning their sanity. They had got the names down to a tee and also a few English words with a heavy Russian accent. Yet again Pete had taken to it like a duck to water and was reeling off whole sentences like a pro. It felt warm for evening. *'The channel isn't much like this,'* he thought as he turned and looked out to sea. There was very little cloud and in the distance he could make out the horizon. It was as if an artist had painted the two lines in blue in front of him, only the bottom one had been done with an old brush and had left yellow streaks. He smiled to himself as he thought of Jan and their honeymoon. Clacton 1972. They, too, had a sunset like this though the wind never really dies down over there. They had huddled together on the beach with a steaming flask of milky tea, sitting there eating fish & chips. For a moment he stopped smiling as he thought of her home alone in London. Maybe she wasn't alone he smiled. Maybe if she settle down with someone new he too would finally move on. His mind returned to his next move. Max the sailor would soon have to turn into Max the 'interested neurologist' writing a PhD. He was sure Australia had someone somewhere that could help him. *'Probably on the other bloody side,'* he thought as he returned to 'below deck' ready to dock.

30

The meeting lasted a little over three hours and as Sam said goodbye to his colleagues he put a hand gently on Angie's shoulder.

"Have you got a minute?" he asked politely. Things had become increasingly awkward between them and he felt it was only a matter of time before the team was going to be affected.

"Sure, but I'd rather not talk here," Angie replied. Sam shrugged and as they walked down the stairs to the main bar he suggested a coffee back at his apartment which was only a couple of blocks down from hers. Angie nodded and smiled for the first time that evening and they headed out into the night air.

After an uneventful but very wet journey across town, Sam unlocked the door to his top floor apartment. It was in a small block in what could be best described as a cosmopolitan area. Despite being 3am the sound of the city still wide awake on the street below drifted up into the open plan living area. On the left as they came in was the kitchen where Sam headed, coming to a stop in front of the fridge. He turned around after checking inside.

"Er, is black coffee all right?" he asked.

"Sure," Angie smiled. The room was big and with the large windows she imagined it would be bright in the daytime. The couch was simple and modern, as was most of the furniture. Organised, clean and tidy but definitely lacking a woman's touch. She had never been to Sam's apartment before but had often imagined what it would be like. The only item standing out was a sideboard along the back wall past the iron circular staircase that led to the second level. It was about six feet long, dark, old, and looked extremely heavy. "It was my father's," Sam said handing over the steaming mug of coffee into her hands. "It's been in my family for years. My father died ten years ago and as the only child I've sort of inherited it."

"Where did it come from originally?" asked Angie. She wasn't really interested but wanted to know anything about the man in front of her.

"England. It was made in the 1800s and my great grandfather bought it in the 1890s as a wedding present to my great grandmother."

Angie smiled and sat down beside him on the couch. There was an awkward silence with both of them clutching their coffee mugs and staring down at the dark contents. "We need to talk," Angie said quietly into her coffee.

'She's so beautiful. Even with her hair soaked,' Sam thought as he looked at her. He put a finger to her lips and kissed her gently on the forehead. Angie sighed as if a huge weight had been lifted from her shoulders.

"How did you know," she asked.

"I wasn't sure," Sam replied, "but you never look me in the eyes these days," he laughed softly. He placed an arm around her and she rested her head on his shoulder.

"You do know there's no way anything can come of this," Sam said quietly.

"Yes," replied Angie as she turned around and kissed him.

31

They didn't have to wait too long moored out on the bay. Captain Yarun had a call on the radio that he could now dock. It was 7pm. They had been expected the following day but calm seas had meant that they were ahead of time. As they neared the dock Max and Pete said goodbye to their newly found comrades. Pete had arranged with two of them to play chess by correspondence which had amused and pleased the captain. In a mere five minutes they would be off the ship and in the hands of customs. The photographs on the passports were old and faded and they were quite confident. The language side still niggled Max. *'Can we pull it off?'* he thought. He felt the side of the ship knock the dock and finally come to a stop. The gangway was being lowered and the crew climbed the ladder to the deck, the two impostors with them, out into the evening light. They crossed the deck in a quiet procession and the rusty sheet gangplank rattled as they trooped across it. As the thirty or so men crossed the quay to the inviting glow of the customs offices Max looked back at the ship. It was the first and last time he would see the vessel that had carried them half the way around the world. It was an imposing black colour and in the faint light he could just distinguish the areas covered in rust, basically most of the hull. *'I'm glad I saw it like this,'* he mused. *'Probably looks like just another rust bucket by day,'* he thought. They reached the doors of the Australian Customs Authority. Once inside they treaded the dull grey carpet toward the long queues by the security gates. They funnelled quickly through with their possessions, passing through the regulation x-ray machines. Max beeped profoundly as he walked through the gate finding it was his hip flask, pen knife and bullet (which had been tastefully crafted into a key-ring whilst on board). He smiled and shrugged at the security guard who simply sighed and held out the little dish while he passed through again. *'Dopey sailors,'* Max guessed he was thinking, and he wasn't far off. The easy part was over with and they rounded the corner and a bright yellow sign gleamed out at them - Immigration. Max followed the rest of the crew who had all joined the queue on the far left. He glanced at each of the officials in turn. They all looked bored out of their skulls. Most of the sailors passing through appeared to be foreign and there was very little dialogue. The bunch in the queue next to them was Italian and the one next to that Spanish. Further across the room were a few queues full of young Asian sailors. All denominations, colours and creeds standing in lines; quiet as mice they were being ushered through at the rate of two a minute. As he came nearer to the front of the queue he noticed there were two officers and the people in the line went to each in turn. They had another group ahead of them, which was just going through now. The first of their crew went to the left hand officer and went straight through. Now the other side - Max couldn't quite see but this one took a little longer, or was it his imagination. As he got closer he could hear why. The sod on the right could speak a little Russian and no doubt out of sheer boredom was having great fun practising. The odds against both he and Pete getting the guy on the left were pretty high. There was nothing they could do. He looked at the clock. 7:20pm. Pete would notice in a minute or two. How would he feel?

Pete had already noticed and was suppressing his panic. Suddenly all he had learnt in the last few days had gone all fuzzy. He breathed deeply and focused on the collar of the man in front of him. He was a tall man and Pete's eyes were at the same level as the collar. It was a pretty clean collar *'But he's got pretty bad dandruff,'* he thought. He tried to close his mind to his surroundings. It wasn't working.

Max was now three from the front. It could go either way. One to the left, one to the right. *'Come on, come on,'* Max urged the guy on the left to hurry up. He was aware that he was sweating and a bead had settled on his left eyebrow. "Next." It was the man on the left. *'Thank God,'* Max thought and stepped up to the counter handing over his passport and papers. The customs officer was slightly balding and had thick round glasses which had slid halfway down his nose.

"Good Evening," he said without looking up

"Cabbage and Gravy, Saucepan," said Max quietly in perfect Russian. The man looked up and smiled handing the papers back to Max.

"Next," he called as Max walked down the corridor. One down, one to go.

Pete was still focused on the man in front's collar. He was close to the front. He calculated that if they went through one by one like this he would get the one on the right. He was willing the pattern to change but left, right, left right it went and it wasn't going to change. He was close now, only one person. The dandruff man between him and doom. "Next." It was the man on the left. He was now at the front of the queue. It would be soon. Any second now. He stared into space in front of him. "Next," came the call. Hold on a minute, it was the man on the left. He was still frozen to the spot. "Next," called the man again and Pete walked quickly to the counter fumbling with the papers.

"Good Evening," came the greeting from the top of the man's head.

"I'd like my steak well done," replied Pete - perfect accent. *'It's the first one that came into my head,'* he thought. The man smiled and nodded and gave back the papers. As Pete turned he could hear the man with the other officer having a heated argument which must have gone on for a few minutes. The sailor growled and followed after Pete and as he did so winked at him. The other officer shouted something after them and Pete wondered what it was. The translation later in a small café was along the lines of "And you can tell those smart asses with the food orders that some of us do speak Russian....."

32

The sunlight woke Sam and he yawned. He blinked the tiredness away from his eyes to see Angie's slender figure slipping into a white blouse and a pair of jeans. She was standing in the bathroom and paused to look in the mirror unaware he was awake.

"Sleep OK?" Sam asked.

"Fine," she replied but he knew she was lying.

"Do you want to go for breakfast somewhere?" he asked trying to break her mood.

"No thanks. I'll, er, see you later," she said as she headed out of the door.

"Angie," he called after her but heard her shoes clanging on the staircase and the apartment door close behind her. Sam lay back in the bed and stared at the ceiling. *'What is it with me and women?'* he thought. *'I'm crazy about a beautiful woman who for once cares for me too, and she ends up sleeping on my couch and treating me like a stranger.'*

33

With three days worth of stubble, Easton looked somewhere between a sleep-deprived stock-broker and a Manhattan tramp. They'd had nothing positive back from any of their contacts. False alarms were into double figures and were frustrating as none looked even vaguely like the pictures of Jones that they had faxed out. Anders had been irritable since the previous Tuesday, stomping around like a caged animal. They were wasting their time. They knew it, their bosses knew it and perhaps many of their transatlantic colleagues knew it too. He missed the smell of Cassie's perfume, especially on her robe. All he could smell at the moment was Anders' after shave which was definitely tinged with a canine element. It was a poky little room too. Lounge, kitchen and dining room all rolled into one. The seats were comfortable though. Oh yes, and the TV only had four channels. He didn't watch much back home but he knew there was always a minimum of fifty. There had been a good 'Duke' movie on a couple of days back. Anders idolised John Wayne and wouldn't hear a word against him. Easton quite liked the slow drawling voice too. Still, all of this would be over by the morning. Just a few more ships had docked that day and the fax remained silent. *'It will take a while to shake this one off,'* he thought and remembered back to Colonel Masters' words, "cushy assignment" and repeated them over in his head. It would be an embarrassing return to the US. He was young though and there would be many more missions. He looked out of the window at a rain soaked scene. "I hope the next one is somewhere a damn sight sunnier," he murmured to himself.

34

Across the street in a similar hotel room three people sat playing cards. They had been there two days. They were bored too. Tom rose from the table and grabbed the coffee jug from the counter. He poured another mug for Sam and himself but Angie placed her hand over hers saying, "That'd be my tenth and I hate to go into double figures in any one day."

Tom chuckled and added, "I wonder if our two laughing chums would like some?"

"Probably," said Sam "from what we know, they are coming up empty on their traces and they have been cooped up for ages."

"Poor bastards," said Tom, "everyone screws up once in a while."

"Well, they are certainly having plenty of time to contemplate their fates," nodded Angie solemnly. She avoided Sam's eyes again and tried to focus on her cards.

"Yep, I wouldn't fancy being in their shoes when they get back to face the big cheeses," said Sam sipping at his coffee.

"Jesus this stuff's strong Tom," he winced.

"Yeah, just how I like it - oh, full house by the way," he said laying down his hand in a neat fan shape. The other two threw in their cards and shook their heads. Tom was on a roll again.

35

The hostel they had stayed in had eaten up $40 of the $600 they had managed to get from Pete's visa card. It was risky to leave any trace, but without money they could do nothing. Besides, they would be well out of Newcastle by this time tomorrow. They were standing outside the central library. The only brief stop they had made was to a charity shop in town. They were both kitted out in jeans and T shirts. The library was a modern building with lots of red brick and glass. They walked through the automatic doors and were greeted with a friendly smile from the lady at reception. After a brief bout of questions she pointed them towards the periodical section.

"What were you on about CDs for?" Pete said puzzled as they climbed the stairs.

Max tried not to appear patronising.

"Well, some of the magazines and journals have made it onto CD ROM and progressive libraries often carry a good selection," He paused as he reached the top of the stairs.

"You mean your newspaper doesn't use CD ROMs at all?" he asked.

"Nope. We've got a word processor but only Milly really knows how to use that," Pete smiled.

'At last,' Max thought, *'something he isn't an expert on'.*

As they reached the periodicals section they saw a small bespectacled man in a collar, tie and cardigan tidying the already quite ordered desk in front of him. He was almost devoid of hair and the top of his head gleamed as he put the items into their places meticulously.

"Good morning," said Max cheerfully.

"How can I help you?" replied the man casting a critical eye over the two of them. How he wished they could introduce a dress code.

"We are looking for any medical journals that you have on CD, please."

The little man did very little to conceal his obvious surprise.

"Are you quite sure?" he asked with a good deal of sarcasm.

"Yep," said Pete quickly before Max could retaliate.

"Ok," the man said slowly, "Have you operated one of these before," he sneered confident that these two would be blissfully ignorant.

"Well," answered Max, "it appears to be a standard Panasonic 2400 quad speed windows driven drive and I believe you are running a HP multi-level menu system allowing random access and multi-search print with storage of multiple data blocks." Max smiled, managing not to sound smug which seemed to annoy the little man even more. He stared at them for a moment then reached into a locked drawer and promptly brought out three CD ROM cases.

"AMA Journal, Modern Medicine and Medicine Today," he said flatly.

Max smiled, picked them up, and again before he could speak Pete piped up.

"Thank you very much," he said quickly and ushered Max toward the waiting machine.

"I didn't know you knew about computers," Pete said quietly as they sat down in front of the PC.

"Just don't tell anyone," Max grinned, "it'd ruin my reputation."

The PC stirred into life and Max loaded the first CD. The menus flicked by as Max tapped away at the keyboard. Pete watched engrossed as Max searched under lots of criteria. 'Neurology', 'Brain Tissue' and so on. It was the term 'cerebral' that came up with the greatest number of articles. He scanned the titles quickly as he went through them on the screen he marked those for printing that he thought might be useful. Then came the next CD and finally the third. After each one he set the printer in motion and by the end the inkjet printer on the next desk had a neat pile of printouts in the tray. Max piled up the CDs and returned them to the counter where the little man was still in an irritable mood. When he returned, he gave Pete half the pile and they moved to a quiet corner.

"OK," said Max in a whisper, "I'm looking for any notable brain experts who appear in the articles - mark them and where they practice or lecture."

Pete nodded and picked up the first article. He was really beginning to admire this big man. Many in his position would have given up a long time ago but he had this dogged determination and ability to think rationally in the oddest situations. They both sat in silence for what seemed like an hour, but was closer to two. Max finished ahead of Pete and helped with his pile. They had come up with a list of eleven and Max noted them on a plain piece of paper.

"To the phones," Max said emphatically and bounded down the stairs two at a time, which drew a glare from the little bald man. He stopped at reception for directions and a $10 phone card. The phone booths were around the corner and Max turned to Pete as they left the building.

"Look, if I get to work on these maybe you can grab us some lunch." He motioned to the shopping mall at the end of the street.

"Okay," said Pete happily. He was glad to get out in the fresh air again. Max found the phones and set about finding the experts. Directories gave him the numbers and he started phoning around the hospitals and two universities. By the time he reached number nine on the list he was beginning to despair a little. Six were now in the states, two had died and one's whereabouts they did not know. He keyed in number ten.

"Hello, South Adelaide State Hospital can I help you?"

"I'm looking for Dr Bradshaw."

"Which department please?" came the terse reply.

"Neurology?" he replied hesitantly.

The phone clicked and started ringing again. It seemed to go on for ages.

"Neurology," said the gruff voice. It sounded like the other person was out of breath.

"Yes, hello, I'm looking for Dr Bradshaw. I believe he works in your department."

"Bradshaw. Bradshaw, doesn't ring a bell," said the young voice.

"Hey Joe, do you know a Dr Bradshaw?" he shouted across the room. Max waited patiently as a brief discussion ensued.

"He used to be the boss here apparently, but he's been retired 2 years now."

Max sighed *'I guess asking won't hurt,'* he thought.

"Any idea what happened to him?"

"Hold on," said the young man who had now regained his breath. Max waited for the negative reply.

"Hi there. My name's Joe. I used to work with the good doctor - can I ask who you are?" The voice was much older and Max had to think quickly.

"James Hughes. I'm doing my doctorate on a new neurological theory. I read some of his work and would have loved to speak to him."

"Hey, you're a pomme, right?"

"Yes I am," Max said in his best Queen's English.

"I'm only here for two weeks doing some research. You wouldn't happen to know where he lives now?" he asked hopefully.

"Sure. I reckon the doc would be flattered. Hold on a moment, I've got it written down somewhere." Max waited eagerly, pen poised.

"Here you go, Napperby.....," Max took down the full details and repeated them slowly.

"Du Rhone Homestead, Empty Creek Road, Napperby near Alice Springs. Ok, how near is near?" he asked tentatively.

"About 150kms Northwest I think," came the reply.

"How about a phone?" Max asked hopefully.

"Phone?" the other man laughed.

"He hasn't got a phone. He wanted to get away from civilisation after his wife died. Why do you think he's living in the middle of nowhere? We get a letter from him now and again. Seems pretty happy out there. If you see him, tell him Joe says Hi."

"I'd be glad to," Max said making a few more notes, "and thanks."

"No worries mate," replied the old male nurse as he put the phone down. *'Hmm'* Max thought. *'This sounds like quite a distance'.* He decided to try the last one on the list. Two minutes afterward the name had a line through it with 'Deceased' scribbled next to it.

"Well Dr Bradshaw," Max said to himself, "I guess you'll just have to do." He carefully folded the page of notes and as he put it into his pocket he saw Pete crossing the street grinning. In one hand held aloft was a brown paper bag and in the other about a dozen packets of extra strong mints.

36

'*For once,*' Easton thought, '*he really does need those sunglasses.*' He looked across at Anders and then out of the window again. The airport bus from La Guardia reaches the corner of 46th and 8th in twenty minutes on a good day. It wasn't a good day, and they had been on the bus close to an hour. To add to the frustration, the air conditioning didn't work and the occupants of the bus smelt like a wrestler's armpit - after a bout. It was with great relief they clambered off the bus into the 35° heat and made their way down 8th Street dressed once more in their dull grey suits. As they approached the nondescript cream coloured building, Easton did his top button up and straightened his tie. Anders, the perpetual martyr, had gone the whole bus journey without touching his collar. They passed the polished brass plate that read 'Southern Electrical Units' and crossed to the reception. '*Now for the usual games,*' Easton thought.

"Good Afternoon gentlemen," said the stout dark-haired man from behind the counter.

Easton smiled and said, "We have a meeting with Mr Lexington-Smythe at 2pm." The man looked at his watch. It was 3pm.

"You're early then," he said quizzically.

"Yes a little." replied Easton, "Do you have anywhere we can freshen up?" he said trying to sound serious. The man smiled and handed him a piece of paper. Easton thanked him and they sat down on a bench next to a row of phones. He opened the note - '*Right hand lift - second floor. Press emergency button and wait twenty seconds.*' Easton read it slowly, took a lighter from his breast pocket and lit the corner. He waited till the flames almost touched his fingers and placed it in the ashtray. They both rose and walked to the lifts. The second lift opened invitingly and they stepped in. Anders looked at Easton and pressed the 2 button firmly. Easton shrugged and when they reached the second floor he waited until the doors closed again and pressed the emergency button. The lights cut out and they were in darkness. The lift lurched downward and they couldn't tell how far down they had gone when it came to a stop. They waited. Soon a small light came on and a panel on the left-hand side opened revealing what looked like an entrance to a vent shaft. Easton sighed and put his bag through the hole and followed it on his hands and knees. Anders did the same. After twenty feet or so of crawling they came to a tunnel twice the size of the one they had been in. Immediately in front of them was what seemed like a go-cart only it had no wheels. It had two seats and a panel with two traced hand shapes on it.

'This gets worse,' Easton thought as he put the bag into the cart and placed his right hand on the screen. As Anders placed his hand on too, there was a succession of flickering lights and a couple of beeps. As they felt some minor vibrations Anders spoke.

"Mind your ....(smack) head." Too late. The dull thud of Easton's head against the sloping ceiling echoed around them.

"Shit!" came the quick reply. Easton looked over at Anders bent forward in his seat. The cart was hovering in mid-air.

"Magnetic field," said Anders smugly as the cart shot forward. The ride lasted a mere two minutes in which time the tunnel had veered left and right so many times they couldn't begin to guess where they had ended up. It was a small room with a single door.

'And a proper frigging ceiling,' Easton thought. They stood up and straightened their suits. The door opened onto a well-lit corridor and a succession of well armed MPs stood at attention beside each door.

"Colonel Masters is expecting you, sirs," said one of them with a firm salute.

'Yippee,' thought Easton and walked to the steel door which the MP had opened slightly. Colonel Masters had his back to them as they entered the room. They stood to attention and the Colonel waited for the click of the door closing before he turned around. He wasn't smiling.

'Ok, do your worst,' Easton thought uneasily.

"It gives me great sadness gentlemen to have to give you these," he said handing them each a sealed white envelope. Both held the envelopes for a moment and then opened them. The Colonel continued.

"Sadness, because if I had my way I'd slap you two dimwits so hard I'd have to redecorate afterwards," he said calmly. Easton reached inside the envelope to find an airline ticket. He glanced at Anders and opened up the ticket. Sydney? He felt and looked a little puzzled. The Colonel spoke again.

"While the two of you were on the bus from the airport I got a call. Our friend Mr Jones and his sidekick are alive and well in Australia. It means you have one more chance and I have to shelve the dressing down I was going to give you." He said with a wry smile. Easton didn't know what to say, neither, come to that did, Anders.

'At least it'll be hot there,' Easton thought.

37

The brown bag had contained a number of hot pasties of varying descriptions. Max went for a contrast, a traditional 'Cornish' and a 'Mexican'. The latter turned out to be a disappointing mix of hamburger mince and kidney beans. They were sitting in the food hall of a large shopping mall. In front of Pete was a steaming coffee as yet untouched. Max's cup was all but empty and Pete got up to get another. Max reached into his pocket and lifted out the map they had bought at the newsagent on the way in. He carefully folded it out and found that no matter which way he turned it a good part was draped over the edge of the table. Pete returned with the second cup of coffee and grinned as he saw Max poring over the map.

"You haven't told me where we're off to next," he said as he sat down.

"Alice Springs," Max answered with very little enthusiasm.

"Good one," Pete chuckled. "But seriously, where are we off to?"

"Napperby, near Alice Springs," Max said irritably. He was having trouble finding the place on the map. Pete realised he was serious and slowly placed a finger on Alice Springs in the centre of the map. Max was still looking at the bottom right hand corner and it took him a few moments for him to notice Pete's hand. He glanced over, paused and checked the scale of the map. A quiet ten seconds passed as his eyes made out the distance between them and their new destination.

"One thousand, four hundred miles," he said slowly.

"Crocodile Dundee may have hidden from the mob in the bush, but at least he was kitted out with the right clothes," Pete said laughing.

"And," Max said sternly, "we're actually going to see one of the doctors on that list."

"Let me guess. An Aboriginal witchdoctor!" Pete laughed.

"Very droll," Max smiled.

"You've never visited here have you?" Pete asked "Do you think you, well we, are ready to head to the outback?" he said in a more serious tone.

"Look. I've got two INXS CDs, seen Neighbours once and hated it and like to gamble which about makes me a bloody citizen."

"Okay, okay," Pete laughed again feigning shock. They thought they would have a lot of planning ahead of them but the map showed the main highways which they guessed the coach companies would follow. Luckily the route was a fairly straightforward one. Dubbo, Broken Hill to the south, then straight up. Max scribbled notes onto the map and Pete lent his basic knowledge of Australia. Between them they produced a map with lots of scribbling on it. As they admired their handiwork Max stood up saying,

"We'd better find a travel agents or something." Pete nodded as Max popped a couple of mints into his mouth. They headed down the mall, Pete grinning and Max crunching. It wasn't long before they found a travel shop and were negotiating two economy tickets to Alice Springs. The agent hadn't heard of Napperby and Max thought it better not to labour the point. The bus left from the main city station at 3pm.

"You know what we need?" Pete said as they left the shop.

"An understanding God?" replied Max.

"And hats," said Pete, "we'll fry in the heat of the outback without hats and suntan lotion." Max spun around and shouted back to the girl behind the counter.

"Is there anywhere local to get a hat......cheap?" he added quickly. She smiled waving her hand to the left.

"Disposals store, across the street two blocks to the left."

The sun was still blazing as they left the mall and Max was glad Pete had mentioned protecting themselves from its wrath. '*Come to think of it,*' he thought as he passed people on the street, *'lots of these Aussies wear hats, stay covered up and have that pasty white colour of people that avoid the sun.'* As they reached the disposals store, the shop next door caught Max's eye. He gave the money to Pete and motioned that he should do the shopping.

"I'll meet you here in five minutes," he said quickly and darted into the shop next door. It was a large cluttered shop and there were two assistants behind the counter. One was probably the owner Max guessed, in his fifties and greying. The other was an acne-ridden teenager who leapt to attention from the magazine he was engrossed in as Max neared the counter.

"I wonder," Max began as he fumbled in his jeans' pocket, "if you have any of these in stock?" he said pulling out the bent bullet now attached to a number of miscellaneous keys. He dropped the bunch into the eager young man's hands and waited as he held it up to the light turning it over and over. After some umming and ahhing he reluctantly shook his head. This seemed to be the signal for the older man to walk over. He took the object of interest and scrutinised it through his half-rim glasses He raised his eyes to Max's and asked blankly.

"You're from Gun Monthly aren't you?" and before Max could answer, "I've heard your questions have got tougher. I got fourth best retailer three years ago you know." The last point was made with such pride that it prompted Max to pause and felt it would do no harm to humour him.

"Oh dear, I guess you have got me," he said trying to sound sincere. He shrugged then raised his eyebrows and looked back down at the bullet.

"Well?" he said with eager anticipation. "Which gun would this have come from?"

"Oh yes," the man said excitedly and with an air of confidence.

"It's a .22 cartridge from a series 4 Baretta. It will have been made in the USA between 1983 and 1992 as they have now been superseded by a newer version." Max jotted the details down on his notepad and had to admit that he was impressed. He felt fairly confident that the skinny man in front of him was spot on though he wouldn't know if he wasn't. As he looked up the two were grinning profusely at him.

"I'll just wander," he said awkwardly making a circular motion with his hands. The man nodded and the two quickly tried to look busy. Max wandered through rack upon rack of guns, crossbows and hunting accessories and pretended to pause and make notes. Shortly he reached the door and called out over his shoulder.

"I have a feeling that you'll do well this year," which was greeted with large grins and a pat on the back for the younger chap.

'What am I like?' Max thought as he bumped into Pete coming out of the other shop. Pete handed him the hat which was a little too small but nevertheless sat on his head quite well.

"To the station and a phone box," he said triumphantly and they headed off down the road at a brisk pace. Pete held out a number of blocks before his curiosity got the better of him. Max filled him in on his brief visit to the gun shop which prompted Pete to give him a mock telling off for having so much front. They got to the bus station with plenty of time to spare and squeezed into a phone booth with some difficulty. Max took some time to be sure about the number and checked the dialling codes. It rang quite a few times before it was picked up and it was evident why.

"This had better be bloody good!" the voice rasped harshly, "do you realise its barely four thirty!"

'Shit,' thought Max glancing at his watch, he hadn't remembered the time difference.

"Hi Andy. Sorry about the timing."

124

"Max?" the voice was confused but now very alert. "I thought you were dead?"

"Pretty close a couple of times," Max chuckled. "Sorry I can't tell you where I am but this is a transatlantic call and I'm pretty pressed for time."

"Sure," replied Andy who was now perched on the edge of the bed.

"I need you to check something," Max said pausing while Andy grabbed a pen and paper. He continued with all the detailed notes he had made half an hour earlier. Andy's voice was slow at the other end of the line.

"I can tell you that straight off, but you might not like it," he said and paused. "There's only one organisation that uses that type of Baretta and it ain't the boy scouts."

"Okay," said Max slowly.

"It's the Central Intelligence Agency," he said pausing again. "Is there anything I can do?" he asked solemnly. Max tried to sound calm but still rushed his goodbyes. He placed the receiver down slowly in an exaggerated manner and he and Pete stared at each other.

"CIA," they said simultaneously then, "Shit", Max and "Balls" Pete together. They both looked around, which was difficult as there wasn't much space inside the booth.

"Look, if they were here do you think that we still would be?" asked Max shaking. Pete forced a smile but neither of them felt comfortable walking to the bus or indeed once they were planted in their seats.

38

The blinds were half-open and the spacious room was bathed in a misty haze that owed much to the clear dawn sky. There were two people by the bed. The closest to the window was a golden-haired woman who was fast asleep. Over her lap was a heavy check blanket and covering her feet leather moccasins with fluffy rims. *'Even fast asleep she looks tired,'* the man on the other side of the bed thought. Very few people (bar the man lying motionless between them) would have seen her pretty face without makeup. She had been there for two weeks now. There when he spoke his last words, there for the first operation, there for the tenth, there for the twenty-three times his bed lay empty, waiting to see if his body would return to fill it once more. He looked at the myriad of tubes that ran from the drips and machines and back at her. He had made sure that he had been there as much as his commitments would allow. Was his sympathy spurred on by the memory of his departed wife or from the fear that the man in front of him was only two years his senior. It was too quiet in the room. He hated the pressure the silence put on him to think. A dozen subjects worthy of his time fought to get to the surface but the feelings of sadness pushed them away with ease. The door opened very slightly letting in a shaft of light. He rose quietly from his chair and crossed to the door. As he closed it behind him he acknowledged the two young men either side and adjusted his eyes to the brightness of the corridor. Business called. It called today in the shape of an immaculately dressed lady with an equally immaculate, if somewhat fierce, short haircut.

"Good morning, Sir," she said, and as they walked down the corridor she added quietly, "We have come up against a bit of a problem." She hesitated a moment as she surveyed his heavily bloodshot eyes.

"Dr. Price will need another donor by Monday and London and Frankfurt have come up blank." She looked down at her clipboard waiting for his reply.

"Transfer someone," he said bluntly.

"I'm not sure I follow," she replied. She did, but for the record she wanted him to be explicit.

"Just get someone, anyone that fits the bill. Do I have to spell it out for you?" The last sentence had been a shouted whisper, menacingly spat out. She nodded and he felt a little guilty. After all it wasn't her fault. If she was hurt she didn't show it merely straightening and delivering a sharp salute.

"Yes Sir." The moral implications of his order reared their ugly head but he held them back. *'Anyway',* he thought *'I'm only following orders too. What the agency wants the agency gets.'* Still, if the man in there hadn't been his closest friend he would have told the precious agency to shove it. He wasn't afraid to be 'retired'. In fact, the idea had become more and more attractive over the past few weeks.

39

The coach they had chosen, or rather had chosen them by virtue of being the cheapest, stood before them. Max checked twice that it was in fact theirs as the haphazard way it had been parked meant it could have been in either bay 15 or bay 16. The tell tale point that swung it was a piece of card with the words 'Alice Express' written in green felt tip that sat in pride of place in the windscreen in front of the steering wheel. Despite the scratches and the rust, there was a certain sturdiness about it that the new clean coaches lacked. They had fifteen minutes before it departed.

'That's if it starts,' Max thought. As they had no luggage, bar one small shoulder bag, they had time to wander and check out the other passengers. In a forty-five seater bus twelve people seemed few, but as the driver explained most of the passengers would join in Sydney.

"It'll be like a Donegal pub during happy hour on St. Patrick's day," he grinned. Yes, their driver was of Irish descent and despite over twenty years of Aussie conditioning, still retained a broad Irish accent. The people on the bus, as Max and Pete inspected them, were a mixed bunch. Five were backpackers of varying description and nationalities. Two of them had more than likely been to Asia recently as flowing garments of coloured cotton covered most of their denim and worn footwear. The other three wore the more traditional creased and stained T-shirts. A middle-aged couple sat conservatively in the middle of the bus and an elderly couple right up at the front, as they invariably do. The last passenger didn't seem to fit in at all. He was a young priest who they later found out was on a visit to a number of Aboriginal settlements in the outback.

He was in the row of seats opposite them, two thirds down the bus. Pete was around the same age as him and the two hit it off fairly quickly. The bus kicked into motion with a sound that few would have experienced, except those that had knocked a dozen tins of nails over in their shed. The driver guided the bus out of the garage accompanied by a low thumping noise from the engine. The elderly couple looked disturbed and the middle aged couple mildly worried. The backpackers were completely unmoved. Max and Pete were too occupied looking for suspicious people in the crowds and masses to take any notice either. It was only when the bus had left the city streets behind and was ambling down the highway that they sat back in their seats and relaxed a little. Pete looked at Max who he could sense was nervous. Actually he could hear his nervousness. He had crunched his way through two packets of mints in the last fifteen minutes. Behind them, one of the backpackers was listening to his Walkman so loud that either he had, or would soon have, a hearing problem. Max had glanced in his direction and scowled a couple of times. He was beginning to get wound up. Pete heard him utter something about relocating the offending stereo but Pete put his arm on the seat in front blocking Max's path to the aisle. Max was about to snap at him but was handed a pen and paper by the young priest. He had been watching the two with interest and guessed it was only a matter of time before Max lost his cool. Max forced a smile back and felt a little ashamed at his anger in front of a man of the cloth. He sat back down and wrote a few brief lines and handed the scrap to Pete who dutifully delivered it to the young man. He edited it on the way adding a 'please' and removing a few of the smaller more offensive words. The receiver of he note was in the middle of a sounding rendition of the subtle classic 'Bring your daughter to the slaughter' and was decidedly pissed off by the contents of the note, however justified. Pete had identified the originator and egged on by his mate he was going to 'teach the cheeky bastard a good lesson.'

"Oi you, note writer!" he baited from his battle position in the aisle at the back. Max got up past Pete and stood face to face with the young man. He walked forward and growled.

"Yes?" with his face a mere six inches from the lad's nose. In a few moments the taste for blood, the macho spur and manly bravado evaporated. Beads of sweat appeared on his shaved head as he examined his foe. No daylight passed him from the front of the coach so he was kinda large. The look on his face revealed that he wasn't having a very good day.

"I'm , er, sorry about the, erm, noise," he stammered.

"That's all right then," Max replied in the same deep growl and returned to his seat. The confrontation had a profound effect on the young man's music listening. The Walkman wasn't used at all for the remainder of the day. The young priest appeared pleased with the outcome and congratulated Max on his non-violent solution to the problem. Max closed his eyes and tried to sleep but his mind was racing. Eventually at around 2am with the highway rolling by outside the window, he fell into a deep sleep.

40

Anders stepped off the plane. His eyes were hidden as ever behind those sunglasses. After him gingerly walked Easton. They had been flying on and off for 20 hours and the latter hadn't slept a wink. They had endured four dismal films, eight mediocre meals and a trio of irritating Scandinavians in front of them who managed between them to deplete most of the plane's 'free' alcohol stocks. Easton could now go to any North European beer festival and hold his head high as he was sure that at least two of their drinking songs were imprinted on his brain forever. It was close to midday and the airport at Newcastle was fairly quiet. For the sake of speed they had assumed the same identities as before and were kitted out in the same drab suits. As they passed through immigration, the officer paused as he examined their passports. As a precaution for each mission they were adorned with a visa for each continent and this surprised the man. He found it odd that such dull looking gentlemen would travel so much.

"You're doing a lot of travelling gentlemen," he said enquiringly.

"Yes we have a new medical discovery that we're very excited about," replied Easton with only a hint of enthusiasm. The officer was about to enquire further when he noticed Easton's heavily bloodshot eyes. He smiled to himself as he stamped their visas in and thought, *'Bloody yanks, can't teach the buggers to leave the in-flight grog alone.'* They headed straight for the coffee lounge and sat at a table in the corner. Easton opened his case slowly to reveal his laptop and various attachments. Plugged into the side was a mobile phone and on this he dialled a long number and closed the case. They both ate a hearty breakfast. Easton had eggs, bacon, sausages and a plateful of toast

131

with a large black coffee. Anders opted for muesli, herb bread and freshly squeezed orange juice. As he started on his third glass Easton moved his tray onto the next table and lifted the case back up in front of him once more. He opened the case and the screen told him that the data he had requested had been successfully transferred. The mini-printer sprung into motion. It was an annoying fact that they had to wait until they had come off the plane but the one time they had ignored the warnings the 737 they were on had developed 'technical problems' and had made a hurried landing.

"There's only seventeen travel agents in the whole town," he said slowly reading from the printout, "and, according to this only three sold pairs of tickets for cash in the past two days," he added a little surprised.

"Not exactly a booming travel industry," Anders agreed.

"Do you think they would be smart enough to buy the tickets separately?" Easton asked.

"Nah," Anders replied confidently, "but if the doubles don't work then we'll try the singles I suppose," he added. They took a cab from the airport into the city and it didn't take them long to find the right travel agent. It was the second on their list. Easton had no problem getting the information from the young lady there either as their two 'friends' were quite conspicuous. Besides, he was a handsome young American, even in such a dull grey suit. They were both smiling as they left the shop; Anders at the thought of catching up with his quarry and Easton at the prospect of a good night's sleep. A plane would get them to Alice Springs in a mere five hours so they didn't have to leave until the next morning.

41

Supermodels Elle Macpherson and Claudia Schiffer had had their differences before but never over a man. The rift between them had grown so wide, the fall of their blooming café chain was rumoured to be around the corner. The flames had dulled a little the past week as the media circus had directed its attention elsewhere, but they were roaring now. Claudia had arrived at the luxurious Karma Lodge hotel with the aforementioned man for a fashion show only to find that Elle, one of his past loves, was staying a few doors down from them. He guessed that it had been done on purpose. Elle had held a candle for him that last year. It was a tragic scene really. He eased back into the big leather armchair and ordered another double scotch. Claudia was near the bar chatting briskly to a couple of beer-bellied media tycoons. She was wearing a daring white figure-hugging dress. She smiled at him one moment and threw evil stares in Elle's direction the next. She, in contrast, was in an excitingly short red dress that showed off those lovely legs. Little did Claudia know he had set up a secret meeting with Elle later that evening. His scotch arrived delivered by a beautiful blond waitress who smiled shyly at him. He sipped the drink casually.

'That's odd,' he thought, 'I can't remember Glenfiddich tasting of blackcurrant.' He looked at the glass and sniffed. It smelt fine. Claudia smiled at him again.

'Ahh, the bliss of having two of the world's most beautiful women in the world fight over you,' he thought as he eased lower into the chair. The chattering was fairly loud but he thought he heard someone calling his name.

He turned around and looked at the grey-haired man who seemed uncomfortable in his dinner jacket.

'He looks familiar. Oh bollocks,' he thought, *'Its my geography teacher, Mr Rawlins.'*

"Come on, what's the capital of Kenya? Well Jones?" The images became blurred and he caught one last glance of Claudia's smile.

Max's head felt heavy and his eyes sore as he opened them to a squint in the brightness. His back felt odd and he found he had slipped half way down in his seat. He opened his eyes a little wider and noticed Pete was not in the next seat but over with young priest. He was calling over to him. Max yawned and managed a barely audible grunt

"Yeah?"

"What's the capital of Kenya Max?" asked Pete for the third time. It was the last crossword clue left in Barry's newspaper.

"Nairobi." Max answered without thinking and reached for his hip flask. He took a swig. *'Shit,'* he thought, *'must get some more Scotch.'* It had run out the day before and Pete had filled it with blackcurrant cordial of all things. Max became aware that the coach was moving. It seemed smoother than before but probably because he had got used to its rumblings. He pulled back the small curtain and an arid landscape whizzed past the window. The earth was an orangey-yellow colour, sparsely populated with trees and shrubs that looked in desperate need of some water.

'How could anything possibly survive out here?' he wondered. There were a few animals on the horizon which Max took to be sheep.

"They're grey kangaroos," said Pete sitting back down next to him and smiling.

"We've seen loads of them. Barry says they're a pain in the ass - especially at night. He has to dodge them all the time. He even hit two on the last trip."

134

"I wondered what the bull bars were for on the front of the coach," said Max

"Yep, they call them 'Roo' bars over here," said Pete knowingly. Within the next hour they passed a lot of kangaroos, mostly hiding from the heat under trees and bushes. They would be in Broken Hill that evening to drop off and pick up more passengers. The bus was fairly full now, but not to the proportions that Barry had predicted. They stopped for lunch and fuel at one of those towns that seem to revolve around the petrol station. The heat hit them as they left the air-conditioning behind. Max's feet kicked up a lot of dust as they stretched their legs. There was a small general store which housed the bakers, the post-office and just about all the other services the place had to offer. It was owned by an elderly couple who both looked as strong as shire horses. They got a few provisions including lunch and more water this time as last time it had run out. They sat on a couple of boulders that were conveniently located under a tree a few yards down the road. They ate and chatted, mostly about what they thought of Australia. As he finished his last roll Max's tone turned serious.

"Pete, I think that when we get to Alice Springs we should go separate ways."

Pete tried to answer but Max carried on.

"Let me finish please. Before we got to here it was the IRA after me, us, and they don't operate outside the UK. This CIA thing is serious. We're damn lucky to have got this far in one piece."

"But they don't know where we're going," protested Pete.

"Yet," said Max, "and besides you've got plenty of background for a cracking story and when this is all over you can have the exclusive."

Pete waited and thought a little before replying.

"You've been thinking about saying that haven't you," he said eventually.

"Yeah," admitted Max. "It sound too corny?"

135

"A little," grinned Pete, "but it doesn't make a difference because I'm staying put, no arguments."

"Okay," said Max, "I would have felt guilty as hell had anything happened to you and I hadn't tried to persuade you to go," he said jokingly.

"Some persuasion," laughed Pete and mimicked Max's serious face, which set Max off laughing too. Their laughter carried quite a distance over the dry flat landscape and seemed to linger, for a moment anyway.

42

Alice Springs was nothing like Easton had expected it. It was circled by a wonderful deep red mountain range and was, in fact, a vibrant town. The streets were full of tourists and hire cars sped around the roads. The first thing they did was to drive up to the top of Anzac hill near the centre of town. It gave them a view over the whole of the town and they got their bearings quickly. The saddest sight that greeted them at each corner was the aboriginal people in small groups. Most of them were clutching bottles or wine boxes and it was only mid morning. They looked for somewhere to have lunch with Easton hoping for a raw steak with a pile of fries and definitely no salad. He reluctantly followed his partner into a café on the corner of the street opposite the bus station and prepared himself for the worst. The town had health food fever, fuelled by the Australian 'Year of Health' which had worked its way to the outback. It seemed only the aboriginal people had been left out, as the menu was dominated by pulses and vegetables.

Sam sat alone in the bus depot coffee shop. To the passer by, he was an average Joe reading his morning paper and listening to classical music on his Walkman. The loud music drowned the voices in his left earpiece.

"X1 - they have entered Marti's café and look like they are getting their lunch."

"X2 - my thoughts too. What do you think, a nice Kanga burger?"

"X1 - not funny X2."

Sam smiled. He did like working in this team, there was never a dull moment. Angie was kitted out as a young mum pushing a pram doing some window-shopping. That guise had been chosen due to the hoards of women with kids in town. It seemed to have a very migrant population. There were a couple of hours before the bus was due and it was just a matter of waiting. Sam bought another coffee and started to read the paper for the second time around.

The bus would be late, despite the fact that it was only an hour out of the town. The bus was at the side of the road and its passengers sat in the shade it created. Barry the driver was underneath fighting with a spanner and jack to get two of the wheels off that had decided to give up and burst on the last bend. To make matters worse, the air-conditioning had packed up two hours earlier. The temperature inside the bus had climbed to a very uncomfortable 50°c. It wasn't too much cooler outside but at least there was a breeze. What really pissed him off was that his Guiness supply for that evening was the latest casualty of the heat. Two cans had already split and the rest had been hurriedly moved from behind his seat to under the bus in the shade with him. He cursed aloud as he heard another pop and spring a leak. His hands were oily and sweaty and the bolts were proving pretty stubborn.

Pete and the young priest had decided the enforced stop was the ideal opportunity to explore the nearby 'bush'. Despite the heat and looking pretty daft in his hat, Max felt obliged to join them and tagged along. Everything was so red. The shrubs that were speckled around looked almost wiry. The sky was so blue and even through sunglasses it was very bright. Pete pointed out the charred earth and rocks, which, he explained, were tell-tale signs of a recent bush-fire. It amazed Max that the landscape they stood in had recently been ravaged by fire. The plants had simply taken it as par for the course and had begun to grow back slowly. As they continued further down the road they looked eagerly for signs of wildlife. They didn't have to wait long as they approached a dead kangaroo by the side of the road. Sitting astride the animal that had probably been hit by a truck was a magnificent wedge-tailed eagle. They had seen a few from the bus but it was only when they were within twenty feet that they realised the real size of these birds. Rather than scare it off they diverted off the road and headed toward a patch of greenery that Pete had spotted.

Barry hadn't struggled for too long before offers of help started coming thick and fast. The more able-bodied people's opinion seemed to be that any way to get the heap moving again quickly should be employed. There was no such luck with the air-conditioning. Barry tinkered with it for about five minutes while two of the lads put the finishing touches to the second wheel. He knew his limits though and decided to leave it. There was a feeble cheer from the mass of bodies sprawled next to the bus as he announced with a cheeky Irish grin that the journey could continue. He was now down to only four cans of Guiness, which didn't put him in the best of moods getting back to his seat. He started to count the passengers on but gave up as they piled on too quickly. The ubiquitous question.

"Are we all here?" was shouted backwards which received a chorus of impatient Yes's and that was good enough for him.

The young priest paused in the middle of his examination of the cluster of flowers in front of him and looked up puzzled.

"Isn't that the bus's engine?" he said slowly. All three of them listened carefully and realised they must have strayed further away then they had thought.

"I hope that means he's testing the air-conditioning," said Pete as he quickened his step.

"He wouldn't leave us here surely, would he?" said the young priest now breaking into a run. Max didn't contribute to the conversation as running fast took all his energy and breath. Judging by the slow speed he went at, he didn't have much of either. He quickly lost ground to his companions and very soon lost sight of them as they disappeared over a ridge. Max slowed to a walk puffing heavily. It was no good, the heat was just too much for a man of his age. He groaned as he reached the top of the ridge holding his side with sweat pouring down his face. The sight that greeted him didn't exactly cheer him up either. The two young men stood staring blankly at the horizon where the only evidence of their bus was a dust cloud in the distance.

"Oh great," Max managed to get out before collapsing onto a rock.

"Erm, at least we've got our bag," said Pete holding it up sheepishly. It dawned on him that Father Vernon's belongings were probably still on the bus and he blushed deeply. The young priest saw this and smiled.

"Oh, mine were sent on a few days ago. I too only have what I am carrying."

Max tried to be angry but he was too exhausted. Pete was waiting for an outburst but was surprised when Max got up and started walking. The other two shrugged and looked at Max who turned and said.

"Look it's 2pm and Barry said we were around an hour from the town. I reckon that means around 50km. We're bound to find a house with a phone inside a couple of hours," he said with surprising optimism. They were both impressed and followed him down the road. They were just far enough behind him not to hear him swearing under his breath.

43

Sam, Angie and Tom were used to waiting. They had once waited two days to snare a Chilean diplomat who was trying to bribe a CIA agent. They had got him and this would be a walk in the park in comparison. They had now changed about. Sam and Tom had switched places courtesy of a visit to the gents. Tom emerged with the Walkman and a copy of Business Week. The music this time was the new album from Harry Connick Junior. Angie had ducked into a nearby shopping mall within reach of the bus station. Inside Marti's café, Anders and Easton were on their fourth round of coffee. Anders was on the de-caf naturally. From where he sat, he could see the road in toward the bus station and every time a coach or bus came along it he would switch the glasses he was wearing to long-sight and check the bus details.

'Marvellous,' thought Easton, 'the Agency can develop the technology to incorporate 16 times magnification in a pair of normal sunglasses, but I can't lay my hands on a decent steak.' He looked down at the remains of cauliflower cheese and fishbake and grimaced.

"OK lets make a move," said Anders quietly and got up from the table leaving the money for the meal (no tip) on his napkin. They walked across the road to the bus station and Angie and Sam moved in closer. Anders walked into the bus café while Easton went to the bay adjoining and sat beside a pregnant woman holding a baby. He hid his face behind a magazine and watched as a tired and pissed off Barry finally brought the bus to rest in the bay. The people rolled off in a ramshackle mass looking worn. He was very surprised when the last person staggered off and Max and Pete were nowhere to be seen. He decided quickly that the driver would certainly know where they had got off. Maybe they had underestimated them again. Lulled into a false sense of security by the easy to trace tickets they'd fallen for one of the oldest tricks in the book. They were probably thousands of miles away by now.

"Excuse me," he said to Barry who was collecting his bag and cherished, if somewhat depleted, Guiness stock.

"Yes?" he replied tersely.

"My two friends were supposed to be on this bus. Both pommes. One 6ft tall and stocky with dark hair. The other shorter."

"Yes?" Barry was tired, fed up and needed a drink.

"Well they didn't get off the bus just now," Easton said slowly.

"Listen pal," Barry said unsympathetically, "Your mates were on this bus an hour ago. I'm the driver, not their bleeding mother. If they've disappeared that's their business. I'm off for a pint." With that he headed off for the nearest pub. Easton forced a smile. So they were coming here, just took the precaution of switching transport before they got into town. He found Anders and filled him in on the developments. They chatted for a moment and reverted to their backup plan (which they had just made).

"X2 - looks like they screwed it up again."

"X1 - nice choice of phrase X2," Angie laughed.

"Looks like they are dealing with two pretty smart cookies."

Max didn't feel like a smart cookie. He was uncomfortable and hot. Ah yes, and he must remember to add sheep after fish on his list of things he didn't like. So far in the back of this truck, two had decided to lunch on his shirt and one had dumped on his foot. He wished the kind farmer who had stopped to pick up the three struggling walkers hadn't had two dogs which occupied the front seats. He was too tired to chat avidly like Pete and Padre over there. Max kept forgetting the young priest's name and Padre seemed much more appropriate. Max guessed they had walked around 5km before they had been picked up (it was actually a little over 2km) and they had been eager to jump in the back, albeit with around thirty sheep. What really pissed him off was that they seemed to stare at him before they tried to eat his clothing. They had chosen their seating positions very carefully, for obvious reason. This meant that Max had ended up on the other side of the truck. His eyelids were heavy and he closed them to rest for a moment. Despite the bumpy ride and noisy co-passengers he drifted off.

Angie and Sam kept a long-distance eye over Easton and Anders as the two went around the town visiting all the inns, hotels and hostels in a methodical way and finally ended up at their own, The Melrose. Their three shadows checked in across the road.

The farmer lived on the outskirts of town and he dropped them off before he turned down the side-road. Padre offered to buy them a drink and they both heartily accepted. It was only a short walk and they were through the door of his hotel within ten minutes. He suggested that they might find a room there too, which sounded like a good idea. They all headed toward the reception in their little group and rang the small bell. The clean-cut young man behind the counter gave them a warm smile.

"What can I do for you fellas?" he said.

"I have a room booked under Father Vernon McDade and these two gentlemen would also like a roof over their heads," said Padre.

"I'm sure we can manage that Father, I'll just get the manager for you," he replied and disappeared. In a moment he was replaced by a man with more waist and less hair than his younger colleague.

"Good evening Father, we've been expecting you. Your luggage arrived yesterday," he said with due reverence and paused whilst looking at Max and Pete.

"Are these two gentlemen with you?" he asked looking a bit puzzled.

"They certainly are," he beamed.

"Well then, there must have been some mistake," he said and added with a whisper,

"I had two fellows in here about an hour ago looking for two guys travelling by themselves. Their descriptions of these two are spot on, but they reckoned you guys were very dodgy characters."

Max swallowed hard.

"Oh man," he said "not those two bozos again," looking at Pete he added chuckling,

"I wonder what they pretended to be this time, CIA, FBI, or MI5," he laughed sourly.

"Oh, they didn't say," said the landlord quickly to make sure they didn't realise he'd fallen for the CIA trick.

"So who are these guys then?" he asked. Max was on a roll now and was waiting for that question.

"Well, about five years ago me and Pete worked in the tax fraud office and we busted those two guys for a time-share scam. They conned hundreds of pensioners out of their life savings," he said, looking disgusted.

"The bastards only got three years and they were out in two. They've been after us ever since," Max added shaking his head.

"Bastards," echoed the landlord. "And they had the cheek to ask me to phone them if you came in here. They slipped me twenty bucks for my trouble too."

Max thought for a moment then whispered.

"Would you mind helping us put one over on them?"

"Nothing would give me greater pleasure mate," he said enthusiastically.

"OK," Max continued, "I'll need pen and paper, a pair of binoculars, and of course a phone."

The landlord grinned. "No worries."

Easton and Anders were sitting in their room reading their respective papers. As ever there was a lack of conversation and it was quiet when the phone rang. Anders answered it with a simple

"Yes?"

"Hiya mate. Its Jack from the Duke here. You know those two guys you're looking for?"

"Yes?" Anders said flatly.

"Well, they came here about twenty minutes ago and headed off to the Rock Lodge out on Valley Road for the night."

"OK where is that?" Anders was getting excited but didn't let it show in his voice.

"It's the first road off the Central Square. How about the rest of the money?" he added, trying to sound greedy.

"You'll get it," Anders assured him, "Just as soon as we get them." He put down the phone and tossed the hire car keys to Easton.

"You can always rely on people's greed," he grinned.

"As sweet as a possum in a pie," said the landlord after he put the phone down softly. Max,Pete and Padre all smiled and, binoculars in hand, went up the stairs to the roof. As they watched Valley Road Max noted the license plate of a red saloon which sped down the road. "Part two," he said as he walked back down the stairs. He went to the phone behind the counter with the others crowded around him. He dialled and a voice at the other end said, "Hello, police service, how can I help you?" In his best Scottish accent Max said, "Ah, thank god. Some sassanach has stolen ma hire car under ma nose. The bastards waved their guns at me as they drove off," he sounded very flustered.

"OK Sir, please calm down. Where are you phoning from and what's your name?" she asked slowly.

"I'm in the Duke. I ran across the road to phone. Me name's Angus McDougal, but they'll get away m'girl," he said sounding panicked.

"Yes OK sir, what's the registration and which direction did they go?" she said calmly.

"Oh yes, sorry, its one of those red Hertz things. UMX-401, a Holden I think."

"And the direction?" she asked again.

"Oh yes, Valley Road," Max replied.

"Don't worry Sir, we'll do our best. You just stay put and we'll get them all right," she said reassuringly.

"Thanks I will," Max said and put the phone down and grinned like a Cheshire cat.

'By the time they get out of that one we'll be well out of here.'

He thanked the landlord who seemed to be as happy with the success of the phone call as Max himself.

Anders and Easton reached the T junction at the end of Valley Road. They stopped the car and were puzzled. It was only a short road and there had only been one hotel on it and that was 'The Pines'.

"Shit," exclaimed Eaton slamming his hands on the steering wheel. He pointed to the left and Anders looked back to see a large boulder with a sheet of paper stuck to it. Anders got out calmly and returned with the piece of paper and read its contents aloud.

"I'm sorry I can't come to the rock right now. Please wait for the tones, leave a message and I'll get back to you, Max." He looked at Easton who forced a smile.

"OK, we've been done. But what did he mean by the tones?" He said inquisitively. Anders didn't need to answer as they heard the police siren behind them and saw the flashing lights. Moments later a loud hailer boomed,"

"Throw your weapons out of the windows and come out of the car with your hands behind your head, then down on your knees."

"Shit," said Easton as he tossed his .35 and Anders' Baretta out of the window. They followed the instructions to the letter and as they kneeled side by side, Easton whispered.

"Have you got your ID?"

"Nope," Anders replied. "Mine's in the motel too. But don't worry, I'll sort out these country hicks."

"X1 - this has got to be a first. Our two friends have only been arrested!"

"X2 - yep, did you get close enough to see them on their knees and trussed up in cuffs?"

"X1 - no X2, but I'm sure it was a real Kodak moment."

"X2 - I guess we'll have to stake out the police station now," Tom laughed.

"X1 - shame we can't interfere and get them out isn't it."

"X2 - yeah real shame."

"X1 - they'll be out by the morning if they're nice to the locals. Now you two boys get some shut eye. I'll cover the station," said Angie.

"X2 - no arguments from me. Nighty night"

"Hicks eh?" said Easton quietly as he ran his fingers up and down the bars of their cell. Anders ignored him and instead focused his attention on the sergeant sitting at his desk twenty feet away.

"Hey, Sarge," he said loudly.

"You realise this will be a major international incident if these two felons escape?"

"Oh good," said the round sergeant without lifting his eyes from his magazine.

"My wife works for the local paper. They've been painfully short of 'major international incidents' in the last few months," he said grinning.

147

"If you'll just retrieve our IDs from our motel you can verify them within the hour," Anders growled.

"Sure. I'll just ring Judge Molten and ask him to pop to the court buildings and whip up a warrant," he said picking up the phone.

"Wait a minute!" he said in mock surprise in mid-dial.

"It's 1 am (looking at his watch) and the judge'll be asleep. Perhaps I'd better not," he said putting he phone back down and chuckling.

"Listen, you'll lose you're job if you don't sort this out, and damn quick. You can be sure of that," Anders shouted.

"All I can be sure of," the sergeant replied still grinning, "Is if I get the old judge out of his bed in the middle of the night I'll be out of here so fast my ass will land halfway across the street," he laughed again. Anders lay back down on his bunk. He was really, really pissed now. No quick death for that bastard Jones now, oh no. He'd rip him to pieces, starting with his head. Easton looked up as a young cop entered the room. He pointed at them and whispered something to the sergeant who burst out laughing. Anders buried his head under his pillow and Easton let out a deep sigh.

'This is going to be a long night,' he thought.

44

Max and Pete got up early. After quick showers they stepped out into the morning sun. There was a bite in the air and not a cloud in the sky. It was going to be a glorious day. Their walk was only going to be a short one but Max still pulled the scribbled map from his pocket. One of their drinking partners the night before ran a 4WD hire place and had drawn them a map to it. Prompted by the landlord and the thirteen cans of VB he'd consumed, he'd offered them a free jeep for their visit to the outback. They quickly accepted, as their funds were pretty low. They found the yard easily.

"Tim's 4 Wheels" proclaimed the big red sign and below it a yard full of shiny Suzukis. In the middle of said yard was an office, or badly erected shed depending on your architectural persuasion. They both knocked on the door. No answer. Max knocked again much louder.

"Coming," came the muffled answer, then a bang (knee on desk) a quiet yelp and a few choice words describing the offending desk. The door opened and a bleary-eyed face greeted them with a big grin.

"Morning fellas," he said as cheerfully as he could muster. Judging by the look of him, his morning had been anything but good thus far. He honourably met his offer of the night before, which he remembered only vaguely. Max drove the jeep out of the yard and headed off down a back street. They were careful to avoid the area that housed the police station and within twenty minutes they were out on the highway, heading Northwest. Pete turned out to be a pretty good 'map man' and Max was content for him to issue directions as and when. Tim had reckoned on them taking around four hours to reach where they were going, with the assumption that they didn't get lost. He'd given them a short lecture about driving in the outback and Max had been very attentive. He'd seen the dents in their coach and sat through a number of Barry's 'disaster' stories. Pete was fascinated by the revelation that there were hundreds of thousands of camels in Australia.

"On account of the bloody big deserts," Tim had said. Very soon the heat of the day was upon them and they were glad of the air-conditioning, however simple. They were undoubtedly driving the oldest jeep from the lot and it had obviously seen more countryside than they had. Their field of vision was that much greater than it had been on the coach, which pushed home just how dusty, barren and orange the landscape was. They had only come across a few vehicles since leaving Alice behind but now in front of them was a line of traffic.

"Must be one of those 'road trains' up ahead that Tim mentioned," said Max and looked up the line of half a dozen cars and trucks ahead. He was quite right. There was a sixteen-wheeler with three trailers attached to it. Some cars had already passed it but those without a death-wish were waiting patiently for a long stretch of straight road. Max decided not to push his luck and after ten minutes followed the stream of traffic around the obstacle and the road quickly became quiet again. Max drove for another hour and then Pete took over. By the time they decided to have lunch they were only 1½ hours from Napperby. Once the engine was off it was lovely and peaceful. They had stopped in a parking area off the highway and sat with their backs to the jeep's wheels in the limited shade that the high sun gave. Another hastily prepared lunch from their bag - cold pies from the hotel the previous evening. Still, the lack of vitamins and minerals and a balanced diet are not usually high on the priority list of people evading the clutches of the CIA. They ate heartily and drank what seemed like endless cups of water.

"Just another few hours and you'll have the answers you need," said Pete as he leaned back on the wheel. Max sighed.

150

"I'm not sure he'll know, and if he does I'm not sure I'll want to know," he said sullenly. It had dawned on him as Pete said those words that he was pinning his hopes, and perhaps his life, on the next few hours.

When the cell doors had been opened hurriedly neither of them had said a thing. They picked up their Ids from the sergeant's desk and walked straight out of the front door into the sunshine. They hadn't acknowledged the chief inspector's presence at all but now, an hour later, they were back to make up for that. Anders stood opposite the chief, only a desk between them. Even before he opened his mouth the chief felt intimidated. His hands were on his hips, his jacket open and the butt of his Baretta jutting out. The chief held his palms up and said humbly, "What can I say gentlemen?"

"How about, 'Jeez we're buttheads, sorry about the fuck-up'," Easton sneered.

The chief was a little taken aback but was locked in Anders' piercing stare.

"Sit down Chief," Anders said calmly. Like an obedient puppy he did just that. Anders placed his hands on the desk and leaned forward.

"I won't waste my time with recriminations. My department will see to that," he paused for effect, then continued. "Firstly I want this whole fiasco kept watertight. If any of this gets to the press I will hold you personally responsible."

The chief nodded.

"Second, all your men are to be issued with photos of these two. In the unlikely event that they come back here, I want them rounded up and held until we come and take them off your hands."

The chief nodded again.

"And finally, I'd like a helicopter fully fuelled here inside half an hour. No pilot."

The last request surprised Easton. He wouldn't admit it but he was impressed. The chief was about to object but Anders' relentless stare reminded him that he was in no position to bargain. He nodded again and turned to the sergeant passing on the orders with a wave of his hand. The officer shot out of the room glad to get out of there. In a little under an hour, Anders and Easton were walking toward a helicopter in the middle of a small field three blocks down from the police station. Anders was an experienced pilot, having flown all manner of 'copters in Korea and Vietnam and on a number of assignments for the agency. Easton had only flown with him once and that had been pretty frightening. At least this time it was daylight and they were the ones that were armed. They climbed into the front seats and Anders laid the .22 rifle they had commandeered behind the seat. It was an odd looking whirlybird. It used to be a crop sprayer in its first life but had been converted for use on sightseeing tours. Whoever had done it had extended its range so they had plenty of fuel. Anders lifted the bird off the ground ten feet, dipped the front and sped off. The gust knocked a number of dustbins over and the sergeant's hat flew off over a fence. Easton glanced back and smiled, then crossed his fingers.

45

They asked in the 'town' about the doctor's house and the deli owner directed them back along the road they had travelled down. The only evidence that the house was in fact there, was a rusted mailbox that stood alone about ten feet off the road. The name on the box matched, so they headed off the bitumen in search of the house. It was two o'clock and it was hot. The jeep was so covered in dust it looked like a moving sand dune. They drove another three or so kilometres and Max realised why the mailbox was on the road.

"How often do you think the post gets out here?" he asked.

"If they're lucky twice, but I reckon once a week," replied Pete, who was busy watching the bush for bird-life. There were so many fantastic birds in the countryside here, parakeets of all colours and patterns. *'Even the crows here are pretty,'* Pete thought, as an orange and grey one darted past his window. As Max drove over the next ridge they saw the house. They were both surprised by its simplicity. A house surrounded by so much land would have been much grander in England. But then Max supposed the little two bedroomed, corrugated iron roofed house probably cost more than the barren land it sat on. By the time they rolled up to the front porch a grey-haired man was standing out on it. He'd probably seen the dust cloud from a couple of miles away. A large Alsatian sat obediently by his side. Max had a healthy respect for well-trained dogs. His left buttock still bore the scars of his childhood neighbours' dog's teeth, a huge German Shepherd that had thwarted a ball-retrieving trip one Sunday morning. They got out of the jeep and walked toward the house stopping a respectful twenty feet from the steps.

"Good afternoon, Sir," said Max cheerfully.

"Good afternoon," replied the doctor and added, "Insurance or Real Estate?"

Max quickly realised the mistake and laughed.

"Neither sir. My name is Max Jones and I would like to ask you a few questions that you may be the only one to answer," he said smiling.

"I doubt it," said the doctor, "unless the questions are 'what did you have for breakfast?' and 'how much milk have you got left in the fridge?'" He grinned

"Besides, I'm retired and according to local opinion I'm an eccentric old man."

"That's fine with me," Max said, "I don't have too many options and you really are my only chance." The doctor sensed the urgency in Max's voice and smiled.

"Well, you're probably in deep shit then, but I guess you can come in for a cup of tea," he laughed. They followed the doctor into the house taking great care that they didn't bring the outside in with them. Once inside Max and Pete felt they were walking around a mini-museum. They both gazed around at the fascinating objects that lined the walls, shelves and other surfaces of the living room. Max was captivated by the fireplace, which was gorgeous marble and by the portrait above it. The woman was stunningly beautiful and the picture looked a good forty years old. Time had not altered the smile and warm eyes that kept watch over the room.

"The kettle is on gentlemen, please do make yourselves at home," the doctor called from the kitchen. Max and Pete sat down on the couch which was a deep green with highly polished mahogany arms. It too had a feeling about it of being decades old. Max's eyes wandered past the portrait to the iron gas lamps that sat either side of it. He wondered if they were in fact functional, as he could not see any other forms of lighting in the room. Pete's eyes fell on the bookcase, which at one end held all medical journals and the other, classical fiction. 'Far From The Madding Crowd - Thomas Hardy' nestled amongst rows of Dickens and Jules Verne. Further on lay the works of Plato, Lenin and a host of other philosophers. Many of them large leather bound volumes that looked a delight to read. In front of the bookshelves was a small table with a chess-set mid-game. He studied it briefly and decided that white just had the upper hand. The back wall was full of certificates and diplomas all in beautiful script. Many were in German though the ones to the right were in English. The doctor emerged from behind a stately grandfather clock that sat next to the door to the kitchen. He was carrying a silver tray with china teacups, saucers and a jug of milk jostling for space with an ornately detailed teapot. He laid it down on the table in front of them and sat down in an armchair.

"I'm afraid I'm out of Earl Grey, so normal tea will be OK I trust?" he said. It was a rhetorical question but Max still said, "Great". He was trying to relax a little and it wasn't working very well. They drank the tea and made small talk, mostly about the house and its contents. The lady in the picture was his late wife as Max had suspected. The gas lamps were real as there was no electricity in the house at all yet. He planned to have solar power in by the end of the year. Max finished his second cup of tea and sat back into his seat. The other two were still drinking, of course, and he decided that now was the time for serious talking.

"My first question doctor is this," he paused, "are you familiar with the fluid Panvidyxcil?" he said looking anxiously at their host.

"Yes, it is a cerebral fluid substitute. I have come across it a number of times during my research," replied the doctor. Max sighed with relief. He had found someone who knew what he was talking about.

"Why would someone use it?" he asked.

"Well, the only application it has is to keep brain tissue in a state of suspension long enough for experts to examine the cells in an 'alive' state. Its very useful in analysing cancerous patients to determine in the last few hours the course the cancer took."

"How long could the tissue be kept in that state?" Max asked slowly

"That's irrelevant really," replied the doctor who was curious as to where this was leading.

"Why?" asked Max.

"Simple. If you left the cells with cancer/disease for more than, say 48 hours they would have changed beyond measure."

"How about healthy tissue, for say, transplants?" The doctor was very curious now.

"Firstly, the cost of storing the tissue in a healthy state for the maximum of around sixty hours would be very costly. Secondly, the chances of matching compatible tissues is around one in fifty. Thirdly, the tissue would have to be extracted within minutes of death. Difficult in itself."

"Unless of course the patient is already in hospital," Max interrupted.

"I suppose so," agreed the doctor.

"Next, in around 75% of cases death itself renders all the tissue useless. Finally," he said slowly, "such a tissue transplant is highly unlikely to be very effective. So far in such operations patients' bodies initially accept the tissue but within a few weeks it is rejected and you are back to square one." Max thought about this for a moment.

"So, it would be possible to keep such a patient alive indefinitely if you were able to line up enough donors?" he asked.

"Technically yes. For the reasons I have outlined, practically no."

"What if you turned some of the odds back in your favour?" Max said solemnly.

"Hmm" the doctor thought. "The only factor you could physically influence..." he paused and cast a concerned look at Max.

"Would be to remove the tissue before the patient is actually dead," Max said slowly. He went on to explain piece by piece the events at the hospital and the records he had kept.

"These people must be stopped," the doctor said in a disgusted tone as Max finished.

"Whatever you need from me you've got it," he said earnestly.

"Thank you doctor," Max said, and took out pen and paper and began to write.

46

'Not a patch on a Hewey,' Anders thought as he sliced through the clear blue sky and kept his eyes glued to the horizon. Many memories of the two conflicts in which he had fought were painful, but they were more or less held back by better images - skimming the treetops and hovering over the lakes collecting his precious human cargo from the jaws of danger. Easton looked away from the stunning scenery to look at Anders' face and saw his past glories being relived. He was too young to have been part of the wars his partner had been in, except as an indirect casualty. His father had made it back from Vietnam and had been altered by its horrors. He seemed all right at first but then came the screams in the night, the mood-swings and the erratic temper. He didn't like to guess what was going on inside Anders' head. The agency was the natural choice for him. Easton turned his eyes back to the scenery. They would be there in half an hour from now. It would be close as to whether they would be in time.

47

Max stopped the jeep at the end of the doctor's drive and thought for a moment.

"It's right back to Alice Springs, Max," Pete said. He was surprised Max had forgotten the way back. *'Still, he has a lot on his mind'* he thought. Max smiled briefly and pulled out left onto the road.

"North to Darwin," he said quietly.

"OK," said Pete trying to sound enthusiastic. Max had been solemn ever since they had left the doctor's front door.

"I suppose Tim can arrange for someone to pick up the jeep from there," he said.

"But I'm sure you thought of that," he added as an afterthought. Max hadn't. He was grappling with his next problem. Now he had the information he wanted, what the hell was he going to do with it?

It was about ten minutes after they turned off left that a large red helicopter flew low over the doctor's house. With no sign of the jeep they were looking for they headed back to the road and Anders brought the chopper to rest by the road a good 100 yards from the post-box and leapt out.

'You won't get away that easily,' he thought as he crouched over the tracks leading into the road. As he suspected one of the sets of tracks led out to the left.

'Got him,' he grinned as he walked casually back to the helicopter. The road in that direction (according to the map) ran plenty long enough to catch

them up. The chopper rose off the ground sending dust flying once more and sped off in a straight line above the road.

Pete was driving now. Max had found he couldn't concentrate on the road and think at the same time. Had he known of the impending danger perhaps he would have had his foot to the floor but he was cautious as ever and respectful of the harshness of the road conditions. Max's hard thinking wasn't getting him anywhere and he decided he'd wait until that evening. A good meal and a couple of whiskeys would get the grey matter moving again.

Anders would normally be holding the rifle. On this occasion he had no choice but to let Easton have the honours. Easton was no slouch but he had seen Anders hit targets that he could barely see himself. They could see the jeep now and Easton loaded the rifle and checked the sights.

"Remember, just take out the wheels," Anders said slowly.

"I know," replied Easton, "and if the crash doesn't kill them then we'll have two prisoners."

'Two corpses either way,' thought Anders and started his descent.

"Oh look," said Pete. "A helicopter way out here," he smiled as he saw the speck get larger in his rear view mirror. Max wasn't listening properly but at the word helicopter he perked up.

"A what?" he said.

"Helicopter," Pete repeated and pointed over his shoulder. Max spun round and saw the quickly descending 'copter. He turned back telling himself not to be so silly. Where would they have got a helicopter from? He chuckled to himself and leant forward to turn on the radio.

"Now!" shouted Anders and Easton squeezed the trigger hard. His face was being blown about and was sure he'd missed.

The back window shattered with a crash and both Max and Pete let out unintelligible screams. Pete somehow managed to keep the jeep on the road and Max cursed himself vowing that from now on he would be a paranoid bastard.

"Keep weaving left and right," he shouted over to Pete. The noise from the road had increased due to the lack of a back window but *'he needn't have shouted,'* thought Pete. He then realised that worrying about being shouted at whilst being shot at was rather stupid.

Easton re-loaded the rifle and prepared to shoot again. He'd actually fired the second shot well wide. He wasn't being helped by Anders in his excitement calling him a 'Bloody Amateur'. He elected to aim for the front wheels this time but instead hit the bonnet. It turned out to be close enough.

Steam gushed out in front of him and made Pete's job of driving near impossible. They veered off the road to the right straight through a bush and down into a shallow river. They probably would have stopped there had the river not been dried up for many years. The jeep rapidly found its way out the other side.

"Tree!" yelled Max as another bullet thudded into the back of the jeep. Pete turned hard right and missed the tree but hit the wall behind it side on. The jeep flipped over and crashed onto its roof.

Easton had popped a few more shots as the jeep had made its way through the bush.

"Bingo!" shouted Anders gleefully as he saw the upturned jeep. He grinned as he noticed it sitting in the middle of a flower bed. As they swooped toward the ramshackle dwelling Easton saw a figure emerging.

'I bet he's pissed,' Anders thought. Another couple of seconds closer and Anders saw the figure raise his arms and before he could bank away fragments ripped through the 'copter sending it into a dive.

"No-one messes my cacti," shouted the man holding the shotgun and shaking his fist at the sky. As he turned and walked toward the jeep he saw that a couple of the wheels were still spinning.

"Urggh," Max grunted as he shifted in his seat. Well one thing was for sure, he was alive. His throbbing leg told him as much. *'Pete?'* he thought and anxiously turned his head, painful in itself, and called out his name.

"Pete." Pete opened one eye and curled up one side of his mouth at the same time.

"We alive then?" he asked sounding surprised.

"Yep, and upside down too," Max replied in a strained voice. He moved again which was a bad move as he slid down a foot or so, just enough to hit his head on the roof (currently doing a pretty good job as a floor).

"Ouch," he groaned and Pete bit his lip to stop himself laughing. Both windows had smashed in the crash and dust blew in and into Max's open eyes.

'That's all I need,' Max thought as he squinted and rubbed his eyes. As he opened them and looked across at Pete he let out a loud 'EEEK' and did his best to jump backward. All this in fact achieved was to rock the jeep and cause him to slip further out of his seat so his head was almost flat on the roof. The cause of his alarm was a dark face with a big grin that had appeared at Pete's window.

"G'day fellas," the man said cheerfully. "You do realise you are trespassing," he said in a serious tone and then laughed.

"Sorry about the wall," Pete said quickly.

"Oh screw the wall. I'm more worried about yer mate's leg there," he said pointing at Max's jeans that were blood-soaked below the knee. He opened Pete's door and helped him out and then they both tried to free Max. His door however had been wedged closed by the impact.

"Any time before Christmas," Max said loudly.

"Oh, a pomme with a sense of humour," laughed the man. "I'll just get a crowbar," he added and headed to the house. Within a few minutes Max was out, lying in the shade with his bloody leg in the air. It was propped up on an empty beer carton and his jeans cut away to reveal a deep gash with excellent scar potential.

"I'll need to stitch it, OK?" the man said matter-of-factly.

"You a doctor?" Max asked hopefully.

"You got a choice?" came the short reply.

"Anaesthetic?" Max smiled.

"My name's Mulwi and you see that log over there?" Max nodded "That's the only anaesthetic you'll get here."

"I'll pass thanks," laughed Max holding his hands up. "Got any Scotch?" he asked as an afterthought.

"Whiskey. Now you're talking like an Aussie. Sure." Mulwi got up and returned with a well-drained bottle that still had a dozen gulps left in it. Max knocked it straight back and gritted his teeth. As the needle was being held over the man's cigarette lighter Max closed his eyes. Despite the numbness of the leg the pain was intense but he was too proud to show it and didn't utter a sound until the last stitch went in. Mulwi was impressed with the big man's bravery and as he tied the stitch off he leaned down and whispered in his ear.

"You're supposed to scream you stupid pomme." Max laughed as he opened his eyes and saw that it was all over. Mulwi ran a bandage over the wound and Max extended his hand and thanked the tall man. Pete had watched quietly and decided to ask about what had been worrying him. He'd half been expecting their armed pursuers to leap out any moment.

"Did you see where the helicopter went?" he asked.

"They crashed somewhere over that ridge," Mulwi replied pointing out to their left.

"Crashed?" repeated Max.

"Yes, with a little help from my shotgun," Mulwi said proudly pointing to an ancient looking device which was leaning against a tree. It looked like a cross between a bugle and a Winchester.

"Why did you shoot at them?" asked Pete amazed.

"They shot at me first," Mulwi replied pointing at a bullet hole above the door.

"And besides, they ruined my cacti," he added turning to where the jeep lay amongst a once beautiful bed of cacti.

"I didn't hear an explosion though," Mulwi said jumping to his feet and heading off in the direction of the 'crash'. Pete and Max followed tentatively. Mulwi had picked up his shotgun and was reloading it from a pouch underneath his T-shirt as he walked. Max winced a little from the pain but his leg wasn't too bad all things considered. As they reached the peak of the ridge they saw a clump of Boab trees, one of which had the remains of a helicopter entwined in its branches. One of its blades hung down and was swaying in the breeze. That was the only movement they could see. The edged closer and as they came to the trunk they saw a lot of broken glass and two motionless bodies.

"Do you think they are dead?" Pete asked taking a step back.

"Only one way to find out," replied Mulwi and began to carefully climb the tree until he was level with the cockpit. He didn't need to check Anders' pulse as his neck was so broken he looked like a limp chicken. He did find a strong pulse on Easton's neck though. There were no apparent signs of serious injury and he began to free the belt and lowered him down to Pete and Max below.

"The other one is dead," Mulwi shouted.

"You get that fella inside and I'll cut this one down." Max swallowed hard as he thought of the dead man but there was nothing that they could do for him now. He recognised the guy that they were carrying from the service station on the M3. As they neared the house Max saw a shed at the back with a convenient looking chair in it. They sat the unconscious Easton into the chair and stepped back.

"Shouldn't we tie him up?" Pete asked.

"I guess you're right," replied Max and headed for the house for some rope. By the time Mulwi had returned with Anders' body over his shoulder Easton was well and truly bound to the chair.

"What you gonna do with him?" Mulwi asked slapping him on the back.

"I haven't worked that out yet," came the reply.

"Would a coldie help the thinking process?" smiled the tall Aboriginal leading the way through the front door.

"Would it ever," replied Max wiping the sweat off his brow.

'Whoever tied these knots must have been a boy scout,' Easton thought as he wriggled in the chair. His eyes were adjusting slowly to the light though he could already tell that his present prison was made out of corrugated iron and had all manner of junk piled around the sides. Small holes and gaps in the sheeting let shafts of light in and it was almost as if he were being held captive in a colander. He remembered the crash vaguely - the shot and the tree and then nothing. There was no sign of Anders.

'Where is he being kept?' he thought. Ironically if he'd been able to turn around he would have seen a dark blanket draped over his partner three feet behind him. It was musky and humid in this little shed and he was itching to wipe the beads of sweat off his nose. Where and who were their captors? He was pretty sure that it wouldn't be too long before he found out.

Mulwi sat fascinated, listening to Max's story explaining how they came to be in Australia and the chase that ended in his front garden. He was finishing an ice-cold beer and looked over at Max who had his hand under his chin in

165

true contemplative pose. The other two were still cradling their beer bottles and Mulwi whispered to Pete.

"He always look like that when he's thinking?"

"Sometimes," Pete chuckled. Max got up slowly and walked to the fridge.

"Can I use some ice?" he said holding up a large piece.

"Yeah sure," Mulwi answered intrigued. "Can I do anything to help?" he asked eagerly.

"Actually you can," grinned Max.

The door of the shed creaked open slowly and the sun shone bright into Easton's face. He closed his eyes from the glare and squinted heavily. He could see the outline of the two figures in the doorway. One silhouette was surely Jones as it matched his bulky frame, but the other looked too tall to be his companion. The two figures entered and partially closed the door behind them. As the light dimmed he saw it was Jones but the man next to him was very dark skinned and distinctly tribal. He wore only a loin cloth and symbols were painted across his arms and chest. In this left hand he held an extremely sharp looking knife. In his right was a spear. They stood for a moment then Max spoke.

"Guess we are even," he said menacingly straight toward him.

"You're pal copped it in the helicopter and my mate Pete got crushed in the jeep." He spat out the words slowly and continued.

"So it's just you and me, and of course this fella here whose house you half destroyed," he said pointing to Mulwi who stood twirling the knife over and over in his hand.

"So you want to tell me what the hell's going on and why you guys want me dead?" Easton stayed silent and stared blankly ahead of him.

"I thought that'd be the case. Your choice buddy. OK Mulwi do your stuff."

Mulwi sneered and held up the knife. Easton shuddered a little to himself.

'Was Anders really dead? Were these two serious?'

"Oh I'm sorry, how rude of me," Max said, "I should explain what he's going to do," Max added, as Mulwi went out the door and returned with a box from which he produced a stone and began to grind the blade slowly and methodically.

"They have an ancient method of slicing pigs which involves razor thin cuts all along the animal while it still lives then letting it run wild. The cuts split wide as it runs and the adrenaline is said to spread throughout the meat." Max leaned closer and continued.

"The animal doesn't feel much until the last cut - so you have a while to choose to talk," he said and sat down on the ground near the door. Easton gritted his teeth as he felt Mulwi make the first incision. He could feel the cold edge of the blade on his skin and the drops of blood run down his back. Jones was right, there was no pain yet but the thought of the cut widening repulsed him. The second cut came and then the third. His determination to hold out was slowly ebbing away. He waited for the next cut but Mulwi came forward and ushered Max out of the door.

"What's the matter?" Max asked puzzled when they were out of earshot.

"All the ice has melted," Mulwi grinned.

"Do you think he's falling for it?" Max asked.

"He's heaps scared," Mulwi said, "but this will put him over the edge," he added, picking up a machete that he had on a hook by the back door. Max chuckled quietly to himself and waited for Mulwi to get some more ice from the kitchen.

"Sorry about that," Max said apologetically to Easton as he came back in through the shed door followed by Mulwi who began to slowly grind the machete.

"He decided he needed a bigger blade to do your shoulders," Max said with a nasty grin. Easton snapped and shouted.

167

"OK, OK, what do you want to know?"

"Why kill me?" Max replied quickly.

"You were getting too close at the hospital," Easton replied.

"So it was the CIA that set me up for McQuinn's murder," Max said shaking his head.

"All we were told was that McQuinn was a threat to the peace process and had to be erased. You had to be gotten out of the way too."

"Kill two birds with one stone eh?" Max mused.

"Something like that," said Easton.

"Do you know what they were doing at the hospital?" Max added.

"No," replied Easton, "except that it was some sort of research."

"Some research," said Max under his breath.

"Why not just get me sacked?" Max asked, "Why set me up?"

"Don't know," said Easton slowly. Max looked at their prisoner. He looked exhausted.

"Pete," he shouted out.

"Grab a few cold ones, our man here looks thirsty - oh and grab a towel too he's soaking wet." Max added.

"Towel?" Easton moaned.

"Yeah," said Mulwi, "this bloody ice melts so fast," he said running a cube over Easton's hands.

"You bastards!" Easton shouted and hung his head. Max chuckled then adopted a serious tone.

"Look I don't mean you any harm, and I'm sorry about your partner, that bit was true. I know you guys were only following orders," he said sympathetically.

I wonder where Pete's got to, he thought only to have two guns shoved in his face the moment he stepped out of the door. Pete was standing a few feet away and also had a pistol shoved in his ear.

"Tell your mate to come out with his hands on his head," said a stern voice. Before Max could say a word Mulwi was in front of them hands held high.

"His mate has pretty good hearing sir," he said as he took his place next to a worried looking Pete.

"Tom, do you want to go and free the prisoner," Sam said as he ushered Max next to Pete and Mulwi. Tom disappeared into the shed and quickly emerged with Easton and told him and the others to all sit on the edge of the back porch.

"Anders appears to have a broken neck," said Tom after a brief examination of the body.

"Would you mind me asking you who you guys are?" Easton asked wearily.

"We were coming to that," snapped Angie, "us 'guys' are Internal Affairs."

"Are these good guys or bad guys?" Mulwi asked Max.

"Good, I think. But then who am I to guess."

"Yes we are the good guys," Sam repeated.

"Can't we just arrest these two and then get back to the states," said Easton.

"Not so fast," said Angie, "We were in time to hear your little story."

"Under duress," Easton pleaded.

"Oh, yeah. Torture by ice cube. I'm sure that'll cut it with the chief!" said Tom.

'I walked into that one,' thought Easton cursing himself.

"Where do we go from here?" asked Max who wasn't sure if things had deteriorated or not.

"Where's your laptop?" Sam asked Easton.

"In the chopper I suppose," he replied and Tom set off to retrieve it. Sam whispered quietly to Angie.

"What do you think?"

"The visit to the doctor checked out. If we get Easton to call in then we'll get the full picture," Angie replied.

"My thoughts too, except don't mention Anders. They may get suspicious. I think the chief was right on this one. The smell is coming from way up."

"Yes, and I think we'd better cover our backs too." Angie said solemnly.

"I've disabled the emergency code just in case," said Tom as he returned with the laptop and briefcase.

"If you co-operate then we'll recommend they go very easy on you," said Sam. Easton nodded and keyed in his access code. Sam typed away and got the message ready for sending.

"Will it be re-routed?" asked Sam.

"I guess so. Yes" replied Easton.

Sam tutted and pulled out his mobile phone. He keyed in the long number and his access code and spoke quickly, "Agent X487329BY - Trace please on remote transmitter after it reaches central switchboard please. Transmission source? Alice Springs, Australia. - Yes I'll hold". He motioned to Easton who keyed in his transmission code and waited.

"Thank you," said Sam and after a few moments.

"Copy of trace to Chief Jackson, internal affairs please."

"You mean you can trace any CIA transmission world-wide?" said Easton bewildered.

"Yep," replied Angie, "not even our big boss knows about that one," she said proudly.

"Looks like big brother has a big brother," Max chuckled.

"What now?" asked Pete.

"Well gentlemen," said Sam, "we wait to see what the person at the other end wants done," he pointed at the screen. They didn't wait too long before the message came up"

NEUTRALISE BOTH TARGETS. ERADICATE ALL TRACES OF ACTIVITY. FILE REPORT 'TARGETS COULD NOT BE LOCATED'. RETURN TO U.S. ASAP FOR DEBRIEF......

"According to this you have to waste these two innocent civilians and pretend that you never found them," said Sam to Easton.

"Does that mean that you're going to let him kill us?" said Pete in a worried voice.

"As far as the person at the other end is concerned you're already dead," smiled Angie.

Sam looked over at Angie and then back to the three civilians.

"You got room for two more lodgers?" Sam asked Mulwi pointing at Max and Pete.

"Yes Sir!" Mulwi answered with a sigh of relief.

"Just for a week or so while we go back and sort things out," Sam added.

"Am I a free man?" Max asked.

"It will take a few days to sort out a credible story for the British authorities. We'll send someone out to pick the two of you up and brief you," said Sam. "Oh and this should cover your expenses," he said handing Mulwi an envelope in which he carefully placed a number of notes. Max turned to Pete and wiped his hand across his brow.

As Tom and Angie walked around the side of the house helping Easton with the body of Anders, Max tapped Sam on the shoulder.

"Can I ask you a question?" he asked

"If it's about this case then the answer will probably be no," Sam replied.

"No. It's just curiosity really. Are you and that young lady, you know together?"

Sam stopped in his tracks and stared at Max.

"No," he replied quickly and then added, "Well, that is, it's not encouraged in our profession."

"Sod the profession," said Max. "If I'm lucky I'll get a second chance. I lost my first wife to my bloody profession. I may have been looking down the wrong end of a revolver for the last half an hour but even I could see the way the two of you look at each other."

Sam was stunned. He was being given personal relationship advice by a man he had just met in very unusual circumstances. He paused for a moment and took a long look at Max. This man had been through a hell of a lot over the last few months and yet..... Sam held out his hand and shook Max's hard.

"Thanks," he said. "I guess I just had to hear it from a complete stranger."

Max smiled and reflected at the choice he had made all those years ago. *'Who knows what could have been,'* he thought. He then told himself not to be so silly and headed for the front of the house.

48

The knocking on the door distracted him and instead of taking the congressman off hold he cut him off. *'He'll call back. They usually do,'* he thought. It had been a shitty day by all accounts and he'd been at his desk since 5am.

"Come in," he called out in a snappy irritated tone. The door opened to reveal Chief Jackson flanked by two MPs.

"Bob," he said surprised. "What a nice surprise."

"Not for me," came the reply. "Here's the warrant, read it," he added in a cold tone.

He placed the warrant on the desk. After a brief glance the man looked up.

"I'll have your balls for this," he shouted getting to his feet.

"We've got you, otherwise I wouldn't be here you dumbass. I know you have friends where it counts so keep you're mouth shut and face the music you composed," he snapped, surprised at his own confidence. He was, after all only internal affairs. The man behind the desk sat down slowly.

"I get my phone call I suppose," he said.

"Unfortunately, yes," came the reply.

49

"What a waste of a good tea towel!" Pete laughed as Max paraded his new outfit.

"Very good," Mulwi laughed, "I'll have a word with the elders, maybe they'll let you become a temporary member of the tribe!" he laughed again.

"Remember this was your idea," Max reminded him as they set off for their walk in the bush all clothed in aboriginal dress. As close as they could get to traditional dress anyway. With only a bag full of beer over Pete's shoulder to link them to the modern world they set off at a moderate pace in respect for Max's convalescing leg.

"To really appreciate the beauty of the bush you have to get close to it." Mulwi said.

"Well my feet certainly are," Max grinned as he glanced down at his already dust-caked toes. The sun was still beating down and it was very hot.

"I walked this area and more when I was initiated as a young boy," said Mulwi.

"How long did you have to spend in the bush?" asked Pete.

"Three days," Mulwi said proudly. "Legend says you go into the bush as a boy and come back as a man."

"Return as a man with loads of blisters more like," Pete chuckled. The air was still and they heard the cackle of a nearby crow. They continued through the stunning scenery for about an hour when Mulwi realised his companions' feet weren't up to much more.

"Here we stop to make a fire before it gets colder," he announced. They actually had ages before the sunset but these two would struggle to get to the next suitable spot. Both Max and Pete sighed with relief and gladly collected the necessary firewood to create a good blaze. They cracked open a beer and Max and Pete listened intently while Mulwi described the 'boat race' they ran every summer in the river that runs through Alice Springs.

"There is, of course, no water in the river at that time of year and the boats have no bottom to them to allow the competitors' feet to run along the ground. They run through the sand carrying the boat between the team of them," he explained.

"That doesn't sound too hard," Max commented.

"Except that to qualify to be in one of the teams you have to drink a whole case of beer beforehand," Mulwi added. "Have you ever tried to run through baking hot sand after that much grog?" he teased.

"Come to think of it I did try and run along Brighton beach after six pints once," Max laughed, "but I didn't get very far." They took turns telling drinking stories and despite being the youngest Pete kept them amused with how he and his girlfriend had woken up with fourteen 'For Sale' signs in her front garden after one of his nights out and various other antics from his university days in Bristol. After a dozen or so bottles had returned to the bag empty, Mulwi attempted to lead them in a traditional aboriginal song. After the somewhat poor performance he shook his head.

"Every frog for many miles will descend on us after that," he laughed.

"So smug," smiled Max, "I thought you might pull a stunt like that, so I took the liberty of bringing along a tune that suits my deep tones much better," he smirked as he got a couple of pieces of paper on which he had written the words for his two friends.

"I hope this will be a rendition of which The King himself would be proud. I'll do one verse then you can copy," he said and Pete smiled and winked at

175

Mulwi who winked back. They both knew the song but didn't want to miss out on hearing Max's solo. They were pleasantly surprised as their large comrade hit every note. Well almost. When he finished they clapped and cheered enough to make him blush. They cleared their throats and Max counted them in.......

'As the snow flies,
On a cold and grey Chicago morn,
Another little bay child is born, in the Ghetto,
And his momma cries....'

The three voices, accompanied by the crackling fire, drifted across the plains. A bush-tailed possum paused briefly at the sight and sound.

'They must be standing too close to that fire,' he thought and scurried off into the night.

50

There was that knocking again. Max decided to face the fact that there was someone at the door. He could hear two voices, too, but not what they were saying. To quote Mulwi he had 'a family of kangaroos living in his head' at the moment. His mouth tasted awful and he guessed his breath wouldn't be all that much better. He hauled himself off the floor where he had thrown himself in the early hours. The walk back had been much easier than the one into the bush. At least he thought so, he wasn't altogether sure. He was about to open the door when he realised he was still in 'tribal costume' and dug around for a shirt. Mulwi and Pete were both still asleep. Unconscious would be more accurate. He ran his fingers through his hair and checked his breath. Bad, bad move. *'Oh well,'* he thought and opened the door. The two smart young gentlemen seemed shocked at the sight before them.

"Mr Jones?" one of them asked tentatively.

"Yeah, for my sins," Max smiled.

"Ah, we've erm, come to debrief you and escort you back to the U.K," the smaller one said.

"OK lads I'll put the kettle on," he replied fumbling.

"We've just had one thank you, sir," said the other. "We have an eight berth roadster nearby. The boss decided we would drive you down to Sydney and brief you on the way there. Is that OK with you?" he added politely.

"Oh sure, whatever. If you can give us a few minutes," Max said.

"Certainly," they chorused, and both turned and headed back toward the road. Fifteen minutes of frantic tidying themselves up and packing and Max and Pete were on the front steps saying goodbye to Mulwi.

"Thanks for everything," Max said. "You've been a mate," he added as he shook Mulwi's hand hard.

"No worries," he grinned. "Besides, with the money they gave me to fix my wall I'll be set for grog for about six months," he laughed. Pete said his goodbyes and the two of them walked up the road to the campervan.

51

By the time they reached Sydney in a little over three days and nights driving, they had their version of events down to a tee. Max's relief at being both alive and free overwhelmed the annoyance and anger at having to adopt the agency's cover up. He'd been little placated by the assurance that those responsible had been 'appropriately dealt with'. Whatever that meant. His return to work had been assured, with a hefty promotion. Max kept his word to Pete who had already begun work on the story and sent word ahead to England. News had also been sent to both of their families and they could look forward to a warm welcome at Heathrow airport. They were sitting in the departure lounge at Sydney and Max was indulging in a bit of reflection. Pete was engrossed in the Sydney Morning Herald.

'A long way round of getting to see a bit of the world,' Max observed. He was looking forward to seeing Jan again. Although they had little in common and led fairly independent lives, they had had a good marriage. He made a mental note to get her something special when they got back. Pete tapped him on the shoulder and handed him the newspaper. It was open at the 'World' section and Pete had circled a certain story.

'WASHINGTON BUDGET NEWS- Following the death of the President at 3:27am Eastern Standard Time on Thursday, the major departments in the government have been rocked with news of funding cuts. The vice president Mr. Henry Forbes was sworn in immediately and as expected wasted no time re-enforcing his personal tough stance on public spending. With an election only a month away he vowed the axe would fall quickly on a number of departments. Defence and the internal agencies are expected to be hardest hit. It has come as a particularly cruel blow to the new director of the CIA, Dan Myers, who has only been in the job three days following last week's sudden resignation of his predecessor. Both the president and his Republican opponent had been in favour of additional security funding. Had the president made it to the election, Myers would have taken over the most prolific internal agency in the world whatever the result. Instead, he faces an uphill struggle. President Forbes defended his tough stance, so soon after the president's death from a brain haemorrhage, saying that the world needed to know a strong man was at the head of the world's most powerful economic nation in the midst of a global recession. Critics have argued that it is purely a vote winning ploy to reverse gains by the republicans in recent opinion polls...................'

52

4 years later.....................

The blackened-out Mercedes saloon sped under the bridge and for a moment you could see the reflection of the lights on the bridge in both the windows and on the dark waters of the Danube. The car was one of the more traditional 1970's style large-engined models with plenty of chrome to keep their drivers busy polishing. Across the river, three hundred feet up, the cross hairs of the night-vision sight of a rifle were fixed on a bend in the road. As the car slowed and came into view the gunman tracked the front window. He was leaning on the battlements of the castle which just forty years before had seen the beginning of a revolution. For a moment he lowered the gun and looked around to check that he was still alone. No traffic on the top of the hill at 3am. He raised the rifle back to his shoulder and once more the car was visible in the eerie green colour of the sight. The car came to stop fifty yards from a green car, which was parked next to the promenade. Two men got out slowly from the green car and waited. They stood respectfully with their arms crossed in front of them. They knew that whoever was in the Mercedes was worth the caution. The Mercedes window on the side nearest the river rolled down giving the shooter a clear view into back seat. He checked himself as the occupant's face came to the window and beckoned to the larger of the two men. He had of course studied every contour of the face of the man he had been sent to kill but there was always that instant of hesitation as he mentally ticked the box. As the large man approached the Mercedes the man in the car reached down and grabbed a package, which he held out.

The package fell to the floor as the force of the bullet whipped the man's head back into the darkness and the approaching man hesitated, then reached inside his long coat for what appeared to be some sort of semi-automatic weapon.

"Karchi" he screamed across to his colleague who already had his shotgun resting across the roof of the car. They both looked around frantically to see what was going on. Although they hadn't heard the shot, when one of Budapest's most notorious criminals drops the best part of $1m onto the sidewalk, even the dimmest of criminals gets the feeling that something must be wrong.

The shooter knew he had a minute and no longer before he would have to disappear. He watched the next thirty seconds unfold with the inevitability of a stack of dominoes falling over. The next life to be erased was the larger man on his feet as the driver of the second car snapped open his door and sprayed dozens of bullets in the vague direction of the first. Two of the bullets caught the man in the chest and one in the stomach. The rest rattled off the car and shattered a street lamp, which cut off half of the nearby light. Karchi ducked, and re-emerged growling and emptied both barrels of the shotgun into the windscreen. The toughened glass cracked under the force but held and the driver's gun appeared with another volley of bullets. Karchi dived for cover but was too slow. The upper part of his jacket shredded as he flew through the air.

The engine of the second car roared into life but as it spun backwards it smashed into the cast iron railing of the promenade. Two more occupants from the first car stepped out over their fallen comrades and rushed toward the crashed car, machine guns blazing. The gunman in the passenger seat wielding a handgun caught one of them halfway there. The other got parallel to the driver's side and peppered the occupants.

Then silence. The last man standing lowered his gun and ran back to check on his colleagues who were sprawled across the road near the first car.

The gunman quickly checked the area around the cars and saw no other movement. As the first bullet slammed into his back, he staggered forward and grabbed the rim of the roof of the car. The last second of his life was spent with a confused and horrified look on his face trying to turn to see where it had come from, before the second shot caved the back of his head in.

53

The market had been deathly slow again for the third day running. Marcus Jones looked at the numbers slowly clicking over on his screen and forced himself to focus. He hadn't slept for two days which wasn't unusual for a broker, but pretty difficult to do without, well, a little extra help. Marcus had gone through most of the steps in the cycle. He joined the firm with the staunch belief that all drugs were out of bounds, then becoming slowly immune to the everyday stimulants like coffee and caffeine pills, then falling behind the performance of his peers who used any combination of speed, crack and heroin in varying quantities. He first tried heroin at one of the parties that cropped up every couple of weeks at one penthouse or converted loft or another. He'd worked through from 7am on the Thursday straight to close on Friday, and headed with a group to Battersea to a beautiful apartment overlooking the Thames. He had made a killing that afternoon on a currency deal and was buzzing.

Too much alcohol and lots of encouragement and goading from the rest and he found himself kneeling in front of the coffee table being shown how to cut a line. He had kicked the habit six months later after an incident with his boss. He often remembered back to how surreal the experience was. The fad at the time was for 'Pink Heroin' which was in fact normal Heroin mixed with crushed pink painkiller. The resulting mixture looked like sherbet, but gave a very different fizzing sensation.

Now he managed to stay off the class-A drugs but would admit to smoking dope to relax. He knew that there was no chance of him being as lucky again. The day that he had snapped two years ago was at the end of a 'Treble' – three days without a break – and he'd been called into his boss' office to explain a dubious call he had made on a short-term option. It began with a shouting match in the confines of his boss' office and finished with him breaking the poor man's nose. Marcus had played rugby for Northampton when he was younger and fitter, and his boss was half his size. The incident was brushed under the carpet and Marcus later found out that it was because the manager concerned had been dealing and didn't want to draw any unnecessary attention to him. He was duly moved to another team and made clear that he'd used up his only pardon.

At about 2pm Marcus's PC emitted a couple of small pings which automatically focussed his eyes on the top-left-hand corner of the screen. A small icon appeared with the NYT.Com logo quickly followed by a small cartoon-like character dressed in blue. It had the words "Roving Reporter" across its chest in large yellow letters. Marcus grinned and double clicked. A small video window appeared on the screen. The scene showed a large five level apartment block with a number of smashed windows and flames pouring out. The camera panned down to the street level as a group of figures emerged through the glass doors. A number of them wore instantly recognisable dark blue jackets with FBI across the back. Two of them were dragging out a figure by the shoulders and others pushing forward three more figures encased in handcuffs. Next to the video stream a text box appeared and as Marcus watched the pictures the commentary slowly filled the box....

"34th Street – the early evening light gives this wonderful City of LA a flattering haze but the relative calm of this up-market neighbourhood is shattered with

185

the sound of gunfire. FBI agents, as we watch live, are just bringing out leading members of the Black Cobra gang at the end of months of planning. Our sources tell us that drugs with a street value of $50m were seized at a separate raid timed to perfection to coincide with this one at a warehouse downtown".

Pete paused for a moment as one of the FBI agents looked directly at the window of the shop across the street where he had set himself up behind the counter. Had he been seen? The man reached for his radio and Pete quickly continued.

"As ever, we are right on top of the action here and it looks like we have been made. I'm sure the pictures will continue for a bit longer as our intrepid cameraman has been encased in that mailbox for the last 48hrs! The man in the centre of your screen now with the wide-ranging tattoos is the head of the Black Cobras – Yeung Durang. He has been on the FBI's most wanted list for over a year now, and they have attributed (as yet unproven) over fifty homicides to him alone. It looks like he put up a heck of a fight judging by the state of his face. The man coming out behind him is Special Agent Johansen who had led the case for the two months since the previous No.1 agent was found executed in his home – thought by many to have a direct link back to the case. The Black Cobras allegedly have over two hundred major money-laundering schemes to cope with the volume of cash generated by their multi-level drugs operations. From PCP for bikers to high-grade crack for our bored middle classes, they had the city pretty sewn up. The question is that now the head of the beast has been chopped off, will we see the rest crumble or is there another charismatic leader waiting in the. .. ... ."

"Hey, there was no need for that" Pete exclaimed as the miniature keyboard was yanked away from his phone by the agent half a second after crashing through the front door of the shop.

"Don't you learn?" shouted the tall angry man in sunglasses.

"Freedom to report" Pete smiled as at least this time they hadn't snatched the phone. He pressed the speed-dial for his editor as he was pushed out of his seat and against the wall. The staff of the shop looked on in amazement as the agent checked Pete over from head to toe.

"Yep, they got me" he laughed into the microphone attached to his collar.

"I guess they have sent a few of their lads off to FBI observation school. Though I assume they missed the advanced class 'cos we still got video".

The agent snarled and pushed back out through the door. Pete watched through the window as the agent grabbed a couple of his colleagues and pointed back to the shop. He continued as he packed up his things.

"How'd we get on?"

"Not too bad. You didn't quite overload the server like last month, but we got around ten million immediate hits. A couple of hundred thousand from across the pond too. Its amazing what a difference it makes when we get the break and it doesn't land in the middle of the night in the UK".

Oscar Randle was Pete's editor. If you rolled up every stereotype of an editor of a major US newspaper into one then you'd get Oscar. Early fifties, greying hair, slim build that came from chain-smoking and the constant nervous energy that keeps most editors bouncing off the walls. Pete had been with the paper for nearly two years but it was in the last nine months that he'd really begun to shine. It had been his idea too. A simple one at that.

Most people want to know about a story when it breaks. The closer to the action, the more captivated the audience. The internet had promised to make

24-hour news a reality, but you still had to update the web pages and you were still relying on the person being logged onto the site at the time. Pete's knack of being at the right place at the right time, which was more down to research than luck, had earned him the nickname of the 'Roving Reporter' – the boys from the copy department had made a bright blue T-shirt up with it on for the Xmas party. Pete had hit on the idea of linking the internet's ability to contact people with the transmitting capability of the new digital cameras and phones. The glue that was to bring it all together was 'Roving Reporter'. A piece of software that people could download free from the NY Times website that put a link on the customers machine that would come alive only when a new story was breaking. That way you could be sitting at your desk at work or in front of the TV (if you had a digital set) and the little logo would appear. Clicking on the little cartoon character would get you into the action as it happened.

Despite a number of run-ins with the authorities, Roving Reporter had become a huge success. The "it could have put the investigation in jeopardy" complaint had come in a number of times from various agencies. At the moment the audience was largely New York and Chicago, but there was a growing following in the UK too. Pete had been a reporter with the Evening Standard in London before he made the move to the states and they had run a piece on the new media hot property in one of their Saturday editions.

"Are you heading straight back?" Oscar enquired.
"Not just yet. I'm working a lead on that drugs link into the Caribbean. I'm sure they're working through a number of the islands there".
"Take all the time you need. I'm looking for another break next week. Can you slip through three or four teasers we can use for the build up?".
"Sure."

That was the other genius part of the process. Pete's 'teasers' were lead-ins to the impending exclusive that would be sent out every couple of days until the story broke. It whet the appetite of the audience. They knew that once there had been a few teasers the exclusive was around the corner. Pete gave just enough not to give the game away, often withholding names and always locations.

Marcus grinned and reached for the phone. He was sure Max had seen the same story but he wanted to wind him up over the crap computer in his office he would have seen it on. His brother really should push for a decent bit of kit, but that was the Health Service for you, still stuck in the early 1990s.

"Jones". Max grunted as he picked the phone up. He guessed it wasn't a work-related call as it had been dead all afternoon and he had finally been able to crack on with the monthly reports.

"Hey little brother" Marcus grinned.
"What's happening at the forefront of medical science?"

"Oh its you" Max smiled. "nothing, much. Curing people and stuff. Which small defenceless country have you bankrupted today?"
Max didn't care too much for currency trading, and made no attempt to hide it, especially from Marcus.

"Touchy. Well it's a Friday I suppose. Did you catch your mate's latest exclusive in your slow moving juddering-picture format?"

"Yep. Must give him a call. He's due over for Easter in a couple of weeks. I must give him a call and check the flights. I can't believe he's been over there two years."

"And four years since you two were in Australia." Marcus chipped in.

"Four years". Max reflected. Pete had gone from local paper reporter to lead correspondent on the New York Times in the same time it had taken Max to become deputy-director at the hospital. Different levels of ambition he mused. He didn't let on to Marcus, or indeed anyone, but he'd followed Pete's career very closely. Read every article and watched every clip. You don't forget someone risking their life for you lightly, and they'd become close friends. Although they spoke on the phone and by email every week, he hadn't seen him since last July as he spent all his time on assignment. He was looking forward to Easter.

54

The moon was trying hard to squeeze past the clouds as the figure dressed in black from head to toe approached the fire escape. There was just enough light to see where he was going – the bulbs from the street lights all smashed or stolen. The rusty pieces of corrugated iron creaked in the breeze as he passed them leaning awkwardly against the bins. They were overflowing with weeks' worth of rubbish. A cat jumped across his path and he paused for a moment, as if deciding whether to go on. It was then that he heard the noises from the apartment on the second floor. It was the only one with lights on at two in the morning. The fire escape was also covered in rust and he took care as he climbed the stairs in case any were worn through.

Some commentators claim that Cuban policemen always dress like they are off-duty. The four men in the beaten up Ford at the side of the curb would back that up. Only one had less than three days of stubble, so you could safely assume that he was the most senior officer, which he was. Sergeant Fuentez grinned as a shiny four-wheel drive pulled up in front of the apartment block a hundred yards away and two figures jumped out. His hands moved slowly over the semi-automatic on his lap and he gave the slightest of nods to the other three. As the two figures disappeared into the block, the car doors opened in unison and they crossed the street swiftly and quietly.

Pete reached toward the windowsill above his head and feeling the cold glass on his fingertips placed the tiny microphone through into one of the small cracks. He turned the unit on and winced as a high pitched whine hit his right ear, and then the faint crackle of three, perhaps four voices from inside. Fiddling with the controls the voices became clearer and he thought he could make out the loudest.

Fuentez took the safety catch off slowly and motioned to his colleagues to do the same. The same scene played out around the world, would have the search warrant nestling in his jacket pocket but there was no need for such formalities here. The men behind the door in front of them were guaranteed to be carrying weapons and drugs and Fuentez just hoped his team would all walk away in one piece. His source placed six of Martinez's men and at least five kilos of heroin in the apartment. With any luck most of them would have been trying out the merchandise.

Pete froze to the spot as he heard the bang on the door. He couldn't make out what the shouting was about but there was a lot of crashing and banging making it difficult to hear. It only took a couple of seconds of gunfire to convince him that he shouldn't be there and he sprang up to run down the stairs.

Fuentez kicked the door in and sprayed the ceiling with bullets. The two men behind the table threw their guns out as did the three crouching behind the sofa. Five pairs of hands emerged.

"Marco you pig. Don't make me come in and get you" he shouted from the doorway as he scanned the faces of the five but didn't see the one they really wanted. Two bags of heroin had split and the dust created a haze. Fuentez edged forward and the three other policemen stayed perched by the door. The tallest of the three scanned the room with the barrel of an abnormally large shotgun. Marco bolted from behind the table and raised his .38 in the vague direction of the front door. Before he could get a round off the shotgun roared and the blast lifted him clean off the floor and into the back door.

The full force of the door caught Pete in the shoulder and face and he thumped into and over the railing. Nobody in the apartment above heard him land in the rubbish bags though if they'd have stopped to think about it, they might have wondered what had got in the way of the door as Marco's body flung it open. The bags had broken his fall but he lay still apart from a small trickle of blood across his forehead.

The five criminals that hadn't been shot got to their feet with their hands firmly clasped behind their heads. Fuentez stepped over the debris to Marco's body and promptly gave it a kick. The low moan signalled that he was still in the land of the living.

"You wearing that vest again huh Marco?" he said as he turned the body over.

The vest had done its job though part of the shot had hit the upper shoulder, which was oozing blood quite nicely. Marco snarled through the pain and then promptly passed out. Fuentez shook his head and motioned to one of his men to give him a hand. As they dragged the body across the room he surveyed the spoils. His contact had been right about the amount of heroin, he could see at least six kilo-sized packets. These jokers would be back on the streets within days but the equipment seized would put one of Martinez's teams out of action for at least a month.

55

"Hey Martin!" Max smiled. He'd spoken to the old sage-like reporter many times when he'd called for Pete. It seemed like he never left the office, and always answered the phone.

"Er, Hi Max" Martin replied. He had really not been looking forward to taking this call. As soon as they'd had confirmation through that Pete was officially missing, Martin realised that there would be a few calls he'd not look forward to. He had already spoken to Pete's mother who had been very distraught.
"Is Pete in"
"Max, he's not here and there is something you'd better know. Pete's still not back from Cuba. There's been a few complications"
"Complications" Max didn't like the sound of this.
"Yeah. It's a bit difficult to talk now. Can I call back in five?"
"Sure"
"Are you in the office?
"Yeah. Talk you in a bit".

56

Martin grabbed one of the dozens of soundproofed 'interview' booths that were scattered across each floor in the Times' offices and closed the door. He keyed in the number for Max's office from his PDA and didn't have to wait more than two rings before Max was back on the line.

"What's going on Martin?"

"Well. It's like this. You know that Pete was on holiday in Cuba?"

"Yeah?"

"Well, it wasn't exactly just a holiday"

"You mean he was there on an assignment?"

"No. You know the Times couldn't be involved in any press activity in Cuba. Look at that team that was held there by the authorities for three months and they were there on an official trip to cover the Salsa world championships"

"So?"

"So Pete had an amazing lead on a story and was sort of unofficially following it"

"Unofficially? The sort of unofficial where if he got caught then the paper would denounce any kind of involvement?"

"Yeah, that kind of unofficial. And the worst of it he's there by himself as he's one of the only correspondents we have that's not on a US passport"

'Typical bloody editors' Max thought

"Ok, so what was he on to". Martin glanced around the office. It was just after lunch and there was a lot of activity with people starting to get their leaders ready for the morning's edition.

"You don't want to know".

"Bullshit Martin. It's me you're talking to. You know as well as I do that if Pete's in trouble you're going to have to tell me the details sooner or later"
"Max. I'm not trying to be an asshole but Pete's really done it this time. It makes that thing he did at the senate committee look tame"

Max forced a smile. He had really been impressed with that one. Pete had got himself inside a cocktail party for the Senate Committee debate on party political fundraising. The issue had been gathering pace in the US media for some months and both the senate and the Whitehouse had been tight-lipped. Dressed as two waiters, he and his cameraman had followed a host of the leading politicians around the room as they joked about the stalemate they had engineered that day between the two sides. Both the Democrats and the Republicans had a vested interest in keeping the millions flooding in because no matter who won the races, all of them benefited from the exorbitant sums of money. Just imagine the effect on his or her standard of living if someone capped the amount of money that could be spent on a Senate or Presidential campaign. Pete had broken his golden rule and had run a two-minute delay on the beginning of the report for fear of it being shut down before any material got out. As it was, it was six minutes of fantastic footage before the security forces had burst in and pinned them both to the floor destroying tens of thousands of dollars of covert camera equipment. The authorities had initially tried a court injunction on the footage reaching the networks, but as Pete's transmission as usual had gone out live on the net there were thousands of copies flying around. CNN ran it as their lead on the six o'clock news the following evening and 60 minutes incorporated some of the sound bites, which called for an independent review to follow. Pete had been very close to criminal charges on that one, but as with most of the incidents with reporters in the last couple of years there were no votes to be gained in punishing the messenger once the cat was well and truly out of the bag.

"What could be worse that that?" Max asked trying to think what it could be.

"He's looking into a possible link between the arms and drugs trades in Eastern Europe and Cuba. He interviewed this guy on Death Row who got caught with a fishing boat full of crack off the Florida Keys. Turns out the guy's from the Czech Republic and got recruited to traffic the stuff out of Burma when he was there as part of a gang shifting arms into the country from the Balkans."

"So where the hell does Cuba come into it?" Max was frustrated and a bit confused.
"Apparently that's where some of their arms gang leaders went earlier this year"

"I don't suppose they were out there on holiday"

"I guess not. The links with Eastern Europe have always been strong and Pete thought there might be something in it. There was no point going to the Balkans and doing a piece on all the arms leaking out of there into Europe and Africa. That's old news. But a story out of Cuba, now that really would be worth having".

"No wonder he told me it was just a holiday. How many people know?"

"Just me and the Editor, but he'd deny it. The background story on this being off his own back is watertight. Nobody would find anything here to link it back. He's on his own on this one."

'And I know how that feels' Max thought.

57

The phone rang in the small villa and it took Easton half a minute to get across the sand and up the worn whitewashed steps. He picked up the handset and listened to the familiar series of beeps that signified that the line was secure.

"Easton" he said trying not to sound out of breath.

"Sir, I have a call for you under code 24"

'I suppose I've had three days of my vacation before they had to interrupt it.'

"Sir, are you there?"

"Sure. Code 24. Put them through"

"Hi Easton". Easton recognised the voice immediately.

"Max Jones" he replied.

"To what do I owe this honour?"

If there was one person Easton hadn't expected a call from it was Max. He'd been in the CIA for ten years now and had come closest to calling in his chips while on an assignment to hunt him down four years ago, when Max had been falsely convicted for murder. Bad things had a habit of seeking Max Jones out and Easton wondered what it could be this time.

Max explained as much as he could about Pete and Easton listened intently. As he did so he could picture the situation Max was in. A man with no shortage of history who owed a huge amount to the young reporter. Pete hadn't directly saved Max's life, in fact he'd done something more dramatic. Four years ago, when the whole world was after Max Jones, Pete had been the only one to believe his side of the story and Easton imagined that Max would stop at nothing to find his lost friend. Max finished talking and Easton began slowly.

"Look Max. I'm not promising anything but I'll make a few calls. We keep everything with the Cubans at arm's length as you can imagine. Most of our work is done through the Brits"

"Perfect" Max replied. "In case you don't remember I'm also a Brit"

"Oh yeah. Like I could forget. I'll do this for you Max but after that we're even."

"Thanks. You know I know you were only doing your job"

"Yeah. But it'll make me feel better" Easton laughed.

58

The buildings lined up behind the gate held Max's attention as his friend leapt out to sort out the day pass. Really they should only have one guest. It was unlikely that any guard was going to stop a Major from coming on the base for a game of squash with three of his mates. It was not like there was anything particularly secret housed within these magnificent old buildings. The naval base at Portsmouth on the very South East of the English coast was home to around five thousand men from the Royal Navy and usually a couple of companies from the Royal Marines. It was, however home to tens of thousands of transient seamen whose ships were docked at the port to replenish supplies or undergo repairs.

Three and four storeys high, the main buildings gave way to the small, more recent additions behind and the sports complex came into view. Jim's Audi purred into the parking space that was marked up for a senior member of staff. He was quite safe taking the space as it was the weekend and most of the top brass were spending the weekend away with their wives, or someone else's.

The man on duty in the leisure centre looked decidedly bored. Understandable really, as he was guarding a couple of squash courts and some showers. Oh, there were Coke and coffee machines in the lobby so technically there was something of value in the building. From the changing rooms Jim and the other two lads headed for court number one, but Max instead grabbed his bag and headed to back of the courts and looked for the storage cupboard that he had been instructed would be there. He took the key out of his pocket and after checking no one was around opened the door and stepped in. Some pretty dingy, though clean, shelving and such exciting implements as mops and brushes greeted him. At the back of the room was what looked like an electricity meter box. Max turned on the light, closed the door and turned the key. The meter box opened to reveal what did look like a very modern electricity meter. There was a keypad into which Max tapped the six numbers that he had been given and after a couple of short beeps the back wall came forward a couple of inches and slid to the side.

Behind the wall was what to the layman looked very similar to a lift. It was. Max stepped in and gave a wry smile as the wall slid back into place. The lights in the lift went out and a series of flickering green beams cascaded in a line above his head. The criss-cross beams slowly came down the walls all the way down to the ground and back up again. They would find nothing untoward in Max's garments although you could have hidden an anti-tank missile in his baggy jogging suit. His bag did contain an offensive weapon though. At least that was what Jim had referred to when Max had shown him his squash racket. Max's fitness level was a clue to the fact that he hadn't played squash for years – fifteen years in fact. Graphite rackets were the stuff of science fiction back then and Max's bag contained a vicious looking wooden contraption that he assured Jim had seen him through his college days.

The lift began to move and Max readied himself for the judder as it would no doubt plummet twenty floors down into the high-security underground office of MI5. He was to be disappointed as less than thirty seconds of ambling later and the lift had stopped and opened to reveal a very ordinary looking office. Baber was there to greet him at the door with that pensive look that Easton had told him he would be wearing.

"Baber, MI5" Baber offered his hand

"Jones, North London" Max grinned and shook the hand firmly.

Baber tried desperately not to wince. Easton had not been kidding when he described this man as big and strong. Needed to shift a few pounds no doubt (like about twenty) but he wouldn't want to mess with him. Easton had briefed him on how he had come across Max Jones and it didn't surprise him at all what he was contemplating doing.
'This is not going to be easy' Baber thought as he led to big man into one of the small back offices.

"I know this isn't going to be easy for you Mr.Baber" said Max almost as if he'd heard Baber's thoughts.

"Please, call me Jack"

"Ok, Jack. But I do learn pretty quick"

"I'm not going to pretend Max. Even if you were the most talented undergraduate at Oxford I still wouldn't be able to teach you enough in the next week to pass you off convincingly as the head of an Eastern European arms dealing syndicate. Lets just concentrate on giving you the basics which with a bit of luck, no scratch that, a shit-load of luck, may just keep you from getting your head blown off. We'll start with two days here then finish off in Budapest".

There was a solemn element to Baber's delivery of his little speech that had a sobering effect on Max. He had made his mind up to do this the day before and the reality he suspected hadn't really sunk in. Easton had called him in the car and explained that there was this Hungarian arms dealer who had been assassinated, but nobody yet knew that the deed had been done. When Max had asked how the CIA had known that, Easton had told him not to put two and two together as he was likely to get four. He had gone on to explain that the Americans has been trying to get into the 'Kovács' gang for years and that their chances were slim if head of the gang, János Kovács was gone. The delicate infrastructure of the arms trade would be shaken by the news. Especially so as 'The Nomad', as Kovács was affectionately known, was one of the world's most elusive criminals. Even most of his own men had never seen his face and the latest pictures of him were many years old. With him gone the rest of the industry would tighten their already close lines and years of work would have been wasted.

What had this got to do with Max finding Pete he'd asked? The interesting thing Easton had discovered was that Kovács bore an uncanny resemblance to Max. It was then that one of Easton's counterparts had come up with the beginnings of the plan.

He stood for a moment while Baber shuffled a few folders of papers and fiddled with a multimedia projector on the desk.

'Screw it. Time to become an arms dealer' he thought, took a deep breath and sat down.

59

Max stepped out of the warmth of the hotel lobby into the driving snow and looked across at the end of Margaret Island. He had an hour to get across town before heading back for his afternoon meeting on the island. He wondered why such an unusual place was chosen, but suspected Baber had watched way too many spy films and decided on a place with a lot of mystique. He headed for the No.19 tram that would take him into the very centre of Budapest. The bright yellow trams had survived throughout stringent communism, sweeping capitalism and the current delicate balance without a falter. Gone were the days where you could travel across the whole city for a single Forint though. Max paused as he reached the road across from the tram stop. His hesitation was spot-on as a large blue bus slid around the corner in front of him clipping the kerb as it passed. He grinned as it whizzed by. Budapest was one of the few places where concertina buses were common. Awkward looking single-deckers twice as long as a normal bus in two sections, joined by what looked like the middle section of an accordion. Hungarian bus drivers were famous for their speed and complete disregard for pedestrians. While zebra crossings were widely accepted as being merely an indication of a good place to cross, some felt these guys used them as effective targeting. As Max boarded the tram and found himself a seat he glanced back at the three men that had also got on. He wondered which of them was the trail that Baber had invariably put on him. He discounted one because he was obviously too young. The second looked like a badly dressed spy so he discounted him too. The third man was dressed in a long black cashmere coat with matching hat and was carrying a copy of Das Spiegel folded far too neatly in one hand. Leather gloves topped off the ensemble and Max suspected the neatly groomed moustache was either grown for the job or stuck on.

The tram trundled into life and slid onto Margaret Hid (Margaret Bridge) and made its way across the river. The Danube was a good half a mile across here and its icy waters appeared to be flowing fast. The tram stopped half way across and the well-groomed man got off. Too many others got on for Max to bother to guess and he looked out across the river back to the other side. The imposing shape of the Castle way up on the hill was difficult to locate through the snowy haze but his eyes finally fixed on the long sweeping perimeter wall. Baber's sources estimated (correctly) that it was that point just a month before that the sniper had chosen to take out 'The Nomad'. Max gave a small shudder as it dawned on him he was walking in a dead man's boots. The team in London had done a remarkable job with Max's transformation and as he caught his reflection in the window it took him a moment to register that he was staring at himself. Kovács' face was marked with two distinctive scars. According to Baber the one above his right eye had been attributed to a member of the Yakuza who had taken out six of Kovács' men and sliced his face before Kovács had discharged the tiny 3mm pistol he took to wearing inside his jacket sleeve into the assassins face. Kovács had apparently sent freeze-dried pieces of the assassin to the Japanese corporation whose ID the man had been carrying. After a month of that a truce covenant between the two was formed. Since then the Yakuza had brokered a number of deals between the Far East and Europe using their extensive Chinese operations. The other scar's origin wasn't confirmed but there were plenty of rumours. They ranged between the plausible and the outrageous. Max's favourite one, and in the guise of 'The Nomad' the one he would choose, was the one borne out of passion. Evanya one of the one time mistresses, a ballet dancer, had apparently opened up his cheek with a broken wine glass when she had found out about his other mistress. While she'd not been naïve enough to assume he wouldn't have other women, she'd objected to him going behind her back with her younger sister. Max ran his fingers over the scar and grinned. He couldn't claim anywhere near as salubrious a love life. One marriage with an amicable (ish) divorce the only major story.

The tram was now following the bank of the Danube and Max unconsciously folded his arms across his chest as they passed the houses of parliament. He could still feel the holster and shape of the gun against his side. Baber has assured him that the links with the Hungarian authorities were extremely good. Cynically he'd suggested that with the decision on EC membership still pending, they were being overly co-operative. Hungary had joined the PFP (Partnership for Peace) in 1998 and then NATO in 1999. Independent observers were hoping the current government would hold on until EC membership was secured, as it was much less likely if the resurgent Communist Party were to get back in. Western style capitalism had come with a price for all of the former satellite states and Hungary was no exception. With the new order had come Western money and Budapest had become the capital of organised crime for Eastern Europe. The fall of the iron curtain had begun the process of freeing up huge stores of weapons in each country. There will always be a demand for the tools of death. The movement of light arms mainly Russian built across to African states like Zaire, Rwanda and Somalia was well documented. Max had read that one particular conflict had seen Hutu rebels attack government troops with anti-tank missiles launched from their shoulders. Allegedly hundreds of Hutus had died as they couldn't read the instructions on the side and were unaware that standing behind the launcher wasn't a particularly good idea – especially when the launcher was being held the wrong way around. That was the tip of the iceberg as Max had found out. Many of the arms peddled to third world countries had not been tested, let alone maintained, with awful consequences.

A jolt of the tram dragged Max back to the present and he could see the imposing structure of the Keleti Palyudvar (Eastern railway station) up ahead. He would get off here and head on foot about three blocks to Beke street.

"He's got another tail" whispered the man Max had discounted as a badly dressed spy.

"What?" came the somewhat startled reply into his earpiece.

"Are you sure?"

"Yeah. Tubby guy in a green puffy jacket. Dark blue trousers and a woolly hat. He's about 6'2"

"Sure?"

"Yes. He's hanging back about half a block on the other side of the road."

"Okay. You keep on our man and Donaldson will be with you in two minutes to watch the other guy"

"Sir. We have a problem."

Marticell Denauvre had waited three years for this opportunity and wondered if he was just being a little paranoid.

"He's got a tail. Maybe one of his own men. Trenchcoat, hat, small backpack about half a block behind"

"No problem. We have another two agents in the coffee shop around the corner. Anything happens and they will be here in under thirty seconds"

His boss had an air of confidence but Deneuvre knew how slippery 'The Nomad' could be. This was the first public sighting in many years and they'd only got onto him through meticulous, some would say obsessive research. Getting copies of all guests' photos from all hotels with CCTV for the last ten

208

months had finally paid off with the match that morning at the Romany. The match had come too late to get him at the hotel, and besides he'd undoubtedly have had a lot of protection. Interpol had good relations with the Hungarian government that would be severely damaged if they were seen to have initiated a bloodbath.

Max walked up to the reception desk and smiled instinctively as he laid his folder on the counter. He had quickly found that his size combined with the facial scars tended to make people very uneasy unless he smiled. The receptionist returned the smile and pressed a couple of buttons.

60

Baber led Max into a small conference room and immediately Max felt four sets of eyes latch onto him. The room was laid out like a formal corporate interview. A small desk was in the middle of the room with a plain chair behind it. It faced two long large tables that had been placed together but at a slight angle to enable the four 'panellists' to sit in a line but still face each other. Max glanced at them in turn. No smiles. Three men and a woman. Baber introduced them in turn as they stood next to the small desk.

"The gentlemen on your far left is Dr. Axif Sanur. Dr. Sanur is one of the leading writers on Western terrorism and arms dealing. Next to him is Jeanine Jackson, a senior lecturer from MIT specialising in short quarter weaponry. Next is Jamie Callaghan a writer with 'Force' magazine and finally Paul Snow senior Eastern European operations for MI5. They have all been made aware of your situation and have taken the time to construct a guide for you, which gives you the rudiments of arms dealing. We thought it would be useful to get you in front of them for an afternoon at least. That way you should be able to digest the information they have prepared a little more easily".

Max smiled at each of them in turn and extended a hand toward the desk and chair. Baber smiled and headed out closing the door behind him. Max felt weird and a little intimidated. Not that he couldn't hold his own in a conversation but he could tell that the combined credentials of the people in front of him meant it would take all of his concentration to keep up. There was a pen and a pad in front of him but he opted to retrieve his palm and keyboard from his jacket pockets and took a moment to set them up.

Sanur and Snow on each end looked like they wanted to be elsewhere, Callaghan was smiling and Jackson looked like she was looking forward to the session.

Sanur cleared his throat in an 'Ok I'm the Chairman' kind of way
"Shall we begin?"
"Shoot" replied Max,which got a smile out of Jackson.
"We've been told that you need a crash course in arms dealing Mr.Jones. This is not the easiest thing to achieve. Arms dealing has gone through somewhat of a renaissance in the last ten years and there are many facets to be aware of." Sanur's voice was tempered and deep and Max could see why Baber had referred to the man with a great deal of respect.
"The end of the Cold War left thousands of soldiers with little to do and much of the military equipment in the former Soviet Union and Eastern Bloc has, how shall I put it" he raised his pen and pointed it at Max, "fallen into disreputable hands".
"You're in the right place to get the ambience," Callaghan added. He had been a reporter for the US military magazine for five years and spent most of his time in the East.
"The black market in Hungary has never been stronger. It's sort of the gateway to the West for many of dealers and of course is the eastern capital for the mob"
"The mob is involved in arms dealing?" Max said surprised.
"Not directly" said Jackson. This was her favourite subject and she jumped in before Callaghan had a chance to add anything.

211

"There isn't much that the mob doesn't control. There is more money to be made in many less dangerous activities but inevitably they get involved around the edges".

"Like?" Max asked.

"Well if you take the land repatriation. Until a few years ago, the Hungarian government owned all of the agricultural land and ran them as huge State farms. The land of course had been taken from the citizens decades before. A few years back, following the exit of the Soviets and the subsequent democratic governments the decision was made to give the land back to the people. The records were no where near accurate enough, nor were the divisions there any more so they had to give all the people concerned 'auction' vouchers. They then preceded to auction off the land in small local auctions all around the country". She paused for a moment to take a sip of water.

"Miss Jackson" said Snow and Max immediately decided that he was either a stuck up toff or he had something quite wide wedged sideways in his mouth restricting his speech.

"Can we please stick to the subject?"

Jackson threw a stare at him.

"I was getting there." she snapped

"Anyway, the Mafia hijacked hundred of the auctions by approaching the people with the vouchers offering them various things to get them to hand them over. Many of the people were elderly so what would they need a block of agricultural land for? So, the Mafia ended up with huge blocks of land and in many areas engineered themselves a tidy little trading route through from the Eastern States. No matter what comes through they have built the infrastructure to get it through."

"So they guarantee the safe passage of those bringing the merchandise through?" Max asked.

"Yep" said Callaghan. "I've even seen them bring tanks over the border from Khazakstan. They have a huge network of farm buildings all over the country to hide them in. The authorities have their hands tied."

"Ok. I follow that. But how do they get the arms into Western Europe?" said Max.

"They don't tend to bother" replied Jackson.

"Their final destination is usually somewhere in Africa. No shortage of local squabbles and the occasional wider conflict" she added.

Max looked straight at Jackson and asked.

"So. Who are the players?"

"They don't play Mr.Jones" remarked Snow.

"Ok" Max sighed. "Who are the top five organisations I need to be aware of?"

"Just Eastern Europe or wider?" Sanur asked looking up from his notepad.

"Wider" Max replied.

"Well, my first vote goes to Black Doctrine" Jackson said. There were nods of agreement from the other three.

"The Black Doctrine are a huge group of ex Soviet Forces men and women who came under the leadership of a disgraced General from the Soviet army in the late eighties. General Wartinichev is believed to have been involved with the Soviet Special Forces, or Speznatz. He took a division of them with him when they were mostly disbanded and used his family money to set himself up in Latvia and operates the group from there. There were no shortage of recruits from the downsizing of the Soviet army and they control most of the shipments from the Russian Federation."

"What type of arms?" Max asked

"Mostly conventional. A lot of tanks. He uses front businesses to launder his money and one of them is a haulage firm".

"Comes in useful lugging all those big chunks of metal around" Callaghan added.

"Sees himself more of a businessman than an arms dealer" Jackson added. "A born again Capitalist".

"Hard bastard though" Callaghan added.

"Oh he's that all right. Ex Speznatz, what do you expect? A community orientated tree-hugger?"

"Next?" asked Max.

They went on to three more groups involved in dealing around the world and covered them in much greater detail. By the time they had finished the third Max had drunk the two-litre bottle of sparkling water on the desk. They were all obviously passionate about their subject, as they had barely paused. Each time one of them latched onto the thread of one of the others.

"And the final group is the Kovács family" Jackson said and Max tried not to react. Baber had given him a detailed background on the family but it would be good to get this four's perspective as well. They covered much of the same ground as Baber had but Max decided to ask a few specific questions.

"Have any of these groups crossed, like for instance have the Kovács ever stepped on any of the others' territories?"

"They tend to stick to what they know," Sanur said and before Callaghan could interrupt "but of course there have been incidents".

"Like?"

"Probably the most notable back in 1988 Interpol busted one of Wartinichev's supply routes wide open and he had to get a lot of merchandise out of Poland very quickly but inadvertently led Interpol to one of the Kovács storage silos".

"Yeah" chipped in Callaghan "that 'incident' cost the Kovács at least five million in merchandise".

"Our sources put it nearer eight," said Snow and Callaghan nodded.

"What did the Kovács' do?"

Jackson stared straight at Max and he could see her pupils clearly against her light blue eyes.

"Kovács rounded up every one of Wartinichev's men and apart from one women, who he left to drive them back to Latvia in a truck, broke every one of their arms and legs".

"Ouch" Max said under his breath.

"Thirty seven men and women with multiple fractures. If the rumours are to be believed János Kovács and his brother did it all themselves with baseball bats as the others watched, knowing they were next".

"None of the other groups wanted to go too near the Kovács' after that" added Jackson.

"I'm not surprised" Max replied.

"Yeah that's certainly one family to stay away from" Callaghan added and Max felt a knot the size of a small orange in his stomach tighten. They decided on a quick comfort break and Max headed for the gents at the end of the hall. As soon as he got into one of the small cubicles he threw up violently for the second time that week.

61

As Max stepped out onto the main road the snow was swirling much thicker than when he went into the building. The trainer, a wiry MI5 agent called Heath had offered Max a coffee at the café around the corner and he'd jumped at the chance. One of Max's passions was good coffee. It was up there with good scotch and just as difficult to find. Hungary was one of those countries that didn't muck about. Ask for instant coffee and you get a blank look and pointed toward a small cup filled with a thick black liquid that will turn you into an insomniac in a couple of sips. Heath stepped out next to Max, tapped him on the shoulder and pointed him in the right direction. In the two minutes it took them to get around the corner and in through the café's front door they had both got covered in snow. Max brushed the flakes off his shoulders and walked to the counter.

"Ket Káve letzives" he smiled and pointed to a table in the middle by the window. Heath headed to the gents while Max sat down and grabbed the menu. The good sign was that it only carried Hungarian. Any place that included German or English would be used to dealing with tourists and Max didn't fancy that.

"He's gone in to the coffee shop with Heath and you're not going to like this, but that tail is on his way in as well"
"I know I thought it might be one of his men but I'm getting a really bad feeling about this. Where the hell is Donaldson?"

"Don't worry sir, he's already in the café"

"Well, get close. Jones has a vest on but that won't do him any good if someone pops him one in the head"

There were two goals that Dimitri had in life. The first was to follow in his father's footsteps and become one of the best agents in MOSSAD, the Israeli Secret Service. He was in a division called 'Metsada' – Special Operations. The second was to bury a nasty piece of crap that had caused his father's death. He was so close, about fifteen feet close in fact. He could feel the adrenaline pumping through his veins and rested his Glock 9mm on his thigh as he took a couple of deep breaths.

Donaldson was a very sensible MI5 agent but somewhat lacking in field experience. He'd been stationed in Budapest for the last three years and the most frightening situation he'd been in up until now was last month when the ambassador's wife had run out of Earl Grey tea.

Max took a quick survey of the small café. Before he got very far a very nervous looking man in a booth near the counter looked like he was trying to attract Max's attention. Instinctively Max reached down and pressed a couple of small buttons on his belt.

"Sir. Jones has acknowledged Donaldson."

"Pity he didn't agree to the microphone implant otherwise we could have warned him about the tail"

'Of course he didn't go for the wire' thought the older agent. 'Any cheap sweeping device would pick it up'

"Well I hope he's in safe hands"

As soon as the waitress screamed on seeing the larger Frenchman draw his weapon Max lunged to the left which was rather a good call. Two bullets from Dimitri shattered the huge window behind him and Dimitri cursed under his breath. He raised his gun and pointed it straight at Max as he staggered towards the space left by the window.

The smaller of the two Frenchmen had blocked the way and had his pistol raised at arm's length, the second's weapon was trained on Dimitri - the sole reason he didn't follow up on Max. There was a lull as the players took all of them in. Donaldson boldly stepped out from his Booth and trained his gun on the Frenchman that had his gun on Max.

'Shit. Four guns and none of them are mine' Max thought and raised his hands to shoulder level.

"Allez" shouted the small Frenchman and waved his gun at Dimitri who glared back and swore something under his breath but kept his gun on Max. Donaldson was sweating like a pig in heat despite the freezing wind that was now blowing into the café bringing the snow with it. Dimitri looked at the smaller of the two men by the door. He could probably take both but that left the one by the booth. He wanted this bastard but he wasn't worth dying for. He took another glance across at the second one and that was the chance Max was waiting for. He threw himself backward over the table by the window trying to slip out the gap onto the sidewalk.

The large Frenchman squeezed his trigger hard and the bullet slammed into Max chest. The force of the impact took Max through the open window and he slid across the packed ice into the centre of the road. A Lada taxi screeched and slid to avoid the body and slammed into the wall by the right of the café.

Inside, it was chaos. Donaldson had headed for the door with Dimitri diving into a booth and exchanged gunfire with the small Frenchman.

Max grunted and gasped for breath. The vest had taken the full brunt of the bullet but it had taken all the wind out of him.

He got up to see Donaldson emerging onto the sidewalk holding his pistol in both hands. He was about thirty feet away but Max could see the terror on the man's face. Max drew his gun and planted three bullets into his chest and Donaldson dropped to the floor covering the fresh snow with splatters of blood. The two Frenchman prepared themselves to venture out onto the street. They were behind an overturned table and had Dimitri pinned inside the booth. From where they were they could see the sprawled shape of Donaldson's body and paused.

The Frenchmen's reluctance to join the man lying on his back in the snow bought Max a few seconds and was now two hundred yards down the street.
"INTERPOL" the smaller one shouted over at the booth.
"MOSSAD" came the reply and Dimitri threw his ID across the café from behind the booth. The larger Frenchman grabbed it.
"Merde!" he screamed slamming the ID onto the floor. He grabbed his colleague by the shoulder and dragged him out onto the street. Dimitri scooped up his ID as he followed them out and ran straight across the road to a waiting white van.

Max was already out of breath as he rounded another corner. Up ahead was a taxi rank with a line of cars sitting with their engines running, their tailpipes spewing steam into the cold air. He ran to the first and opened the driver's door. The driver got out and was about to shout abuse when Max shoved the

219

gun in his ribs. The man threw his hands up and retreated rapidly stuttering something in frightened Hungarian. Max didn't catch it but suspected it was something along the lines of 'Shit, take it, it's only a Skoda'.

The two Frenchmen rounded the corner as Max pulled away and got half a dozen shots off. They took out a couple of taillights and the back window but Max managed to keep the car on the road with a little bit of help from a barrier. The wheels were spinning in the slush and Max wrestled with the steering. He rounded another corner and found himself running parallel with the Danube, not that he was in any position to admire the scenery. He eased up on the gas and looked into the mirror. A white van was careering down the road and catching up with him. He decided not to take any chances and floored the pedal. As he did so a car pulled out of a side street and Max swerved to avoid it but quickly ran out of road mounting the pavement. The pavement rapidly turned into a sea of people and Max swung the car onto a ramp to the left, which led down to a cruise barge. It wasn't wide enough for a car and the wheels dropped off the sides and it slid another forty feet on the underside of the car before it slammed into the pod at the bottom. The impact smashed the windscreen and left Max sprawled over the bonnet. He was a little dazed but the adrenaline gushing through his veins kept him conscious. With both sides of the car hanging over the water forward was the only open direction.

The white van screeched to a halt and Dimitri and three of his colleagues leapt out. Pistols at the ready they ran to the edge of the promenade. Max clambered over the bonnet of the car and crouched down just in time. Dimitri threw his arm over the wall and took aim and pumped half a dozen bullets in through the back window of the car. Some rattled off the bonnet and a couple thudded into a mooring post behind Max.

'This is not doing anything for my blood pressure' Max thought and pulled out his Walther. He ditched the nearly empty bullet clip and loaded a fresh one from his jacket. One of the Israeli agents sneaked round the wall as the others laid covering fire. As the bullets hailed down all around Max he took a deep breath. He swung the gun onto the bonnet and emptied the full clip in the general direction of the shore. The advancing agent yelped as one of the bullets slammed into his shin. He fell to the ground and began to crawl back to his colleagues.

Max looked at the motor launch tied to the side behind him. He loaded another clip and reached back to untie the rope holding the launch to the mooring. It was as the rope began to slip through his fingers that he realised that the current of the river was plenty to move the boat and it began sliding away from him. Another couple of bullets pinged around his ears and Max hesitated for a moment. If he didn't move soon then the launch would be out of his reach. He grinned and took a flying crouching start.

Dimitri glanced past the wall and saw Max diving for the boat. He got another shot in which slammed into the side of the boat as Max flung himself off the edge and into the bottom of the boat. Dimitri spun around the corner and began to run down the ramp dropping his empty pistol and reaching for the semi-automatic strapped to his left side. Max had found the ignition to the launch and it kicked in on the second attempt. He smashed the lever down and the launch lurched forward. Dimitri took another couple of seconds to reach the wreck of the car and clambered onto the roof with his gun trained on the launch.

It was too far but that didn't stop him letting off a few dozen rounds that splashed into the water thirty feet or so behind the boat. He cursed under his breath that they had only brought close-quarter arms with them as the launch pulled further away. Max took a moment to look back and could make just out the figures against the shoreline. He could also hear the wail of police sirens and could see half a dozen police cars streaming over the bridge ahead of him. Dimitri had heard them too and instinctively sprinted back to the van. He slammed his fist against the side as he climbed in and the van pulled away with the back doors flapping. One of his colleagues threw a package out onto the roadway into the path of the oncoming police cars. A sports bag wrapped around what looked like a bomb. It was a bomb, but with a couple of wires loose it didn't pose a threat to anyone but it certainly looked like it and would hold them up long enough to get some distance between them.

Max scanned the other side of the river and could see a jetty in the distance. He had to get off the river and disappear as fast as possible. The weather was getting worse which although it was playing havoc with Max's sense of direction it was probably the key reason he made it to the jetty and away into the snow-covered back streets. He ducked down a side street and into a clothing store. Two minutes later he emerged in a brown, full length leather coat with a hat firmly over his head. The shop assistant had been surprised that the man in the expensive looking cashmere coat had wanted another coat and had decided to wear it there and then. Max dropped the bag with his old coat in it into a bin two blocks down the road and headed towards the underground station.

62

Petra had taken three hours to get home on 'that' day from the court. In the last eight days she had paid up her tenancy and moved across town to a new apartment and maintained a two hour trek into and back from the office. She was certain she hadn't been tailed and she had left no trace at her old apartment but nevertheless she was still terrified. She had thought she was tough as nails. Daughter of a beat cop. One of Washington's finest. She had grown up around guns and cops and the only thing that had stopped her becoming one was a promise she made her father on her fourteenth birthday. He had been wounded in a drive-by shooting and made her swear that she wouldn't follow him into the force. She could still picture him on the bed in the Maryfield hospital. Tubes and wires hung from both arms and he looked half the man she remembered in that familiar blue uniform. He had died two days later. 'Complications' they had said. So, she had kept the vow and in her mind did the next best thing and became a lawyer. Unlike the majority of her fellow graduates from Harvard she specialised in taking on the gun lobby and gained a reputation as a hard case.

It was Friday night and as she switched trains on the subway for the third time she wondered if she dare venture out in her new neighbourhood. As she pressed herself against the dim side of the carriage and sank her chin under the high collar of her jacket a couple jumped onto the train holding hands. They curled themselves around one of the poles in the centre of train and Petra saw the girl close her eyes, content in her lover's embrace. She stared for a moment then stood up straight and released her bunched up red hair from its bun and strode into the middle of the car. They weren't going to break her. She leaned out of the doors as the buzzer sounded.

"Screw you!" she shouted at the top of her voice out onto the empty platform. As the doors closed she caught her reflection in the glass and found herself grinning. Petra Harrison was back.

63

Max held his head under the cold tap for three minutes as his mind raced.

'Come on. Get it together!' he urged himself. He slowly turned off the tap and let the water drip off his hair before he walked across towards the hand drier. Half way there he stopped and looked at himself in the mirror. Not quite the cold killer he was supposed to be. Just some overweight guy with wet hair. He kicked the trash can which was nowhere near as solid as he had thought and it clattered across the white floor tiles and bounced off the far wall sending soggy hand-towels across the restroom in an impressive arc. Three of them stuck to the wall and this brought a strained smile to Max's lips. He shook his head hard and headed to the drier.

Within a couple of minutes he was back in the corridor heading down to the training room where he had a debrief session scheduled with agent Heath. As he was about to pass the conference room he had been in ten minutes before he heard voices from within. The four specialists were still in there and Max could just about make out what they were saying, as the door was slightly ajar. He stopped and listened to Jackson who was mid sentence.

".........to the Middle East?"

"No. I reckon he's definitely up to something in the Eastern Bloc" disagreed Callaghan.

"Important enough for them to drag us all in here?" Jackson argued.

"What do you think Dr.Sanur? What do you think this Mr. Jones is going to do?"

"You mean you didn't notice the resemblance?" Sanur replied.

"No way!" Snow laughed.

"What?" asked Jackson.

"He's the splitting image of János Kovács" Snow laughed.

"Exactly!" said Sanur.

"But he's not been seen for years, no, more like decades" said Callaghan.

"You think that's maybe it?" Jackson asked.

"No chance" snapped Snow. "It's just a coincidence. I admit there is an uncanny likeness from the pictures of fifteen years ago but that's stretching the bounds of reality!"

Max breathed a sigh of relief. Baber had warned him to stay away from the subject and had hoped they wouldn't make the connection. These were good people who could be trusted but Baber had used the old cliché, 'loose lips cost lives' and reminded him that only a select few knew about the plan. He was about to walk on when Callaghan piped up.

"Hypothetically, say Mr. Jones was going to play the part of an international arms dealer what would you expect him to do?"

The question wasn't aimed at anyone in particular and there was an uneasy silence as they all chewed it over.

"Simple" Snow said solemnly.

"I'd expect him to die".

64

This was definitely a great place to see Margaret Island from. Max took another sip of hot coffee and leant against the railing. The tower in the middle of the islands had been there for centuries and despite being added to still retained some of its charm. Max had only just made it in time for the meeting with Baber and as he sat in the small lookout room at the top of the tower he reached into his jacket and took out the passport he was travelling under. 'Martin Johansson' was the name under the picture and Max smiled as he wondered whether he qualified as a schizophrenic yet with his three identities.

Baber was dressed in a Barbour jacket and from the moment he got to the top of the stairs Max could tell he wasn't in the best of moods. He checked the staircase before speaking despite the fact that he had closed the entrance door to the tower and locked it before he had come up. It may be the new millennium but $20 was plenty to encourage the attendant to go for an early lunch-break. He approached to about six feet from Max and stared at him.

Max smiled and drank some more of the hot coffee.
"Easton said you were a lucky bastard," Baber said finally.
"Complimentary as ever" Max replied.
"I wouldn't have needed to be so lucky" he continued "if your security had been up to scratch".
"Our security was fine. How the hell those boys from Interpol got on to you I don't know and we're still trying to identify that other group"

"I don't call six gunmen trying to waste me 'fine'" Max snorted.

"Where were your agents?"

"Well you know where Donaldson was" Baber snapped. "You were only supposed to shoot him in the chest once for realism. As it was you broke three of his ribs and the pain knocked him out cold. Why did you have to hit him three times?"

"Ah." Max felt a twinge of guilt.

"You put yourself in the same situation. You're an internationally renowned thug with very little respect for any form of life and you've just been ambushed. You really think Kovács would have left it at just one shot"

"Well,....maybe"

"Maybe my arse. I was a little concerned that the fact that I hadn't popped him in the head would look staged"

"Oh you don't have to worry about your cover, that's well intact. The wires have been jumping for the last three hours. Its not every day that a there is a running battle on the streets of a major European city that isn't gang related. Interpol are seriously embarrassed. The word is that they underestimated the manpower they would need".

"That other group wasn't mucking about though" Max added

"I know. Kovács wasn't, sorry isn't, a very popular chap" Baber smiled and took a seat next to Max.

"We have another two days of intensive training for you here Max and then we can get you off on the route to Cuba".

Max stood up and finished the coffee with a gulp.

"I don't think so. Every day I take now could be vital. I want to get on the way tonight"

"Mr. Jones" Baber got up and put his hand on Max's shoulder.

"You may think you are ready but you have only really scratched the surface"

"It's my call" Max said sternly.

"Well actually it's not. We have to consider your role in the overall operation".

"My role eh?" Max laughed.

"Just get me back to England tonight" he shouted over his shoulder as he headed down the stairs.

Baber watched the big man go down the stairs and shook his head. He reached into his pocket for his mobile and pressed a shortdial. It connected and a voice at the other end said.

"4-4"

"4-4. This is Echo five. There has been a change of plan. The package leaves tonight. Prepare the route."

He snapped the phone shut and shook his head again. The odds for Mr. Jones had just shortened again.

65

Max decided that the first thing he would do when he reached dry land would be to check if there were any links between the ferry company and a corrugated cardboard manufacturer. Why else would all the cabin walls have been made so thin that he could hear every moan and whinge of the family across the hall until three o'clock in the morning. He had never travelled on the Liverpool to Belfast ferry before, having flown the two previous times he had been across to Ireland. He had sensed trouble when the departure terminal turned out to be a slightly oversized port-a-cabin. It did have a coffee machine, which to his surprise worked, and only tasted as crap as normal machine coffee. Security came in the form of a young lady whose face piercing would have set off any self- respecting metal detector.

"Did you pack your own bags?" she had enquired
"Yep"
"Are you carrying any illegal substances, like drug or firearms?"
"No"

What an intense grilling. Once he had survived that, it was time to play with the car deck (floating multi-storey car park) – no simple drive on drive off concept here. Another designer with a sense of humour.

The cabin was pleasant enough, if you're into that sort of thing. Four beds (all made with an anorexic midget in mind) were laid out in bunk style with Max managing to squeeze into one of the bottom ones in the foetal position. After testing the bed he was pleasantly surprised to see power points for his laptop. He dumped his things down and headed for a wander around to check out the facilities.

Thirty seconds later, he arrived at the restaurant having seen all of the rest of the amenities on the way. That's a little harsh as they did have a TV lounge, bar and a shop with four different books in stock. This was the sort of ticket that had dinner thrown in and the menu was short but encompassing most tastes - provided you like chicken and egg. It was seven o'clock and they didn't sail for another two hours so he asked when dinner was due to be served.

"Possibly eight, maybe later. Depends on when we get enough people to serve it to" came the confusing reply. Max must have looked as if he needed it clearer than that as the young man in a painfully burgundy waistcoat explained further.

"Once the food is out, it can't be put back – we have to have enough people to serve it to".

Fair enough, Max thought. With all the modern advancements man had come up with he would have thought more flexible food could have been available, but he was too tired to argue the point. He was obviously going soft. Just another hour and fifty eight minutes to go to departure. The first leg in a trip that would take him to the Caribbean, via Belfast, Frankfurt and Amsterdam.

66

Max had gone over the meeting a hundred times in his head at the hotel and dozens more on the way to the airport. Why they wanted to meet him there he couldn't fathom, but it was a public place which had to go some way to making it safer. This was all assuming he would survive the taxi ride. Cuba was one of those countries where all the old cars you don't see any more at home seem to end up. The Volkswagen they were in had to be thirty years old if it was a day, and the interior could no doubt tell a thousand stories. The interior trim was a 'wipe clean' mock leather in tasteful dark beige, and the door locks were those thin chrome ones that old cars all seem to have. There was no partition between the driver and the back, presumably because the driver didn't speak to him at all. The meter ticked away but Max had taken the tourist guide's advice and agreed the fare before getting in. It was hot. Max didn't usually have a problem sweating, but a man of his build in this heat with no air-conditioning is a simple equation. He looked once more at what he was wearing. Chinos, white shirt and a casual jacket. He had no idea what people in Cuba wore, so had taken his fashion tips from a coffee commercial a couple of days before. The ensemble was rounded off by a pair of boots and some very conspicuous sunglasses which he'd been given by Easton in a 'they-could-come-in-useful' James-Bondy kind of way. The sign for the airport showed two more miles.

Gorino was also confused. Why Martinez had sent him to meet the Hungarian he could not understand. Maybe it was deliberate. He knew about his late night partying and perhaps this was his way of winding him up. It meant he couldn't have a fix for at least another couple of hours, and he was getting annoyed. Gorino stood six foot tall but his slouching made him look a lot shorter. Despite wearing a silk suit, and an Armani shirt, he looked scruffy. He hadn't changed from the day before, and the creases looked like they had been there a week. Dark hair, steely dark eyes and heavy stubble he looked the part. Martinez knew he was an amateur though. Inherently lazy, with a cocaine habit he was only just controlling. His attitude problems made him a liability. But he was one of the cartel leaders' half-brothers. Sending him out to the airport to fetch someone meant he was at least out of the way for a while.

The main airport in Cuba sits uncomfortably two hours away from the capital Havana. You will find it fifteen minutes away from the tourist area in Varadero where the beach has a dozen all inclusive resorts, catering for anyone that doesn't have an American passport.

It is the type of airport that has one lounge, and in the country famous for its cigars, the concept of no-smoking areas has obviously never come up.

Gorino sniffed and pushed the few locks of greasy hair that had escaped from his ponytail off his face. He reached into his jacket pocket taking out a crumpled packet of Camel cigarettes and a silver embossed lighter. He casually tossed the cigarette and caught it in his mouth in the way he had seen in many films, and practised intensely. After the first drag he realised he had it the wrong way round and had lit the white filter. Despite the fact that no one in the airport lounge was remotely interested in his attempts at being tough and cool, he proceeded to smoke the cigarette the wrong way round. If you have ever tried to do this you will know it doesn't work very well and he finally gave up and threw it smouldering into the trash can next to him. It wasn't going to be his day. The half-smoked cigarette found a discarded newspaper and within seconds flames were starting to emerge. He ran across to the kiosk and bought a handful of cokes and put the flames out by pouring them one by one into the trash until it was sodden. Again, no one had batted an eyelid. Gorino looked around uncomfortably and leaned once more on the pillar.

Max paid the taxi driver and walked over towards the terminal building. By the looks of things there were some flights due to go out as the entrance had three tourist buses spewing out people and cases in all directions. A hoard of smartly dressed porters were 'helping' the bemused tourists get their bags onto trolleys for the long trek to the check in desks. As Max came through the doors into the departure area he realised that the aforementioned long trek was in fact only about a hundred metres. No sooner had the porters got to the growing queues (travelling time approximately twelve seconds) then they parked the trolley and looked expectantly at the 'customer'. Max suspected that they all knew exactly what "No I don't want any help with my bags" meant, but language-based ignorance was such an excellent tool.

Max looked around for his contact. You couldn't see for sunburnt tourists and matching luggage but the guy in the green suit stood out a mile. Most Cubans were dressed for the weather. Casual and simple but inherently smart and tidy. From across the terminal Max could see him puffing away on a 'smoke' and looking like a throw-back to the yuppie late –1990s computer consultants who had too much money and not enough taste.

'Oh, shit. He's got a ponytail' Max thought. It was the only personal appearance decision that Max despised more than untidy beards.

"Excuse me, do you have change for a $20 dollar note?" Max said the pre-arranged line with as much enthusiasm as he could muster.

"Of course" Gorino replied grinning. He reached inside his jacket and pulled out his wallet that predictably was a flash burgundy leather job with a huge GUCCI tag. He pulled out 20 one-dollar bills, which was his agreed sign. Max thanked him and headed to the car park. Gorino followed a minute or so later into the sunshine, slipping his aviator shades on as he approached the white 1956 Chevy. Max was leaning on the car with his bag resting on the roof.

"Hey man. This car is a classic, don't be putting no dents in it" he laughed gesturing at Max's size. Max smiled and stood up and faced up to Gorino until he was a few inches from his face. He had maybe four inches in height on the Cuban, so he looked down slightly when he spoke.
"Listen. I chew up and spit out little shits like you on a regular basis. If you want to screw me around then I'll either waste you and charge your boss for my time, or get on the next plane off this little island and onto the next place they have a need for what I specialise in. Which do you prefer?" Max growled.

To say Gorino was taken aback was an understatement. He was sure he had the hard gangster look down to a tee, and rather than back off he rallied.
"I don't think so". He stammered.
"My associate Carlos has your head in his rifle-sight as we speak. All I have to do is give him a sign and goodbye fat man". Gorino was surprised with his front, but immediately realised that this man in front of him would more than certainly see through his bluff and, despite all the practice, he couldn't draw his gun anywhere near fast enough. A tingle of fear ran down his spine as he waited for a reaction.

He wasn't the only one. Behind the mirrored sunglasses Max's eyes darted left and right. There was no way he was going to see, or avoid, the gunman. Damn. He shouldn't have been so bold. Okay, yeah, he was supposed to be this big-time arms dealer from Eastern Europe with an iron-fist reputation, but out here he was alone. He cursed Easton for firing him up to play the character so much.

Gorino's pulse began to race. The big man in front of him was surely going to do something to him. Would he really kill him at the back of a car park in the airport? Despite the very bright sunshine and the scores of people in the near distance, if he had come prepared with a silencer on a small pistol he could easily waste him without getting too much attention.

Max swallowed hard. Think. Think. Max threw his head back into a huge laugh. Gorino paused a moment, then forced himself into an uneasy laugh too.
'Damn that was close' *Max* sweated as he held out his hand to the Cuban.
'For God's sake Gorino, you wanna get yourself wasted' the Cuban thought as he grabbed Max's hand and shook it hard.
"Let's do it" Max said tapping Gorino on the shoulder and turning to take his bag off the roof. Gorino frowned and walked around to the passenger side of the car.
"Why don't you drive? I'm sure it's been a while since you've driven a vintage American car" he pointed towards the driver's side.
"Whatever" Max replied as nonchalantly as he could and climbed in tossing his bag onto the back seat. His focus for a moment turned to the dials in front of him. The position of the late afternoon sun meant the tops of the chrome dials glinted in a row in front of him. Whatever kind of bum this guy was, he sure knew how to look after his car. Max had heard that there were more vintage US cars in Cuba, per head of population, than anywhere else. The wonderful

climate where even winter saw constant sunshine meant minimal erosion. Coupled with the fact that sanctions limited the numbers of new cars coming in and you had a formula for great old motors.

67

For the first hour of their journey toward Havana on the coastal route as the sun began to set barely a word passed between the two. Gorino was doing his steely, no expression on my face because I'm so tough routine and Max was trying to go over his background story in his head as many times as he possibly could. Gorino motioned Max to turn into the petrol station and while the attendant added the $20 to the tank Gorino disappeared to the toilet. The dust off the road had used up the window washer's tank. Max decided to fill it back up and found a half-full watering can. He lent into the car and pulled the lever that he thought opened the bonnet, but the boot flipped open. He tutted to himself and walked round to the back of the car. Max reached out for the boot lid and stopped dead. In the boot of the car was what looked suspiciously like a body bag. Max glanced over at the small shack next to the main building, Gorino was still in there. He looked under the bag and found rope, tape, acid and a variety of tools that he didn't want to even speculate about. Someone was going to get murdered, and probably tortured too. He shut the boot quickly, and turned to run but Gorino emerged from the shack and headed straight for the car.

He frowned at Max and pointed for him to get back in the car. They pulled away and after another ten minutes Gorino pointed at a turning off the coast road. They were not far outside Havana now and seemed to be heading for the nearby hills.

68

Petra Harrison wanted to punch the air with delight but managed to keep her composure.

"Thank you Your Honour" she said loudly and confidently and placed here file into her tan briefcase. It had taken three years and every hour of every day but at this moment it had all been worth it. She knew she had set a precedent as well. The Senate Arms Committee hearing a case raised by a small-town lawyer and siding with her research. The directors from the arms contractor looked dejected as they trailed out of the court and Petra forced herself not to feel sorry for them. Their prototype weapon would now never hit the production line. She was on such a high she realised she hadn't visited the bathroom all morning and due to her nerves had polished off a whole jug of water during the last mornings testimony. She hurried out into the corridor and into the restroom. She flew into a closet and before she sat down heard male voices come in. She glimpsed through the door and on seeing the urinals realised in her rush she had run into the men's. She quickly closed the lid and crouched on it holding her briefcase. She could clearly hear the two men laughing.

"Hook line and sinker"

"Yep, that'll keep the Senate off our backs"

"Inspirational idea feeding that hick lawyer with that report. Took a little longer than I'd have hoped for the little cow to get it nailed but she got there in the end"

'Hick lawyer' Petra thought. 'It couldn't be, could it?'

"The first shipment goes out on Thursday, four thousand units"

"Wouldn't want to be on the opposite side of those bad boys" he laughed again.

'Shit, that's Mark Duggan.' Petra thought. Duggan was the CEO of the arms contractor that she'd just got a production veto on and it sounded like they had already made them. Petra felt suddenly afraid and slumped onto her backside and began to sob.

'What the hell am I supposed to do now?' she thought.

69

Max had noticed Gorino getting twitchy and as they climbed higher into the hills and as Max had turned the lights of the car on he was getting more nervous. His passenger still had his sunglasses on in what Max thought was an act of defiance. Max kept his on too and concentrated hard as the sun disappeared and he could just make out the road markings as they wound round the tight corners.

Gorino was grinning and when they rounded the next left-hand bend Max looked down to see the handgun on his lap.

"And that would be for?" Max asked

"You were very stupid to come here by yourself Mr.Kovács. We know you have the main supply line into Eastern Europe but I'm sure we can deal with your people" Gorino replied without looking at him.

"My people wouldn't give you the time of day." Max snarled

"Look. You can make this easy or difficult. You can tell me what I need to know now and bow out quickly. Or...."

"Or?"

"Do you really want to know? Most people regret asking that question."

'Oh, you do this all the time I bet' *Max* thought and began to panic. Beads of sweat were slipping over his eyebrows and he reached up to wipe them away. As he did so he knocked the side of his sunglasses which kicked out a small beep. Fortunately they were on a straight piece of road as the night-vision mode kicked in because Max's focus on the road was thrown off. From a dim outline of the road Max could now see every nuance of the road as if he were driving in daylight. He sneaked a glance over at Gorino who was still fiddling with the gun in his lap. Max's mind was racing and then it hit him. He could see but Gorino couldn't. He plucked up the courage and reached down.

70

Petra grabbed the half-full bottle of white wine and headed for her study. It was a mess with thick legal books strewn open covering the desk and most of the floor as well. There was a large noticeboard above the desk that was covered in newspaper clippings and yellow post-it-notes with her erratic scribble on them. She pushed a couple of the books onto the floor, poured herself a glass of wine and grabbed a note pad and pencil. Petra was a creature of habit and always planned her days the night before. She had to face it though; the last three years hadn't taken too much planning. She had spent the time divided between her study and the various courtrooms that it had taken to get her in front of the committee. She reached for the report that was marked 'internal' and headed up Axkon Confidential. How could she have been so stupid? It had been too easy to get hold of the report. She played the sequence of events back in her head. Bumping into the temp at that coffee shop around the corner from Axkon and finding out over a cup of coffee that he was working in the department down the hall from Duggan. Hindsight was a wonderful thing but she really should have realised that it was all too convenient. That he was drinking in the same coffee shop, that he tried to hit on her and convinced her to let him buy her a coffee. She shuddered as she remembered the weekend they had spent in that cabin in the mountains, where he finally agreed to snoop for her. Were they watching her every move? Was sleeping with her part of the assignment? She took another gulp of wine and sharpened her pencil in the electric sharpener on the side of the desk.

71

"What the hell?" Gorino screamed as Max turned off the lights as they flew toward another tight corner. Max said nothing as he turned the car at the last moment. Gorino's knuckles were white on the door and dashboard and as they hit another small straight he tried to reach over to the controls. Max grabbed the light switch and yanked it down snapping it right off. He threw the broken handle over at Gorino who had pulled his sunglasses of and was scrambling to point the gun at Max.

"Stop the car now" he shouted. Max smiled as he pumped the gas pedal as they went into another bend, turning the wheel at what seemed to Gorino to be the last second. He knew that on the other side of the very flimsy barrier was a drop of hundreds of feet.

"Are yyyou mad?" he screamed.

"No. Well, I suppose yes." Max laughed.

"Don't worry, I can see the bends in the road from the road markings. Oh, I hope they haven't done any repairs recently" he smiled

"If you don't stop now I'll blow your head off!" Gorino shouted. He was holding the gun in both hands now and visibly shaking.

"You really haven't got a clue little man" Max growled. He could feel the fear and sensed that this was his chance to nail him.

"You waste me and there's no way you'll stop this car going over the edge". He continued as they spun around yet another corner a split second before the edge. For Max it looked like an easy drive in the midday sun, and he was getting used to the light orange tinge to everything. He was going pretty slowly at the corners but to his passenger the pitch black put the real speed right out of proportion. Max smiled to himself then noticed something flashing in the bottom right hand side of the display – Warning: Battery Low. 'Oh shit' he thought. He hadn't a clue how long that would last so he frantically looked across the hillside to see what was ahead. There was a corner with a lot of bushes coming up and then a long straight stretch of road.

"You wanna put that gun down," he said. It came out more of a suggestion than a question. Gorino didn't answer at first, it was almost as if he was considering his options.

"I will kill you, ..you pig" Gorino stammered. All menace had disappeared from his voice. Max wondered if it was his imagination but the display seemed to be flickering. As they approached the next corner he timed his turn so that the side of the car scraped heavily against the bushes.

"Oops. I guess the line was a little close to the edge there" he laughed.
Gorino grabbed the door handle with one hand the gun flailing around in the other.

"You are mad" he screamed as they pulled into the straight. Max saw his chance and slammed on the gas pedal and they lunged forward.

"Drop the gun asshole" he shouted across at Gorino – 400 yards to the corner.

"Nnno.." Gorino stammered as they flew towards the darkness.

"Last chance" Max screamed as he accelerated again. It was then that with a small click the night-vision disappeared. Max's world plunged into darkness and everything seemed to slow. He could hear Gorino blubbering in the darkness and wondered how many seconds he had before the edge of the road.

"Drop it now!" he screamed into the darkness. After what seemed an age he heard the clang of the gun as it hit floor and he slammed on the brakes.

Max was one of those people that passed their driving test and then immediately forgot all the statistics in the highway code. As they skidded toward the corner, rather than his life flashing before him, his brain was grappling with;

'You're doing fifty miles an hour, that's 150 feet per second, no, yards per minute, no...'

He held firm on the steering wheel as the car began to slide to the right. They were now a mere fifty feet from the edge. He made out the shape of the two trees a fraction of a second before they hit them. Silence. Max reached up and removed the sunglasses. It took his eyes a moment to adjust to the light. The car was perched six feet from the edge of the drop with the passenger door wedged into a small tree. The back end of the car was about two feet closer to the edge, also nestling against a tree. All Max could hear was his breathing and his heart going ten to the dozen.

Gorino wasn't moving. Max wasn't sure if he'd fainted or knocked unconscious as there was blood trickling from a small gash in his forehead. He quickly reached across and picked up the gun from the floor. The safety catch was off. Max was almost relieved.

'Look's like he'd have done it' he thought as he stepped out of the car and saw just how close they were to the edge.

'Thank God for trees' he smiled and walked round to the back of the car.
'At least some of this lot will come in handy' he thought as he opened the boot.

72

Gorino had given Max the silent treatment for about ten minutes then saw no point in delaying the inevitable. He gave him the directions into the back of Havana, but stayed silent for the whole journey. Max had tied his hands and feet and sat him in the back of the car.

By the time they got to Marcelos street, Max's left shoulder was numb. He'd driven that last couple of miles mostly with his right hand and he began to lose all feeling in the arm. He guessed he'd trapped a nerve or something when they hit the trees. He couldn't claim that things weren't going to plan because, to be perfectly honest, he didn't have one. Max pulled up at the side of the street and he could hear the thumping beat of a Mambo band coming from across the road. Max motioned to Gorino and he nodded. The restaurant was smaller than Max had imagined. Max got out of the car with his arm dangling limp at his side and headed to the door.

You know that feeling when you've moved into a new area, you've settled in and decide that its time for your first pint 'down the local'? Except its not your local yet and the moment you show your face through that door for the first time it feels like the whole bar instinctively knew that the next person through would be an outsider. They must get an extra-sensory split second warning that ensures that they have the 'you ain't from around these parts' looks on their faces the moment you appear. Well, double that and you begin to get the feeling Max got the second he walked through the doors of the Club Juliet.

Before we pause to consider this, it should be pointed out that a tied and beaten up member of the Langusto family had immediately preceded him through the aforementioned entrance.

Emile Langusto stared straight at Max across the card table and wondered if the day had arrived when he would regret the 'no firearms' rule he held so dear in the club. The man standing behind the crumpled figure of Gorino looked large and menacing and the long coat he wore could easily contain a formidable weapon.

"I believe this is yours" Max growled kicking Gorino's backside which sent him careering down a small set of steps leading down to the bar. The reaction was instant. Out of nowhere a medium build dark skinned man leapt the bar wielding a knife. Before Max could react the blade gleamed as it cut through the air and connected with Max's left shoulder. Max felt a searing pain – at least he would have if he could've felt anything at all on that side. Instead of flinching he grabbed the extremely surprised man who had followed the knife in and spun him around and into the side wall. The thud of skull on wood echoed across the room as the man slumped to the floor.

Max took two steps forward.
"Allesandro, you are really beginning to disappoint me" The comment was directed at a middle-aged man at the left of the table who stood up and held his hands open.
"János" he replied in a welcoming tone.
"Boys, back off" he added as the remainder of the Langusto family rallied and looked ready to pounce.

Max cast his eyes around the dining area. There were no customers to be seen. There was a group of four men in the corner some way from the main table but he suspected they were also connected to the family. Allesandro gestured for Max to come forward and as he did so he extended a hand. Max smiled and reached up to his left shoulder and grunted slightly as he removed the knife that was still firmly embedded. He smiled again and turned toward the door. Slowly and methodically he cleaned the blade of the knife on his trouser leg and took the blade end between his fingers. With a flick of his wrist the knife slipped through the air and hit the centre of the front door with a resounding "thunk". Max turned back again and took Allesandro's outstretched hand.

Max sipped another Mai Tai and the enormity of his current situation began to grab his attention. He tried to ignore it but he couldn't escape the fact that here he was in the den of one of Cuba's, and probably the Caribbean's most powerful families. Luco's voice broke the spell.

"Did you like what you saw on the DVD's?"
Luco was Allesandro Langusto's right hand man and younger brother. He was around six foot two inches tall with trademark dark skin and a very neat moustache below jet-black wavy hair. Allesandro was perhaps ten years his senior, around fifty and probably just how Luco would look in a decade or so.

"Some of it" Max replied.
In fact, he'd been impressed by the whole package as soon as his contact had been made with the Langusto family that previous Tuesday. The disc had been dispatched via DHL. Max reached inside his jacket pocket and retrieved a sleek silver portable DVD player that contained the aforementioned disc and flipped it open on the table. Max was more computer literate than many men his age

(just the wrong side of forty) but the multimedia set-up on the disk had him whistling through his teeth the moment he had first loaded it up.

The disc contained some of what Max decided was an obscenely wide range of military hardware available from the Langustos. The catalogue was heavily indexed and you could search by section or just type in what you were looking for. Max typed
TORNADO
on the tiny keypad attached and the screen came up with a full list of statistics;

Maximum Speed	800 knots
Length	17.2 metres
Engines	2 Turbo Union RB199 Mk103
	Reheated turbofans with integral thrust reverse

Beneath these the buttons PRICE, AVAILABILITY, VIDEO and of course ADD TO BASKET were emblazoned in red and yellow. The concept of adding a $10m plane into a shopping basket had amused and bemused Max the first time he had seen it.

Allesandro smiled as Max clicked on the video clip and a thirty second movie of a jet blowing seven bells of crap out of various inanimate objects filled the screen.
"Good choice" he smiled
"Yep. I first came across them when the Italians took them in 1982, and then in the early nineties with the Saudis," replied Max "but you seem a little light on stock"
"Light?" Allesandro frowned.

"I had my eye on half a dozen"

"Six?"

"Yes, perhaps settle for five and a Phantom if you're really struggling, though my client was pretty insistent on all six".

Luco leaned across to his brother and whispered something into his ear.

"I'm well aware of your credentials János, or should I call you Nomad?"

"Whatever. János is the name given by my parents. Nomad was given to me by my wonderful and faithful following in the press" Max laughed and they joined in.

"Well, János, you should appreciate that whilst your request is not a problem in terms of stock, the stock just has to be, how should I say, 'acquired'" he smiled.

A wave of relief swept over Max. In going through the inventory with Easton's friends at MI6 they had tried to find some items that would buy Max at least a week or two of time.

"And the amount of time required to 'acquire' the merchandise?"

Allesandro once more looked to Luco who reached for his laptop and punched away at the keys Max silently hoped he would have a fortnight at least. The various authorities had had a month to find Pete without uncovering the smallest of traces but he suspected they hadn't looked very hard. Journalists were not the most highly regarded breed, even those with a Pulitzer prize under their belt. He had to hold on to the hope that Pete was alive somewhere. His gut told him he was, but then his gut had had a dodgy chicken sandwich in the airport so might not be in a position to venture a strong opinion either way.

"Ten days" Luco announced with a surprisingly large flourish. Max tried not to look so pleased.

"That long?" he mused.

"I suppose I have other less exciting business to take care of in the meantime. I hear that Cuba has a few distractions to keep me busy" he smiled.

"And delivery?" asked Luco.

Max knew this was a critical question as six jets wasn't the easiest of cargoes to shift around.

"Well, I've got this small warehouse in East London" Max replied with a straight face. Luco looked very concerned until the old man across the table from him began to laugh. Max broke into a smile and the table ran into hearty laughter.

"Irony, irony" (pronounced EYER-RONY) said the old man and winked at Max.

"I understand that Qatar is particularly nice this time of year" he added.

Luco mimicked a grimace and returned to his keyboard.

"We must continue tomorrow, Mr.Nomad" Allesandro smiled.

"I see now why you broke your rules and came yourself"

"It isn't every week I get to spend $40m of someone else's money" Max smiled.

"Where are you staying?"

"Well, apart from the place down the quayside called 'concrete blocks around your ankles' that young Gorino had me booked into I thought maybe the Grande"

Allesandro looked a little offended and Max thought.

'Cheeky git. His asshole of a nephew decides to whack one of the most dangerous men on the planet and he gets pissed off at the man being a tad annoyed by it'

"Good choice, I trust you'll accept our suite with my compliments" he paused. "Under the circumstances"

"That's most gracious of you" Max smiled as he got up out of his seat.

"Luco will drive you over" Allesandro motioned to the door and Max took that as a sure sign that this first audience with the Langusto family was over.

73

Havana was beautiful. At least the parts between the centre of town and the Grande on the seafront. Max had been to Cuba once before in the early eighties and despite some developments the centre has remained much as it had been back then. He wished he could say the same for most of his favourite European capitals. It hadn't occurred to him before but the exclusion of anything American had a whole lot to do with that. No fast food restaurants, no commercial shopping chains, though he must admit he thought he saw a branch of Bennettons flash past at one point. Walls and buildings were still adorned with pictures of Castro and Ché Guavara. Max didn't know much about the country's history but at that moment felt a twinge of admiration for the country that had resisted the allure of the west for a number of decades. They passed another Lada, the most common car on the streets of Cuba and pulled into the opulent entrance to the Havana Grande. The seafront area of Havana was mostly concrete and it struck Max as almost part of the luxury of the hotel to have the only green patch for someway located right in front of the hotel. He wondered if that meant the rooms facing the sea would have an even more enhanced view.

As the doorman moved toward the car Luco stepped out and the man seemed to find a couple of extra gears. Perhaps surprised to by the fact that Luco was doing the driving. The man dressed head to foot in burgundy, gold braid and stripes bounded to the boot to get the cases.

The foyer of the Grande was a shrine to Italian marble and Max's steel capped Doctor Martin boots (DMs) clicked as they crossed to the reception. As they drew nearer to the counter staff backed away and what Max assumed was the manager appeared dressed in a light blue shirt and very conservative tie topped off with a blazer. The man and Luco exchanged knowing glances. He handed the manager a white A4 envelope and introduced Max as their "distinguished guest Mr.Nomad".

'Almost extinguished' Max thought which made him chuckle and then shudder a little. A tiny (4'5") bell boy whose nameplate proclaimed him to be 'Juan' grabbed Max's two large cases – one of the which Max observed was almost big enough for the little man to climb into – and they headed toward the lift. The lift was one of those terrible new pristine chrome edifices with built in 'patronising' voice. Not only did it inform the occupants that it was now 'on the ground floor, foyer' but counted out loud the floors as they headed to the penultimate.

"Eleven, Twelve, Fourteen" Max smiled. The tradition of not having a thirteenth floor had been adapted for the lift as well.

A sound not unlike the "shhhhkk" of the door on the Starship Enterprise greeted them on the 21st floor and Max half expected Spock to emerge from around a corner, raise an eyebrow and quizzically ask "Captain?". Instead Max was shown to one of just eight suites that covered the whole floor of the hotel. It was rumoured that the top floor contained one huge suite that Castro himself was prone to entertain in. The lift certainly looked like you needed extra passkeys to get up there, and there were no stairs. Guests, of course, tended to arrive via the helipad on the roof. The lift was really just for the staff.

The door of the suite opened to reveal what looked like four rooms to Max. The lounge was probably large enough to have a half decent game of five-a-side football he guessed. He tipped Juan with US$ which the little chap made a point of grinning at, but Max decided that he was probably used to it from the guests. The Cuban dollar was more or less at parity with its US big brother and most people didn't worry which they used. The buck was always favourite though.

Max set down his bags and glanced down at his watch. He worked out that the time delay with Washington was negligible and fired up his laptop. He sent a 'hey guys I'm online' ping to Easton and, despite the fact that it was the middle of the night in London sent one across to Baber. He changed into a bathrobe (heavy, monochromed 'Havana Grande' and definitely nickable) and fixed himself a scotch from the vast bar. He had just made it to the sumptuous sofa as he heard two beeps that told him that both the guys were online.

B – Hey chaps, London calling.

E – Washington here, what's cooking?

M – Havana, home to the anti-tank crew.

E – Hey Max, still mouthy even across the net.

M – That's me. As un-personable in text as in the flesh.

B – What's happening, you've been offline for two days?

M – Unintentional, had a bit of a welcoming party.

E – Serious?

M – Nah – I'd better get to it. The Langusto's took the bait on the Hurricanes.

B – What, all six?

M – Yeah, seemed hesitant at first though.

B – I'm not f-ing surprised! We know he can get his hands on four out of Iran, but where the heck the others are coming from I'm stumped.

M – Well, the RAF had better watch its ass 'cos I'll have them in 10 days.

B – Ten!

M – Yeah, No Typo. 10 days. You were right about the clan – close family, but a few weak links.

E – We've had Luco Langusto under surveillance for six years now.

M – Seems like a nice enough fella.

B – Oh yeah, when he's not redecorating rooms in 'hint of brain'

M – He killed many then?

E – He's their hitman, and Allesandro's No.2. Our count is up to thirty where he's actually pulled the trigger himself. Careful as hell, he never leaves a trace.

M – Ouch – he's not a bad driver either.

B – Eh?

M – Drove me over here – I'm on floor 20 of the Grande.

E – Shit, they have bought into this one.

M – Yeah – took a little persuading.

Max typed as he stretched his left arm out which was now pounding. The knife wound had been sewn together by one of the Langusto henchman. That was one of the funniest things he'd ever seen. A huge muscle-bound frowning man in dark sunglasses reaching into his jacket pocket for a small needlework kit. He gave Max an admiring series of grunts as he didn't flinch once while the man set in a dozen deep stitches. The truth was that although he had been getting the feeling back into his arm it still felt more like he was being tickled than sewn up. Once sewn the whole area had been strapped – a little too tight for Max's liking.

E – I've left some more background in your drop-box – see what you can get on their missile capabilities

M – Sure, I know I'm here courtesy of your ticket guys, but I have a friend to find...

B – Yes, and we're working on that too. You might want to get to the golden sands restaurant tomorrow around six – we have a man in Havana – Tremiere – Anglo/French. He may have some news for you.

'Our man in Havana' Max thought. 'How bloody passé'. He could tell by the way that no new information was being handed over that:

a) they had some news but were holding it so he could concentrate on the arms.

b) they had jack and were keeping him upbeat by introducing him to the local man.

He suspected it was the latter as although Easton owed him he knew he couldn't count on Baber in the same way.

B – Max, you still there?

M – Yeah – I'll be there – how will I know Mr Tremiere?

B – Don't worry. He'll find you. You're not exactly inconspicuous.

Max agreed but Baber was still a cheeky git. 'That is always a problem for security personnel' Max thought. 'They always assume that everyone else sucks at the whole spy thing'

74

The room was dark apart from the outline of the three sides of the door which let a little of the hazy light of the corridor into the hallway. It wasn't enough to see by but the black-suited figure didn't need such luxuries. He'd been in a thousand hotel rooms just like this. Nevertheless, his heart missed a beat as he crept into the bedroom and saw the figure on the left side of the huge bed. He raised the muzzle of the 9mm Sig Hauer and pumped a couple of rounds into the midriff. The silencer did its job and the only sound was a small 'phutt phutt'. The sound of the impact was all wrong but before he could react a fist flew out of the walk in wardrobe to his left and connected with his temple. The Sig dropped from his hand and clattered onto the side table as a foot appeared whipping through the air and planting itself heavily into his chest. The impact took him back out of the bedroom and into a set of bookshelves. Clambering to his feet another fist came out of nowhere into his face and he felt his nose snap. His hands flew to his face, which was instinctive but a very bad move. A series of blows rained in on his stomach and chest relieving him of what wind he had left and a knee into his chin sent him out toward the balcony door. Sadly for him a foot followed at the end of a spinning roundhouse kick. Careering four floors the black-suited man drew one more breath before his body slammed into the trees behind the hotel.

It took Cassandra nearly half an hour to find a suitably safe location for the body and make the call to her backup team. Though she'd had to kill before in self-defence – it came with the job – she hated it, and wondered if the bulky man had a wife and children waiting for him at home. Moving the body had worn her out, as the guy must have been 220 pounds and well over 6ft tall. She was no slouch but its amazing how heavy people get when they're dead. She had gathered her things from her room and disappeared into the network of small streets that made up the Velado district of Havana. It would be too dangerous to return to her hire car – if they'd found her at the hotel then they would probably have the car covered. She'd been so careful too, obviously not careful enough.

75

For someone who didn't like firearms, Max was having some serious fun. The outskirts of Havana had given way to a wooded area that stretched as far as the eye could see. About five miles into the countryside and they had passed through a large set of gates set into a huge fence. Max was pummelling a series of targets with an Uzi that would have been at home on the mean streets of LA – or at least the parts that Max imagined were ravaged by gangs. As the hundreds of bullets sprayed the target he realised how inaccurate a lot of the gang films were. There was no way you could hold one of those babies in one hand at arm's length and get any sort of accuracy. He had both hands firmly on the gun as it peppered the targets but also the surrounding posts and structure. They moved onto shoulder-held anti-tank missiles with which Max took out a sizeable group of pine trees. He was accompanied by a couple of Langusto henchman and been shown a variety of small arms. All questions around larger kit were palmed off – they'd had their orders. Max noted that most of the people around were in military uniform of some sort. He wondered what bribes it took to get a military facility for the day.

Lunch consisted of some very tasty char-grilled chicken and lobster pieces with large bowls of steamed rice. Max tried to make small talk with the two henchmen but they made trappist monks seem talkative by comparison. He did get out of one of them that the afternoon's schedule was to be played out at the Langusto villa, which was, quote, "in the hills". Being in a foreign land worried Max. Being in a foreign land and away from the hustle and bustle worried him more. Being in a foreign land, away from the hustle and bustle, and shut away in the headquarters of the Cuban equivalent of the Cosa Nostra took him beyond worry. The countryside was pretty calming though. The route to 'Nirvana' – scriptural reference more likely than musical preference – took them via the coastal road before heading once more inland. They passed a gaggle of oil wells in two-tone green and rust that swung like pendulums back and forth. Max switched his mind back to the briefing with Baber on this, the largest of the Caribbean islands. The oil wells did produce oil, but until fairly recently most of the islands oil had come out of Soviet Union. With its break up the supply had switched to Venezuela. Max had asked Baber if he was winding him up when he had said that Cuba even imported milk, which came from Holland. Apart from the obvious cigars – high visibility, low GDP – the biggest export was sugar which seemed to make sense as all they'd passed since leaving the coast was miles and miles of sugar cane. Max had asked the henchmen their names and got No22 and No23 in return. He assumed someone in the Langusto organisation thought that it was terribly sophisticated, but Max thought it was lame so insisted on calling the taller one Bob and the shorter one Fred. He wasn't sure whether their resultant grins were out of amusement or annoyance, but at least it had provoked some sort of facial expression. Black suit, black shirts and black ties and the requisite Ray-Bans in this heat? A slightly retarded 'Men in (completely bloody) Black'.

Bob was driving, moderately well and carefully, while Fred sat in the other front seat turned at an angle facing Max in the back. The car was a black (naturally) 1958 Chevy. Max suspected Bob and Fred spent a good part of their day polishing the car, as all of the panels were shiny to mirror proportions. That didn't distract any from what these guys were primarily employed for and Max wondered how they were armed. As if reading his thoughts Fred reached in to his jacket holster and removed a rather impressive Glock. Max had learnt more about guns in the past couple of weeks than he'd come across from dozens of thrillers and movies. The Glock had a clip that held an ample ten with one in the chamber. Fred proceeded to check the gun over and fit and remove a sleek silencer that he had produced from his other inside jacket pocket. Perhaps he thought this show would intimidate Max but he'd gone past that stage. Max wasn't a particularly brave man but he owed his life to a friend who had now been missing more than five weeks and he was determined to find him, or die in the attempt. Baber hadn't understood that but Max just viewed it as evening out the odds. He'd had four extra years courtesy of Pete so in his mind he was already ahead. Max had never carried a weapon 'other than my rapier like wit – hah, hah' but today he had three. A shoulder holster housed a Walther PPK (and yes Baber had rolled his eyes when he asked for that – the same as James Bond for the uninitiated). His pen and lighter (both functional) clipped together to form a 2mm pop gun that Baber warned needed to be used at extremely close range. His belt contained cheese wire that Baber had insisted on, but Max doubted he would come across any vicious Edam, Cheddar or Brie on this visit - or perhaps he thought he couldn't bring himself to use it.

76

She'd seen the three of them leave the Grande that morning but decided it wasn't worth following. Two goons and a client that looked strangely familiar but no major family members. Instead Cass had attached a rather simple tracking device to the underside of the Chevy. She loved the concept of recruiting within the family. It generally created heavily committed yet technically inept pawns. She actually attached the two units connected with electronic tape while they had grabbed breakfast that morning. Following cars in places like Cuba, due to the lack of cars and severe lack of roads was pretty tough. On the busy streets of London or New York you can easily blend in with the traffic. In Cuba, anywhere outside Havana, half a dozen cars is considered a jam. The fact that the car had headed out of town, toward a known military zone was enough to change her mind. She had them on the tracking console now after lunch and they were heading out to the Langustos. 'This guy must be important' Cass thought as she kept the Lada ticking over at a steady 50. They were about 2 miles North of her heading into the hills.

According to Fred, the Langusto residence used to belong to a former foreign minister of Cuba, Heraldo Sanchez, and one of the most secure buildings on the island. Sanchez was monumentally paranoid and surrounded the huge sprawling villa with a deep moat to the South. Nature provided its own battlements to the North and East with sheer drops of around 400 metres to the valley below. To the West was the road approach across a ravine to a 3-metre wall with huge iron gates. At the gates was a security checkpoint, no doubt manned by some cousin or nephew carrying a suitably threatening semi-automatic. The gates had already begun to swing open as the car approached with the 'as yet unidentified cousin/nephew' waving the incoming Bob and Fred through.

Cass knew not to get too close to the villa and pulled into a side dirt track. She flipped open her palmtop and checked to see if Tripoli has processed the pictures of the European she had taken that morning in front of the Grande.

77

Luco met Max at the door of the villa and took him via a metal detector where the Walther was confiscated. Strangely, the fact that the other makeshift weapons had been left didn't give Max any comfort. The walk through the villa to the veranda was a gallery of dark-skinned suited guys doing their best Godfather impressions tipping Max small nods without the merest hint of a smile. The veranda itself had a generous sized pool with a bar at the end, which he noticed had the rest of the senior family members deep in conversation.

'Shit' Max thought.
'100% dark suits, and I look like a cross between the man from Del Monte and Dr. Livingston'
Cream suit, cream hat. 'The Nomad', he knew had had a penchant for pastel suits and while Max understood the need to stay in character he resented feeling like he looked like a twat.
"Ah, János".
Allesandro stood as he saw the three of them approach – looking like the start of a zebra crossing.
"Let me introduce you to the boys" he added and began to point them out one by one.
"Andre" – dark, short and plump.
"Pauli" – dark, tall moustache, nice scar across the cheek.
"Tony" – dark, tall, ponytail, missing two fingers on his left hand.

"and Little Marco" he laughed as they pointed to the huge man that was nearly as tall as Max before he stood up. Max wondered if Marco had ever thought of trying out for the NBA or NFL, or perhaps he had and they hadn't let him in on account of him being too big. Each man shook Max's hand though Marco nearly took Max's arm off at the shoulder. At around 6'8" and roughly at a guess 24 stone (none of which Max could identify as anything but muscle) he was what the phrase "built like a brick shit-house" was coined for.

78

Cass sat in the front seat of the battered old Lada staring at the screen with a stunned expression. The left hand portion of the screen had an unflattering photo of Kovacs in combat greens with a breakdown of 'The Nomad's' illustrious history.

> János Kovács – aka 'The Nomad'
>
> Born Pécs, Hungary, 17th August 1955.
>
> First class honours Oxford, MBAs at Harvard and MIT.
>
> No.6 on CIA's all time most wanted list.
>
> Interpol file dates back to 1985 when he is rumoured to have brokered a deal for 40 T-80 tanks from somewhere in Eastern Europe (possibly Czech Republic) to the Yemen.
>
> 1987 linked to the terrorist groups in East Africa, mainly light arms.
>
> 1989 linked to the coup in Namibia.
>
> 1990 CIA file opened following strong association with parts for Pakistan nuclear program – a shipment of plutonium hijacked in Turkey.
>
> 1990 shot four times in assassination attempt – gunmen and two associates (Indian) killed in the raid.

'Wow' Cass thought, 'The Indian Government sure didn't appreciate his involvement in the nuclear race'

1993 briefly detained by authorities in Dubai but released on a technicality (arrest warrant had a typing error quoting a statute from 1981 when it should have read 1971)

Net estimated worth $625m – mainly in haulage industry, Budapest, Geneva and Chicago.

British and Hungarian passports.

'Now what the hell is he doing in Cuba with the Langusto brothers' she thought as she clicked the palmtop closed. She was well aware of Dimitri's hate of the man and that gave her an added reason to bring him down.

79

What he was currently doing in Cuba was playing three-card brag, or at least trying to teach the rather drunken group of Cubans the intricacies of the game.

"Why do they call it 'Bastard Brag'" Tony laughed trying to look serious.
"Err, maybe the bloke that invented it had dubious parentage? "

They had begun playing spoof for healthy measures of rum and after an hour of that decided they could handle something a bit more sophisticated. All except Marco of course. The basic idea behind spoof (that of three coins each, placing 0 to 3 in your closed hand and then guessing the total number of coins being held. The person guessing correct dropping out then repeating with those left) was way beyond him. He lost six straight games before Luco suggested he dropped out. Even a man his size felt what was the best part of a bottle of Cabanas. Tony had whispered to Max that Marco's nickname was Rex (as in Tyrannosaurus) – big, but brain the size of a pea.

'Trying to negotiate an arms deal when you're pissed is both inadvisable and difficult'
Max thought as he wiped his brow. They were sitting in a large long room with a table in the centre that at a push would seat 24. Max felt a little like an interviewee with him on one side of the deep oak table and the six brothers across the way on the other.
"So we are agreed"

Luco checked his computer printout slowly flipping the pages over as Max did the same with his copy.

"$2m to cover additional armoury for the Hurricanes and $5m across three categories of missile. Air to air, air to ground and heat-seekers"

Max confirmed.

"Topping up to the $50m mark with small arms as detailed on pages 5 through 11"

Luco added.

"Yep, that sounds about right" Max smiled. If it wasn't for the incident with Gorino Max felt they would have asked for a slice up front, but Allesandro had insisted that Max's agent transfer the money on receipt of the planes in Qatar.

"I've spoken to Klaus in Geneva and the transfer is cleared and ready to go" said Max and added.

"Thank God there's no VAT on this little transaction"

which was greeted with six bemused faces.

"Oh, sales tax" he laughed and the others joined in.

"I'm not too sure it would go down that well with certain of our politicians"

Tony smiled. Max thought he saw Luco throw him a stern stare and changed the subject.

"Well, János, will you be staying in Cuba until the deal is complete?"

"I thought I might make the most of the hospitality"

he grinned looking over at Gorino who was sulking in the corner.

"I have some clients to meet and my golf swing could probably do with some serious practice"

Max smiled.

"Well then, I recommend a course out at Varadero, not far past the airport.

"What's your handicap?"

"Apart from my habit of slicing, I play off an eight"

Max lied. He had played a few times but felt destined to be a habitual beginner. He guessed that golf was a given for an international arms dealer.

"Ah, with me playing off a ten that would be some match"

Luco grinned.

'Yeah, and you'd be over the moon when you'd do me by twenty shots'

They arranged a game for the following Thursday. Hopefully Max would be long gone by then. As they walked toward the front steps the others headed back to the veranda.

"Luco, I wonder if I could ask a small favour"

Max said and turned to face him on the top step.

"Name it"

Luco replied.

"I am trying to find someone, here in Cuba that I suspect would much rather stay lost if you follow my drift"

"Do you have any idea what region of the island they are in?"

Max had no idea, but Pete was last seen in Havana.

"Havana"

Max said in a confident tone.

"Ah well, that's easy" Luco replied and reached into his jacket pocket and retrieved a small stack of cards. He thumbed through them for a moment and passed him a shiny blue card with light yellow block print.

JULIUS MANTON – Chief of Police

Max raised his eyebrows and Luco laughed.

"Second Cousin. Just tell him Luco is calling in one of his cards"

80

"You are bloody kidding"

The young man said as he huddled close to the phone. It was raining hard and he didn't believe what he was being asked for. He hoped the rain was distorting the line and he'd not heard properly.

"But that was so much easier. They were being decommissioned"

The voice on the other end of the line became sharp.

"We can always find ourselves another source" he snapped.

"Okay, okay but I'll need a month. I'm not a magician"

"You have a week" the man snapped and put the phone down. He began to protest but realised there was no one at the other end. He slammed the phone down and gave the base a kick. He looked three blocks down to the grey building and began to make his way back shaking his head from side to side.

81

They were on the move again. Cass waited two minutes after the sleek back car had passed her on the road and pulled the Lada out sending wisps of dust up into the air. It was four-thirty. He'd been at the villa for three hours. They were heading back into Havana and she decided to take the inland route back to the Grande hotel.

"Oh and book me a room at the Grande" she added "as high up as possible".

She held on the line while her colleague made the booking.

"Floor 18 – the best I could do"

Tamian was very efficient and a good agent but persistently making advances.

"I don't suppose you want some company"

Cass cringed but decided to be polite.

"Much as I would enjoy your charm Tam, I need to stay focussed, especially after last night".

"I suppose so. The colonel is very concerned about you getting made"

"Ah, that's very sweet but he need not worry. I've picked up a fresh passport and cut and dyed my hair"

"Oh, not your hair surely!"

"Yup. Had to go one day" Cass laughed running her hand through the jet-black hair that now barely touched her shoulders. Since she had been a child she had long flowing hair to her waist and she felt somehow naked without it. It was a straight piece of road and Cass stole a peek at herself in the mirror.

'I suppose it'll dry faster' she smiled to herself.

82

Max walked through the front doors of the police station and couldn't help wondering if this is how a cat would feel wandering the corridors of Battersea Dog Home. Cuban policemen seemed very laid back and he wondered whether Havana suffered much from crime. In fact, apart from a few established syndicates Cuba was relatively crime free. The large man behind the counter asked Max what he wanted in the time-honoured tradition of all desk sergeants. He looked up from his pad and raised an eyebrow about half an inch with a 'Yeah?' look on his face.

"Julius Manton"

Max said pronouncing it just the way Luis had. The man's expression changed ever so slightly to 'Oh, ok?' and picked up the phone.

"Captain........................" he said in a monotone. Max's Cuban was poor but he was sure the man said the word 'ice' in there somewhere.

"A man dressed like an ice cream?" Julius Manton laughed the kind of barrel laugh you'd associate with, well, a barrel shaped man. He was a little on the plump side from the last fifteen years driving a desk, but nevertheless the laugh didn't quite fit him.

"Send him in" he laughed again.

The sergeant nodded and pointed to a corridor off to the left then held up three fingers. Max set off down the corridor before he got to the third door a tall broad shouldered man with a dark blue uniform stepped out into the corridor.

"Not many people ask for me by name"

he smiled holding out his hand. Max removed his hat, shook his hand and replied.

"Kovács. János Kovács."

"Mr Kovács, please come in"

Manton showed Max into his office that was fairly roomy with two small leather settees facing a large carved desk. The walls were covered in paintings and photographs, mostly black and white of Castro and what Max assumed were high-ranking politicians.

"Iced Tea?"

Manton asked and gestured for Max to sit in the nearer settee. Max wiped the sweat off his brow.

"Thank you"

he smiled a little relieved. He hadn't got used to the heat. Manton reached into his sideboard behind the desk that contained a small fridge. From it he produced a jug of iced lemon tea and a couple of frosted glasses.

"So what can I do for you, Mr Kovács?"

"I was referred to you by Luco Langusto"

At the name Manton's face became a little more serious.

"He said you owed him a favour" Max paused

"or two, and I happen to be in need of a favour" he smiled.

"He did, did he?" Manton eyed Max up and down warily.

"Well, although I'm familiar with Senor Langusto, my dealings with him have been extremely limited" Max felt his hopes slide.

"However, as a welcome guest of our country" Manton winked

"I am happy to oblige you within the scope of my normal duties".

Max breathed deeply in and out. He reached into his pocket and retrieved a 6"x4" card with Pete's picture and vital statistics. He'd run off a couple of hundred through a mate of his at print studio.

"Pete Smalt" Manton read off the card. "And you believe he is in Cuba?"

"He was last seen in Havana about five weeks ago"

Manton slowly shook his head.

"Mr.Kovács. I assume someone has already explained that for missing persons the first 48hrs are critical. After one or two weeks the chances of finding someone are small at best. I see that the young man in question is a journalist"

"Yeah. New York Times, though he's English I think"

"He was here on holiday or working a story"

"He was working a story and the reason I need to find him is that he may have some 'research' "– Max motioned quote marks with his fingers – "that could be somewhat damaging to my organisation"

"I see. What is it that you do Mr.Kovács?"

"Import-Export" Max smiled.

"Ah" smiled Manton seeing the connection with his cousin. Although he didn't agree with what Luco and the other family members were involved in, he couldn't judge as his growing pension fund wasn't completely from the right side of the fence.

"Anyone else looked for him?"

"Yes, sort of. You might want to check with the British Embassy for records. I'm sure they have them but I'm not in a position to gain access"

"OK, I make no promises but we'll do our best. What value would you say such information would be to your organisation?"

'Oh here it comes' Max thought. He lent forward and scribbled $5,000 onto the desk pad. Manton sighed and added a 1 to the front, $15,000, and looked at Max with a questioning look. Max felt nautious at the fact that he was bidding for information to find his friend. The fact was that Max's budget was limited. His basic expenses were being covered by MI6 and the CIA in return for the information on the Langustos and bribe money had to come from his own coffers. He'd sold some investments and a quick re-mortgage had freed up a chunk but at $15k a time that wouldn't last long. Max paused, leaned over and changed the 5 to a 0, hoping he wouldn't piss off Manton. $10,000 Manton wrote and smiled.

"And your mobile number?"

Max wrote it on the pad.

"Thank you" he said. As he headed towards the door with a sheet from the pad which had a set of numbers to a Swiss bank account.

83

Max headed back to the Grande in a taxi and was in a bit of a subdued mood. He hadn't made that much progress and the meeting with Manton hadn't exactly filled him with confidence. As he headed up in the lift he wondered if he had bitten off more than he could chew. He stepped out onto the 20th floor and immediately realised something was wrong but couldn't put his finger on it.

Cass had made it to the Grande ten minutes before Max and after a quick change of outfit in her room went up the four flights of stairs to the twentieth in her cleaners outfit. She found a cart at the end of the corridor and made her way towards the lift.

As Max stepped out of the lift the first thing he saw was the cleaner and her cart. He smiled and walked towards her as his room was at the end of the corridor – he still couldn't figure out what was wrong. Cass smiled back and had her hand on her pistol underneath the pile of towels in front of her.

Max looked past the cleaner as a large man dressed in black turned the corner dressed in a long black coat. Cass felt the barrel of the shotgun in the small of her back and froze. Max paused and looked at the scene in front of him.

"Back off Senor. This doesn't concern you," said the man slowly.

"Botchanot, en nem besselek Angolul" 'Sorry I don't speak English' Max said in Hungarian and carried on walking. Two more steps and he could see the gun.

The man in black swung the butt of the shotgun against the back of Cass' head and she flopped onto the cart.

"I said back off" shouted the man at Max and pointed the shotgun at his stomach from ten feet away.

Max stopped and waited. He had guessed it might come to this. If he was going to die then at least he would go out fighting. He smiled and the man looked confused. He threw himself forward and landed on the front of the cart that shot backward into the man's stomach. The shotgun clattered on the floor and Max dove for it. The man in black scrambled backwards and around the corner. Max headed after him and fired towards the fire exit as the man pushed through the door. He heard a scream and a thump. He reached the stairwell and pushed the door. The shotgun had taken a chunk out of the frame and judging by the crumpled heap at the bottom of the stairs, out of him too.

"Damn!" Max said loudly then realised that there was an innocent unconscious cleaner in the hallway and ran back. The woman was lying on her back and as Max bent down he saw the pistol in her hand.

"Damn!" he said again.

84

Cass's head was pounding. She opened her eyes slowly. She was propped up sitting on her bed, at least she thought it was her bed, it looked like her bed.

"Hey" Max said and threw her some ice wrapped in flannel.

"Hey?" she replied slowly.

"Coffee's by the side of the bed. You want to explain what you were doing with a gun and dressed as a cleaner?"

"Oh". Cass didn't know what to say. Things like this didn't happen in her profession. Cold blooded arms dealers didn't make you coffee and ask you questions.

Max was sitting at the small table and waved his pistol.

"Well, I'm here to arrest a pig of an arms dealer call Kovács, and I guess that must be you" she snapped.

"Arrest?" Max said, "You're from the Cuban police?"

"No" Cass smiled. "Mossad".

'Oh shit' Max thought.

"So get it over with you bastard because you are not going to have your way with me" she growled.

"Ah." Max replied. There was no way he was going to get out of this easily.

"Here's the thing. Let's just say for argument that I wasn't exactly the man you think I am"

"Oh, yeah sure, János Kovács is a real nice guy" Cass laughed.

"János Kovács is dead," Max said flatly.

"You look pretty alive to me" Cass replied.

"How much do you know about János Kovács?"

"Enough to know you fit the bill" Cass snapped.

"Do you know what he has on his left shoulder blade?"

"Er, a tattoo of a black panther"

Max stood up and removed his shirt.

"That doesn't prove anything. Tattoos can be removed" Cass argued but Max could tell there was doubt in her voice.

"Okay, would János Kovács do this?" he smiled and threw his pistol over onto the bed next to Cass. She grabbed it and checked the magazine. The clip was full. She pointed the gun back at Max.

"So. You have my attention. Make the story a good one."

Max talked for half an hour straight. He started with the background on how he met Pete back in Oxfordshire while he had been on the run. Max had been framed for murder four years before and despite only meeting him by chance, Pete had stuck by Max across two continents and through a bunch of dangerous situations. Pete and Max had travelled across Australia to get the evidence needed to clear Max and had even had some dealings with the CIA. Cass interrupted Max a couple of times to get him to repeat certain parts of the story. If he didn't come across so genuine she wouldn't have believed him. When he finally finished he looked at her and smiled.

"What now?" he said.

"I could really do with something to eat?" She replied.

"Sure" Max said relieved.

"I'll tell you what. You freshen up while I go and sort out your friend from earlier"

"You've got the guy from the corridor. That's great. I really want to get some information from him." Cass replied jumping up from the bed and heading towards the door.

Max put his arm out to stop her.

"Sorry. The only thing I'm going to get from him is a hernia. He's a heavy bastard. It's funny, is it me or do dead guys weight more"

"Shit. I could really do with finding out how Martinez is keeping tabs on me," Cass said.

"Next time I'll aim for the legs, ok?" Max said over his shoulder as he walked out of the door.

85

Max was more nervous about the fact that he hadn't had a decent night's sleep in the last two weeks than the fact that he was in a busy restaurant. The Uno Habana was a magnificent building that had been used in many ways over the three centuries since it had been built. It's most decadent feature being the huge glass domes, six in all that gave it such an amazing level of light. This last iteration as a restaurant followed a particularly successful reign as Havana's main musical venue. Evidence of that remained with wonderful prints of Salsa dancers and grinning musicians which adorned the walls. Max smiled. His ex-wife had insisted he joined in the Salsa craze that had swept North London in the late 90s. He had managed to get quite good. Not from natural ability but from a pig-headed stubbornness that saw him get through a host of dance partners. His wife had had enough after the second broken toe and refused to dance with him until he had mastered the difficult moves. Such a shame really, they had only squeezed in three or four evenings on the hardwood before the divorce came along. Were they still dancing together? Not a good move dancing with your ex, especially as they got on so well. They had even less in common now then when they were married, which didn't stretch too much beyond sharing a name - and with a name like Jones it wasn't exactly exotic enough to want to hold on to either. There was no animosity created by large alimony payments. Jan was an accomplished lawyer and had always earned more than him and there were no kids to complicate matters.

He looked at Cass and smiled. She was studying the menu and he couldn't help focusing on those lips. She was wearing a print dress that was very well cut for her slender figure but flowing enough to conceal the undoubted arsenal she had strapped to herself at the hotel. The walls in the small motel were thin enough for Max to have been able to hear her getting ready in the morning and was in no doubt that she had more than the single pistol that he had inside his jacket.

The waiter ambled up to the table and Max realised that having spent the past few minutes staring at Cass he had no idea what was on the menu. He didn't really need to look, as variety was not a word Max would associate with Cuban cuisine.

"Mademoiselle?" the waiter enquired. French was not the mainstay here and it irritated Max that the guy was trying to be hip. He looked a little funny too. Max couldn't quite put his finger on it but he was sure there was something amiss. He was probably getting a little paranoid though. People trying to kill him always seemed to have that effect.

"Chicken Salad please" Cass smiled

"I'll go for the same" Max added and looked straight into the waiter's eyes. This drew no reaction apart from a cursory "Oui Monsieur" and the waiter headed for the kitchen.

"There's something about that waiter" they both said under their breath and then laughed.

"Apart from the bad accent and the hairstyle that is definitely looks like a Syrup, there's something else"

"Syrup?" Cass smiled.

"Oh, hair-piece, Syrup and Fig......wig. Rhyming slang" Max replied. He must try to avoid colloquialisms like that. Cass's English was excellent but she'd be hard pressed to have picked up that one.

"You think?"

"Possibly, though he had better have kept the receipt because one day he'll look in a mirror and realise he looks like a 1980s footballer"

"Ah yes, Glenn Hoddle" Cass winked and it was Max's turn to be surprised.

"Don't' tell me you're a Spurs fan?" he asked in mock horror.

"No. My brother studied in London and would always take me to games when I visited him"

"Makes sense, but why Spurs?"

"Oh no, not just Tottenham. He loved football and we would go to any home game in London"

Max must have looked a bit dubious because Cass then preceded to recount half a dozen football chants which brought blushes and plenty of head shaking to a nearby table of what Max guessed were Canadians. He still had not got used to being in a foreign country that had no American tourists.

The food arrived and they chatted more about football and Cass's hometown a stone's throw away from the West Bank. Max had that knack of being a great listener and adding just enough to a conversation that company felt he was fully involved but afterwards found they had learnt very little about the big man. He signalled to the waiter for the bill in the time honoured tradition of waving his hand in the in the shape of a wild signature.

'It may look stupid but it works' he thought. It was as the waiter walked towards him that he saw the glint of metal under the tray. It was way too big to be a pen and the waiter had a distinctly focussed look on his face.

He had six seconds before he reached the table and they were over in a blur but to Max they seemed like they went on for ages.

One and two he spent flicking his eyes around the room and picked up on the fact that there were at least ten sets of eyes trained on their table. Yes he was an interesting sight in his cream suit but not that bloody fascinating.

Three was largely wasted as the 'run' option was raised and immediately dismissed.

Four and his covered the rest of the scene, down - the floor - and then up to the stunning glass dome.

Five and his pistol was out and pointing towards the sky.

Six was an interesting second because two things happened. The waiter got within six feet of the table and was lowering his tray to reveal a semi-automatic pistol. At that point Max's gun thundered a bullet straight up within an inch or so of his own face.

As the waiter recoiled Max leant forward and pushed Cass hard in the chest sending her careering backwards and underneath the adjacent table. Her head reached its safety a split second before the thousands of pieces of glass from the shattered dome engeulfed the dozen tables in the centre of the restaurant.

From that moment it was chaos. Although the domes central panels had long been replaced by safety glass the force of the bullet had created a domino effect and apart from a few small panels at the sides the whole ceiling caved in. Max felt the full force of the falling glass on his back and the back of his head and was not far away from being knocked out. The waiter wasn't so lucky as he had instinctively looked to the source of the noise and took the glass in the face. Cass leapt to her feet and grabbed Max's arm. It took a moment for him to respond but within half a minute they were out of the side entrance of the restaurant. Two of Martinez's men were right behind them. That number could very easily have been worse as there had been a total of nine in the restaurant. Mostly at nearby tables. Martinez knew full well that Cass had earned her reputation and despite protests from his men had insisted that all available be involved. He would not be pleased to be proved right but would no doubt have been amazed by the real reason that only a couple of his men were now pursuing Cass through the narrow streets of Old Havana. Sure, Max had created the diversion but he was stumbling along the road almost being pulled along by Cass. She spun Max into a doorway and turning with her gun aloft sent half a dozen shots back in the direction of the two men who dived for cover. Max shook his head and steadied himself against the doorframe. Cass held the gun tight as she reached into the strapping on her left thigh, removed a new clip and swapped it for the spent one in an effortless movement.

"You okay Max?" she shouted.

"Been better" he replied and took up a position on her right shoulder.

"They are about a hundred yards down the street. One behind the corner and the other on the far side of that blue car"

Max looked past her but could not see either man. 'They'll keep under cover if they know what's good for them' he thought. Glancing back he saw a small road with what looked like a market sprawling into it about fifty yards down its length. Max motioned to Cass and she nodded. Still no movement but the unmistakable sound of sirens made the decision for them.

Three bullets rattled into the stonework at the end of the narrow street but Cass and Max were already within yards of the throng of the market. Martinez's men hesitated as they reached the edge of the market and the larger of the two veered off to the left, which unfortunately for them was the opposite to Cass and Max who were making their way quickly towards the railway station.

They ran into the main terminal building and Cass made a beeline for a train that was just leaving the third platform. Max was having great difficulty keeping up and when he clambered aboard the train he was four carriages behind Cass. They made their way towards each other through the crowded cars but there were so many people that it wasn't until the third stop that they reached the same car.

86

"Send a bunch of peasants to do a man's job!"

Martinez screamed at the six of his men that had made it out of the restaurant. The other three were among the large group of people ferried to the state hospital.

"One hundred thousand dollars to the man that finishes this, and I mean FINISH!" he slammed his fist on the table and sent his wine glass over the edge. As the glass hit the ground and shattered the six men in front of him winced.

87

Max laid eyes on Cass and without thinking gave her a huge hug. No sooner had he wrapped his arms around her he let her go and smiled awkwardly. Cass's face carried a frown that quickly turned into a grin.

"You are a very dangerous man to be around" she laughed as they stepped out onto the small open area in between the cars.

"I don't look for it. Honest"

"Nevertheless, it seems to find you" Cass added.

"That wasn't Langusto's men. I'm sure I recognised one of them but I can't place him"

"How many of them were there?"

"At least five, but I didn't get a good look on account of someone pushing me under a table"

"Well excuse me" Max replied

"Oh, don't get me wrong. I'm pretty pleased you did. I got a bit of the ceiling in my left leg" she lifted her dress to reveal a two inch gash in what Max admitted was a tanned shapely thigh.

"I was lucky" Max replied feeling the back of his head and finding a raft of bruises and pulling a face.

"Let me look at that" Cass grabbed his hand and for a moment they paused. Hand in hand with the beautiful Cuban countryside rolling by and then her hand moved to his head and she was behind him.

"No harm done. Bruises and cuts but you'll live, again"

"You said that with a hint of the inevitable" Max said as he turned back to face her.

"I have a funny feeling you're pretty good at it" Cass replied and reached inside her waistband and removed a tiny mobile phone which she punched a few numbers into. She raised the phone to her ear and after a few moments rattled of a series of instructions which, as they weren't in English Max couldn't understand.

As she put the phone away the train pulled into the next station and Cass jumped onto the gravel. Max followed and sent plumes of dust into the air as he landed heavily.

'Not exactly Mr.Stealth' Cass thought and headed for the small group of taxis huddled under the limited shade at the front of the station.

88

Eight weeks locked in the confined space had taken its toll on Pete and he could have easily passed himself off as a hunger striker. He looked more gaunt than a catwalk model, well perhaps not that bad. There had been no physical cruelty since his captors had decided that he had nothing interesting to reveal. They had not got far into their repertoire of methods of making people talk before they realised he knew nothing. The broken fingers were healing nicely but he wondered how his typing speed would be affected.

"I'll never be able to play the piano again," he said out loud and the guard outside shouted for him to shut his fascist pig mouth. 'Charming' Pete thought and added in a whisper. "Not that I knew how to play the f'ing piano before anyway!" and immediately chided himself for the use of the cliché. This had gone well past just a good story and he was beginning to wonder if he would ever get out.

89

There were twenty-seven men in total on the quiet airbase in Northern France. Charlotte was a small town about a hundred miles from Normandy whose history was steeped in things military. In the Second World War it had been a regional headquarters for the resistance. The picturesque town square and seventeenth century church held plenty of stories. Tonight, however, Charlotte's place in history would be marked for a very different reason.

In the centre of the airfield were two concrete hangars. They were large enough to house a dozen or so small aircraft but very plain and un-inspirational to the external observer. The tower was nothing special either. Four of the men were in there, a further eleven around the perimeter, two inside the hangars and ten asleep.

There were just eight in the 4x4 by the south gate of the airfield. Eight against seventeen awake. They had spent the previous day and night watching and recording every move and pattern since the planes arrived. They had come in the dusk and at first Durant had only counted three. It had been a painstaking five minutes until the fourth had arrived. He was relieved his information was good. It had been out though on the number of troops at the airfield. He had been told forty, but was pleased his contact had over cooked it.

'The key to the operation iss speed and stealth' he reminded himself. He prided himself in ten years of stealing military hardware he had not lost a single one of his men. True, they had not taken anything anywhere near like this before. He flipped his night-vision glasses over his eyes and glanced around his men. They all looked composed, but he knew the adrenaline was pumping through their veins.

"Remember gentlemen, I have no desire to rise higher on Interpol's list because one of you is careless. Lets do it"

He checked his watch.
"0-2:00, mark"

As his watch emitted a small beep the 4x4 rolled through the small gate and towards the back of the unused hangar. No lights and a muffled engine.

90

"I really don't like this," said Colonel Letract as he paced up and down in the command trailer. "That's my men in there," he said pointing at one of the bank of video screens on the desk.

"You know the importance of this mission Colonel" Agent Baber was annoyed at the interruption but had a little sympathy for the man. The radio operator at the controls raised his arm and spoke softly into the microphone hooked around his head.

"Subjects have just passed through the perimeter fence"

91

They reached the hangar in a little under a minute and Durant opened the back doors. They filed out two by two and six of them made their way around to the South of the building. The largest of the bunch, a stern faced German called Mantz headed towards the tower. The small Frenchman went straight towards the main building.

Mantz reached the base of the tower and as he did so one of the soldiers emerged with cigarette and lighter in his hands. Still running Mantz raised his pistol and the soldier hit the wall and fell forward crushing his cigarette under his chest. Six more steps and Mantz was inside. He checked his watch. Forty-five seconds before 2:03. He took the grenade from his belt and checked the pin. He tried not to think what he would do if another came down the small staircase. He regretted having to shoot the first one but you couldn't plan for everything.

The Frenchman was standing outside the dormitory and took a moment to peer through the small pane of glass. Thirty seconds to go. Four of the team were now by the open doors of the main hangar and they could see all eight of the men inside. They were working on one of the planes and Durant cursed under his breath.

'I really hope that it's a service' he thought. They had got this far and the last thing they needed was for one of the planes to be in pieces. Fifteen seconds.

The last two had set up the scrambling unit. It was extremely heavy and they were thankful that the unused hangar had a large sturdy table in the office. They had taken the precaution of putting the unit down as they entered which had proved to be a good move as there were two guards inside. Fairly vicious blows to the head and they had been taken care of and were bundled into a corner of the office. They completed the initiation sequence that would bathe a five-mile radius in radar static. Five seconds.

92

Baber was watching the monitor trained on the tower as the grenades went off. At precisely three minutes past two the hangar, main building and tower were a mass of smoke. The force of the blast in the tower caved two of the windows that drew a sharp intake of breath from Baber.

"Shit!" he said quietly as the four men in the trailer were glued to their screens.

Colonel Letract headed for the door but Baber signalled to his burly colleague who blocked the way.

'Get out of my way!" the Colonel snapped, but the man in the dark suit made no movement.

"You know we have to let this run its course" Baber said without emotion. Inside he was worried though. He knew that this was a make or break situation for him. Not only had both the British Defence Minister and Home Secretary been involved in the briefing, but both had expressed grave concerns. Not for the planes as they were due to be decommissioned in a few years anyway, but for the NATO troops involved. If it ever got out that the British had sanctioned this then the consequences could be dire. Most of the men stationed at Charlotte were French, naturally, but four were Italians, four British and a Norwegian.

93

The eight men moved quickly in the hangar. After a brief check that no soldiers had made it past the gas, they had converged on the planes and paired off two to each aircraft. Durant took a moment to smile to himself.

'We're actually going to do this'

He placed a hand on the cold grey steel of the wing. His partner was checking the wiring underneath the panel that had been open when they came in and signalled that everything was ok. He bolted the panel down and they got into the cockpit.

The unexpected delay had cost them four of the five minutes he had set aside. The engines roared into life one by one and they rolled out onto the runway. There were no runway lights to guide them but the four pilots were experienced enough not to need them. The blue and orange flames of the jet engines erupted and the first jet soared into the air closely followed by the second and the third. Durant looked back at the hangar as they taxied onto the runway. The helmet giving him a steady flow of oxygen limited his vision.

'Four Tornadoes' he thought 'and clean once again' he smiled as the force of the takeoff pinned him back into his seat.

94

Baber had never met the deputy director of MI5 other than at social functions. Claire Wilson was the youngest woman to have risen to her current grade in the secret service and many tipped her to take the top job in the next five years. She was thirty-eight, tall athletic and had worked her way through a number of tough consular assignments. These included stints in Kosho, Zaire and Northern Ireland. It was widely known that she had a thorough knowledge of ballistics that formed part of her major at MIT and post-grad at Harvard. It was also know that she despised tardiness and Baber had been a good fifteen minutes early for their meeting, despite his office being in the adjacent building. He had been sitting in one of the huge brown leather armchairs opposite her desk for five minutes before she looked up from the files on her desk and removed her gold rimmed glasses.

"In your own words, Mr.Baber, perhaps you would like to summarise the operation of two nights ago"

Baber straightened slightly in his chair and in a flat tone said.

"Operation 129A was completed successfully. Four RAF Tornado aircraft, known to be sought by the Langusto arms syndicate were stolen from the Charolotte airfield at shortly after 2am and are currently thought to be en route to Qatar"

"Currently thought?" Wilson raised an eyebrow.

"I take it from your choice of words and the lack of contrary information in my files that you don't have a fix on the aircraft at the present time?"

"No Ma'am" Baber answered and had he been able to show any emotion he would have been grimacing.

"Well" she paused "Let me give you the feedback I received from the Home Secretary this morning" Wilson stood up clutching a large file and started walking around the room.

"Twenty four men admitted to hospital with severe smoke burns, five of whom are still in there. Two concussions and, as you are probably aware, one young Frenchman with gunshot wounds. The vest he was wearing saved his life but looks unlikely to have saved his right arm.

Baber stayed silent. He had heard about the wounded man immediately after the raid. Colonel Letract had ensured Baber watched as they loaded him into the field ambulance. His Kelvar vest had done its job with the first bullet but the second had hit him in the shoulder. Baber had felt numb as they had carried the young man on a stretcher. He wouldn't have gone through with the operation if it hadn't been for Durant. It was so out of character for Durant's men to use their weapons. Stun guns were the traditional tools he used and that was the reason Baber's team had engineered for the information on the whereabouts of the planes to be leaked to Durant's right hand man in Milan.

'Maybe he had difficulty getting a team together at short notice' Baber reflected.

"And you view this as successful?"

Wilson snapped. Baber took this as a rhetorical question and was relieved when she continued.

"Thirty million pounds worth of aircraft and you are gambling this on this Jones gentlemen? I've read the file Mr.Baber and I'm rather surprised you got this through." Baber winced. He'd cut a few corners, no wait, a lot of corners, and pulled in all his outstanding favours to make this happen.

"The question is can you trust this man to follow through?"

She had both her hands face down on the desk and was staring right into Baber's eyes.

"I'd stake my reputation on it" he replied in a confident tone.

"Oh, don't worry Mr.Baber" she smiled.

"You already have"

95

Max was having trouble sleeping. Being shot at by Cuban thugs had that effect on him. He was safely back in his suite at the Grande. Cass had assured him that as it was the Langustos' territory, Martinez's men would stay well clear. He wasn't sure but he was beginning to get the feeling that he would have great difficulty not paying attention to her. His mind was just starting to drift to thoughts of her three floors beneath him when his PDA began beeping in the living room.

He swung his legs over the side of the bed and reached for his robe. He fastened it around his waist and sat down on the sofa. He reached into his open briefcase and flipped open the PDA.

B: Max?

M: Hi. Do you realise that it's 3am here?

B: Sorry. We have a situation.

M: Where's Easton?

B: Easton's not on the call. It's a little delicate.

M: Hold on. Easton's running this little show?

B: Technically, yes.

M: Technically?

B: Technically. This doesn't concern him.

M: Well it concerns me. What's going on?

B: We've lost the Tornadoes.

M: Wasn't that the general idea?

B: No, I mean we really lost them. We were all set to track them across Europe but we lost them somewhere over Finland.

Max looked at the screen and began typing a reply. He stopped and held down the delete key. This was not good, definitely not good.

B: Max?

M: Yeah I'm here. If anything surfaces this end I'll let you know.

He clicked the enter button. He had a really bad feeling about this.

96

Cass's hair was still wet from the shower when the phone rang. She instinctively drew her pistol from its holster lying on the bed and stood with her back to the wall before lifting the receiver. It was one of the first things they had been taught - if you want to attack someone, get someone to phone them. As well as distracting it also telegraphs where they are in the room (unless they have a cordless) and means at least one of their hands is occupied.

"Si?" she answered.

"Ah Bueno" said the hoarse voice on the other end.

"Itsa Uncle Guiseppe. How's about that breakfast?"

Cass grinned at Max's awful accent.

"Si. Fifteen minutes" she replied. He was early, but nothing this big man did surprised her. She dressed in a plain white blouse and slacks and sprayed some L'eau Dissey perfume on her neck. She realised she was standing in front of the mirror fiddling with her hair and she shook her head for a moment regretting having cut those long brown locks.

97

"Hey its 'Our Man in Havana" Max tried to sound enthusiastic. In the first two weeks he had met with Tremiere twice and talked with him on the phone a dozen times with little result.

"What you got for me?" he asked.

"We think we've found the last place he stayed in Havana"

He certainly had Max's attention.

"Where" Max asked.

"It's a flea pit of a hotel downtown. We're pretty sure it was him. The manager of the hotel gave us a good description.

"How on earth did you find it?" Max was curious.

"To be honest" Tremiere sounded a little embarrassed.

"A little bit of luck. One of our contacts picked up a small time pickpocket using one of Pete's credit cards. He had claimed he found it in the trash so we did a door to door check of the hotels in the area"

Max didn't particularly like Tremiere but was thankful for the lead.

"Hey Tremiere, thanks"

"No Problem Mr.Jones"

Max put the phone down and wondered whether he should tell Cass. He had about two hours before he was due at the Langustos for dinner.

'I'll just take a little look' he thought and put on his jacket.

98

The taxi was a Lada and Max had found it about two streets down from the hotel. He doubted the Langustos were having him followed, but it never hurt to be sure. He was right though. The manager of the Grande was keeping Allesandro up to date with his comings and goings but the Langusto family had too much going on domestically to waste the manpower. Despite Luco's cousin's influence in the Police Force, there was a marked increase in the police activity in Havana. Income from their loan-sharking operations was down 30% and Allesandro knew that the other families were being hit too. The focus on drugs was hitting Martinez hard, followed by prostitution, which hit everybody. Max hadn't seen evidence of either, not that he had been paying much attention.

The taxi pulled in front of a grey building that was identical to the dozen or so others on that street. Max handed the driver a five-dollar bill and stepped out. The words 'Hotel' and 'Vacancy' were barely readable from the sidewalk they were so small. 'So much for Marketing' Max smiled.

The six crumbling steps led to a heavy set panelled door with two long panes of glass. Both were cracked and dirty and Max closed the door behind him carefully. The "reception" was a small hatch in the wall and what Max assumed was the manager sat glued to a small black and white portable TV on the back counter. He had his face pointed away from Max and every couple of seconds emitted a small chuckle. There was an episode of the Three Stooges that had been dubbed in Spanish, badly. Max rang the little bell and the man turned his head slightly so he could see Max out of the corner of his eye.

"Yes?" the man said as if getting an answer was the last thing on his mind. Max held up a twenty dollar bill and that seemed to be enough to get his interest. Max reached into his breast pocket and retrieved a fifty. At this the man got up from his seat and came to the counter.

"Ok, Ok. What kind of girl do you want? I can get big, little, black, white, Asian. You like fat? I got fat womens too" the little man grinned. Max wondered if this little man who was all of five feet tall would be suspicious if he didn't play along.

"I like BIG women" Max laughed.

"and give me room eight". Before the man could answer he added "My lucky number" and laughed. The little man grinned and took both of the bills.

"One hour" he said in an excited tone.

"Okey dokey?" he added.

"Okey dokey" said Max and took the key.

There was no lift and Max noticed that the door to the fire escape on the second floor had a padlock on it. The corridor was dim due to only one of the light fittings being on. It was an overstatement to call it a fitting - 'wire with a bulb' would be more accurate.

The lock on the door of room 8 was set very low in the frame and Max had to bend to get to it. He saw that it was the fifth location of the lock and guessed that there was more plastic wood than real wood left in the door. The room itself was sparse and had a dreary layout with a bed, a small wardrobe without a door and a chest of drawers with two missing drawers – a chest of drawer in fact. The curtains were a nasty bottle green but still competed for the most pleasant feature of the room, closely followed by a cigarette stained coffee table. Max closed the door and began to search the room. It didn't take long and he was beginning to think that he had wasted his time when he got to the waste-bin. It was almost empty but had a few scraps of paper in the bottom. Max carefully took them out and unfolded them onto the table. He recognised Pete's handwriting straight away and felt a pang of excitement. There were two pieces of what appeared to be a list of notes. Max laid them together and grabbed a pen and pad from his jacket and copied over the words.

MARTINEZ

DRUGS FUNDS ARMS

HAVANA – COLUMBIA

VARADERO

BACARDI?

Max looked at the page in the notebook.

'Bloody shorthand' he thought and wondered what Pete meant.

At that moment the door opened and Max leapt to his feet.

'Ola senor' said the woman that filled the doorway, literally. Max was a little stunned. Whilst the woman was pretty short, that was the only dimension in which she was lacking. She was wearing a skin-tight dress and Max guessed that she would qualify as having a circumference. As she stepped into the room her huge bosom bounced wildly and Max was reminded of the bouncy castle his brother had hired for his nephew's fifth birthday party last summer. She shut the door with her bottom and it shook heavily – the door not the bottom. Well, actually, the bottom as well.

"You like?" she asked as she gave Max a Meringue shake. For the first time in years Max was speechless. He immediately thought of the padlock on the fire escape door and took half a step backward and glanced out of the window. The roof of the adjoining building was about ten feet away and fifteen feet down. He shuffled over to the other side of the room and the woman grinned.

"Shy boy, shy boy" she laughed and retrieved the door key Max had left on top of the chest of drawer and locked the door. Max raised his hand in protest and she laughed again. He stepped forward and reached for the key but she quickly slipped it into her large cleavage, wagged a large stubby finger at him and shook her head. Max looked at her arms and calculated that although there was enough flesh on them for a dozen supermodels, he didn't rate his chances against them.

He raised his palms in submission and pointed to the bed. The woman giggled and rolled onto the bed and hitched up her dress. Max seized his chance as her bulk was obscuring her view, but he knew he only had a few seconds. He grabbed the window and slid it up and was straight out onto the ledge. He looked at the roof below which now seemed miles away, and he hesitated.

"Senor?" the woman called from the bed. A mental picture of his head being crushed in between those huge thighs was enough to inspire him and Max leapt across the gap and the dark street below.

He landed in a heap on the roof and rolled to a stop. He felt his right shoulder where the wound screamed out at him. He reached down and immediately realised he had ripped a few of the stitches and blood was seeping out onto his cream shirt.

"Damn" he said under his breath and struggled to his feet.

99

An empty Tornado weighs 14,500kg, which generally means they aren't the easiest things to move around. The simplest way to transport them is to fly them to their destination, but that option is also fraught with problems. You need a good pilot, no scratch that, you need a bloody good pilot. Why? Apart from the fact that this is a pretty powerful piece of aeronautical engineering, it's also stolen which means that you need to be able to fly it below conventional airspace or it will inevitably get caught on radar. And what don't you want to do if you are dealing in stolen fighter planes? To get caught on radar. Colonel Riley was just that type of pilot. He was just about old enough to have seen action in the Gulf War and until two years ago he would have gladly given his life for his country. The thought of flying along a few hundred feet off the ground heading for an abandoned airstrip in Northern Qatar in a stolen plane would have disgusted him. Charles Riley was a patriot through and through but he had one little problem. Well, about two hundred and fifty thousand little problems to be precise. His weakness for Tequila and gambling combined had left him in debt to a loan shark in Philadelphia and he was pretty desperate. His wife had cleaned him out after she found him having sex on their sofa with their son's primary school teacher. Well, she was cute. She had taken the house and their savings and he was just left with his Mustang. Not that that wasn't enough of get him a string of women in the six months since they separated. He was having a second youth and was determined to enjoy it. Its just that he enjoyed it too much and the day he found himself on the floor of his apartment with a broken nose lying in a pool of his own vomit after a visit from his creditors he knew he had to find a fast way out. As he brought the Tornado around and lined up with the dusty runway he told himself that he only had a few more trips to do and he would be free.

100

Cass opened her hotel room door cautiously with her pistol at her side. She relaxed when she saw that Max was alone and ushered him in.

"You're early again," she said as she walked back across her room towards the bathroom.

"I'll be a little while yet," she added as she leaned over for her hairdryer. She was wearing a thick hotel dressing gown and her long dark legs were glistening. Max saw her black dress hanging on the wardrobe door on a hanger and let out a quiet whistle. He could picture what she would look like in it. He forced himself back to the present.

"Hey Cass. We have a few problems," he said loudly and she stopped drying and came out of the bathroom.

"What was that?" she said.
Max sat down in one of the armchairs and Cass sat in the other.

"You know these arms that I'm supposed to be buying from the Langustos?"

"Yes" she said and began combing her hair

"You know I said that it was, err, quite a large shipment?"

"Come on Max,you know you don't have to tell me the details" she laughed.
"you know I would have to report it back and your government wouldn't be too keen on that"

Max nodded.

"I know. But I need your help and you can't do that unless you know more"

Cass put the comb down.

"Okay, but you know the rules"

Max nodded again. He told her about the Tornadoes and how they had lost them. He had her full attention and when he finished her eyes were wide and she sat back in her seat.

"Shit." She said. "I bet MI5 are pissed"

"Understatement" Max said

"So what can we do?" she asked.

"We need to find out where the planes are being stored"

"Oh, just that" she laughed. "And has the wonderful London got any ideas how the hell you are supposed to do that?"

"I've been told to get the information to them by Friday. Three days. I figured I would try and get it in casual conversation with Luco on the golf course tomorrow"

"Sure he's really going to let that slip," she said with a heavy dose of sarcasm. "Don't kid yourself Max. These guys don't mess about. I still can't believe you guys lost the planes. We'd never do that"

"Ah, but would you have done it in the first place?" Max snapped. He didn't know why he was being so defensive.

"Probably not" she conceded.

"We'll just have to get the information tonight. I've got the blueprints of the house and we can narrow it down to one of their studies"

"One of?" Max asked.

"Yes. Luco and Allesandro both have their own studies on separate sides of the house".

"Two studies, two of us, no problem" Max laughed.

Cass gave him a mock sneer and got up to go to the bathroom. She stopped and turned back.

"What was the other problem?" she asked.

"You got a needle and thread?"

Cass put her hands on her hips and grinned.

"Why, you lost a button?"

"Err, not exactly" Max grimaced as he took of his jacket and revealed his blood stained shirt.

"How on earth did you do that?" Cass exclaimed and helped Max remove his shirt.

"Oh, it's an old war wound" he said as Cass reached into one of the drawers and took out a fresh towel.

"And this?" she asked pointing to the heavy bruising around his shoulder and side.

"Fell out of a window" Max smiled and winced as Cass splashed some Iodine from a brown bottle she had taken from her vanity case.

"Ouch, that stings" Max said.

"Good" she snapped.

He could sense she was annoyed that he had gone off by himself.

"I hope it was worth it," she said as she finished cleaning the wound.

"Not really" he replied and he retrieved the notepad and passed it to her.

"It's from Pete's hotel room" he explained. She looked at the words.

"Drugs funds arms" she read.

"That figures. We always had Martinez down as a player. The Langustos stay away from drugs, they leave that to Martinez. The connection with Columbia is interesting. I'll run that one back to Tel Aviv and see what comes up".

"What do you think he means by Varadero and Bacardi?" Max asked.

"Maybe it's a name of a hotel in Varadero" she suggested.

"Nope. Tried that. Our boys are working on it though" he said and tried to look hopeful.

101

He was pushed roughly into the chair and he felt the rope burns into his wrists as his hands were lashed to the arms of the chair. He tried again to open his eyes but the light was still too bright and pointed straight at his face.

"Who are you?"

"Who do you work for?"

The same questions over and over punctuated only by a punch in the ribs or a slap around the face. His answers were mumbled for his jaw was swollen and his lips cracked in a number of places. He could taste blood again and found he couldn't swallow.

"Water?" he asked quietly.

"Agua?" laughed the burly man behind the light.

"But of course Senor" and a glass of cold water was held up to Pete's mouth. He guzzled at the cold liquid but almost immediately spluttered and shook violently. The chair toppled and his head hit the floor with a thud. Salt and lemon juice. 'Bastards' he thought as they left him lying on the floor. He had told them the truth on the second day but they had not believed him. Their paranoia combined with the fact that all Pete's identification had been made to look like he was a research assistant for a horticultural institute made for a difficult to credit story. Most of the questioning centred on the Cuban authorities that of course Pete knew relatively little about. Two men grabbed the chair and set it straight again.

"Now" said the same voice.

"Let's try that again".

102

Cass and Max walked out of the front doors of the Grande arm in arm and were greeted by the black shiny Cadillac and the two henchmen Max had spent the day with at the military facility.

'Hello again boys' Cass thought. As she got into the back seat. She wondered if they had found the tracking device she had used and sat back in the leather seat and smiled.

Oh they had found it all right. Or rather, the head of security at the house had found it. It had set off one of the sensors when they had taken it into the garage that had been converted into a carwash. They had both been penalised a month's wages and security at the house had been stepped up.

The route out to the Langustos was very beautiful at night. The lights of Havana drifted away in the background with the dark hills and the infrequent lights of the houses dotted by the roadside. The two in the front didn't say a word and Max was uptight. He wanted to talk to Cass and could feel her arm linked into his but apart from a few smiles the trip passed by without incident.

The house was more impressive than Cass had imagined. The plans didn't do it justice. Four towers, one at each corner with a central pointed roof with a smooth white dome. They passed through the gates and Cass felt uneasy and somehow naked without her guns. Max got out and opened the door for her and she stepped out, the gravel crunching under her heels. Luco Langusto was standing at the top of the steps and extended a hand and friendly grin.

"János" he beamed.

"And?"

"Oh, this is Katherine Derrick" Max smiled and held Cass's hand as she walked up the steps.

"Charmed" said Luco and lightly kissed her outstretched hand.

"You old dog" Luco whispered into Max's ear.

"Where did you find her?" he asked.

"Wife of a Venezuelan oil baron" Max grinned.

"Met her in a bar. Husband is hopping around the islands on business apparently". He nudged Luco on the arm as Cass stopped at the entrance to the Veranda.

"Katherine, this is Allesandro and Emilio" Max introduced her to the two men who had risen as she approached. She put on her best smile but she struggled to hide her disgust. She knew Allesandro Langusto. She had seen his work first hand in Tel Aviv, in Penang, in Hong Kong.

'Oh how I wish I had my Sig now you oily little bastard' she thought.

She realised she was pausing a little too long with her greeting and took a step towards the bar.

Allesandro stepped forward and offered a drink and Max and Cass perched on the tall bamboo bar stools and surveyed the long mirrored bar.

"Mai Tai" Cass purred and stroked Max's arm.

"Oburn single malt if you have it" Max added.

The barman mixed Cass's drink and as he was pouring it into a large glass with some fresh mint she noticed something odd behind the bar. She didn't have long to dwell on it though as Luco asked her a question.

321

"So Katherine, what brings you to Havana?"

She picked up her drink and as they walked across to one of the tables she replied.

"Oh, some tedious business" she said demurely.

"But I'm succeeding in finding things to keep me amused" she smiled and threw a glance at Max. Luco grinned and looked at Max.

'You lucky bastard' he thought.

103

Dinner was a lavish affair of six courses and contrary to everything Max had heard and experienced of Cuba's limited cuisine. It was 95% imported of course. The Langustos spent a small fortune on food. Allesandro's wife Maria had trained as a restaurant manager and their chef was one of the best in Havana. They had closed the restaurant for the evening and half of the staff were up at the house.

The meal finished and Maria, a striking dark-skinned woman five years younger than her husband, offered to take Cass on a tour of the house while the men headed for the billiard room for brandy and cigars. Max hadn't smoked for about fifteen years and the taste of the world's finest cigars was nothing short of heaven.

"So, how progresses my purchase?" Max asked.

"Manjana János. It is all in hand. We are in fact ahead of schedule. The merchandise will be in Qatar by Sunday" Luco replied.

Max tried not to show his panic.

"Sunday?" he asked. "I will call Klaus and move everything forward to Monday".

Luco and Allesandro exchanged satisfied looks.

That left Max just four days to find Pete. He would lose tomorrow afternoon playing golf with Luco, which meant three days.

104

"And this is the eastern tower" Maria used a sweeping arm motion as she led Cass into the base of the tower. Identical to the other three except this time they climbed the stairs to the second floor.

"János tells me you have a wonderful library," Cass said as they reached the landing. She had done her homework and Maria's eyes lit up at the mention of her great passion. She collected classic novels and over the years her hobby had cost Allesandro a lot of money. Even with his income and lavish tastes he had balked when she had spent £20,000 on a Dickens first edition at Sotheby's.

The library doubled as Allesandro's office and Cass pretended to be looking the other way as Maria keyed in the security code by the door. 342632. His wife's measurements at a guess. The office was decadently done out in walnut. No veneer here. The desk was the size of a table tennis table and three of the four walls were covered from floor to ceiling with books. The bay window overlooked the canyon and the veranda and in the middle of the bay stood a magnificent wooden globe.

"This is a complete set of the works of Beatrix Potter" Maria lifted the delicate works from the shelf onto the desk. Cass kept smiling and giving words of encouragement. "Beautiful", "Magical", "Stunning". Maria was in her element and Cass had about twenty minutes to case the room. The desk had huge drawers that weren't locked. Maria had slid one of them open to get a pen to note down a few of Cass's suggestions for additions to her collection.

105

When they rejoined the men they were playing poker in the lounge. There was a bottle of Courvoisier on the table, which was nearly empty, and Cass wondered if that was the same one that was full just two hours before. It was just five of them left now and Max was looking very worse for wear.

"Ah Katherine, you've come to save me from these scoundrels" Max grinned.

"I hardly think you are in a position to call these darling gentlemen scoundrels" she twinkled.

"You however, will go severely down in my estimations if you don't get me back to my hotel".

Marco shook his head and tutted.

"Bad Kovács" he laughed and Max grinned.

"I have my orders gentlemen" he got up and headed towards the door with Cass on his arm.

"I'll see you at the club at two" he shouted over his shoulder and Luco waved a hand.

"Si, Si. Two o'clock" he called back.

106

The same car and men took them back to the Grande and Max wondered whether they had been standing outside waiting the whole time. The journey back was just as quiet. Cass's mind was racing. She was sure there was something in that office that would incriminate the Langustos. Max was asleep. Scotch, wine brandy and the heat once they had left the air-conditioning of the house had knocked him out. He awoke as they came to a stop in front of the hotel.

The manager winked at Max as they walked across the lobby and got into the lift. As the doors closed Max whispered.
"Nice act"
"My life is an act" Cass forced a smile and steadied Max as he stumbled.

They reached the 21st floor and Max fiddled with the key to his room.
"Why don't you stay?" he asked, surprising himself with his boldness.
"Okay" she said simply and walked over to the wardrobe and retrieved one of Max's large T-shirts. Her dress slid off her shoulders and she slipped off her bra and clutching the T-shirt went into the bedroom. She smiled as she saw that Max was face down on the bed snoring quietly. She looked at him sprawled on the bed and warned herself that this wasn't a good idea. She managed, with some difficulty to get Max's clothes off and under the sheets. She put her arms around his big frame. Murmurs of contentment came from Max's side of the bed. Cass had lived on her nerves for several years and she

realised that here, now, with this sleeping drunken Englishman she felt calm. For the first time in years Cassandra Yillette slept through the night.

107

Max wasn't sure where he was but he was sure he hadn't invited the family of kangaroos that had taken up residence inside his skull. They seemed to be having a party in there. He counted his limbs and found he had three arms. Closer examination revealed that the third was not his, and came with a head of black hair which was resting on his stomach. His head was really pounding. He tried to move his arm a little and the head of hair became a flash and he found himself with the barrel of a pistol shoved up his nose.

"Oh Max,I'm sorry" Cass said as she hastily removed the gun and placed it on the nightstand.

"Good morning to you too" Max said trying to lighten the mood.

"I guess I'm used to sleeping alone" she said sheepishly. Max had no idea how Cass had ended up in his bed, but he was extremely happy about it nonetheless.

"I'll order some breakfast" she smiled and headed for the lounge. Max gingerly rose and sat on the side of the bed. He looked down and saw that he had a pair of South Park boxer shorts on. They must have been in the pocket of his suitcase and the maid must have unpacked them when he arrived. His brother had given them to him for his birthday. The cartoon face of Cartman was looking up at him telling him to "Respect My Authoritah" in large yellow letters.

"Oh by the way" Cass shouted from the shower.

"Nice Pants!"

108

Durant knew why he was anxious. He had five million reasons to be precise. That was his share after the team had been paid. He would retire on this one. He had said that before, but his decision had been made for him after the debrief and Mantz's admission that he had popped one of the soldiers. He would be way up the wanted list by now. That stupid pig. Ten years and no casualties and he has to go and shoot someone. The Cubans had confirmed the exchange would take place on Monday and by Tuesday morning he would be the new owner of a little town nobody had heard of on the Northern coast of Brazil.

109

Max mixed two sachets of Resolve into his orange juice and used it to wash down a couple more Ibuprofen. Cass was already halfway through her eggs and was reading the front page of the Havana Times.

"I got a fantastic look around Allesandro's office last night"

"You did?" Max replied glad that the awkward silence had been broken.

"Yeah. I'll try and get back in there when we go back for dinner again in a couple of days. I must admit I'm looking forward to the golf tomorrow".

"You joining us?" Max asked surprised.

"Thought I might" Cass smiled. "Played a little when I was at university".

"Is there nothing that the lady cannot do" Max smiled and braved a mouthful of egg.

"Drink quite as heavily as you?" she grinned.

"Cheap shot" he said and pretended to sulk.

"Did you notice something at the bar last night?"

Cass asked.

"The twenty different types of Scotch?"

"No. There was a bank of bottles with their labels removed. Clear spirit, vodka or something"

"That's weird" Max agreed. "Wouldn't have thought they were into home brew"

"No they had branded bottle tops"

"What brand?"

"Don't know. It was some kind of a crest"

Max grabbed a pen and a sheet of hotel notepaper. Cass drew the crest and handed it to Max.

"Used to be a barman me" he added a few more lines.

"BACARDI" he wrote below the crest.

Cass jumped up and shouted as she reached the door.

"Back in a minute".

When she got back from her room she had a set of briefing notes which weren't a lot of use to Max as they were in Israeli.

"I knew I had seen that somewhere before" she said.

"I'm annoyed I didn't pick up on it in Pete's notes. The Martinez family runs part of the small island of Bacardi not far from the Dominican Republic. The rivalry between the two families is such that all references to the Martinez family are banned"

"You're telling me that it goes as far as taking the labels off bottles of rum?" Max asked.

"Oh yes. Bacardi Island is a big part of the Martinez's history".

Max stood up.

"We've got to get out to that island," he said.

110

By the time Cass and Max drove the two hours out to Varadero and the golf course their itinerary for Friday was set. They had chartered a plane from Havana to Puerto Plata on the Northern Coast of the Dominican Republic. From there a hire car to the town of Cabarete where daily tourist trips went out to the Southern bay of Bacardi Island. They turned off the main road and Max looked at the mansion on the coast ahead of them. Max could see at least five holes with water and made a mental note to get a lot of spare balls. They got their clubs and headed to the first tee where Luco and his caddy were waiting. Luco looked genuinely surprised to see Cass and he smiled.

"I see we have an audience" he laughed and tapped Max on the shoulder.

"No sir" Cass replied in a syrupy voice.

"You have some competition" she raised an eyebrow and reached in the cart and retrieved a three wood. Luco grinned but looked confused. As she walked to the tee she whispered to Luco.

"I have to do something with my days, and I can't abide tennis or horse-riding. I find them both so unladylike".

Luco and Max both stared as Cass smashed her ball down the middle of the fairway. Luco gave her a 'lucky hit' look and Max shrugged his shoulders.

111

Eighteen holes later and they headed back to the clubhouse following behind Luco's cart. Max had got through half a dozen balls – one straight into the ocean on the tenth hole. Luco had lost just three. Cass, however had her original ball in her bag and had taken them by eight shots. Max had been three shots off Luco's score. It would have been much more but for a couple of lucky chips which had rattled into the hole.

"You didn't need to beat him so badly" Max said quietly.

"I know" said Cass "but I enjoyed making him squirm," she said through her teeth.

Luco had come with a stretch Mercedes and Max and Cass made a quick call to the hire car company who agreed for their car to be left at the golf club. It was an interesting ride back to Havana with Luco explaining in detail his family's sugar beet empire for Cass's benefit. He in turn listened to her stories of her husband's oil business and Max decided that either the person who had put together Cass's cover had done an excellent job or she was very, very thorough. Possibly both.

112

They had dinner at the Langustos restaurant and Max wore a sharp dark blue suit with Cass in an ankle length red dress. Max found it difficult to take his eyes off her the whole evening. Once again at the end of the meal the ladies separated off and the men sat in the corner.

"I have another interested party" Max said to Allesandro as he lit his cigar. "although not on the same scale of course" he added.

"Okay" Luco replied. "What's the shopping list?"

"Missiles" Max said.

"Missiles?" said Allesandro.

Max removed the cigar from his mouth and gestured with it.

"That a problem?" he asked.

"No" said Luco quickly "Just a little unusual".

"Unusual is my game" Max smiled.

"Fine. What sort?" he asked firing up his laptop.

"Cruise, anything in that arena"

"How many?"

"Around a hundred"

'At around a $100,000 a piece that's a cool $10m' Allesandro thought.

"Which types were you particularly interested in?"

'Oh Shit' Max thought, 'he's testing me'

"Well, I need to get some SAM surface to air missiles and I would normally go for something like SA11 Gadfly – its got a range of just over 30km and you can get 4 of them on the loader"

"Nice" replied Allessandro. "And how about air-to–surface?"

"AS-18s."

"Oh yes. That's 500kg each".

'Max smiled. He knew what he was trying'

"Well, the warhead is about 320kg but the whole thing weighs around 960kg"

Allesandro smiled. He couldn't resist testing people.

"And for Anti-tank I favour the AT-9s" Max added.

Allessandro grinned and tapped the keyboard.

"So you sure we can't tempt you with something to launch them off?" He turned the laptop around.

Name	Ka-50 Hokum
Type	Attack helicopter
Year	1982
Engine	2 x TV3-117VMA turboshaft, 2x2200hp.
Wingspan	7.34 m
Length	15.6 m (rotors turning)
Height	4.9 m
Rotor	4.9 m
Weight	9800 kg/10800 kg
Max. speed	350 km/h
Op. Range	450 km
Ferry Range	1100 km
Crew	1
Armament	1 x 30 mm gun 2A42 (500 rds),
	12 x Antitank missiles AT-9,
	80 x 80mm or 20 x 122mm Rockets
	AS-10 Anti-radar missiles,
	UPK-23-250 Gun pod,
	GUV-8700 Machine-gun pod

Max smiled.

"No thanks. There's plenty of them knocking around"

Allesandro turned the laptop back and found the full list.

"These are your alternatives".

Easton had taken Max through all the different types of missile that the US authorities were interested in. Max saw all of them on the list.

He made a mental note of each with the stocks.

"I'll confirm on Monday" Max said and turned the screen back.

"I think we'll have a deal" he smiled.

113

Max left Cass in her room while he hooked up his PDA to transfer. He opened the dialogue with the missile list and Baber was the first to join two minutes later. Max had wondered why they used the PDAs but Baber had explained that this way their transmissions were encoded and that mobile phones were still too easy to hack into.

B. Nice list Max! Any news on your friend?

M. Have a strong lead but nothing yet. Any luck with those planes?

B. Zero. I gather you got nothing from the Langustos.

M. Not yet. We'll be there Saturday and will try again.

B. What do you mean "we"?

Max cursed himself for the slip.

M. The royal 'we'. They're treating me like royalty.

B. Don't get too excited. If I was spending $50m I'd get treated like The Queen as well.

E. Good evening gentlemen. I'm afraid I have some bad news.

B. What?

E. This operation is officially over. Effective immediately.

B. On whose authority?

E. Don't know. All I know is it's a lot higher than me.

M. Bullshit. You can't just pull the plug.

E. It's over Max.

M. Like hell it is.

B. Max if E says it's over then its over. I'll have Tremiere arrange a flight for you tomorrow.

M. I'm not going anywhere.

B. Don't do this Max. We can't help you out there.

Max typed the words 'Then SCREW YOU' but thought better of it.

M. I'll sort out my own flight tomorrow.

Max flipped the cover over the PDA.

'Why did they have to lose those planes' he thought and threw the PDA hard onto the bed. It bounced off and cluttered into the headboard and split into a number of pieces, two of which fell onto the floor. Max sighed and grabbed the pieces and froze immediately as his eyes caught the word 'detonation'. He placed the three pieces carefully onto the table and ran out of the room.

114

"I'm very impressed," said Cass as she fiddled with the wires with a tiny pair of tweezers. She had a magnifying glass attachment over her right eye and was examining the back of the PDA.

"And its safe is it?" Max asked. There were beads of sweat on his forehead.

"Oh yeah. I've disconnected the power for the moment. Clever little thing. The right command and the timer starts running".

"Let me guess. The command can also be sent remotely?"

"Clever Boy" Cass said and ruffled Max's hair.

"And which side would I be on?" he fumed.

"Max" Cass said solemnly. "Sides don't matter, everyone takes out insurance"

"Remind me to beat the crap out of Baber when I see him next"

"He might not have known. This is a very tidy piece of work. You're rather fortunate you didn't remove the floor of this hotel when you threw this".

Max shuddered. He didn't feel all that lucky.

"I think I can reprogram it to only take a local command"

"Oh Goody" Max said. "Why don't you just trash it?"

"Two good reasons. First, they will get very suspicious if you suddenly go offline and second, it might come in useful."

115

"Macedonia!" Baber's voice was verging on the pleading.

"James, I don't have a lot of choice here. It was that or the Ukraine"

Steve Parkes was Baber's boss and a fairly new breed as MI5 goes. He had been amazed when the Americans canned the operation, but MI5 were the ones that had lost the planes so weren't in too strong a position to argue. Wilson had asked for Baber to be assigned 'As far away as bloody possible'

"You're lucky you're not being suspended" Parkes said sternly.

"You know that's not right" Baber argued.

"You leave on Wednesday. Be ready. I need a full write up on this farce Monday morning"

"Yes sir" replied Baber and headed out of the door.

Parkes didn't say anything to Baber but he wasn't too comfortable with this. He had sensed Wilson wasn't either. Something stank.

116

Puerto Plata was a fair sized airport with a main runway right on top of the sea. The flight from Havana was quick but uncomfortable. Max hated small planes. It had been twenty years since he'd been in a Cessna and had jumped out of that one. To be fair he had thoroughly enjoyed the parachute jump and gone straight back up for another. This wasn't quite Swansea airfield.

The rental 4x4 was waiting for them and as soon as they left the main part of the town Cass double-checked the rear-view mirror.
"We've got a tail," she said calmly.
"Don't turn around" she said quickly as Max went to turn his head.
"We need to lose them before we get to Cabarete" Max said.
"No chance" replied Cass.
"Its one road. We will have to lose them in the town itself"
Max guessed it was Langusto's men and he was sort of correct. The first tail in the black jeep was two of Allesandro's men but the blue car had four of Martinez's men. They had been placed at Havana airport to keep an eye out for Cass and couldn't believe their luck.

Cabarete was not a large town. It consisted of a mile-long beach, a market of sorts and a few dozen interwoven streets lined with stalls selling knock-offs and cheap cigars. Max knew from the Lonely Planet guide that almost everything peddled through these very similar stalls was fake – even the cigars. You got what you paid for, if you wanted a Rolex for $50 what do you

341

expect. Most of the merchandise was mass produced in the capital Santa Domingo and shipped out to the resort towns.

They parked the jeep and joined the throng of tourists jostling through the streets. For about an hour they moved around and until Max put a hand on Cass's shoulder.

"Hey, I'm frying here!" He was really struggling in the 40-degree heat. They ducked into a small bar and hid in a booth at the back.

"This is no good" Cass smiled "But I have an idea". She told Max to stay where he was. And went to the next table and said hello to two backpackers. They were a young couple and after a few questions Cass found out they were French.

Max wondered what she was doing but didn't have to wait long to find out.

"Max this is Francois and Yvette" Cass introduced them.

"They are going to do us a little favour" Cass smiled.

Martinez's men had split into pairs and it was the two by the beach that saw Max and Cass come out of the café. They quickly called the other two on the cell-phone.

Langusto's men were back in their jeep watching the other jeep. They had figured that Max had to come back to it eventually and sure enough, they were just coming round the corner.

"Marco. Do you see those four men getting into that blue car?"

"Yeah" he said uninterested.

"One if them I recognise. It's Manny Rodriguez"

"Shit" exclaimed Marco and looked closely.

"Martinez's hitman. You'd better get on the phone and get some help"

Marco slammed the jeep into gear and sped after the blue car.

"We don't have anyone over here" Marco said solemnly.

"You're right. Let's just follow. Probably nothing will happen" he added but didn't believe a word.

The blue car was closing in on the jeep, which was gaining speed. The road was running close to the ocean and as they emerged from the trees the jeep swerved off the road onto the beach.

"Damn" the driver of the blue car hit the brakes and the car slid in the sand. Ten seconds later the other jeep with Marco sped past the car and along the beach. Ahead of them Max's jeep had appeared to have stopped. As they got closer they could see the jeep had been abandoned and the occupants were a couple of hundred yards into the sea – even from that distance Marco knew it wasn't Kovács.

117

Max and Cass stepped off the small boat and onto the beach on Bacardi Island.

"I hope those two youngsters are ok" Cass said feeling a little guilty at putting them in danger.

"I just wish you'd have picked someone a little bigger" Max replied. Cass stopped for a moment and couldn't help laughing. The only thing that had fitted was the bamboo strip hat. The shirt left part of Max's stomach exposed – white and pasty – and the shorts were tight and he hadn't been able to get all the buttons done up.

"Oh hah hah" he said and walked awkwardly to the bar on the edge of the beach.

"As soon as the guide has finished his introduction and they all head off to the scuba diving we can get round to the other side of the island" Cass replied.

118

Allesandro Langusto smiled to himself.

'Sixty million dollars in sales, and I haven't had to kill anybody yet'

He was putting the final touches to the small arms shipments. He had needed to borrow from one of his consignments to Namibia and although that had cost him over the odds the last of the guns would be with his agent that afternoon.

The phone rang and he grabbed it.

"Yes?"

It was Marco.

"What do you mean Rodriguez was in Cabarete?"

Marco was at a phone back at Puerto Plata airport.

"Just like I said, Rodriguez and three goons" Marco repeated.

"Stay put" Allesandro said and slammed the phone down. His mind was racing.

Martinez was trying to screw up his deal.

'This time he had gone too far' he thought.

119

The Martinez villa was smaller than Max had expected, but he reflected that every brick would have been carried from the beach and taking that into consideration it was pretty impressive. It looked deserted but Cass wasn't taking any chances. They spent an hour and a half slowly edging around the perimeter which revealed three guards, four rooms and a wine cellar.

120

"I want a meeting" Luco said coolly. He glanced over at the rest of the family who had all gathered in the restaurant. Martinez was on the speakerphone so they could all hear.

"Want is a strong word". Martinez's voice was cocky and confident.

"Five o'clock at the central library"

"Just me and you Luco?"

"Just you and me". Luco clicked off the phone and under his breath.

"He could do with spending some time in there the little illiterate sonofabitch". Nobody laughed. It was well known that Luco despised Martinez all the more because he has built his empire through mindless violence and lack of finesse. Luco liked to think of himself as a gentleman criminal and cited Martinez's lack of a formal education as the reason why his methods were so primitive.

121

Max felt useless as he sat two hundred yards from the villa. Cass had reminded him that it was what she did, but he couldn't help feeling worried for her. The first guard was sitting on a tree stump reading a book when he got a blow to the head and toppled into the undergrowth. Cass slipped around the side of the veranda where the other two were playing cards. She tossed a small stone in through an open window and it clattered across the wooden floor. The two men dropped their cards and went to draw their pistols. That was all the time Cass needed. Neither of them saw what hit them. The first got Cass's fist into his temple and the other her foot in his face. The first went down like a sack of potatoes but the second stumbled clutching his shattered nose. Cass spun around and unleashed another kick to his midriff. This sent him back into a glass cabinet that smashed and fell forwards on top of him.

Max could hear the commotion and headed towards the villa. Cass came out onto the front steps and motioned for him to hurry up.

122

Allesandro and Luco rode in the back of a red Cadillac to the central library. The caddy had been 'modified' with armour plating and four inch glass windows.

"I don't like this" Allesandro said.

"Even he is not so stupid to try something here"

The central library was directly opposite the main police headquarters and the square outside was packed with police cars.

The library itself was a wonderful cream building rebuilt in the 1950s. Luco pushed through the glass doors and smiled at the librarian behind the counter removing his sunglasses and hat. He could see Martinez sitting at a large oak table in the middle of the fiction section. He had his arms folded and resting on a large hardback copy of 'Das Boat'. Martinez was a wiry figure who worked out incessantly and Luco noticed that he never seemed to age much. He knew he was thirty-eight but he had to admit that he looked good for his age. His hair was shaven short and his dark eyes never left Luco's as he came over to the table and sat down.

"It has been a long time"

"Eight years" Martinez agreed. Martinez had worked for Allesandro originally running operations in Old Havana. That was until he saw more money in going independent. Martinez's band of cousins along with his two brothers gradually took ground from the Langustos. He was purely a domestic operator, but dealt plenty of drugs from most of the South American countries. He had fewer connections than Luco but made up for it in ruthlessness. Even a cold killer like Allesandro was wary of the man.

"Let's cut to the chase" Luco said.

"I want you to back off my client. I have a lot riding on this - enough to risk a confrontation with you"

"Your client? And that would be?"

"You know damn well who" Luco snapped quietly.

"Indulge me" Martinez smiled.

"Okay. No bullshit. If you go anywhere near Kovács again I'm coming after you"

"Kovács? János Kovács?" Martinez let out a low long whistle. Although he only dallied at arms Martinez had heard of Kovács. Everyone had heard of Kovács.

"Come on Luco, I'm not that mad"

"Don't bullshit me. Rodriguez was on his ass yesterday"

"Rodriguez wasn't even in Havana yesterday" Martinez argued.

I know he was chasing down Kovács in the Dominican."

Martinez paused for a moment then grinned.

"I heard he had a weakness for the ladies but this is priceless"

"What?" said Luco.

"Rodriguez wasn't there for Kovács. He didn't even know who the guy was. He was there to ice that little Israeli bitch"

"Katherine Derrick?" Luco asked but he was beginning to get the picture.

"She's Mossad. Israeli intelligence. She's killed one of my best men already" Martinez scowled.

'Oh shit' thought Luco. 'How could János have been so stupid. Still, she fooled all of us'

He had to find Kovács and fast. Luco got up to leave and Martinez grabbed his arm.

"If you get to her first, promise me that she will suffer. It was my cousin that she killed" Luco removed his hand from his arm.

"Don't worry. She will take a *very* long time to die" he said and headed to the door.

123

It took all of five minutes to search the four rooms and they found nothing. They had to search two of the guards before they found the keys to the pantry and the wine cellar.

"Max" Cass shouted to him as he checked the pantry.

"There are boat keys on this set. You check the cellar and I'll find the boat"

"Oh and take these"

She tossed one of the guards' pistols and a torch and ran out onto the porch. Max unlocked the thick wooden door with a big iron key and it creaked open.

There were about twenty steps down and Max shone the torch into the darkness. He guessed the villa had been built on top of a rock and that they had used a natural cave as the basis for the cellar. It was slightly damp and Max took care not to slip on the steps as he made his way down slowly. He reached the bottom and found himself in a main room with three rooms off it. Each had a wooden door similar to the one at the top of the stairs except these had been cut to fit the openings in the rock.

One of the doors was open and when he shone his light in Max could see that from the floor to the ceiling were racks full of dusty wine bottles. Max opened the second door and found a large storage room and moved on to the third. That one was locked and it took Max a few guesses with the bunch of keys before he found the right one. The room was small and very dark. Max shone the torch around. In the corner was a mattress with a pile of rocks on it. Max stepped closer and the pile of rocks moved. The bunched up figure on the mattress was shielding its eyes from the light.

"Pete?" Max whispered. This thin figure couldn't be him.

"Mmmmm" the figure mumbled and Max gently lifted him into a sitting position. Max could hardly recognise Pete's face. He'd been so badly beaten it was little wonder that he could only mumble. His left eye was completely closed from swelling and his left arm hung limply by his side.

"Pete. It's Max mate. You're ok now."

Max checked him over briefly and he guessed a broken collarbone, at least two cracked ribs but at least his legs seemed intact. He got Pete to his feet and helped him through the door. It took a few minutes to get to the top of the steps and Max heard Cass call.

"Max, we'd better get out of here. You find anything?"

Max walked onto the veranda and Pete's legs gave way.

"Jesus!" Cass exclaimed as she saw Pete.

"We'd better get him to a hospital" Max said. Cass nodded.

"Their boat will get us back to Puerto Plata. I've tied the three of them together but no doubt someone will realise soon".

Max put Pete over his shoulder and carefully they headed to the boat.

"There was enough in the house to take down Martinez" Cass said as they got to the speedboat.

'Well at least we have that' Max thought and smiled. They laid Pete flat on the floor of the boat and sped away from the island.

124

"Any news" Allesandro asked as Luco walked back in to the lounge.
"Nothing" he replied.

It had been eight hours now and it was beginning to get dark. In less than two days they were due to complete an extremely profitable deal which wasn't going to happen unless they found their client.

125

When they got to Puerto Plata, Max phoned the British Embassy in Santa Domingo and explained that Pete had been in a car accident and his documents were missing. He arranged for a private hospital in Mexico city. It was close enough until they could get him back to New York. They couldn't risk using the main airport themselves so Pete boarded the plane on a stretcher accompanied by two nurses.

126

"Where to Senor?" asked the cab driver.

"Santa Domingo" Max replied.

"No" said Cass.

"Himenetta" she told the cab driver. Max turned to Cass.

"Why Himenetta?" he asked. He'd never heard of the place but it sounded small.

"We can charter a plane to get us back to Havana" she replied.

"You must be kidding. It's over. We've found Pete, you've got Martinez. Time to go home" Even as he finished the sentence Max could see the look in her eyes.

"Without you I can't get back into the Langustos."

"Suits me, you'll be safe." Max said.

"It's what I do Max. I can't, and I won't change that"

Max sighed.

"One more evening at The Langustos. The deal doesn't hit until Monday so we could be out of the country tomorrow," she added.

He wasn't convinced but nodded slowly.

127

Allesandro and Luco were sitting on the veranda when Luco's cell-phone chirped.

"Visitors at the gate sir".

Luco checked his watch, seven p.m.

"Who is it?" he snapped.

"Senor Kovács and the Senora. Shall I let them in"

Luco put his hand over the receiver.

"It's him" he said in a surprised voice "and the Israeli is with him"

"She's with him?"

"I forgot they were coming to dinner".

Luco waved them quiet.

"Si, si bring them in," he said quickly.

Marco stood up with his pistol drawn.

"Hey" Allesandro said. "She doesn't know we know about her. Let's play it clever". Marco holstered his gun and sat back down with a disappointed look on his face.

Max and Cass came into view across the lounge.

"János, how was your day?" Luco asked as they stepped onto the veranda.

"Did a little touristing on the islands" Max smiled.

"Their cigars are definitely not as good as yours" he laughed.

Luco joined in. "Drink?" he asked and motioned to Marco.

"Yeah. Could do with a scotch. I must be getting paranoid but I could have sworn we were followed today".

Allesandro glanced at Luco.

"Bloody inconvenience. Lost one jeep and had to hire another one." he laughed. "At least they were amateurs." He smiled.

"Its better safe than sorry" Luco said as he handed Max his drink.

128

Dinner was a quieter affair than the previous evenings – pizza on the veranda. Max wondered how many of the Langustos were out searching for him.

'They must have been going nuts' he thought.

They had dessert out by the bar that was lit with dozens of small lamps as the light was fading. As Max had tried to sit down Cass had shuffled him into a chair facing the bar with his back against one of the four pillars of the barbecue area. After a few drinks Cass disappeared off to the powder room.

129

Baber was sitting at his new desk in Skopje feeling sorry for himself. His laptop beeped and he saw he had a PDA message. He clicked open the box and a single line of text stared back at him.

M: Planes @ Gresnock airfield, S.Africa.

130

"Get your hands off me" Cass screamed as Marco dragged her through the house by her hair. He threw her against the bar and Max turned as she clattered onto the floor.

"What's the meaning of this!" he shouted.

"Perhaps Mrs.Derrick would like to explain" Marco snapped back.

"János" Luco said and placed a hand on his shoulder.

"She's a spy," he said coldly.

Max froze. They knew. 'Shit!' he thought.

"A spy?" he asked trying to buy some time.

"Si. A very good one it seems"

"How could I have been so stupid" Max shouted and flung his scotch glass so it smashed a foot away from Cass's head. He grabbed her by the shoulders. Marco lunged forward but Allesandro motioned him to wait.

"What did you find out bitch!" he screamed as he shook her. Cass spat in his face.

"Nothing you pig!" she shouted, then whispered.

"Hit me and throw me over the bar quickly". Max was stunned but did as he was told. He hit her hard across the face and she let out a wince of pain. Marco smiled. He was glad Allesandro had called him off. Max grabbed Cass's shoulders again and threw her over the bar. She crashed into a couple of bottles and disappeared behind the bar.

"Come here you bitch!" he shouted and went behind the bar.

"What now?" he whispered. Cass shook the glass out of her hair and checked her watch. 'Another twenty seconds' Max was confused but stood up and began kicking the underside of the bar.

"Come on you whore, get up!" he shouted. The Langusto brothers looked on and Luco thought.

"He's a vicious bastard all right" he turned to make a comment to Allesandro but he didn't get a chance.

The explosion ripped the side of the house apart and four of the Langustos were thrown into the bar with huge force. Max was pinned against the back of the bar and was hit on the shoulder by an ashtray. His head smacked into the bar wall. Rubble rained down on the veranda and a large section of the railing overhanging the canyon had been blown away.

Cass leapt up and checked the surroundings. The blast had caved in the main roof and taken out the four walls of the library. There were books everywhere. There was screaming from inside the house and Maria came running out with Luco's wife Anna. They rushed to their respective husbands who were both at least unconscious.

'Worse I hope' thought Cass. She quickly took a piece of glass and sliced her forehead and smeared the blood across her face.

"Get an ambulance" she screamed at the two women and Maria ran back into the house. Max was trying to get up and Cass gave him a hand.

"What the fuck was that!" he stammered.

"Come on" she shouted at him and dragged him into the house.

"Where are we going?" he managed to get out as they raced up the stairs. Before he got an answer Cass kicked open a door and Max saw they were on the roof. In front of them were two power gliders.

"Surely not?" he said as Cass pushed him towards the closer one.

"You told me you'd flown one of these before" she complained.

"That was ten years ago, and besides I was with an instructor on a fun flight, not two thousand feet up a bloody mountain".

"Can you start it?" she asked as she strapped herself on behind him.

"I think so" Max replied and pressed the ignition. The hang glider roared into life but they didn't move.

"Well?" she shouted.

"Brakes I think" Max shouted back and he tried all the levers until the glider lunged forward and off the roof. Within a second they were flying alongside the canyon with the villa a smouldering heap behind them.

They heard the engine of the second glider kick-in and Cass turned around to see the glider leave the roof.

"Step on it" she shouted to Max.

Max was trying desperately not to look down. Not that he could see much below them in the half-light.

"How are we supposed to land in the dark?" he shouted.

"Just fly it" Cass screamed and clutched the pistol she had taken from Marco's body. She suspected Marco wad dead due to the huge piece of glass embedded in his back.

She fired a couple of shots that drew a dozen or so in return. A couple were close, with one clipping the metal frame of the glider making an annoying pinging sound.

"Don't worry" Cass screamed. "They won't be here for long" she laughed. Sure enough within a few seconds they heard the engine of the other glider splutter and cut out. The two figures inside tried desperately to restart the engine but it was dead. Cass had cut the fuel line when she had discovered the hang gliders earlier.

Max let out a sigh of relief that proved premature. Whatever weapons the two had grabbed they now employed at Max and Cass.
They were too far away to aim but the odds were high that one of the dozens of shots would hit the mark.

Max felt the sharp pain in his side and for a moment let go of the controls. He gritted his teeth and grasped the controls again. He had not been shot before and although in a lot of pain, had expected it to be worse.

He shouted back to Cass "I'm hit in the side".
He thought he heard her reply "I know" and twisted his head around to see Cass slumped back in her seat. There was lots of blood on her dress at the same height as his wound.

"It went through her before it hit me," Max said to himself. He turned back to the front and continued to follow the side of the mountain towards Havana. Ahead of him the lights of the city were beginning to flicker on and he willed the small glider to go faster.

131

The scene at the Langusto house had calmed down and an eerie quiet had descended. Luco was still unconscious. Allessandro was talking to one of the two men in the glider on his cell-phone. They had landed on the main road up to the villa and were waiting for Allesandro to reach them in a car.

The ambulance was on its way, though it would be a good twenty miles at best. Marco was alive, just. The huge piece of glass was still embedded in his neck. Allessandro knowing not to remove it in case it had severed an artery. "Get every available man and when they land kill them" he shouted.

He closed his phone and went to Luco's side again. He didn't like the look of his big brother. He had been under a mound of rubble and was looking like his back might be broken so they decided not to move him. He and Marco lay where they had fallen.

He swore under his breath. "You will pay for this Kovács."

132

Max was starting to feel dizzy. He knew he was over Havana, he knew the Langustos would be searching for their glider but most of all he knew he was slowly losing blood. In a moment of inspiration he turned the glider around and headed for the castle.

The El Morro Castle was built in 1589 and is a very popular tourist attraction. At night it is lit up beautifully. This feature made it very easy to see from the air at night. The other important attribute of the castle is that it was within a quarter of a mile of the British Embassy. This kernel of information jumped out at Max as his brain processed the limited background reading he'd done on Havana. It wasn't as big or lavish as many of the other Embassies around the world but nevertheless it had a large Union Jack flying above it and Max hoped that once circling the castle he would be able to see it.

The Langustos' men had located the glider in the sky and had two cars tracking it through the streets. It was moving too fast in public to take the shots necessary to down it but once they landed they would have them.

133

Martin Beaumont was extremely bored. To say that Cuba was an uneventful posting was an understatement. It was a good stepping stone he kept telling himself. Forty five with mousy brown hair in a centre parting dressed in a tailored navy pinstripe suit, crisp white shirt with subtle pink stripes and a conservative deep pink tie he looked every part the diplomat. His gold rimmed glasses, which he knew added years to his appearance, sat halfway down his nose. Martin didn't need them as his eyesight was 20-20 but he felt they gave him that extra air of authority and intelligence so he wore them whilst in the embassy and at functions. He placed his tea cup lightly down onto its saucer and leaned back into the leather chair. He sighed slightly as he contemplated another quiet uneventful evening.

Deputy Ambassador here and maybe, if he was lucky, Ambassador of a small country somewhere next, he just needed to keep his nose clean which wasn't going to be difficult here. He looked out of the window and smiled as he looked down to the car park where his 1956 dark blue Chevy gleamed in the lights of the Embassy. Now that was one perk he did like.

He watched in horror as a large contraption skidded across the car park and slammed into the side of the Chevy. He ran down the staircase to the lobby. He hesitated at the front door peering through to check the scene. His eyes slowly tracked across the crumpled heap embedded in the side of his beloved car.

Four embassy guards stood about twenty feet from what looked like some sort of glider. They had their weapons drawn but were understandably reluctant to get any closer.

The fabric of the glider moved a little and a large man in a cream jacket staggered out and fell onto the ground.

"Put your hands up" shouted one of the guards and steadied his pistol with both hands. Max looked up into the man's eyes then across to the front doors straight at Beaumont.

"Get a Doctor" Max said.

"I said put your hands up sir," the guard said louder this time.

Max got to his feet, put his hands above his head and walked straight to Beaumont.

"You look like a sensible fella," Max said quickly as he stood three steps below. "Please get a Doctor and fast".

"There is an Israeli diplomat in the glider. She's been shot and if she doesn't get medical attention she might die, and you wouldn't want that would you?"

Beaumont was taken aback.

"Peterson" he shouted over his shoulder. "Get out here".

"Thank you" Max said.

"You just keep your hands up," Beaumont said in a stern voice. He noticed the man's shirt was covered in blood.

A young man with a doctor's bag ran out to the front doors, with two of the guards he lifted Cass out of the glider.

"Martin" Peterson shouted back to the doors.

"She's lost a lot of blood. She needs a hospital".

"No" Max snapped. "Do you have a medical bay?"

"Yes, but its not that well equipped. Besides who the hell are you?" Beaumont said turning to Max.

"Look just get her stable and we can call London".

"What you're a spook?" Beaumont said.

"A spy? Not Exactly." Max said.

Peterson and the guards were carrying Cass past Max and he turned to Beaumont again.

"One call to MI5 and its sorted." Max said. Max was feeling really weak now and sat down on the steps. As he spoke a half a dozen police cars came speeding around the corner and lights blazing pulled up at the gates.

"Sir" a woman came running up to Beaumont.

"It's the Chief of Police on the phone. He says he wants his two prisoners back".

"Oh wonderful." Beaumont said clasping his hands together.

"Tell him he'll have to wait a few minutes".

"And get me Tina Althorpe on the phone."

His assistant Peterson reappeared through the doors and Beaumont turned to face him.

"Peterson, get this man searched and see to his side."

As Beaumont turned toward him Max forced a smile and then passed out slumping onto the steps. Peterson threw a glance at Beaumont who shrugged and motioned towards the group of guards.

The medical bay in the Embassy only had two beds and tonight both were full. Max was awake and looking over at Cass who was in a bad way. They had cleaned the wound and concluded that, although no organs had been hit by the bullet they had removed from Max's side she needed to get to the hospital.

Beaumont walked into the medical bay and gave Max an uneasy smile.

"We have a bit of a Mexican stand-off here."

"London have acknowledged that they would like to get you and the young lady across to the US safely.

"However the local authorities insist you are not going anywhere."

"What does the Doctor say about Cass" Max said slowly.

"She's extremely weak" Beaumont replied.

"We have to get her to a hospital before the morning."

"Thanks" said Max.

"Let me talk to the police."

134

Max's mind was racing. In five minutes he would be talking with Manton. He did not have time to go through the documents and disks Cass had taken from Allessandro's office. They sat on the table next to her bed. He wondered how good his bluff could be?

'It'd better be bloody good' he thought and got up

"Kovács" sneered Manton voice on the intercom. He was standing twenty feet from the Chief of Police and the huge guards in between them gave him little comfort.

"A lot of people want you dead" Manton continued.

"Tell me something new" Max growled.

"You have nowhere to go Mr Kovács. Stop wasting everyone's time and I give you my guarantee that you and the Israeli will die quickly."

"How long have you been in the police force?" Max asked.

"Twenty five years" said Manton proudly.

"And have you seen the inside of Havana's jails?"

"Oh you won't see those Mr.Kovács"

"I was thinking of you actually," Max said.

"We have documents from Allesandro's office with your name all over them"

"Bullshit!" Manton snapped.

"Just give him a ring" Max replied and hung up.

Max waited by the intercom. It was the longest five minutes of his life.

Manton had a problem. He weighed up the facts. He knew about the explosion at the villa. He knew Kovács had gained access to Allesandro's office. He also knew that Allessandro kept detailed accounts. He had been involved in a lot of heavy shit in the past. If he went to Allessandro he would deny it either way, but if the Hungarian was going to take the Langustos down anyway he would do well to distance himself from them.

"Okay" Manton said as Max held the intercom to his ear once more.

"I want a statement signed by you and the Ambassador giving me immunity from all aspects of this should anything get out".

Max let out a long deep breath.

"You got it. In return I want a police helicopter and a jet waiting at the airport with fuel, a medical crew and facilities on board".

"Okay. You are a ruthless calculating bastard Kovács" Manton said with a hint of respect in his voice.

Max glanced back toward the embassy where Cass lay pale and fighting for her life.

"It's what I do." he said simply and hung up the phone.

135

Max stayed by Cass's side through the night on the plane and once she had been set up in a hospital bed in Mexico City. She had received a blood transfusion and was still on an IV but the doctors were pleased with her progress. The following morning at about six am Max was sitting in an armchair at the side of her bed. He still held her hand despite having drifted off about an hour before. He opened his eyes and stretched his back. His side was still sore and he winced a little. He glanced at Cass who had her eyes open and was smiling at him.

"Hey" he said quietly.

"Hey" she whispered back.

"How long have you been awake" he said and held her hand in both of his.

"A while" she said, "I didn't want to wake you."

"Listen to her. Watching over me again" he smiled.

"Where are the papers?" she asked.

"Oh they're here. Yesterday I made copies of everything and put them in a safety deposit box. I sent a second copy over to Easton. He wants to talk to us".

"I bet he does" Cass's eyes lit up.

"Did you find out what the Yukon base was?" she added.

"Yep. When I saw it on lots of the paperwork I checked with Martin at the NY Times. Apparently he's been sitting on an amazing story from a small-town lawyer, Petra something. Her research shows a huge link between a Chicago based company and the base. It's a US air base and most of the Langustos arms seemed to pass through there".

"I knew it!" she exclaimed.

"The irony. The US government involved with Cuban arms dealers" she shook her head in amazement.

"Oh that's not the half of it" Max leaned over and grabbed a couple of sheets of paper from a folder on the windowsill.

"Look who else is involved."

Cass took the papers and scanned over them. Her eyes reached the box on the bottom right hand corner. She lowered the sheets and looked straight into Max's eyes.

"Oh my God" she said slowly.

136

The Director of the CIA was enjoying a rare escape from his office and the fact that he had lofted an 8 iron shot from the seventh tee to the edge of the green meant that he was enjoying it all the more. He passed the club to his caddy, got into the golf cart and the driver set off down the fairway. Thirty yards ahead of them a dark suited man raised his hand to his ear and reached inside his jacket. As the cart got nearer he raised his hand and the driver slowed. The suit handed a small silver cell-phone to the Director.

"Yes?" he snapped. "What do you mean I'd better take the call. Can't you deal with it?" he was annoyed at having his 'quality time' disturbed.

"Ok, put him through."

The voice on the other end of the line spoke clearly and with conviction.

"Very interesting Mr.Jones" the Director said when the caller finally finished.

"And in return for your discretion, you would be wanting how much?"

The Director of the CIA steadied himself and removed his sunglasses. He knew Jones was genuine. He'd had the briefing. He had not been expecting to take the call himself as he had assumed it would be about money, and a lot of it. It wasn't.

"Your demands have a note of finality," he said.

"Yes" replied Max. "That they do. Let's just call it my contribution to prosperity" he added and hung up.

137

Pete wasn't sleeping. He was just resting his eyes. His strength had gradually come back to him but his ribs were sore and heavily strapped. He opened his eyes at the knock on the door.

"Come in" he called.

The door flung open and Max stormed in pushing Cass in a wheelchair.

"Max!" Pete exclaimed and grimaced in pain.

"Hey buddy, take it easy" Max laughed and came round to the side of the bed.

"No time for that. We have a present for you"

"We?" Pete smiled across at Cass.

"Oh, sorry this is Cass. Cass, this is Pete"

"Hi Pete" Cass said giving him a wink.

"You look much better" she smiled.

"Come on, come on" Max said "Open it".

He thrust a large box into Pete's hands.

"Quick" Max said.

Pete pulled off the ribbon and lifted the lid of the box. Inside was a laptop connected to a mobile phone. The screen was on and the familiar blue and yellow figure of the Roving Reporter was at the top.

"Roving Reporter" Pete smiled.

"Go on then. Click on it" Max urged.

Pete moved the mouse and clicked on the icon and a video and text box opened in the middle of the screen. The video box had a pair of white doors in the centre of the picture. Max handed Pete a sheet of paper and a keyboard connected to a PDA.

"Go on then. Get typing" Max said to Pete who shrugged and started.

138

The two men studied each other across the large table. They had dismissed the guards from the room about five minutes before and had sat in silence. The younger man gestured towards the ornate coffee set at the end of the room. The old man nodded and George got out of his seat and poured two cups of steaming black coffee. He put one in front of the old man and took a seat at his side. He cradled the coffee cup in his hands and stared deep into the thick black liquid as if looking for inspiration.

"I suppose you are as uncomfortable with this as I am?" he said.

The old man took a sip from his cup and sighed.

"I have seen sparks of revolution and years of defiance, but somehow in my heart I knew this day would come".

George nodded and lifted the cup to his lips and paused.

"Did you think it would come in your lifetime?" he asked.

The old man shook his head slowly.

"No" he said solemnly. "We are sure this is unavoidable?" he added but he already knew the answer. George nodded and they both rose and headed towards the big white doors. George put his hand on the old man's shoulder as he reached for the door.

"Come on. Let's make history".

139

You are here live with Pete Smalt on this historic occasion. You join us at The Whitehouse where in a few moments time history will be changed forever. Two nations who have been separated by a huge political divide have broken down the barriers.

Pete looked at Max who motioned for him to keep going.

In an exclusive interview with the two leaders they gave the reasons for the shock announcements. Relations have been improving slowly over the past decade and with a major recession looming the trade opportunity for both could not be ignored.

The white doors in the video stream opened and George W. Bush and Fidel Castro stepped out onto The Whitehouse lawn. They smiled and shook hands in front of the single video camera - and the 127 million people watching on their PCs across the world.

The End

Also from MX Publishing

Eliminate The Impossible

"Alistair Duncan knows his Holmes, and he brings a fresh eye to this 240 page survey of the Canon and its film and TV off-shoots. Eliminate the Impossible is well written and entertaining. The story summaries are concise and accurate, and the notes are frequently incisive. Most interesting, to my mind, and most controversial, are the comments on film and television portrayals"

The Daily Messenger
Sherlock Holmes Society of London

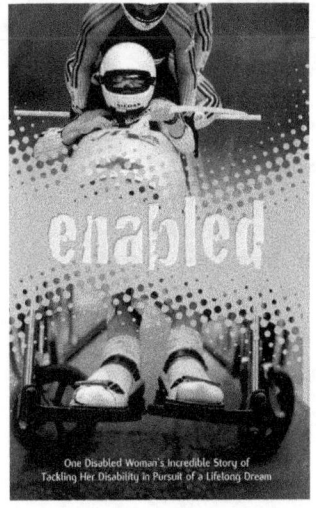

Enabled

One Disabled Woman's Incredible Story of Tackling Her Disability in Pursuit of a Lifelong Dream.

Ruth Merry's dream was to tackle an Olympic bobsleigh – a tough enough challenge for an able-bodied person but seemingly out of reach for a lady that has spent her life in a wheelchair. A fascinating insight that will surprise and inspire.

Also from MX Publishing

Portuguese Property Guide

"Contains a great deal of information of interest to potential buyers and people thinking of moving to Portugal"
Destination Algarve

"This book has a great deal of information for anyone looking to buy property in Portugal. It has been well researched to provide the latest information on living and working in the country"
Portugal Magazine

Seeing Spells Achieving

"For anyone with dyslexia, and any parent or someone involved in learning, education and health, these processes of visualisation integrate so well with existing teaching methods and they do give us all another tool, a new choice for growth and development to achieve new goals"

National Family Learning Network

Also from MX Publishing

The Gift – Real Life NLP

"It can be used in so many different ways from helping businesses to giving people the skills they need do better at school, while also being useful for treating phobias and helping people lose weight or stop smoking".

Daily Record

Performance Strategies for Musicians

"If you suffer from stage fright and performance anxiety then help is at hand."

The Pianist Magazine

Also from MX Publishing

Hurghada Property and Egypt's Red Sea Riviera Real Estate

From leading property writer Nick Pendrell comes a comprehensive overview of the Egyptian property market.

Brazilian Property Guide

From the same team that created the bestselling Portuguese Property Guide comes a comprehensive guide to living, working and buying property in one of the world's most exciting emerging markets.

Already causing a stir in the property market the guide is essential reading for anyone considering Brazil as a potential destination.

Also from MX Publishing

Succeed In Sport

Five times British Archery champion Jackie Wilkinson brings us the secrets to enhanced performance across all sports. Contributions from leading Olympians and leading athletes from Athletics, Running, Golf, Karate, Archery, Show Jumping, Cricket and more.

TOK258 – Morgan Winner at Le Mans

"I would recommend this book to anyone. It is the story of how skill and personal determination can beat the most elaborate, expensive and sophisticated machinery, the story of David versus Goliath. I warmly hope that it inspires the reader to try and achieve their own personal dreams"

Charles Morgan
Chairman, Morgan Car Company

Also from MX Publishing

The Beekeeper - Beautifully illustrated children's book also available in German.

GUS – An endearing story of a day in the life of a Beagle called GUS. Simply gorgeous illustrations.

ABOUT THE AUTHOR

Michael Phillips Mann has been a cab driver, a shrimp fisherman, a swim coach, a stone carver, a college instructor, a concierge—and through it all—a writer. He has a B.A. in Creative Writing, an M.A. in Literature, and a Graduate Certificate in Women's Studies, which he taught for several years. He currently lives in Nashville, Tennessee, where he can be found rolling along the Music City Bikeway on his Gary Fisher Wingra, or sipping coffee and filling pages at East Nashville's Portland Brew.

Follow Michael Phillips Mann on Twitter: @michaelpmann and visit www.wanderinginthewordspress.com for author news and updates.

Martha Cole

ABOUT THE COVER ARTIST

Bryan Holland has worked professionally as an artist, a graphic artist and a college professor. His work has been in numerous exhibitions, from solo to regional and national juried and invitational exhibitions. His work has been published in several journals and is part of many collections. Bryan's most recent work is a mix of painting, collage, found art, image transfer techniques, and a variety of other experimentation. His work is influenced by graphic design, vintage art, painting, photography, mythology and a little bit of science and philosophy.

For more information about Bryan and his art, visit www.bryanhollandarts.com.

Follow Bryan on Twitter: @bryanhollandart